S0-ANP-377

Will You Still

Love Me Tomorrow?

WILL YOU STILL

BENJAMIN

STEIN

LOVE ME TOMORROW?

St. Martin's Press
New York

This is a work of fiction. All characters and events portrayed in this book are fictitious, and any resemblance to real people or events is purely coincidental.

Lyrics from "Ballad of a Teenage Queen" by Jack Clement copyright © 1958 by Songs of Polygram International Inc.

Lyrics from "Another Brick in the Wall" by Roger Waters copyright © 1979 by Pink Floyd Music Publishers Limited.

Lyrics from "Forever Young" by Bob Dylan copyright © 1973, 1974 by RAM's HORN MUSIC. All rights reserved. International copyright secured. Reprinted by permission.

WILL YOU STILL LOVE ME TOMORROW? Copyright © 1991 by Benjamin Stein. All rights reserved. Printed in the United States of America. No part of this book may be used or reproduced in any manner whatsoever without written permission except in the case of brief quotations embodied in critical articles or reviews. For information, address St. Martin's Press, 175 Fifth Avenue, New York, N.Y. 10010.

Design by Judith Dannecker

Library of Congress Cataloging-in-Publication Data

Stein, Benjamin.
    Will you still love me tomorrow? / Benjamin Stein.
       p.   cm.
    ISBN 0-312-05389-4
    I. Title.
PS3569.T36W5   1991
813'.54—dc20   90-48355
                                                                          CIP

First Edition: April 1991
10 9 8 7 6 5 4 3 2 1

For Martha Wyss, who gave me Trixie, and for Susan Gayle Reifer, who made it all come together, and for Betsy, who swung up into the sky on her swing, and for Kay, the Drum Major, and for Alex, who sees and understands.

1

L A N D I N G

December 20, 1987

Nicole Miller pulled the bottom edges of her chinchilla coat over
her knees. As she did, she brushed a tiny piece of paper off the
hem of her red Chanel skirt and shivered. There was something
wrong with the heating system on the Falcon. She was sure of it.
Barron had told his ground crew at Van Nuys to check the
damned thing five different times since Thanksgiving, but they
never quite got it right. Once the plane was above twenty thousand feet, either it would get as cold as the inside of a refrigerator
in the passenger cabin, or else it would be warm enough to toast
oat bread. Nicole had asked Steve Gage, the pilot with an Arkansas accent that would have made Chuck Yeager sound like a
Hasid, to fix the thermostat, and that hadn't done any good
either. From Palm Desert airspace to Denver, the cabin had been
like an oven. After the refueling at Denver's Stapleton Field, it
was like what a martini should be, but rarely is.

It would have been all right if there had been someone for
Nicole to talk to, to distract her from the cold, but there wasn't.
She had planned to work on comparative advertising costs and
productivity and so she had planned to be alone with her tables

and her H-P 12C. In fact, she had been far too jacked up to work after takeoff. The radiophone did not work either, even though it was a brand-new Wolfsburg Six. Whenever Nicole dialed, she got a polite woman's voice telling her that she, the polite woman whom Nicole would never meet, was terribly sorry, but the circuits were all busy. The voice apologized at least three times on every call. Needless to say, it was recorded. No one in real life was that polite.

The portable NAD CD player worked like a jewel, though, as always. Nicole had listened to Mozart for the first three hours—almost all of *Così fan tutte,* the version with Leontyne Price singing and Erich Leinsdorf conducting, an analog-to-digital, but still good, clear, clean notes, and then to the first act of *Die Zauberflöte.* She rummaged around in the darkness and listened to genius, slept off and on, glanced at *Town & Country* until she saw a photo of Saundra Thomas at a party at the Icahns, and then tossed the issue into the wastepaper basket. Barron Thomas's wife was on her mind enough. She did not need to see her grinning above a river of pearls at a party in Westchester County, looking entirely too content for a woman who had her problems with alcohol and men.

After Mozart, when the plane had turned into a leather and chrome Popsicle, she had reached for *Hotel California* and then *Desperado.* Barron hated for her to listen to rock music. He considered it anarchic, especially compared with Mozart. But Barron wasn't there, and damn him anyway. He couldn't even get the thermostat fixed on his own plane. There were a lot of things that Barron couldn't do, and if Nicole wanted to listen to Don Henley, that was up to her, even if she was on Barron's plane. Don Henley had something to say to her today that was just as important as what Wolfgang had to say.

"Lines on the mirror, lines on her face . . ." said the song, and Nicole picked up *Vogue* and leafed through it. It was amazing. Almost all of the models were bosomy. Really bosomy. They pushed their breasts together to get even more cleavage. Where had all this bosom stuff come from? Just a year ago, the models were still razor thin. Now, all of a sudden, out of total nowhere, there were great big milky bosoms pushing through silk, crowding up above strapless gowns, jiggling underneath three-hundred-dollar bras.

Nicole Miller thought it was about time. She had been teased about her large breasts for as long as she had owned them, which was about since she was fifteen. For all of the time since college, when she was working her way up in Los Angeles, when she was broke in Los Angeles, she had tried to hide them, to keep them down, so to speak, so they did not embarrass her with their presence, their radically visible femininity. From the days at the University of Tennessee to the days just before she met Barron, when she was living in a third-floor walk-up in Hollywood, every one of her roommates had clucked because Nicole was too short and too bosomy. Poor thing, they had said. Can't wear top-of-the-line clothes. Can't look like Twiggy. Can't look perfect in jeans.

To hell with them all. Barron had told her the first time he had seen her body that she was exactly perfect just as she was, and that was the end of "poor thing." "They're jealous," Barron had told her that night in her small bedroom looking out on a nail salon. "They don't have your blue eyes. They don't have your perfect nose or your cheekbones or your hair or your forehead. They don't have that little blue vein on your temple that flutters when you get excited. They don't have thighs that feel like they're waiting for a man, not getting ready to strangle someone. They don't have the look of a woman. You have that. You have 'woman' all over your body, and they don't, and they're jealous."

"Perfect just the way you are." That was what Barron, the man on the cover of *Forbes,* her lover, had said about her figure and everything else about her.

The only times that Barron ever criticized her appearance were back when she wore something he thought was too revealing. He did not like her to wear anything with a low neckline at Morton's or anything that was too tight at Sam's Cafe. "You have a naturally classy look," he told her. "You don't need to look like you're fishing. You look perfect, just exactly perfect, like a princess. If

3

you show too much, you're working against yourself." That lecture was some time ago, and Nicole was a quick learner, so it did not have to be given twice.

The maddening part was that Barron was right. She did look better in business suits or in Chanel or in Valentino than in anything low cut or really tight. She gave Barron a look, but then went back to her closet and fished something out—usually something Barron had bought her—and she took off her low-cut outfit and stood in front of Barron in her panties and her thigh-highs and her bra and held each dress up in front of her until Barron found the one that he liked the best.

Sometimes, he would take the dress out of her hands, carefully hang it back up, and then pull Nicole to him. He would slide his hands inside her panties and press her against him. "God," he would say, "I can't believe I ever found you."

Then they would be late for Spago or La Scala, and Barron would hold her hand all the way to the car, and all the way through dinner. Once or twice it had even occurred to Nicole that she might have unconsciously planned to wear clothes that Barron would take off precisely so that they could have those minutes holding each other before they put on their party faces and went out into Barron's world.

The door to the cockpit opened and Steve Gage walked out into the cabin. "We're getting near the Knoxville airport," he said. "We'll be on the ground in five minutes."

"I can't see one single light," Nicole said.

"I think that's why they call it Tennessee," Steve Gage said. He was stocky, with a muscular build and an affectation of military bearing, even though he had never been near the armed forces. He smiled and pointed out the window. "Right ahead there," he said. "At twelve o'clock. That's where the airfield is. Get ready."

Nicole laid down her magazine and picked up the receiver of the radiophone again. She hit the speed-dial for Barron's office in New York. This time the call went through. The perversity of inanimate objects, she thought. These things weren't even supposed to work at low altitude. The perversity of everything.

K.L., Barron's secretary, had once worked as Snow White at Disneyland. She still talked as if every caller might have magical powers that were indispensable to her and to her boss. In a breathless whisper, she would always promise to put Nicole right through to Barron, as if by connecting them, she might be presented with at least eternal life.

"Nicole," K.L. said. "Nicole, Barron has been waiting for you to call. I'll put you right through," she added, as if she could somehow actually physically put Nicole right on Barron's desk. Nicole wished she could.

"Nicole," Barron said as he picked up the phone. "I have been so busy. I miss you, and I'm getting my head kicked in by at least twelve different law firms and fifteen government agencies, and I need you and I'm sorry we got into a fight."

"The phone hasn't been working."

"I know. I've been trying to reach you."

"Barron," Nicole said. "I want to tell you something."

"Anything. Anything from a friendly, sweet voice. God, let me out of this M and A business and back into bed with you."

"Barron, I know you don't like to hear this."

There was a tangible crash of silence on the other end of the radiophone. It lasted ten seconds. Then, in an entirely new voice, the flat, negotiator's voice that Nicole had heard Barron use so many times on buyers and sellers and in depositions with lawyers, Barron ended the silence and asked, "Can it wait until you get to New York?"

"No, it can't," Nicole said. "Barron, what am I doing flying around in a Falcon? What am I doing in a chinchilla coat? What's going on in my one and only life?"

"It's only a Fifty. Last year's model," Barron said.

"I get the joke," Nicole said. "You know what I mean. What are the pearls for? What's any of it for?"

Barron let out a long sigh, audible clearly over the phone. "The

pearls are for one year of sobriety. The coat is because you suggested something on the L.A. Chemical Company suit that saved
me over a million dollars in legal fees. The plane is because it had
to come here to pick me up anyway, and Tennessee is on the way.
Basically, it's all because I love you so much. That's the bottom
line. Because I love you. Because you are the lover of a man who
can afford these things. It's really not that complicated." Barron's
voice still had a good Texas twang, mixed with the Arkansas
softness that came from his mother, Maggie.

"Barron, these people don't know about last year's model.
They know it's a private jet. Private jets are for a maharaja or for
the President. They haven't ever even seen a chinchilla coat
before. As far as they're concerned, real pearls don't even exist
except maybe on the Queen of England. People in Jonesboro
can't even imagine what a prospectus is. They think it's something to put on a tractor to keep cow patties from flying up in
their face."

As she talked to Barron, she could see the lights of Knoxville
snap into view in the clear Smoky Mountains night air. People
in Los Angeles and New York could not even imagine that air
could be so clear. It would just not even dawn on them that at
night the sky would be bright with stars and not with anticrime
lights reflecting on smog. She would take the clear air over the
prospectuses any day.

"They're your family," Barron went on. "They want to believe
you. They've seen me on TV. They've read about me in *News-
week*. They know me. They know that if you do even a little
something valuable for me, it amounts to a lot of money. That's
all they need to know. They're not the IRS, Nicole. They're not
auditing you."

"In a way, they are. It's Christmas. We'll all be opening presents under the tree. They're going to be giving each other
blouses from Spiegel, and I'm going to have a diamond and
sapphire bracelet from Fred."

"What makes you think that?" Barron asked in a rush.

"I think that because I went into Fred to look for something

6

for you, and one of the salesmen, a guy named Cameo, told me that you had just been in there buying a bracelet for your wife, and he showed it to me, and he said you had told him it had to go with really intense blue eyes, and I know Saundra's eyes aren't intense blue, and I know that you're too goddamned busy scaring the hell out of Westinghouse to even think about another girl." She paused for a minute. "That's how I know."

"I can't tell you what I'm giving you for Christmas," Barron said. "They were probably thinking of another Barron Thomas." By now he was teasing, cool, back in charge. That was the edge that money and the ability to buy presents from Fred conferred.

"I don't know," Nicole said. "I know I shouldn't be bothering you with this when you're working so hard on your deal. But please, Barron, who am I?"

"I don't understand the question. You are the girlfriend of a wealthy middle-aged American man. I have to tell you again, it's not that complicated."

Nicole tightened her seat belt across her waist. "You're good to me," she said, barely audibly. "That's the problem. Like in Cambridge. That's what makes it so damned hard." She could see the lights of the downtown skyline, such as it was, reflecting over Loudon Lake. The only tall building, the Howard Baker Tower of the University of Tennessee Medical Center, reflected its lights on the still water. No surfing here, unlike in front of Barron's places on Malibu Road or Point Dume. Just slow canoeing and sailing and watching.

"You're my girlfriend. You're my inspiration. You're my dream girl. You saved me when I was drowning."

The Wolfsburg Six was now making up for lost time. It was transmitting so clearly that Nicole could hear Barron swiveling around in his chair. She figured that he was probably looking out on the New York skyline across Fifth Avenue from his office, in his building. He could probably see the Christmas lights on Bergdorf Goodman, maybe even see the top of Rockefeller Center and its magnificent Christmas offerings.

"You're my dream girl," Barron continued. "My dream girl."

7

"Yes, I'm your dream girl, but it's my real life. I'm living out your dream, but this is my real life, and I don't know what I'm doing in it sometimes."

Nicole smiled to herself. Steve Gage could tell from the LED on the dashboard that she was on the telephone. He knew he would lose the connection on the ground. He had put the Falcon into a slow circle around McGhee-Tyson Airport, so that she could finish the call.

"But don't I make it like a dream for you, too? I wouldn't even bother doing all of this except that I think it makes you a life like you always dreamed of."

"I always dreamed of a life like this, flying around in a jet, doing important work, making a difference in the world. I always dreamed about that. You're right. But I never thought the man in my life would be married to another woman."

There was another avalanche of silence on the end of the phone. Then there was another blizzard of silence and then there was a sigh, and finally Nicole said, "I'm sorry. I shouldn't even be bringing this up when you're having such a hard time with your deal. But it's making me crazy. I'm about to see my parents and my sister, and what do I tell them about who I am?"

"Tell them life is complicated, but that you have someone who loves you and who takes care of you, and that isn't so bad. That you do important, challenging work for thousands of shareholders of BTA, for good wages, and that's not bad either." Barron was starting to get an edge in his voice. He did not like it when things did not go his way. He also did not like it when conversations did not end on an upbeat, happy note. Like all men who had made it in business, he was a little boy who was used to having his way. A Presbyterian prince. "I do take care of you, don't I? When was there ever a time when I didn't take care of you?"

"Look, you take care of me, and you love me. But that's what pimps tell the girls who work for them on Seventh Avenue, and I don't mean to say that you're like them . . ."

But it was too late, because by the time that Nicole realized she had gone far too far, the Wolfsburg was already flashing that

8

there had been a disconnect. Probably right after the words "Seventh Avenue," Nicole realized, and instantly, she was overwhelmed with remorse. How could she have done such a thing to Barron? How could she have compared him with a pimp? Barron, who had been the kindest to her of any man in her life, who loved her unconditionally, who loved her more than she could have imagined possible, who took her from being a loser to being a winner, from temping at software companies to getting the best table at Spago, the one over in the corner next to the kitchen, the Freddy de Cordova table, from being alone to being loved.

Something came over her when she went home to see her parents. That must be it. It wasn't Barron's fault. Barron was the man who had told her that until he met her, it was like listening to music in mono, and then when he was with her, life was lived and heard and felt in stereo. Barron was the one who told her that he had felt alone all his life until he met her, that his wife and he filed a joint tax return, but that he and Nicole filed a joint emotional return on everything.

Real-world consequences: She hit the RCL button on the phone. K.L.'s Snow White voice wafted through the receiver.

"Did you get cut off?" she asked solicitously.

"I think Barron hung up on me because I was being a bitch. Can I talk to him?"

"He just went down the hall to a meeting with a group of lawyers and accountants from some bank or somewhere," K.L. said breathlessly. "Shall I call him? They all looked very serious."

What a smoothie you are, Nicole thought. "No," she said. "Just tell him I'm really sorry. I'll call him later tonight."

"Okay," K.L. said in a chirrup. "I'll give him the message."

Nicole hung up the phone. Steve Gage put the jet on a line heading for the strobe lights of the runway at Knoxville. They flashed in perfect sequence until the Falcon was on top of them, and then on the tarmac.

For just another moment of escape, Nicole put the headphones of the NAD Compro back on her head and hit the PLAY button.

9

"She wonders how it ever got this crazy. She thinks about a boy she knew in school . . ."

That was too on the nose. She hit the SKIP button and another song popped up. The noise of the brakes was so loud that she could barely hear the lyrics. The only refrain she could make out was "You're afraid it's all been wasted time . . ."

At least that was off base. Whatever else she could say about her life since the day she met Barron at the meeting in Cedars-Sinai, it had not been wasted time. No, unless you counted time on a roller coaster wasted time, or time on top of the mountains overlooking Maroon Bells wasted time, or time when everyone at La Scala looked at you as if you were a goddess wasted time, it hadn't been wasted time. Not unless you called time being loved and cared for in the city of Angels wasted time.

No, it still wasn't wasted time. For close to two years now, she had spent every minute knowing that a man loved her. She had spent more than a hundred nights lying against the back of a man who excited her just when he looked at her. ("You always excited me," she once told him. "I followed you down to the phone at the meeting because I liked the look on your face. I never like to admit it, but you always turned me on.")

No. Definitely not wasted time. But also, time where something was wrong and very wrong at that. Barron's dream. Her life. That was the problem in one phrase.

When the plane wheeled up in front of the Ryan Aviation terminal where Barron's plane always parked, there was a small knot of people standing in front of the hangar. Even from a hundred yards, Nicole could tell that they were her mother, Julie, her father, Ray, and her sister, Ginette. (Nicole mentally thanked God that she had been given the pretty name. Imagine having to go through life as Ginette.)

Her mother looked well. Her father had the extremely handsome, perpetually distant, slightly weary look that he always wore, as if he were under the influence of some kind of mild anesthetic. He had not been smoking for almost five years because of his colitis, but he still looked slightly breathless. He had always looked either distracted or distant. Muscular, well disposed if you could run or kick or throw, otherwise you were barely a routine to be gotten through before he got home to watch whatever game was on ESPN that night. He had on the suede jacket from Brooks Brothers that she had sent him, but it looked startlingly new. Probably her mother had made him wear it and he had put it on, only barely conscious of what it was. After all, it wasn't a Volunteers coach's shirt, which is what he had always wanted and dreamed of. Maybe Barron could buy the University of Tennessee, break it up into its most salable pieces, turn the Vols into a large limited partnership, and then have Ray Miller head up the football team. She had better not suggest it to Barron. It was just the kind of thing he would try to do to please her. If he was still speaking to her after what she said to him.

The plane lurched forward again and moved to within about twenty feet of her family, and Nicole stood up. It was colder than ever inside the cabin now. Chinchilla was warm, and Chanel was warm, especially the red wool suits that Barron loved on her. But she was still oddly cold.

Steve Gage stepped into the cabin and said, "Show time."

She smiled at him. He knew more than he let on. He and Barron had been together for years now, and he could probably have bought a small airline with his percentages of various spin-offs and restructurings. But he liked the sky. Free bird.

Steve picked up her T. Anthony bags from next to the head. In the dim light of the cabin, the royal-blue canvas against the tan leather piping looked especially durable. It should. She wondered if her mother, in thirty years as a teacher in Jonesboro, in East Tennessee, had ever in one month earned as much as one T. Anthony bag cost, teaching little demons who did not want to know about Wordsworth and Keats.

The door snapped open, and a blast of fresh air brought Nicole Miller back to her senses. She remembered that she had not applied any new makeup. In one instant, she touched her lips with her Princess Borghese Etruscan Red lipstick, stuck it back inside her bag, and walked down the flight stairs to her family.

"I want a real hug," her mother said, smiling her toothy smile. "A real hug right up against Mother."

"I'm glad to see you, Nicole," her father said. She could see that his mind was already at work on whether he could get home in time for the game, whatever game it might be tonight.

Mom hugged her. Dad touched her lightly on the cheek. Ginette, bearing up bravely under her name, visibly goggling at Nicole's pearls, squeezed her sister and rubbed her hands against the coat.

"Is this mink?" she asked in her startlingly deep Tennessee drawl.

"Chinchilla."

"Does it cost a lot?" Ginette gasped.

"Yes. A lot."

"Ginny," the mother said. "Ginny, how common."

"I just want to know," Ginette said as if she had rehearsed it. "I just want to know, because my big sister is my only way of knowing about a whole way of life I never can even imagine."

"It's still common to ask how much things cost," Julie Miller said.

"I just want to know about her life, because just Nicole, all by herself, is the most exciting thing that's ever happened to Jonesboro since the Civil War." Maybe Ginette was practicing for an essay contest.

In the car, a 1982 Buick Regal—come to think of it, the first American car that Nicole had been in except for limousines in almost a year—Nicole watched the Falcon take off again for New York. She watched the lights of the University of Tennessee slide by, and the statue of Andrew Jackson in front of the main admin building.

Then the endless sprawl of Jack in the Box and Foster's Freeze and McDonald's and Church's Fried Chicken, and then suddenly, like a neon light that snarls and then goes out forever, Knoxville came to an end, and there were the trees and ridges of the Smoky Mountains, lit up and washed with white moon and blue phosphorescence in the late December night.

"I know you're sleepy," Ginette whispered to her sister in the backseat. "I know you probably are sick of hearing this question."

In the front seat, Ray Miller had the radio on to an endless sports wrap-up. Julie Miller just turned around and beamed at Nicole. "Don't bother your sister," she said. "She's tired. She had a long flight."

"On a private jet," Ginette gushed. "I just have to know what it's like being rich. What it's really like."

"I'm not rich. I work for a rich man."

"Same difference."

"Wouldn't it be pretty to think so," Nicole said, and poked her sister in the side.

Later that night, when Nicole stepped out of the little modular Sears Most Durable, Do It Urself shower that she shared with her sister, Ginette was already playing with her cosmetics. In front of a vanity that had once belonged to Nicole's mother, Ginette sat on a vinyl stool and looked through Nicole's Hermès bag. She plucked out first one lipstick, looked at it, dabbed it on her lips, and then took out another and did the same with it. While Nicole toweled herself dry (amazing the difference between ancient Montgomery Ward towels, with their worn, thin nap, and the new, thick towels that Barron picked up at Polo, which seemed to literally suck the water off her skin), she wondered if the girls who had just gotten off the bus at the Trailways Station in Hollywood marveled at the pimps' Cadillacs and Jaguars.

Finally, Ginette picked out Chanel's Midnight Red and applied it with surprising finesse to her lips. The effect was electric. With those two little swipes, the hillbilly was transformed into a movie star. Just that rich, lustrous red was all it took. So easy. That's all it took. You didn't have to dismember Westinghouse or issue zero-coupon bonds or float convertible preferred. Just sixteen dollars in 1987 money for a tube of Chanel Midnight Red, and the process was begun. The way that Ginette looked at herself in the mirror with her new lips made Nicole want to cry. All the things that you think are so fixed, all the paths that you think would be so hard to be on or to fall off—it's all so easy. People are so hungry.

And yet, Barron had told her that until he met her he was a mole living underground, and that from the first day he talked to her at the AA meeting she had switched on the sun. He had told her that he had been a one-eyed man and now he could see depth, that the world was black and white and she had made it color— rich and red and blue and yellow and even sometimes dazzling perfect white, whiter than any white he had ever known when its only opponent was sickly black.

"When I'm with you," he said, "it's like I'm plugged into an electric socket all the time. That's how I feel. Like I'm in an electric chair, only it feels good. Just looking at you." That's what Barron, who made her feel today as if she had broken glass in her stomach, had said.

"Can you buy as many of these as you want?" Ginette asked, hefting a fistful of other lipsticks from Chanel and Borghese. "I mean, do you have to worry about what it costs?"

"You always have to worry about what everything costs."

"All right," Ginette said, laying down the cosmetics and jumping into the little maple single bed across from Nicole's. "Mom and Dad have gone to bed. It's just us. You can tell me. You're his girlfriend, right? There's nothing wrong with it. God, look what it's gotten you. The girls here pay for the beers. But tell me, 'cause I'm your sister, what's it like? What's he like? What's the whole thing like?"

Outside, on a hill somewhere in the Smoky Mountains, a wolf sobbed. "C'mon," Ginette said. "Tell me everything, like how it started and how you first met him, and when you could tell you liked him, and what he's giving you for Christmas and everything."

But by then it was too late for Ginette, because Nicole Miller was already adrift in her own thoughts in her own maple twin bed, not in the silk pajamas that Barron had given her for the trip, but in a pair of J.C. Penney flannels she had found in the bottom of the old pine chest she had used since she was a child. Just for that night, flannel felt perfect. Under its reassuring familiarity she could dream unconflicted dreams about a tall gangly financier with an unlikely country boy's smile and blue eyes and light brown hair that belonged in a cornfield and not on Wall Street.

2

A   BOY'S   LIFE

"All history is the history of class struggle." It was and is an interesting, thought-provoking line. Barron Thomas was gripped by it the first time he read it in *The Communist Manifesto* in his Contemporary Civilization class at Columbia University in 1962. Barron, a gangly, pale Texan in a school filled with chunky, aggressive Brooklyn and Bronx boys lugging around organic chemistry texts, liked the rhythm of the words. "All history." So this one phrase explained *everything.* "Is the history of class struggle." So fighting, struggling, combat, determined everything.

For Barron, just out of St. Mark's School in North Dallas, not to be confused with St. Mark's School in Southborough, Massachusetts, the idea that one theory might explain everything important that had ever happened was dazzling. In his youth, in North Dallas, life had seemed to be just a series of randomly connected dots.

His father, a gruff former B-17 gunner and now a part-time real-estate developer and dabbler in selling used private planes, disappearing for days on end to make fanciful deals in Oklahoma real estate. His mother, Maggie, a startlingly beautiful tall, thin former Pan Am stewardess from the days when "stewardess"

16

meant smart and beautiful, a flying model from Fifth Avenue, not a flying cocktail waitress from a Holiday Inn lounge. Maggie keeping Barron and his brother Austin well clothed and well read, making sure that they read at least one chapter from *The Count of Monte Cristo* or *The Three Musketeers* or *Huckleberry Finn* even before they were in the first form at St. Mark's. Maggie, always cool, always in control, always able to deal with everything, from a missing mortgage payment to a teacher who kept Barron back because Barron corrected her math in an algebra problem about two trains approaching each other from two cities at different speeds. Maggie spoke to the headmaster and had Barron advanced one grade in math.

(That had been another dazzling epiphany for Barron: the possibility that mathematics might explain the seemingly jumbled nature of life, the reason that he felt so confused so much of the time when nothing bad was happening. That god had failed when Barron got to plane and solid geometry, which seemed to explain nothing that had any connection with why Kathy Black or Neely Rasmussen, the two cutest cheerleaders from St. Viviana's, wanted to go out with boys with grease under their nails and a perpetual reek of 10-D-40, even if they were rich, and wouldn't even return Barron's phone calls. In other words, mathematics as an explainer had not survived love, and that should have given Barron a clue.)

The seemingly random series of blips flashing across the enormous Dallas sky: the father and mother who got divorced when Barron was in the third form. The father who flat out told Barron when he left that he guessed he just wasn't cut out for being a dad, but that a kid as smart as Barron could be his own dad, he guessed. He told that to Barron in the family room while he packed up his shotguns and watched the farm report to see if his futures contracts had come into the money. Of course, they never did. Of course, Barron would never watch the morning farm report again.

Maggie telling them that they would have to move to an apartment. Barron volunteering to get a job at a department store moving merchandise and taking inventory and really taking a job as a moving man so that he could earn twice as much per hour. Maggie would have never permitted it if she had known. Her son did not work with his hands.

Barron debating the Kennedy-Nixon election at St. Mark's, taking the Kennedy side in a school that thought that the first plank in Kennedy's platform was compelling all Texas white women to have sex with blacks and raise the children as Catholics. St. Mark's was Presbyterian. Barron so soundly defeating his rival in the debate that the rival waited for Barron after school and hit him with a hockey stick. Barron refused to go to the hospital because he had to take the college boards the next day. He still did well enough to get into Columbia, although his mother would have preferred Princeton.

"Princeton is for boys who already have money," Barron said. "Columbia is for boys who want to make money."

"Life is not about money," Maggie said, and that, too, was a random little red dot. As far as Barron could tell, and he certainly intended no disrespect to his mother, life was more or less entirely about money, at least in Dallas.

It was a lead pipe cinch that when Barron was in the sixth form and looking for a date for the Petroleum Cotillion, the girls at Hockaday were a lot happier to go out with a Hunt or a Cullom or a Davis that they had never met than with Barron Thomas, who for a year had been helping them with their term papers on the causes of the Civil War.

If his mother thought that life was not about money, she must be the only one. It sure was about money when Barron wanted to buy a car and his mother said that he could alternate using her Dodge instead of having his own Ford.

All history is the history of class struggle. Maybe that explained everything after all. It sure looked as if it explained what he had been doing in a school filled with boys far richer than he was, far worse students than he was, far better loved and preferred by girls, faculty, and staff than Barron. Maybe it explained life everywhere.

18

The Marxist phase of Barron's life lasted about one semester. In that time, he joined the Congress of Racial Equality. He drove down to Cambridge, Maryland, in an ancient Chevrolet with red-diaper babies from Columbia and picketed in front of a crab house that would not sell its crabs to blacks at the counter, but would allow them to take out fried crabs. The leader of the demonstration was a charismatic black man with a huge head of hair. The black man had the unusual name of H. "Rap" Trefoil.

While Barron was talking to Rap, at about the time the demonstration was going to break for lunch, Barron saw a caravan of Maryland state troopers pull up in front of the Delmarva Crab Palace. Within half an hour Barron was in a crowded room at the Dorchester County Jail. The white demonstrators were in one large cell, divided down the middle for men and women. Across a dank cement hall the black demonstrators, men, women, and children, were all crammed into a far smaller cell. The heat in the jail was overpowering. All around him, Barron could smell sweat and human flatulence and fear. Across the hallway, in the black cell, three women fainted. Others started to moan and keen.

Barron watched as the white deputies laughed and giggled and talked about "coons" and "nigger lovers." Surely this, as well, was a form of class struggle. Perhaps at that very moment, some major turn of history was being decided by what was going on in the Dorchester County Jail in September 1962.

Just as Barron was thinking about his luck in being part of the class struggle, two events happened almost simultaneously. First, across the thin partition between the women's and the men's white jail cells, through the wooden dowels separating staff and distaff, Barron caught sight of a girl whom he had seen two nights before at the West End Bar on Broadway. She was a tall, thin girl with a round face and long, straight autumnal gold hair, and light, watery blue eyes. The girl had been with a famous grandson of wealth, "Tweedy Eddy" Stewart, her hand in the pocket of his Paul Stuart blazer, looking up at his chiseled features. She had barely acknowledged Barron when he started to remind her that they both worked at the college radio station, WKCR, and she had then passed on in stately procession. Barron thought she was the most nearly perfect girl he had ever seen. She had basically cut him dead.

Now, in the holding tank at the Dorchester County Jail, she looked at Barron through the wooden bars and said, "I'm so glad you're here. I'm starting to get really scared."

Barron had said to her, in a voice that sang a confidence he did not feel, "They can't do anything to us. The whole world is watching."

It had just the right combination of poetry and practicality and reassurance. Barron had seen a look of relief pass through her eyes.

Yes, Barron thought. This is the place I am supposed to be at this moment. Never mind whatever losses I took in the past. Never mind anything but this moment. Columbia with its insensate premeds is on another planet. North Dallas with its girls who did not know I am alive is on the dark side of the moon. At this moment, I am in the center of whatever is supposed to be happening to me. I'm in the center of everything that's happening to everyone.

One instant later, as two more black girls passed out, Barron started to ask a deputy if the black people might be given water. Just the look of obstinate hatred in the man's eyes had so startled Barron that he thought of the times in his childhood that he had been so frightened that he had simply fallen to his knees and started to say the Lord's Prayer.

Acting on an impulse which Barron could not have fully explained even twenty-six years later, Barron had taken the hands of the two Columbia men standing next to him, pulled them to their knees, and started to pray in a loud, deep voice: "Our father, who art in heaven, hallowed be Thy name . . ."

In three seconds, every prisoner in the jail was on bended knee, saying the Lord's Prayer in a strong, resonant voice. When the words ". . . the power and the glory, forever and ever, Amen" came out, Barron could see that Rap had picked up the cue. Without missing a beat, he led the whole group, now standing, in singing "Oh beautiful, for spacious skies, for amber waves of grain . . ." and then in "God Bless America."

In ten minutes, the sheriffs, some with tears in their eyes, were processing the prisoners for release on their own recognizance.

That night, Barron drove back to New York City with Katy Lane, the girl with the round face and the hair like autumnal gold. The next morning, as he lay next to her in a room at the King's Crown Inn and ran his fingers through her hair and touched her breasts as she slept, Barron decided that perhaps all history was not in fact the history of class struggle.

Maybe, instead, all history was those randomly connected little dots. Maybe all history was coincidence, not explained by any one force like gravity or class struggle. Or if there was one force, as far as Barron could tell, it was some kind of mysterious amalgam of luck and timing and unexpected inspiration. Bearing all of those waves was a tidal current of human longing for authority and power and money and belonging and, above all, love. Maybe all history was the working out of chance events mingled with human need. Vague, but then Barron was in college.

How else explain that he was in the hotel room with Katy Lane? Maybe the little red flashes of randomness had turned in the right direction for once. Maybe coincidence was in the driver's seat, and had taken a turn off the sere landscape of North Dallas and down a lush country lane on the Eastern shore—with an occasional detour.

Barron had been an almost total loner at Columbia. His sole connection with the rest of the school community had been through his reading a fifteen-minute wrap-up of the foreign press on Sunday nights. He would go to Times Square and buy copies of the London *Times,* the *Manchester Guardian,* the *Melbourne Gazette,* and the *Toronto Globe,* and read selected stories from them into an immense microphone, and then return to a lonely room in Furnald Hall with a roommate who was always in Butler Library studying (what else) organic chemistry.

Katy Lane's cousin, Grant Phillips, was the president of the most exclusive fraternity on 114th Street. The Alpha Delta Phi did not have the richest boys on campus, who were in the ZBT house, or the most arrogant, who were in St. Anthony's Hall. A.D. Phi had the best dressed, most literary, most cosmopolitan, coolest, most envied boys on a campus not at all noted for cool of any kind. A.D. Phi had the boys who had the prettiest girlfriends from Vassar and Sarah Lawrence and Barnard.

Within twenty-four hours of his return from Cambridge and his morning with Katy Lane, Barron had been asked to rush the A.D. Phi House. He was elected president of his pledge class. In the pledge class was a boy named Harrison Turman III. Harrison was a shy, rotund boy with a way of clamming up and saying nothing when he was around a girl.

Barron felt a kindred spirit in Harrison Turman, who was just as lost and fearful on the outside as Barron was on the inside. Barron took Harrison under his wing. He persuaded Katy to fix Harrison up with a shy but attractive girl in Reid Hall by the name of Annie Bright. It was love at first sight, and Harrison was forever grateful. He had, as he often told anyone who would listen, been introduced into the world of women by Barron Thomas, and for that, he would always be Barron's friend. (When he was drunk, he would say that Barron had led him into "the world of pussy," but Harrison was rarely drunk.)

Harrison Turman's father was chairman of the Department of English at Columbia College. He was also the teacher of Barron's Intro to Eng. Comp. class. Previously, on Barron's first paper, an essay on someone he had never even heard of named Alfred North Whitehead, Barron had gotten a D minus. A note had said, "I hope you plan to be a scientist, because your ability at verbal expression is pitiful."

That was before Harrison Turman had taken Barron to lunch with Professor Turman, a distinguished gray-haired man who could have played the Marlboro Man as an Ivy League teacher, if the Marlboro Man had been an Ivy League teacher. At lunch, at the Faculty Club, Harrison had told his father that he would probably have dropped out of college had it not been for Barron taking him under his wing.

22

Harrison's father, Harrison II, had nodded. Between bites of boiled fish, he told Barron that he had observed that he had a certain "unique exuberance" in his writing style. Harrison II hoped that Barron would take direction to "refine" his writing style and make himself better understood on the written page. Barron had assured Harrison II that his entire effort from then on would be to learn from a man who had won the Wells Prize at Williams in 1937. Harrison II had no idea that anyone in the world besides his wife knew that he had won the Wells Prize. Barron said that he knew about it because he made it his business to know something about the men who had sacrificed high-paying jobs in private industry to teach him.

On his next paper, on someone whom Barron had also never heard of named Benjamin Disraeli, Barron took special care to sound refined. He used "rather" instead of "very" and inserted the word "tended" whenever possible. He got a B plus. The same week, he changed his major from geology to English Lit.

That was Barron's career at Columbia. Katy Lane was his girlfriend from the day in Cambridge until one month after graduation. Barron lived in the Alpha Delta Phi house for three years. He took high honors in English and wrote his senior thesis on Jack Kerouac. He had Harrison II for five classes and got A's in all of them. He was not Phi Beta Kappa, but he was close enough to graduate cum laude.

On his last night at Columbia, Barron walked across the bridge that connected the Law School, on the east side of Amsterdam Avenue, with the main campus, west of Amsterdam. He stopped and looked over the traffic flowing uptown and downtown.

Barron walked into a lounge off the lobby of Livingston Hall and sat on a red leather couch. He looked at the marble fireplace across from him. On it were carved the words "Hold fast to the spirit of youth, let years to come do what they may . . ."

Barron felt frightened. It was the summer of 1966. He was about to go to Washington, D.C., to work at the Department of State's Arms Control and Disarmament Agency. After that, he would start at Yale Law School.

Barron frankly had no clear idea of why he was going to the ACDA or to Yale. He knew many young men who had gone into law. He guessed that the law was a harsh mistress but that she paid well and could support one more single man, to coin a phrase. He knew that young interns had a good time in Washington in the summer. But why should he go to Washington or to Yale instead of going back to Dallas or going to spend a summer in Europe or spending a summer doing research on an ice floe in the Antarctic?

If it were all just connected dots of randomness, with the connective tissue as the ongoing rush of time, with one dot attached to the other simply by the fact that the dots happened and that the man they happened to was still alive, then the future was a dark blur. All of the luck and success that Barron had enjoyed predicted nothing about what would happen to Barron the next day or the day after that.

On July 4, 1966, in Washington, D.C., Barron and Katy, who was interning at the Pentagon, in the office of the Assistant Secretary of Defense for Procurement, went to a party. It was a black-tie party for the Junior Foreign Service Officers' Association. Barron had bought a ticket in the State Department cafeteria two days before, because he and Katy had no plans for Independence Day.

Katy and Barron went through a receiving line where they shook hands with a weary Dean Rusk. Then they went into another line to get rumaki and pigs in blankets. Then they danced to a band from a high school in Arlington.

At nine-thirty, fireworks began to explode in the southeast, above and around the Washington Monument. The guests, neat and trim and earnest in their cocktail dresses and tuxedos, lined up against the balcony to watch the red, blue, green, and white nebulas form, disappear, and re-form above the obelisk.

Katy stayed inside to talk to a friend from Barnard about where she would apply to graduate school in foreign relations. Next to Barron, at the railing, staring at the fireworks, stood precisely the most beautiful girl Barron had ever seen, an order of magnitude beyond Katy Lane.

She was tall and thin, with burnt auburn hair. Her facial features were model perfect: high cheekbones, perfect, full lips, soaring delicate eyebrows, and even, gleaming, almost smiling teeth. When one particularly earthshaking salvo went off, followed by dazzling blue light, the young woman said to Barron, "Think what it would be like to be inside one of those things and watch it explode from the center."

Barron was struck by the woman's soft Southern accent. He did not exactly understand what she could mean by the remark about the fireworks, but it showed an inventive turn of mind. In Barron's life experience, women that beautiful, including Katy Lane, rarely said anything unless in extremis. For this woman to both look like a page out of *Vogue* and sound the way she did, in content and accent, was bewitching.

"I think you'd probably never forget it," Barron said. "But I think it would get very tiring." That was the best Barron could do on short notice.

Still, the young woman seemed to find it thought-provoking. "That's just it, isn't it? When you're in the center of things, it wears you out. That's what my father says, anyway."

Again, the voice and the face in combination were overpowering. And familiar. But it was not until the fireworks ended, and Barron walked into the dining room with the young woman, whose name was Saundra Logan, that he realized why she had a haunting quality of familiarity.

Saundra Logan, who looked even better in better light, who had that gossamer look of perfection on close inspection, was the face, figure, and voice of the 1965 and 1966 Mustang convertible. He had seen her on TV, in magazines, even on billboards a hundred times. In her tight jeans, standing in front of a red convertible and saying, "For the rebel inside you, put yourself in the rebel outside you," or some similar line, in her soft Southern voice.

He had even seen her interviewed on what it felt like to be a famous model, a spokeswoman when she was seventeen and a senior at the Madeira School.

But here was the miracle. This woman, this icon of beauty, femininity, and nationally ranked allure, hung on his every word. She was at the ball with a young foreign service officer whom Barron recognized dimly, who was in turn talking animatedly and smoking many cigarettes with a Marine guard.

As far as Barron could tell, this vision from paradise wanted nothing more than to spend the evening talking to him, Barron Thomas, famous nerd loser of St. Mark's School in North Dallas. It was as if Sandra Dee had stepped off the screen and said she wanted to go home with Barron instead of with Troy Donahue.

Of course, for a Barnard girl, Katy Lane was pretty. Of course, she was a nice girl. But compared with Saundra Logan, the Mustang Girl? Compared with a woman who got paid thousands of dollars just to show her face to a camera?

Not only that, but Katy, to be frank, complained a lot. She even complained about Barron's snoring, and about whether his shirts were ironed well enough.

But Saundra Logan, who was clearly at least one sheet to the wind, laughed and smiled with gusto at every word Barron said.

And, even in this snooty crowd, everyone was looking at Barron. Just to be with Saundra made him a star. Not only that, but Saundra's father was Carstairs Logan, direct descendant of a famous Civil War general on the Rebel side, and now U.S. Ambassador to the Sudan. Her mother was Lolita Logan, a famous party-giver in the capital.

This woman was actually making Barron promise to keep talking to her after she came back from the ladies' room. This woman was actually asking Barron to get her a drink.

This was a vision from nirvana wafting down into his life. This was a woman who took away all of the fear and ambivalence he felt about his life and replaced it with smooth, flowing euphoria. This was, in a word, too good to be true. Katy Lane, and their moment in Cambridge, Maryland, had been at the extreme end

26

of the spectrum of earthly delights. Now, Barron was in outer space.

After about an hour, during which Katy was still talking to her friend about Johns Hopkins School of Advanced International Studies, Barron said to Saundra, who, it turned out, was just about to enter Vassar College, "Why are you bothering to talk to me? Is this to make your friend upset that he's talking to the Marine, or what?"

Saundra, who was by then at least two sheets to the wind, pulled him behind a pillar, and in a voice which erased every memory he had ever had of humiliation at the hands of women, said, as she brushed her nose against his neck, "Because you're the sexiest man in the room. Because you look so smart, and to me, smart is sexy."

Saundra Logan was eighteen years old. She had about her all of the energy, the enthusiasm, the girlishness of youth. It was as if she could recall him to his own youth and rewrite it. What fear? What ambivalence? With the Mustang Girl by his side? Are you crazy? With Eileen Ford's prize hanging on his every poor joke? Forget about it.

It took Barron about one hour after the dance to realize that he was with the wrong girl. Katy Lane was a fine woman. Would make someone a great wife. But to compare her, who had, so to speak, reached the point of diminishing returns, with Saundra Logan—well, that was truly a joke.

Barron broke the news to Katy after he and Saundra had been out surreptitiously a few times. After a night of drinking and spareribs at Trader Vic's, after a night of drinking and fried chicken in Frederick, Maryland, after a weekend in Rehoboth Beach when Barron had lain next to the softest, youngest, smoothest Rebel skin he had ever imagined, Barron told Katy that maybe they should spend some time apart.

Katy took it well. She told Barron she wished him well, demanded all of her letters back, and told him that she was probably going to spend a year in Bangkok as an intern at Air America anyway.

On a dewy morning one week later, Barron got a call from Katy Lane's roommate at a rented house in Georgetown. Katy Lane was dead. She had been in the passenger seat of a Triumph Spitfire with a "new guy she was dating just to upset you" and she had been struck by a pickup truck from Fort Myer going the wrong way on the George Washington Parkway.

The same day as the funeral, Saundra Logan told him that it was not his fault, but that if he wanted to take a few months to think about life and not be bothered by a "pesty little girl" (!!!), she would just write to him from Poughkeepsie and not call him.

He told her that would be nice. (It was a time in American life when people still had some consideration, Barron recalled long afterward. A time when there was dew on the grass next to the brick sidewalks on Capitol Hill, and life was young, and people thought that consideration and forbearance were not just for Mother Teresa. In twenty years, when Barron was in depositions, it would seem like the days of the Sun King.)

A few days later, Barron packed up his Chevrolet sedan and headed up to New Haven. On his first night there, he could not find anyone in the dorms to have dinner with him. He ate pizza alone, like Warren Beatty in *Splendor in the Grass,* missed Katy and Saundra, and felt like a thought criminal.

Within three months, Barron was the most miserable law student at Yale. Constitutional law, contracts, torts, civil procedure—they were all impenetrably dull. The students were ambitious and aggressive on a scale which made the organic chem students from Flatbush seem like sprightly wood nymphs. New Haven was dreary and flat. Above all, Barron was racked with guilt over Katy.

After the first month, Saundra Logan came to see Barron every weekend on a bus of Vassar girls who were discharged into the horny embraces of Yale students across from the Taft Hotel. They lay in bed together, and Barron had fits of panic and terror over his life at law school. They sometimes drove into New York for the weekend, drank, took amphetamines—which were the rage at Vassar that year—and Barron stayed up at night fearful, guilty, and confused.

He felt as if he were on the edge, looking into adult life, looking down into a black, seething pit called being a grown-up. It scared him. The dead hand of law scared him. The classmates who were twice as ambitious as Sammy Glick scared him.

Saundra Logan tried to make his life as easy as she could. She never nagged Barron to study. She never told him what he must do for his career. She was just there, telling him what she thought would soothe him, doing to him what she thought would soothe him, her skin just as soft as a spirit in the night. "I'll be like a baby chicken," she said. "I'll just follow you around and I won't bother you. But I'll be there when you need me."

In the night, lying next to Saundra in the Sterling Law dorms, Barron knew he was with the most miraculously kind creature, as well as the most beautiful creature, on God's earth. It didn't really make any difference. He fell farther and farther into a delirium of internal anarchy.

He was not helped by a visit to the school psychology clinic. A doctor there gave him a medley of powerful phenothiazine tranquilizers. Barron had an allergic reaction and went into shock. When he awoke, one day later at the Yale Psychiatric Institute, Saundra was next to him.

"Get out of here," she said. "I'll be waiting for you no matter what. Just get out of law school and get some change."

But where? Somewhere far away. Somewhere the memory of Katy could not reach him. Somewhere he could still be young. Somewhere he could actualize the rage and fear he felt about the precipice of adulthood.

On one weekend in November 1966, Barron took an indefinite leave of absence, signed by Dean Henry Varnum Poor himself. He shipped most of his goods to his mother in North Dallas. He drove to Poughkeepsie before dawn on a Sunday and woke up Saundra. He told her he was going to Marine Officer Candidate School in Quantico, Virginia.

She cried and said that she would pray for him night and day. She said her whole life would be a prayer for him. She said she wished he wouldn't, but she would never tell him what to do. "I won't date anyone else," she said. "I'll write to you every day."

Unearned grace, Barron thought as he headed south. This is what Saundra is. Unearned grace. For a woman that spectacular to love me, to be that devoted to me. There's no reason for it. It's just a miracle. That much love from a girl who came down from heaven in a Mustang convertible to love me: That's unearned grace.

Every day that he was getting swatted with pugil sticks, heaving up his guts from running up and down sandpiles with full field pack, giving a sergeant with a gold tooth fifty push-ups when he thought his arms would break, he got a letter from Saundra. Every day that he was feeling exhausted, defeated, confused, he got a letter from Saundra.

The day that his unit flew with the other First Division jarheads to Saigon, he got a letter from Saundra. She also called him, and in as moving and girlish a Southern accent—a hallucinatorily beautiful Southern accent—as he had ever heard, she sang to him a song she should not even have known.

" 'I'll be seeing you in all the old familiar places, that this heart of mine embraces, the whole day through, in a small cafe, the park across the way, the children's carousel, the wishing well . . .' "

Barron could not stop sobbing into the pay phone at Andrews Air Force Base. "I'll be thinking of you every minute, every morning, and every night," she said. "I'll pray that you come home safe." Her voice was breaking up into little college-girl tears and sobs.

"I love you, too, Saundra," Barron said. "I'll never forget the way you stayed by me through all of this. No one else in the whole world would have done it."

"Any woman would have done it for you," Saundra said, crying. "Call me as often as you can."

Barron was in un-Marinely tears until about Wake Island, when he had to start making sure that his men's web gear was in decent shape. As he looked at their young black, white, and brown faces, he realized that in some way, every one of them had someone like Saundra back home, and a lot of them would never see her again. At that moment, Barron started to pray minute by minute that God would let him see Saundra again, and let them have a life together with this craziness far, far behind.

Within about nine months after reading that he should "hold fast to the spirit of youth, let years to come do what they may," he was leading a platoon of Marines from the Second Battalion, First Division of the Corps, along a trail in the U Minh Forest, just east of the Iron Triangle, fifty miles south of Saigon.

Barron was just poking at what looked like an unusually straight branch across his path when there was a deafening explosion and a flash of searing white light. When Barron woke up, he was under a pile of the bodies of his own men. Blood was dripping from two of them onto his face. As far as he could tell, he was the only one of his platoon alive. Also, as far as he could tell, he was almost deaf in both ears, and his elbow was shattered so painfully that he could hardly believe he could feel such keen pain and live.

For twenty-four hours, he lay motionless under the pile of bodies in an unknown clearing in the U Minh Forest. Fewer than twenty feet away, five Vietcong sat by a campfire, ate the dead Marines' rations, urinated on the Marines' bodies, read to each other from a slender pamphlet in Vietnamese, cleaned their AK-47's, checked their sappers' supplies of C-3, batteries and wire, and slept. Then they threw piles of their shit onto the bodies of the Marines, and moved on into the jungle.

It took Barron almost forty-eight more hours to drag himself to a Regional Forces outpost near a village so small that it had no name. Just as a souvenir, when he was carried back for his men's bodies, he took off the ground a slender pamphlet that Victor Charles had been reading and had discarded, apparently as unworthy of being toted through the jungle. It turned out to be a book, a translation that began, "All history is the history of class struggle."

After a morphine interlude of a week at a hospital at Cam Ranh Bay, Barron was airlifted to Camp Lejeune. He was there for almost two months. In four separate operations, his ears were repaired to about ninety percent of normal hearing. His elbow was fitted with a prosthetic plastic hinge. He was given a number of pep talks by a hospital psychiatrist who wanted to recruit him for an antiwar movement on the base.

But most of all, through the ether and the fluorethane and the pentothal, there was Saundra Logan. She had dropped out of Vassar for that semester and taken an apartment in the town of Camp Lejeune. She came to the hospital every day and sat by his bed, or played cards with him, or just sat silently while he slept. Whenever he had to go in for surgery, she was there. When he had to come out of the recovery room, she was there.

The other patients, most wounded far worse than Barron, most without limbs, thought that Barron was probably the luckiest man in the world. "You must have done some major good karma in your last life to deserve her," said a black man in the next bed who did not have a left leg or a right arm below the elbow. "She is much too good-looking for a jarhead asshole like you."

Barron thought she was much too good for a jarhead asshole like him, too. Whatever gift from God she had been when he left, now she was unique in all the world.

"You have to go back to school," he would say to her. "This isn't right."

"Yes, it's right," she answered. "This is the only place I want to be."

One day, after he had been at Camp Lejeune for six weeks, Barron looked at Saundra reading a book about life in Sussex between the wars, and he said to her, "Saundra, when I get out of here, will you marry me?"

"Yes, I will," Saundra said. "I was wondering how long it would take you to ask."

For the remaining two weeks at Camp Lejeune, Barron had as much clarity as he had ever enjoyed. He realized that he did not have to have a reason, an explanation for what life was about. That was for college teachers.

Life was to be lived, and the object of any one day's life was to make it until the next day. Anything more complicated than that was a waste of time. Also, Barron realized that he was probably the luckiest man in the world. Not only did he survive an explosion right in front of his face, he also came back to the United States to find himself with the most beautiful, most devoted woman in the world.

What more was there to think about? Just go for it. Be a short-order cook. Be a valet car parker. Be a printer's assistant. Be a law student. Just to be alive was the idea, and everything else was second-order material.

Barron and Saundra were married at the Fort Myer chapel on July 23, 1968, one year after Barron returned to Yale, more or less, two years after they had met, also more or less. Saundra walked down the aisle in a tightly fitted floor-length white dress with a train, holding the hand of Ambassador Logan. She looked to Barron like a society girl-bride from a *Life* magazine cover in 1940. She was twenty years old.

After Victor Charles and prosthetic surgery, law school was comically easy. Barron made friends, and gathered a circle of law students around him who were politically active. Saundra and Barron played bridge with different couples every night. They smoked marijuana, a habit Barron had picked up "in country," and laughed as the snow fell on the New Haven Green.

By the fall of 1968, Barron had made himself into a leading organizer of antiwar demonstrations. He was one of the only men at Yale who had seen the war up close and had an idea of just what the waste of life was all about. He could tell names and dates and faces that were gone forever, thrown down the rathole of a well-meant but hopeless and never thought-out foreign policy adventure.

Word spread through Berkeley College and Timothy Dwight,

down Morse and Styles, up to Silliman, that over at the law school was a guy who had been there. Barron could count on half a dozen undergrads waiting for him at lunch at the graduate commons every day. He knew that if a poster with his name on it was posted next to Hungry Charlie's, right across from Mory's, he could pack Linsly-Chittenden Hall with five hundred undergrad war protestors.

By that time, Yale was coed. Many of the antiwar protesters were women. They looked up at Barron when he talked about the flying intestines and shattered kneecaps as if he were the Maharishi Mahesh Yogi.

In the campus firmament, Barron's star grew ever more lustrous. He was an honorary Black Panther, working with Huey and Bobby and Angela. He was on the organizing committee for the New Mobe. He picked up tear gas canisters in front of the Vietnamese Embassy and tossed them back at the D.C. police.

He sat on national committees with Bobby and Renny and Abby. He was asked for his opinions by the *New Haven Register* on antiwar issues. He was a leader of men and women, with the most attractive woman in New Haven by his side.

It would be easy to say that Barron and Saundra's life in New Haven was idyllic. But it would be wrong. Saundra was the most devoted of wives when Barron was in trouble. But when he started to become a folk hero at Yale, right up there with Richard Balzer and Mark Rudd, Saundra did not react with enthusiasm. She put distance between herself and Barron. She stayed late at night in the library reading Chaucer and Wordsworth. She joined a women's rights group which had as an article of faith that wives must be cool and curt to their husbands. She refused to clean their tiny apartment on Lynwood Place. She refused to cook. If Barron was hungry, she said, he could make something. If he thought there were too many dustballs on the floor, he could vacuum.

In a way that Barron never understood, his being a campus star, not just *her* star, angered Saundra Logan Thomas. In some way, his assertion of himself—largely made possible by the confidence that he grasped from her love—made her resentful and jealous. That, in turn, hooked perfectly into the women's movement, a supposedly political group which in fact served mainly to give a larger forum for generalized anger owned by women.

But Saundra's anger took more than the form of generalized coolness and reproaches and refusal to clean—which is standard behavior for anyone with responsibilities he or she does not want.

Night after night, often starting in the late afternoon, Saundra drank. She stopped at the Drama Deli after her classes and had a couple of glasses of wine. She went with her pals from the movement to the Howe Street Pizza Parlor and had two or three beers. Then, at night, she had vodka and orange juice, vodka and tonic, sometimes just vodka. She had transferred to Yale, as wives of graduate students were allowed to do fairly automatically, so she was in New Haven around the calendar. Barron noticed that in her first year on campus, she had been to more bars with her pals than he ever knew existed. With a thoroughness that impressed him, she had even managed to find out when the various campus places that served beer or wine opened and closed.

Within a year, on about three nights out of seven, Saundra went to bed buzzed. On at least two of the others, she started out to read in bed and simply passed out after a few seconds.

Barron had never lived with a heavy drinker. Maggie was a teetotaler from her late teens. Barron's father occasionally had a beer with the pilots and the other real-estate developers and commodities traders, but didn't ever get drunk. Even Barron's roommates at Columbia had been too busy studying for the med boards or for the GREs in English Lit. to waste time getting plastered.

When Saundra began to nod out during dinner, Barron at first thought she was sick. When, on a regular basis, her mood would change from helpful and cheery to angry and sarcastic during dinner, usually after the second vodka or the third glass of wine, Barron was mystified.

For example, and it's only one of many in Barron's third year at Yale Law School, imagine Barron speaking to about four hun-

dred undergraduates in the Law School Auditorium. It's an or-
nate room with wood paneling and upholstered theater-type
chairs, a fan-shaped room with the stage at the center. The
undergrads are in jeans and sweatshirts, carrying the heavy coats
and jackets they wore against the February cold of New Haven.

Barron is pointing at a map of Vietnam with a pointer. He's
showing that except for a few cities, and maybe except for just
a few neighborhoods in a few cities, the South Vietnamese do not
control an inch. Forty thousand dead Americans, he says. Over
a million dead Vietnamese. Hundreds of billions of dollars that
came out of the paychecks of taxi drivers and factory hands. The
result is nothing but loss.

"This is a war waged by people who are either cynical on a scale
that can hardly be imagined or are terrifyingly stupid. No matter
how many more lives are lost there, the result will always be the
same: We'll be out on our asses, and Ho Chi Minh will be
running the show.

"I'm not saying I like the Communists. In fact, I hate them.
They're stone pigs. Stone butchers. Stone psychopath mur-
derers."

At this, a number of bearded students hiss and boo.

"Fuck you," Barron said. "I've been shot at, kids. I'm not going
to run away because a few punks hiss at me when I tell the truth."

This always gets a great response, because after all, the kids in
the black-and-red flannel jackets and the torn Levi's and sweatshirts that say OFF THE PIG may be Yalies, but in their little hearts,
they're still Americans.

"My job up here," Barron says, "isn't to make you hate America. It's to make you say that your brothers are getting killed and
having their nuts blown off by mines for no reason at all except
that some war criminals sent them there and some other war
criminals won't bring them home.

"When I tell you to end the war in Vietnam and bring it home
to Babylon, as our brothers in the Black Panther Party have said,
I'm not saying to hate the guys who are there in Pleiku getting
blown up by mortar fire. I'm asking you to help save their lives

36

so they can grow up to have families and live as well as we do here at Yale.

"When we lie down in front of cars in Washington, we're not doing it for the Communists, and we're not doing it because we don't love America. We want to take this country back from the people who just use it to get elected, take it away from people who ride around in limousines on the blood of their own children, and give it back to the people who love it."

Meanwhile, there are girls in the front rows who are staring at skinny Barron from the wrong part of North Dallas and literally rubbing their knees together under their long skirts. In the middle of them is sitting Saundra Logan Thomas, in unusually well fitting jeans, very, very alert because she has taken a white cross before the seminar (amphetamines happen to be very in for two years running), but she looks almost more angry than alert.

She's copping looks at the women in the audience, who are so hip to what Barron is saying that it's almost eerie. Especially to someone who actually might have taken maybe one and a half white crosses.

"When we surround the South Vietnamese Embassy, we're not doing it because we hate anyone. When we tell Tricky Dick to stop the war, when we tell Henry Kissinger to kiss our asses, we're not doing it to bring America to her knees. We're begging Americans to get up off their knees and to stand up and say it's useless, it never made any sense, too many have come home in the body bags. Let's come to our senses. Let's take back America for people who love life. Let's take back America for people who love their own children."

Then Barron stops, and he says, holding up the index and middle fingers of his right hand, "Peace now. It's up to us."

The audience cheers and stamps its feet and afterward a knot of undergraduates and maybe even a few law students want to talk to Barron about "tactics" and "strategy" and "game playing." So Barron and Saundra go over to Hungry Charlie's and have a few chili dogs and Barron has a draft, and Saundra has a few drafts.

On the way home, across the parking lot in front of the Yale

Co-op, Saundra says, "Can't you think of something new to say?"

Barron asks, "Did I ever say those exact same things before?"

"I don't know. It's just complain, complain, complain, so a few girls with big tits can stare at you. That's the bottom line, and I'm so sick of it."

Barron is stunned. "I thought you were totally behind the movement."

"Barron, the movement is for you to show off. That's the movement. What do you care about those guys who are still in country?"

When they get home, Barron takes a shower to get the smoke from Hungry Charlie's out of his hair. He's ready for a go with Saundra. She's lying in bed, and he says, "If you really don't think I'm sincere about ending the war, I've made some big mistakes."

"I don't know what I think," Saundra says. "I have an incredible headache."

When Barron goes into the kitchen to get Saundra water and aspirin, he notices that the ice tray is out of the freezer. He also notices that the Wolfschmidt's vodka is out on the counter. When he brings Saundra the aspirin, she's already asleep. Next to her side of the bed is a mostly empty glass of straight vodka. It's cold out, so Barron and Saundra sleep with the windows closed. The room smells like a bar.

In the morning, when Saundra gets up, she makes Barron tea and tells him what a fabulous speech he gave and how proud she is of him. She also says she still has a righteous headache. She also wants to pick up more white crosses so she'll be ready for her exams.

Barron was bewildered, confused, even dazed by her behavior. He assumed that it had to do with the stress of change in the world, the peace movement, the women's movement, basic envy.

Because Barron had no idea of what to do, he did nothing. By the time of graduation, in June 1970, Saundra pulled off her all-time coup: When Barron gave the graduation speech at the law school, she fell asleep before he finished, a paper cup filled with vodka still in her hands.

"We learned the law here," Barron said to his fellow graduates. "Now, let's teach some law, some law of human brotherhood, some law of the Constitution, some law of respect for life, some law of love thy neighbor, to the people who run this country. Peace now. It's up to us."

Half of the grads and a number of bystanders raised their hands in a clenched-fist salute.

Saundra was asleep in the third row, next to Maggie, who was applauding wildly.

Jesus, Barron thought. What the hell is going on with my angel? What's next?

Aloud, he picked up the chant from his fellows: "End the war in Vietnam. Bring it on home to Babylon." He clenched his fist and tried to look determined.

3

BARRON THOMAS
AVIATION

What becomes a campus legend most? What do you do with a law degree, the need to earn a living, a long, shaggy haircut, and a nationally known bad attitude toward authority? What do you do if you are Barron Thomas and you want to practice the law you have been studying, but don't want to change your attitude?

Luckily, Barron left law school in 1970. In that day, the legal woods were filled with jobs for young people with law degrees who wanted to expand legal protection to people unprotected by the umbrella of legal rights. There were jobs working for public defenders, jobs working with prison inmates, jobs at environmental defense foundations, even jobs teaching at law schools to produce more antiestablishment lawyers.

In those days, as remote from the late twentieth century as the days of Cato the Censor, lawyers were almost expected to spend some time making law reach new territory. The days when being a lawyer meant almost exclusively the insulation of the rich from the processes of black-letter law had not arrived, and would not come until they were unpacked from the trunk of an itinerant actor who had turned his hand to politics.

(The trunk had been packed by some magicians in Chicago,

and even they did not understand what would happen when their baggage actually met fresh air.)

For his part, Barron chose to work in the field of consumer protection. More or less by chance, a close friend from Dallas, Arthur Weiss, who had also attended St. Mark's, had graduated from the University of Texas Law School in 1969 and was happily practicing advertising law with the Federal Trade Commission in Washington. Weiss, a tall, gangly fellow with the largest smile that Barron had ever seen, got Barron an interview with Terry Hutzler, the head of the department of consumer protection at the FTC. Hutzler, who had posters of Che Guevara and Mao Tse-tung on the fiberboard walls of his office, stroked his long red sideburns and assured Barron that he had found a home.

"We think of ourselves as a little cell operating to break down the structure of protection that the big consumer companies got for fifty years from the FTC. We're out to make sure that they don't make little kids into robot consumers of shit that's bad for them," said Hutzler.

When Barron left the office, Hutzler flashed him the peace symbol and said, "Power to the people."

There was good news and bad news about Barron's job as a staff attorney for the FTC. The bad news was that Barron's first assignment was to sue the Fab-Cola Company, the third largest soft-drink bottler in America, for false and deceptive advertising. The gravamen of the complaint was that Fab-Cola had said that consumers would "get more out of life" if they drank more Fab-Cola, and that "your spirits will rise as you lift your can of new, fresher Fab-Cola and drink it dry."

The complaint, signed by Terry Hutzler and a majority of members of the Commission, said that in fact there was no evidence at all that consumers of Fab-Cola were happier than other persons similarly situated. The complaint also said that there was no clear evidence that consumers' spirits did rise in any direct proportion to the amount of Fab-Cola they drank. Finally, the Commission said that the claim that Fab-Cola as of June

1970 was in fact any fresher than it had been at any earlier time was a false claim.

It was Barron's job to make a hearing examiner believe that these allegations were meritorious and that anyone was injured by Fab-Cola's alleged lies.

At first, Barron thought that the complaint might be a joke. Perhaps Arthur Weiss, a notorious prankster, had it sent to his office all officially done up in order to make Barron laugh. When he learned it wasn't a joke, he went to Terry Hutzler and mildly protested.

"I'm not sure we've really got much of a case," Barron said after slapping five with Hutzler. "I think a lot of people really probably didn't take these claims too seriously. They might not have thought they meant much besides obvious hype. Anyway, who cares?"

Terry Hutzler leaned back in his chair. "It's not exactly a perfect case," he said with a low chuckle. "But think of all the aggravation we're going to cause those pigs at Fab-Cola. Think of how we're going to keep them too pinned down with this litigation to spread their filthy drinks, with their processed sugar, into Central America. Think of this as guerrilla warfare, one small unit waging war on the colonial force."

Oh my God, Barron thought to himself. Oh my God.

"Anyway, it'll be good trial practice for you," Hutzler added with another lewd chuckle.

Barron did not at that time know about job switching. He had given a three-year commitment. He thought commitments meant something. He wandered down to his lime green, window-less office, and put his head in his hands.

For over three years, Barron waged the battle of Fab-Cola. He traveled across America seeking and finding expert witnesses. He spent nights and weekends in the law library, desperately trying to find any scrap of law that might support his case.

He fought tooth and nail with Fab-Cola's counsel from Box-wood & Nimrod, a major Washington litigation firm. He sat in

42

dreary rooms and argued bitterly with far more experienced counsel, and felt desperate.

By 1973, a scant three years after he had been on a pedestal of achievement and prestige at Yale, he was a low mole in the most forlorn part of the federal bureaucracy, creeping through humid streets in his pitiful Subaru, wondering what McFate had in mind by sending him to law school in the first place. A man's surroundings, especially the airless confines of a futile cause, can affect a man powerfully. Barron, only a few years from the godhead, was cast down into civil service hell.

At home he lay in bed and watched TV, or else spent hours reading the *Wall Street Journal* cover to cover. In some way, the descriptions of great economic events, transactions of billions of dollars, great enterprises run by human beings much like him, gave him some relief from his feelings of hopelessness—the long, underwater swim that every bureaucrat comes to know.

In a tiny rented row house on Thirty-fifth Place, N.W., in Glover Park, north of Georgetown, Barron lay in bed and stared at the shadows made by the street lights coming through the venetian blinds. Barron and Saundra rented it for two hundred dollars a month, and Barron wondered if his good times were over.

On the other hand, Saundra had stopped drinking.

By prodigies of hard work and extra courses, Saundra had graduated from Yale as an undergraduate just as Barron graduated from the law school. ("The best of both worlds," she quipped. "A Yale husband and a Yale degree.") In Washington, she went to work in Anacostia, a startlingly poor neighborhood within easy sight of the Capitol dome, as a remedial English teacher.

In most places in America, that might have meant teaching English as a second language to Iranians or Cubans or Dominicans. In Southeast Washington, D.C., it meant teaching English to black people whose families had been in America for as long as Thomas Jefferson's family. But these people had been the victims of vicious blows, first inflicted by others, then by themselves, for hundreds of years. One consequence was that they could not read or write.

Other consequences were that they lived with rats the size of kittens and sometimes full-size cats, did not know their fathers, saw their mothers turning tricks when they came home from school, and knew violent death at first hand from the second grade.

But Saundra worked only on the reading and writing part. Every morning she drove off to Martin Luther King Jr. Elementary School and spent six hours with kids who had never even heard of the Eileen Ford Agency or Yale Law School. With a patience that brought Barron to tears, she struggled with each eight-year-old who could not read even "John and Mary walked up the hill" without severe difficulty. Each day, without protest, she retaught the children the same things she thought she had already taught them the day before—but which had been terrorized out of them by a mother's drunken boyfriend.

For a reason that Barron did not understand, Saundra was fearless. Rape was a way of life in her school, and armed robbery was commonplace. But Saundra feared no evil. She figured that if she were doing right by the people, the people would do right by her.

And because Saundra had stopped drinking and Barron was no longer a folk hero, she was no longer angry at walking in his wake. She seemingly was no longer angry about anything. She did her job, loved her heartbreaking charges, and kept her perfect, aristocratic nose clean. She even took up cooking and cleaning the Thomas house, although only on occasion.

Yes, to Barron they were defeated, lost, in a state of free-fall into obscurity and mediocrity, but to Saundra it was just life. The monkey was off her back, and she could breathe in and out without white crosses or vodka.

In 1974, Barron joined the Public Defender's Office in Washington. The Fab-Cola case had been settled with Fab-Cola's solemn promise not to explicitly tell people that their lives would be improved by drinking the beverage or that it was "fresh" in any sense comparable to, for example, a fresh orange. Barron was so sick of Fab-Cola that he became nauseated when he passed a display of the product, with its spokesman, the famous nightclub comic Jack Joey Jr., standing on his head drinking a bottle of it.

At the courthouse on Fifth Street things were considerably more subdued than the life of Jack Joey Jr. and considerably more colorful than at the Commission.

Barron's standard defendant was a black man arrested for transvestism and soliciting for lewd and immoral purposes. The number of these men, who dressed in orange wigs and high heels and falsies, and trolled for customers on Fourteenth Street, right near Henry Kissinger's favorite restaurant—The Empress—was staggering.

Burly ex-Marines, steamfitters by day, clerks in the GAO, hairdressers, by the dozens every night, winter and summer, they were out on the pavements looking for money. They had names, too. "Ooh La La Perkins." "Sweet Jasmine Caldwell." "Couchez Avec Moi Robbins."

There was nothing illegal about their dressing as they pleased. This was a lesson later learned by a famous singer named Cher. But when they copped joints in their lipsticked mouths, there was a problem. That was against the law. That was a lot like prostitution.

"Why?" Velvet Peters (a name much envied in his circle) demanded of Barron. "Why is that different from a lawyer or a dentist hanging out his shingle? We just doing what we can to make peoples feel better."

Barron stood before a judge who could have frozen hell with his boredom and argued with an equally bored prosecutor that his charges should be allowed to get off, so to speak. Sometimes because of a lack of procedural safeguards in their arrests. Sometimes because of novel Constitutional claims such as that the right to privacy includes the right to try out new sexual identities and that denying remuneration for same is confiscation without compensation. Barron's favorite standard argument in that era was that dressing up to perform sex acts was neither more nor less than exercise of a First Amendment freedom of expression, much like dancing topless or writing the Constitution.

Incredibly, sometimes the judge was so dazed by his daily work that he granted Barron's arguments and let off the defendants just for the excitement of being reversed by a higher court.

Barron was thirty-two years old and still on that job, still living in a tiny rented house, when something happened that could best be described as a miraculous opening of an escape hatch from bureaucratic/public service/legal hell. It was one of those experiences that told Barron that there was life beating and pulsing outside of the confines of his own losered-out days.

To set the stage for the miracle that was about to transform Barron, imagine him as he was on a July night in 1977, driving from Glover Park down to the Watergate Hotel, with visions of envy racing through his febrile brain. Saundra was at home reading a novel about life in Kent in 1936 in a wealthy English Catholic family, seemingly an inexhaustible trove for novelists. He was in his Subaru going down Massachusetts Avenue by the capital's embassies and grand homes. The fireflies were out. So were crickets. So were strollers in their cutoffs.

Barron was thinking that he had made a mistake. For the thousandth time that year, he was thinking that he should just have gone into private practice in New York or D.C., gritted his teeth, and done what any other halfway intelligent lawyer would do—make money.

This public service, "serve the people" shit might sound great when you were living at Yale, living the life of a folk hero, but when you were thirty-two, living on what would be tips and gratuities to a partner at Cravath, you had to wonder who was the fool.

In law school, everyone lived pretty much the same. A rich law student lived about the same as a poor law student, and both were coddled equally by the endowment of the school. No matter how broke a student might be, he still ate in the dining room off china on tables with white tablecloths, and studied in a wood-paneled library.

The only real gradations in law school living were how much adulation you could get by becoming a folk hero.

In real life, things were different. The war was over, thank you, God. There was no Movement of any kind. Now, serving the people didn't mean getting huge rounds of applause from fist-shaking coeds on the New Haven Green. Now, serving the people meant waiting in a holding tank that smelled of vomit and flatulence to argue your heart out for a Lewanda Lewis who had blown an undercover cop in Lafayette Square across from the White House, maybe getting "her" off the charges, and never getting thanked by anyone.

When you were thirty-two and still in public service, it meant being short of everything you should have—economic security, self-esteem, a halfway decent work environment, nice people to work with.

Well, maybe people at Covington, Burling were not all that nice to work with, but they surely didn't have clients who offered to pay for writing appeal briefs by going down on them.

Public service might be fine for Ted Kennedy, whose father had been the biggest bootlegger in the history of alcohol, but it didn't really quite fly for someone who had to make a living.

That was what Barron was thinking as he drove into the parking lot next to the Watergate Hotel and prepared for his swim in the long, dimly lit Watergate Health Club pool.

As he did his laps, dodging the lumbering geriatrics who swam by his side with goggles, oblivious to such things as lanes, no doubt numbed by recollections of glory days with Harold Ickes, Barron could feel his funk get more funky.

His only experience was in defending transvestites and suing the Fab-Cola Corporation over what had to be the lamest complaint in the history of jurisprudence. He could not imagine who would want to hire him. Plus, he had gotten to be known for a certain sarcastic quality that did not really endear potential employees to potential employers.

Well, Barron thought as he got slammed for the third time by a woman swimmer whom he knew to have been a typist for FDR, McFate had apparently planned all of this. Who was Barron to possibly defy her edicts? Probably soon someone like Bubbles Turner would simply murder Barron because Barron did not get "her" off on her latest charges anyway, and that would be that.

In the sauna that Barron usually visited after his swim, the usual crowd of cave dwellers discussing who was worse, Jenner or Bricker, was absent. Instead, there were two neat men, with black hair that lay perfectly in place even in the sauna. They were apparently visiting from New York, staying at the Watergate Hotel.

In furious, animated tones, they discussed a topic that made them crazy, as they kept saying. Their job, as vice presidents at Morgan Stanley, was to advise a client's management on how to make the company's shares show some approximation of the underlying asset value of the company.

As Barron learned from the conversation, the company in question was a rust belt conglomerate. It made heavy-gauge industrial wire, railway car parts, brake shoes, and huge cement pipes. The company lacked the glamour that Wall Street liked in those days—when it liked anything. In addition, every time there was the slightest breath of fear about oil prices, the company "took a dump," as the investment bankers said.

"Just the goddamned real estate of the company is worth more than the whole capitalization," the first man said.

"Just the real estate plus the cash plus the receivables are worth twice the capitalization, and the business makes money year in and year out. And it doesn't even have a dime of long-term debt," said the second investment banker.

Barron listened to the plans for a public relations campaign, for a stock buyback, for a name change, for acquisitions in the field of high tech, for a possible merger with a small oil services company that supposedly had discovered a major oil field in the Rocky Mountains north of Steamboat Springs.

Barron cleared his throat. "May I make a suggestion?" he asked. "I'm a lawyer, and I own a few little shares of stock, and I have an idea for you."

"We'd like to hear anything," said the first man, whose name was Regan.

"Why not liquidate the real estate, or at least put it into a liquidating real-estate trust, and then spin it off to the shareholders. Then why not sell any part of the company that you can sell for a greater multiple of its separate earnings than you could sell the company as a whole for, and pass on the proceeds to the shareholders as another liquidating dividend. Then you'll be left with a core business that the market might not value very highly, but from what I've just heard, it throws off a lot of cash flow. By that time, the market will be able to see exactly what kind of a company you have there, and the market will value it strictly according to its cash flow, and then you can feel pretty sure you'll start getting the kind of multiple the company deserves."

"I don't get it," the other man said. His name was Todd. "Surely the efficient market already knows about everything the company owns."

"Fuck the efficient market," Barron said. "The market tends towards efficiency. It never gets there. You have to help it along by telling it in simpler terms about what you've got. The market is a lot of analysts who are too busy to pay much attention to any one company. Make it easy. Make it show and tell. And get some cash out of what's not working."

Barron spoke with the perfect glibness of a man who has nothing to lose, who has been reading the *Wall Street Journal* for years, and who was motivated by a desire to show himself that he knew something more than about how to get transvestites out of Lorton.

"My family is in the airplane business," Barron said. "We almost always found that with a plane that wasn't selling right away, we could break it up for parts—engines, interior cabin, avionics, tail assembly—and sell it for a lot more than we could possibly have sold the whole plane for."

The two men looked at each other. They were moved, as most people are, as much by the enthusiasm of the speaker as by what he said.

"But," Barron said, "any of the buyers of the plane could presumably have done exactly the same thing. The problem is that they were looking at it as a flying machine. My father was looking at it as replacement parts for other flying machines. Same thing with corporations. Analysts know to value flows of earnings. They don't know to value parts. These are inflationary times, and parts can get a lot more than earnings. People see parts and they don't discount for inflation. They *add* for inflation, and that makes a big, big difference."

The two investment bankers looked thoughtfully at each other.

"How would you like to come to New York City to talk to some of our people?" Todd asked. "Maybe lay this out for them."

"We'll pay your usual hourly charge, of course," Regan added. "Could you make it next week?"

Then something great happened to Barron. In that sauna underneath the building where history was made, he felt merging in his person three powerful currents of confidence, carrying along his own intellect.

First, there was pure Fourteenth Street jive con man at work, the most basic kind of sidewalk bunco effrontery. He had learned it from past masters with names like "Wetine" and "Lipps," as they were waiting to go before the judge.

Then there was the hint he picked up from the two men that maybe their jobs or their futures or their bonuses or their asses were truly on the line. He had the feeling of power that the grocer always has when confronting the hungry. It's basic, innate.

Third, there was the mesmerism of hearing his own voice talk in big concepts, big ideas, big numbers—and having eager, sweaty faces respond. He was talking about arbitrage between asset value and stock price, but he might as well have been talking

50

about surrounding the Pentagon or picketing in front of the Kline Biology Tower over chemical warfare research.

The subject, Barron realized in a flash, was by-the-way. It was his ax, as a musician might say. That he was speaking and being heard—that was the payoff.

"I don't know, guys," Barron said. "I don't usually do this kind of law work for other people. I have my family accounts, and I use this kind of analysis for their investments . . ."

"Of course," Todd agreed. "But we wouldn't be talking about your hourly fee here. If it's all right with your partners, we would be talking about other participation."

"My standard would be ten percent carried interest," Barron said. "Plus fees and expenses for out-of-pocket crap. That would be ten percent of your ten percent," he added.

"Our ten percent?" Regan said. "We're the bank. The company is the client."

"Why?" Barron asked. "Why, if you're so sure the company is such a buy? Why not buy it yourself and break it down into its parts? The guy who makes the money isn't the guy getting one percent. It's the guy getting a hundred percent. You'll be an equity player, and you'll get partners, and I'll be your partner inside your part of the deal." In fact, Barron just happened to have read an article about a deal structured just that way and the furor it was causing in Singapore where it was being done. Where had he read it? Probably *Barron's*.

"It could fly," Todd said after a while. "There's a new boy running corporate finance who likes taking down pieces of deals. It could fly."

"Well, call me if it can," Barron said airily. He handed them a piece of paper with his number at his miserable cubicle at the PDO. "This rings through directly to me. This is my deal. It has nothing to do with anyone else at the firm." Like Ray "Lanolin" Turner, he thought.

From the phone booth next to the parking lot entrance off Virginia Avenue, Barron called home. "I have some incredible news," he said. Saundra sounded only faintly interested, but correctly upbeat. "This could mean a major change in our lives," Barron said. "This is like a chance to fly. In fact, it's a lot like flying right now."

"Good," Saundra said. "Tell me about it when you get home. I'm watching 'Mystery' and I'm just about to learn who did it."

In the Subaru, hurtling along the Whitehaven Parkway, Barron thought about how his deal might work. He thought about what it would feel like to have clients who would pay him real money, put him in an office he wouldn't be ashamed of, pay attention to his wants and needs—and also pay for his first-class airfare. The Public Defender's Office made a major stink about paying for parking near the courthouse.

By the time Barron pulled up in front of his rented house, his brain was afire with the possibilities of beating down the doors of his captivity. Yes and yes and yes! Freedom and the land of milk and honey! The exit from the nightmare of his daily life!

In his bedroom, Saundra was asleep. Next to her on the nightstand was a mostly empty tumbler.

Barron picked it up and smelled it. The old familiar scent. Vodka. The same scent, bio-organically processed and mixed with carbon dioxide, came from Saundra's mouth and permeated the bedroom.

Barron left the next afternoon for New York for two weeks of meetings with people from Morgan Stanley and NatSted, the company whose fate had been under consideration in the sauna.

At first, Barron thought perhaps some hoax were taking place. The people he was working with were simply too dense to really be running the affairs of a major investment bank and a major industrial corporation. Barron kept expecting that at any moment the *real* corporate titans would appear, dismiss their office boys who were playing roles, and approach each issue with real depth and thought. It was not until a whole week had gone by, in which Barron's main function seemed to be to make something very simple even simpler and then to repeat it to the same person ten times, that Barron realized something:

52

The people he was talking to *were* the real executives, partners, and overseers of American industrial life. There were no geniuses behind the scenes. These ordinary bozos, in no way at all superior intellectually to Barron's fellow lawyers at the PDO—and often not to his clients—were running Wall Street. Distinguished primarily by several factors—a certain harrumphing arrogance, a disdain for doing anything at all new or different, family connections, a tolerance for long days, an even greater tolerance for trivia, above all, simply by being there—these people controlled huge amounts of the money and power that Barron wanted and deserved.

In the two weeks of meetings that sealed the fate of NatSted, Barron laid out every detail of his plan—usually improvising from 10-K's he had read the night before. He explained away every objection. He thought of a device to give public holders a "stub" interest in the sale of the various divisions. He explained the economics of the thing, about liquidating arbitrages between stock price and asset price.

Then, he did it over again. And then over again.

When the deal was closed with handshakes all around and the decision that the liquidation of the company did not require a vote of its shareholders, Barron was told that he would be General Counsel of NatSted Holdings, N.V. (Netherlands Venture). His salary would be exactly ten times what it had been in the PDO and he would have his carried interest of ten percent of Morgan Stanley's twenty percent. By his math, in two years he would have two million dollars, more or less.

In fact, his math was wrong. The wire division sold for far less than had been expected. So did the concrete pipe division. And charges for laying off workers with pension claims were larger than had been anticipated. But the company also happened to own almost five thousand acres in Rancho Mirage, California, virtually adjacent to Walter Annenberg's estate. It also benefited from a European competitor's wish to get into the auto parts business in a desperate way. Finally, it benefited from the sale of only a forty-nine percent interest in its Japanese affiliate, which had a warehouse near the Ginza, with almost eighty thousand square feet of ground space, one of the largest incompletely developed parcels in Tokyo.

Counting the proceeds from the sales, the putative value of the spin-offs, and the stake that Barron had in the new, slimmed down, but highly valued company, Barron's share, by 1980—three, not two years later—was worth between five and seven million dollars. This was even before an attempt had been made to sell the company's headquarters—the NatSted Tower at Fifty-second and Park Avenue.

God save the Watergate Health Club and all who swim in her waters.

In a market gasping for air, with adjustments for inflation down more in ten years than in the 1929–1939 market, or even the 1929–1933 market, the NatSted "stub" took off like a rocket. Issued more or less as an afterthought by everyone except Barron, who remembered something about managers being trustees from a class at Yale, the security had gone from seven dollars to almost thirty within three years. The entire transaction was the subject of a *Harvard Business Review* colloquium entitled "Fairness to Stockholders—Making It Work for Managers?" Barron sat on a panel in Boston on a sticky day in July 1980 between two reverend professors of finance, each one seemingly trying to sound more obscure than the other, each one seemingly competing to be more unaware of how markets work than the other.

At Harvard, as at Morgan Stanley, Barron had the distinct feeling that he was being played with. Professors Rheingold and Schnelling surely were imposters playing business school professors. Surely men whose main ability seemed to be in selecting wildly mismatched suits of clothing—plaid jackets with horizontally striped ties with vertically striped shirts—could not be senior faculty at a famous business school. Of course, they were. Of course, both offered their personal consulting firms' services to Barron for help with his transactions.

What a novel concept, Barron thought as he left the auditorium at Baker Hall. That someone who knows his business, who has demonstrably done well at his business, would want to hire someone who knows absolutely nothing about his business to assist the knowledgeable one in running the business.

The iron law of consultants: Their assurance at offering their services is exactly proportional to the visible likelihood that the services will be worthless.

The platinum corollary: The charge for such services will be inversely proportional to their value.

On the other hand, it would be a nice gig for the consultant, Barron thought. Of course, it would be different in litigation, where experts were cash in hand to a party. But then Barron certainly expected no substantial litigation other than the usual plaintiffs' nuisance suits for a good long while.

In the fall of 1980, Barron made a new deal with Morgan Stanley and NatSted Holdings. By the terms of the new arrangement, Barron would supervise asset distribution and liquidation, would attend all finance committee and board meetings, and would be free to take on any assignments he wished at any noncompeting industrial company.

His only obligation to Morgan Stanley was to bring them any deals he found first, for purposes of their investment or arrangement of financing.

It was a good deal for Barron. Just in the three years he had been working in the NatSted vineyards, he had found dozens of other companies on which the "ongoing liquidation," "show and tell" method of management would obviously work. He wanted to make it work for himself and Saundra, and make the kind of money that accurately reflected his ability to make it for others.

Moreover, the law of bureaucracies was working against Barron at Morgan Stanley. True, he had brought them a situation whereby they had put up less than ten million dollars of their firm capital and had at least forty-five million three years later. But this excited far more envy and anger than gratitude. Had Barron been an insider with prospects for promotion, his colleagues might have appreciated him more, since gratitude is basically no more than the expectation of future gifts. But since he was an outsider, and usually in no position to pass out raises, bigger offices, or bonuses, he was simply considered either a very lucky wise-ass or, worst of all in the world of investment banking, an unpredictable smart guy. The motto of Wall Street or at least its more seignorial firms had long been "Smart People Are Dangerous." Had there been anyone to whom it would have applied, an even more scarlet emblem would have been "Smart People Who Care About Stockholders' Rights Are *Really* Dangerous."

Barron Thomas just might have been such a person, and so Morgan Stanley was happy to see him go off on his own. Again, with the proviso that should his rather ungentlemanly wit find another deal that paid five-to-one in three years, they wanted a slice of the pie.

Fine with Barron. By that time, he lived, with Saundra, in a three-bedroom penthouse on the Promenade in Brooklyn Heights. Night after night, Saundra would return home from a tiring day teaching at the nearby public elementary school, P.S. 60, where reading and writing of English were only a dim memory, settle down in front of her best friend, her Sony, tuned to any show that had tigers, rajahs, murders in small English villages, or ballet, a large tumbler of vodka and tonic by her side, and drift into oblivion. She rarely spoke to Barron, except to ask him if he "had made enough money today," followed by a lewd chuckle.

Barron for his part went over screens of companies whose assets were substantially below their stock and debt capitalization. He created a program, with the help of a Pakistani programmer named Bradley Singh, that would allow him to figure out whether—after capital costs and transactions costs, and assuming various times for liquidation of assets—a deal was doable.

He did three small deals that involved buying defunct real-estate investment trusts—basically mutual funds that owned shopping centers and office buildings instead of stock—and reselling their pieces. The deals were so small that they barely made it into the *Wall Street Journal*. Still, they made enough money so that Barron became known as a good borrower. If he asked a bank for twenty million for a deal, the bank knew for sure that they would get their money out. For his part, by June 1982, Barron had tripled his nest egg. Much more important to him, since he basically cared only a small amount about material things now that he was past the humiliation-level minimum, he had enough credit to do deals quickly, to get the wherewithal to make a realistic offer in a promising situation.

From his father, Barron had learned that a seller, any seller, wants to hear the words "cash" and "offer" in the same sentence, and everything else is secondary.

Many times in the five years since he said goodbye to the Public Defender's Office, Barron tried to explain what he was doing to Saundra. They would be lying in bed together on a Sunday morning, and Barron would point to a story about a company.

"Look," he would say. "These guys just announced that they're shelving a proposed financing. They're not going to be able to raise money. This means they're in trouble. It's like a homeowner having to sell his house because he's in trouble and he can't get the bank to refinance the house. He's still got the house, and that's worth something, but he's in trouble, and he wants to get some cash, fast."

"So, you buy him out and he loses his house," Saundra said, possibly with a trace of humor.

"Only in this case, it's not someone's house. It's the stockholders, and usually their management is so feckless and screwed up that they desperately welcome anyone who'll come along and cash them out with something, anything, so they won't just have a dead loss."

"Barron, it doesn't sound that complicated. Certainly not complicated enough for you and those guys at Morgan to get paid as much as you do. It sounds like your work at the public defender's was a lot harder."

"Intellectually, practically any law work is more challenging than any financing deal. Deals are just numbers. The hard part of a financing deal is getting all of the personalities to do something voluntarily. In a legal case, everyone is under the court's supervision and everyone is under someone else's thumb, so there's some pressure from somewhere all the time. But in a financing case, you've got a lot of wild Indians and no clear rules of who anyone is. It's always the people who are tough and the numbers that are easy."

"I don't know. Which part is easy?" she asked. By that point, she was usually back to one of her two extremes—reading *W* or grading her sixth-graders' heartrending efforts at arithmetic.

Barron would look over at her. She would stare straight ahead into her magazine or her homework.

By the spring of 1982, Barron had taken to spending ever more time at his office, or flying to visit shopping centers and warehouses that belonged to failing REITs.

Invariably, he felt far less alone in a Hyatt in Tucson, watching the local news about police raids on frat parties, than he did with an unconscious or uncaring Saundra. Still, he always told himself, she was going through a phase. She was adjusting. Surely, no man who had been kept alive by the devotion she had shown him fifteen years earlier could ever complain. Especially about just a few drinks. Besides, he was a big boy, and big boys played with big dollars, and big boys didn't cry.

In June 1982, Barron had a visit in his office at 60 Broad Street from a man who wanted to talk about his company, a small airline. It ran on an unusual hub city plan. From the small town of Salisbury, on the southern tip of Maryland's Eastern Shore, it ran spokes out to Baltimore, to Richmond, to Charlotte, to Atlanta, to Washington, to Boston, Philadelphia, Buffalo, Cleveland, and Toronto.

Because it ran out of a semirural airport, it was staffed by nonunion, startlingly productive pilots and mechanics. The owner was, like Barron's father, a former Flying Fortress pilot. He might have even known Barron's father.

"I'm tired of riding herd on all of this," the patrician, silver-haired man, Colonel Brooke Lee, said. "I'd like to get rid of it. But I'd like to get out and keep some stake in the business for my grandchildren and their children. I know I've got a good operation here, but I don't want to just let it be gobbled up by a big operation that'll put it under to keep out the competition. The folks who work for me are good people. They trust me, and I know that sounds like a joke here, but that means something to me."

"It means something to me, too," Barron said. "Let me ask you a question. Salisbury's about thirty miles from Cambridge, right?"

"About forty," Colonel Lee said.

"I had an adventure there a long time ago," Barron said. "Maybe I'll have another one. Would you like to sell me your airline?"

Barron called Morgan Stanley the next morning. He proposed to the directors of corporate finance that they raise money for him to buy control of Lee Aviation. By Morgan Stanley standards, it was a tiny deal. Ninety million in long-term bonds, which was a morning's work for junior people. In return for Morgan's financing at investment grade rates, Barron gave them warrants for fifteen percent of the company. He likewise sold back to Colonel Lee warrants for another fifteen percent of the company, exercisable only if certain cash-flow targets were met. Colonel Lee stayed on as managing director of flight operations.

Barron immediately broke the company down into three major parts: First, he sold most of the older airplanes to a limited partnership. He took the money from the sale and used it to pay off about half of the Morgan Stanley bonds. Then he took the gates and hangar operations and sold them to another limited partnership. With the funds from that sale, he bought routes that extended to Chicago and to Florida.

The partners who bought the airplanes and the gates got a steady cash flow and solid tax write-offs. Lee Aviation's new routes allowed it to use its aircraft about twice as efficiently as it had before, since longer routes allowed jet aircraft to burn fuel vastly more economically than short routes.

The cash flow from the more effective use of aircraft far more than offset the new external rental cost of new leased planes, gates and hangars. In addition, since the costs of rental were all tax deductible, Lee Aviation could and did avoid any tax liability for four years running.

At the end of the first year of operation, cash flow per share of equity was running at about triple what it had been before Barron restructured the company. Barron had put one million dollars of his own into the deal after his meeting with Colonel Lee. In 1983, one year after his assumption of control of the company, Barron offered the public twenty percent of his seventy percent of the company. It sold in a hot market for seventy-five million net of underwriting fees. That valued the rest of Barron's holdings at roughly three hundred million. It also allowed Morgan Stanley, for no money down, to own warrants suddenly worth roughly one hundred million. Colonel Lee, who had gotten what he proudly called "a righteous price" for the airline, also owned about a hundred million of warrants. The magic of increasing cash flow, plus the magic of the market raising the price/earnings multiple of the stock, made Barron rich.

On the day that the registration became effective, Colonel Lee handed Barron a gold card case. When Barron opened the case, he saw that it contained only one business card. That card read, in flowing cursive script, "Barron Thomas. Chairman, Barron Thomas Aviation."

As head of flight ops, Colonel Lee had already made the shops repaint every 727, every 737, every BAC-111 with new blue and white colors and the name BARRON THOMAS AVIATION.

"Because it was your name and your brains that made it fly," Colonel Lee said, "it should have your name on it. I've already filed the papers with the FAA," he said as they sat on his veranda overlooking the Manokin River in suburban Salisbury. "It's yours in every way now."

"I don't even know how to turn the key in the ignition of an airplane," Barron said.

"Big planes don't have keys," Colonel Lee said. "You just take over the controls and press the start button."

Barron flew back to New York the next night on the Barron

Thomas Aviation flight that connected in Salisbury from Orlando. In the first seat in first class, right next to the aisle, Barron read an article about himself in *The New York Times* business section. "Former Poverty Lawyer Flies Into Affluence," said the headline.

A tall, red-haired stewardess sat on the edge of Barron's seat. She had large, full breasts. Her smile was filled with promise, and even her teeth had an unusual liveliness to them. She looked like a mentally and physically more voluptuous version of Saundra as she had been in 1966. Her name was Lori.

"You've turned into a household word," Lori said to Barron. "It's a big day for us, too. We all have stock in the ESOP, and it means something to us."

In fact, Barron reflected, the employee stock option plan had an unregistered preferred with almost no voting rights, but still, it was nice to be noticed. And, in further fact, if the airline kept doing well, Lori would see some real money from her tiny sliver of the ESOP.

"We're all going to be partying over at the St. Moritz later," Lori said. "Come on over and join us."

"I'm not that much on parties," Barron said.

"I'm not either, really," Lori agreed. "I'll probably just go out to a late dinner all by myself. It's pretty scary going out in New York by yourself. I'll bet you know all the good places, though."

"Yes, but I have to work so your stock gets to be worth something," Barron said, smiling.

"Well, if you feel like celebrating," Lori said with a slightly pouty look, "my name is Lori Holland, and I'll be at the St. Moritz."

Later that night, in his bedroom, looking over the East River and the harbor toward the Statue of Liberty, with Saundra passed out next to him, Barron wondered how he could have been so stupid.

What would have been so wrong in going to dinner with Lori? Saundra had not even responded when Barron told her about the naming of the airline except to wisecrack that now Barron would have to get new luggage tags, and then she was back in her book about ball gowns of the English raj. Of course, Barron would never have touched Lori. But just to see a pretty, enthusiastic face over a good meal? Just to feel a flush of interest coming from a beautiful woman? Just to flirt and get the itch that something good is coming your way if you want it? Something human and warm and female?

What would have been so bad? Anyway, it would have been better than the total frustrated deflation he felt after getting an airline named after him, as if he were somebody, only to be ignored by his wife. *That* made him feel as if the blood were running the wrong way in his veins. Surely, dinner with Lori would have been better. It wasn't as if that kind of thing would ever lead to anything. After all, even if Saundra had rebuffed him for a long time now, and even if he could not clearly recall the last time he and Saundra had had sex, there was a bond from a lot of years, and nothing could touch that. Nothing.

4

B A L L A D   O F   A
T E E N A G E   Q U E E N

There's a story in our town,
Of the prettiest girl around.
Golden hair and eyes of blue,
How those eyes would flash at you . . .

F*or Nicole Miller, the Johnny Cash song had gotten to be a virtual*
anthem in Jonesboro. The whole high school, Kefauver High, as
it was called then, would sing it to her when she began to conduct
the school band at football halftime. They also crooned it to her
at band shows to start the basketball season and to mark Christmas vacation and Homecoming and graduation.

Because, after all, that girl out there on the field, or in the boys'
gym, was Nicole Miller, the Drum Major of Kefauver High, and
the hottest thing that Jonesboro had seen since General Braxton
Bragg marched through in 1864 on his way to try to turn the tide
in the Shenandoah Valley or Lookout Mountain or somewhere.

Nicole Miller would step out of the band dugout under Panther Stadium in her outfit. It was the fall of 1977, and Nicole
wore a short felt skirt, red with black piping, high white leather
boots, a red wool blazer with a white cotton blouse underneath,
and a hat. The hat was a tall grenadier's cap, with a huge, enor-

mous, incredibly unlikely cavalier's feather arching at least eighteen inches above it, waving and twisting in the East Tennessee breeze coming off the Smoky Mountains. Nicole would step out as if she were directing the movements of the Queen's Own Household Cavalry, with just that much pride, with just that much authority. Her sixteen-year-old chin would jut straight out, and her blue eyes would catch the sparkle of the East Tennessee fall sunlight or winter sunlight or the lights on the ceiling of the basketball court, and Nicole would lift up her arms, as if she were controlling the movements of the stars and the planets, and wave her baton—an orchestra conductor's baton, not a tacky majorette's baton—and then march out onto the field.

Then the whole band, two hundred and ten students out of a high school student body for the whole consolidated school district of only five hundred, would march out after her.

Suppose it was Homecoming, the afternoon when Jonesboro played against Knoxville Central High School, and the maples and poplars on the other side of the field still had a few golden leaves on them, drifting lazily onto the nearby grass. The band would come out with Nicole at the head and would march straight out until they formed a triangle on the field. And at the top of the triangle would be Nicole Miller, still looking straight ahead, with the band behind her, leading them not by looking at them, not by waving orders at them. Just by being there. Just by being Nicole Miller at Kefauver High School.

Then, in a maneuver Nicole had practiced all summer, under the leadership of the music teacher, Ricky Wurst, who had been trying to seduce Nicole all year, the band would do something really fancy. Like a dissolving crystal, the band would abruptly melt and fall into itself, with Nicole leading the dissolution. Then the band would re-form itself into the same triangle, only this time with the point of the triangle facing the cement bleachers, and Nicole Miller would raise her arms for the performance to start.

It was at just that moment, just in those ten seconds when the band was about to begin, that the whole school would start waving at Nicole and sing, completely a cappella, "Dream on, dream on, teenage queen . . . ," with pretty good agreement on the melody, because these were kids whose mothers and fathers had been playing Johnny Cash all their lives.

Nicole's mom and dad, Julie and Ray Miller, would beam with pride, literally rock back and forth with glee at what the whole town thought about their little girl. Julie would hold up Ginette so that she could see her big sister, hear the crowd in love with her, share the glory of being the sister of the teenage queen of Jonesboro, Tennessee.

Nicole would just scowl above the chinstrap of her grenadier's cap, set her aquamarine eyes with even more authority, and lift her arms up even higher. Then she would start to tap her right foot and begin to lead the day's program.

While this was Jonesboro, Tennessee, Estes Kefauver High School, the program was not "Tie a Yellow Ribbon 'Round the Old Oak Tree" or "Roll Out the Barrel" or even "Dixie." The program would begin with the first movement from Mozart's Symphony No. 38, then go on to an Impromptu by Chopin, then the Rachmaninoff Prelude in G minor. Nicole knew every note, every instrument's role by heart. Nicole was not just a Drum Major. She was something like a symphony conductor on a grassy field in East Tennessee, in high white leather boots and a totally unlikely grenadier's cap with a foot-and-a-half feather of pure white waving on top of it.

After twenty minutes of this classical invasion of Jonesboro, the band would lower their instruments. Nicole would take a deep breath, then she would lift up her arms again and lead the band in playing "The Star Spangled Banner." The crowd would stand and hold their hands over their hearts, except for the few recent grads in the Army or Navy, who would stand to in a snappy salute.

As the band finished the last flourish of ". . . and the ho-ooome of the braaave," Nicole would be high-stepping in place, arms already raised again, and then with one decisive motion, she would lead the band back into its dugout, and the show would be over.

65

Through it all, one thought would go through Nicole's mind in a thousand different variations. "This is really happening. There are two hundred people on the field, and two thousand more in the stands, and I'm in charge of all of them. I'm in control of everything that happens right now."

It's not wrong to feel that way, Nicole thought. I'm not hurting anyone, and everyone out there is hearing great music, and I'm in charge, and that's how I like for it to be. That's the way I'd like things to be forever.

Then Nicole would sit on her bench in the girls' locker room and breathe deeply and let it all out for ten minutes, the sweat and the dust and the excitement.

The other girls in the band, Elizabeth Eastland, Cheryl Longin, Julie Capretta, all the heavy hitters on oboe and violin, would slap Nicole on the back in the shower and tell her how great she was. Nicole would smile as the hot water washed over her blond hair and would tell Cheryl how great her solo had been and Liz how fantastic her violin work had been, and the four of them would laugh as they toweled themselves dry with the threadbare towels that public schools use, and then the three girls would start humming "Ballad of a Teenage Queen" while Nicole put on her jeans and her T-shirt and her red wool Spiegel sweater and her leather-and-wool band jacket, and head out to the bleachers to meet her parents. Once again, when she walked down the steps to see her parents, a ripple passed through the crowd. "Golden hair and eyes of blue, how those eyes would flash at you . . ."

Men from the post office, women who waited tables at the Volunteer Cafe, little kids from down the street that Nicole baby-sat, old people who came to the football games from the Cumberland Convalescent Home, the boys from her Latin class and her English Lit class, and everyone who saw her would just start to whistle "Ballad of a Teenage Queen" when she passed by.

When she got to her parents, her mother would hug her and say, "Nicole, now give me a real hug," and her father would say, "That was fine drum majoring."

Nicole would take her seat just in time for kick-off. As the music died away in her head, she felt as if this was the way she was destined to always feel. Only in someplace a lot bigger. She had not even gone to the first three tryouts for Drum Major. She had only started to read music in seventh grade. If she could be a Drum Major, and the best Drum Major in the history of Loudon County, according to Ricky Wurst, she could be Drum Major of a much bigger band in a much bigger town someday, and not that far in the future, either. How long? Not long.

Jonesboro was cute. The people were sweet, the way they sang to her when she marched out onto the field. But she had done Jonesboro. She needed a bigger world. She needed a challenge, to be Drum Major for something that made a much bigger noise than the Estes Kefauver High School Marching Band. She needed to get out and get up.

For the past two years, she had been studying magazine ads, especially for airlines. She had classified in her mind what the points of appeal were, what the art was supposed to evoke, what in many different ways the airlines were telling their potential customers about why TWA was different from Pan Am, and why Delta was better than United or vice versa. Which appealed to business people? Which spoke to single women?

For a year now, she had been making up her own ads for airlines and for cruise ships at her desk in her commercial art class. Her teacher, Miss Moseby, said that Nicole's work was as good as what was appearing in *Fortune* and *Cosmo.* Miss Moseby said that while she personally did not know anyone in the ad game, she read the advertising section of *The New York Times* religiously, and she knew for a fact that there was a major shortage of advertising talent in both New York and Los Angeles—especially talent that combined drawing and theme work with words.

"With your looks and your charm," Miss Moseby assured Nicole, "it won't be long before I'm reading about you in *The New York Times.* 'Local girl makes good.' That's what it'll say, and I'll tell the kids who are here then that I knew you when."

Of course, there was college in Knoxville, and that would be fun. And nobody said that the advertising business was easy. But how hard could it be for her, Nicole Miller, the Drum Major of Kefauver High School? How different could life be from taking charge of that band?

Then she would be out there, out of that valley no one had ever heard of. Leading a much bigger band—people who sold things and people who bought things. Then she would have a real wind at her back.

Nicole felt the warmth of sitting between her mother and her father as she watched the Panthers play in the autumn afternoon. Above her, she could see the American Airlines flight to Los Angeles that always passed over Jonesboro at about two in the afternoon. How long? Not long.

5

THE REALITY PRINCIPLE

In June 1982, on a day when investment bankers in New York were having lunch at the Recess Club with the owners of regional airlines, Nicole Miller snapped shut the last lock on her five pieces of light blue Samsonite featherweight luggage. She sat wearily down on her pine bed and wiped a line of perspiration off her brow, just above the fine arches of her blond eyebrows.

"It's just too hot," she said to her sister, who looked at her, swung her legs over the edge of the bureau where she sat, and drew on a can of Tru-Ade grape soda.

"Well, you've been packing for a week," Ginette said. "I still think you're making a big mistake. You've got it made in Tennessee. Out there in California, there's gonna be an earthquake."

"Yeah. When I get there," Nicole Miller laughed. "I'm the earthquake."

She stood up and smoothed her jeans, which had bunched around her knees and her ankles, and which were worrisomely tight around the waist. She just would not eat any more hamburgers or cheeseburgers or anything even remotely like them when she got to Los Angeles.

In fact, she would not eat anything but salads and maybe an occasional grilled fresh fish, the kind she read about in *Cosmo*, when she got to Los Angeles. In Tennessee, it was okay to be five or ten pounds overweight. In Los Angeles, you had to be at least five pounds underweight. She had read about it in *Vogue,* seen it in action on "Knots Landing." She was going to stick out in L.A. by her ability and her looks, not by being a fat hick.

She walked into her bathroom, noticed a jar of Pond's Cold Cream she had forgotten to pack, and ripped off two self-help signs she had written to herself and posted on the mirror in recent days. "You're fifty thousand times too fat," said one hand-lettered piece of typing paper. "You are so fat you make me sick," said the other. She had learned the message. She would not need these in Los Angeles.

"You have Jeff Boone madly in love with you," drawled Ginette when Nicole walked back into the room. "You have a job offer at First Tennessee Bank, not as a yucky teller or anything like that, but in the advertising department right in downtown Knoxville. Jeff Boone was the best-looking boy in Sigma Chi."

"Jeff is a good-looking boy. But he's a cracker. He thinks that going to work at his father's John Deere dealership is a cool thing to do. In Murfreesboro. He thinks that having a Mercury is cool. He thinks I should just move into a little split-level house like Mom and Dad's and have babies. That's not why I went to school. That's not why I worked all those summers at the bank and that advertising agency."

"Yeah, but at least with him, you know what you're getting into. In L.A., it's find 'em, fuck 'em, and forget 'em. That's what I hear."

At just that moment, Julie Miller walked into the room. She stared at her eleven-year-old daughter in a mixture of real and mock horror.

"I can't believe my ears," she said. "Where did you learn that horrible language? Where?"

"I learned it from the kids at school. That's the way people talk at Oakwood Elementary School," Ginette said matter-of-factly. No one in the Miller household was afraid of Julie Miller.

"Well, I have taught at that school for fifteen years," Julie Miller answered, "and I have never heard anyone talk like that. I don't want to ever hear anyone in this house talk like that again. We are not K-Mart people."

"Good luck," Ginette said in a monotone.

"Anyway, Nicole does not need your advice," Nicole's mother said as she sat on Nicole's still unmade bed. "Nicole was always a good girl."

"Not always, Mom," Nicole said. "Just what you knew about."

"Well, to me you will always be a good girl, and I will always know that you are being a good girl. When you were at U.T., even with all those stories about drugs and drunken fraternity parties, I always knew you were being a good girl. I knew you wouldn't fall into trashy ways like some redneck trash."

"You didn't know it," Nicole said cheerfully. "You just hoped it, and that's a lot different."

"What do you think she was doing with Jeff Boone all that time?" Ginette demanded with a lewd child's giggle.

"Jeff Boone is a direct descendant of Daniel Boone," Julie Miller said.

"Christ, Mom, half of the people in Tennessee are direct descendants of Daniel Boone," Nicole laughed.

"Well, that's as may be," Julie Miller said. "But you are a direct descendant of Andrew Jackson's brother, and only a few people in all of Tennessee can say that and mean it."

"I've heard all of this before," Ginette said. "I'll start loading the car." With surprising strength, she took two of her sister's smaller suitcases and headed toward the front door.

Julie Miller watched Ginette go with a wan smile on her face. She wore a blue cotton suit and a white cotton blouse. It was what she always wore for farewells. In her life, goodbyes were not something for pajamas and bathrobes. Goodbyes were major ceremonies. Goodbyes were like funerals, except that the departed might possibly return. Julie Miller fingered the plastic pearls around her neck and looked at Nicole as her daughter started to take down the clippings from the Jonesboro *Telegram* about her days as Drum Major, with the photos of her in her grenadier's cap, leading the band.

"Please don't do that," Nicole's mother said. "Please don't take them down unless you really plan to put them up wherever you live in Los Angeles. They mean a lot to me. When you go, I can come in here, and Ginette and I can sit and read them, and . . ."

And then Julie Miller broke down and sobbed. She sobbed until Nicole held her in her tan arms. She sobbed until Ray Miller could hear her over the sound of the baseball game and came in and patted her lightly on her still blond hair.

Ginette did not come in, but that was only because she had seen her friend Dottie on a bicycle and had stopped to talk to her and could not hear her mother's sobs.

"Mom, I'll call you every night from every place I stop until I get there," Nicole said. "And when I find an apartment, I'll let you know that number, too, and I'll be back for Christmas, and it'll be fine."

"I know you will," Julie Miller said after she had cried for fifteen wet minutes. "I know you're going to call. It's just that you're not only a Miller, you're a Jackson, too. And the Jacksons are a high-strung family. Things happen to them. They get real nervous. They're sensitive."

"I know, Mom," Nicole said softly. She took her mother's right hand and held it against her cheek.

"My own mother was just like you. She was lead-pipe-cinch certain that the world was her oyster. She graduated from East Tennessee in 1925, and she was going to go to New York City and set the world on fire. And she went there, and all she did was drink and dance and stay up nights, and when she got back here, she was a changed person. And my grandmother used to tell me that she had been just fine before she left Tennessee. But she fell in with a fast crowd, and it was just too much for her. She pulled herself together enough to marry a boy whose father owned a lumber mill, and they were quite the young couple in Jonesboro for a few years, but underneath, there was something wrong."

"Mom, it's not going to happen to me. I never drink," Nicole lied. "I know how to take care of myself. I didn't get that B.S. in marketing because I'm a fool."

"My mother wasn't anybody's fool either," Nicole's mother said. "But it wasn't a year after I was born that she came down with chronic pneumonia, and then she was in that hospital for another year, and I was with my aunt in Jackson, and when I saw her, she didn't even look like the same woman. And then she told me and my brother that Dad had left her and moved to Canada, just like that, and she was too sick to be a mother, that she wanted us to be well cared-for, and there wasn't a thing we could do about it. So I went off to live with my aunt in Jackson again, and then when I was about six, my mother came to visit me in Jackson with some rich man from New York. He was always using long distance to call his broker, even right in front of me. And then it turned out he was busted, and he went to jail, and Mom came to see me, and she said she didn't have any more pneumonia, and she looked like she was a young girl again, like in the pictures I saw of her when she was in high school. She looked so happy and so cheerful, and so young, in a sailor suit kind of dress, and then she took the train back up to Knoxville. Just before she got on, she told me things were going to be better than they ever had been, and the bad times were over."

When she paused, Julie Miller looked as if she were the loneliest human being in the world for just about ten seconds. Then she wiped at her nose with the pink Kleenex she always carried balled up in her left hand.

"Then she went back to Knoxville, and just walked out to get a cold drink and got hit by a Ford taxicab, and I didn't even get to go to the funeral," Nicole's mother said with a loud sob, and then she said softly, "and I had to live with my aunt, who used to whisper that the Jackson side of the family always had been brilliant but weak, and she was awfully happy she was my father's sister and not my mother's sister. And I had a letter with a check for a hundred dollars every Christmas from my father, but I never saw him again."

"Mom, that's not going to happen to me. I'm not going to Los Angeles to live it up. I'm going to get a good job and make something out of myself in advertising or commercials. I'm almost twenty-one years old. I haven't been Drum Major for four years. What am I supposed to do? There's nothing I can do here except teach school or work in a bank, and, frankly, I want to do something that's bigger than being Drum Major was. I want to do something that'll make being Drum Major seem small. I want people to read about me in the *Wall Street Journal.* Be a star."

"Don't ever say that," Nicole's mother retorted. "You were the best Drum Major there ever was in this town, and Nicole honey, there's nothing wrong with teaching school—"

"I know that, Mom," Nicole said, hugging her mother. "It's a great job. But I want to be in a bigger world. I want to see bigger things. I've done what I can do here. I'll be careful, and you'll be proud of me when you see me in the *Wall Street Journal.*"

"I couldn't be any prouder of you than I am right now. I couldn't be any prouder of you than I was when I'd see you out there leading the band."

"Well, that's the past, and that's history. I can't go back and lead that band again. That's a fact. I'm looking for the future, and I'm Nicole Miller, and Nicole Miller can take care of Nicole Miller in Jonesboro or in Los Angeles, and now I have to boogie if I'm going to make Memphis by tonight."

"Isn't Jeff coming over to say goodbye?" Julie Miller asked. "I should think he would. After all . . ."

"We already said goodbye over the phone," Nicole said. "I told him to look for my picture in *Advertising Age.*"

"And that's it?" Ray asked.

Nicole looked up in surprise at her father. "Yes, Dad. That's it. He doesn't owe me anything, and I don't owe him anything, and that's modern life."

"I guess it is," her father said.

74

At the car, a tiny yellow Toyota coupe, a high school graduation gift from Julie and Ray, with a stereo cassette deck from
Ginette, Nicole paused to look at the grass and the hills and the
neighbors' identical red-brick-and-white-wood-trim ranch houses.
She looked to the north at the Smoky Mountains. For just a
minute, she started to feel a stirring of fear, which instantly
exploded into a fireball of panic. How could she be doing this?
She couldn't be in her right mind. Who did she even know in
Los Angeles? One sorority sister from Theta had a brother who
was a sound engineer at the Raleigh Studios, which was supposed
to be somewhere near Paramount. After that, she was on her own.

For one full minute, while she went through the motions of
saying goodbye, hugging her mother, kissing her sister, kissing her
father, checking to see that her American Express card was in her
wallet, she felt acute terror. I can't believe I'm doing this, she
thought. I can't believe I'm doing this.

Her mother took her hand and held it and Ginette's hand. Her
father took her hand and Ginette's hand, and her mother said,
"Dear God, we pray that you will watch over our little girl and
keep her safe. We ask it in Christ's name, Amen."

Then Nicole added, "And look after Mommy and Daddy and
Ginette, thank you, and Amen."

For an instant, the thought had actually crossed Nicole's mind
that she might change her mind, that she might suddenly say,
"You know, you're right. I am going to stay here and work in the
advertising department at First Tennessee Bank." But then she
was in the car, letting out the parking brake, starting it up, and
heading out the driveway. For as long as she was on Lookout
Drive, she could still see her mother standing in the driveway, her
shoulders riding up and down with sobs as her father held her
tight. Ginette rode her bike alongside the Toyota for as long as
she could, pedaling furiously, waving goodbye with both hands,
until Nicole got on the access for the interstate, and even then,
she could hear Ginette shouting, "We love you, Nicole! Good
luck!"

Then it was all gone. Home and parents and clippings and little

75

sister and hugs. What lay ahead was anonymous blacktopped interstate, fast food, the cheapest safe motels in the Auto Club guide, a day's side trip to the Grand Canyon, the magnificent cactus of New Mexico, and the searing desert. Just about forty miles east of Palm Springs, Nicole realized that she could pick up more than five FM radio stations. From every point on the dial, there was rock 'n' roll, all news, all oldies, all heavy metal, Spanish, classical—even a station playing Mozart's Symphony No. 38. She also noticed that the air was a steadily darker brown, and the drivers of cars looked steadily more grim, more determined, as if they would kill for a burrito. Nicole was in Los Angeles.

*T*he reality principle of moving to Los Angeles from Jonesboro, Tennessee. Here were the bad things that happened to Nicole in her first month in Los Angeles:

First, her Toyota broke down just as she was pulling off the Hollywood Freeway onto Barham Boulevard to look for a motel room. It cost four hundred dollars to have the fuel and water pumps fixed, get a new battery, and have one bald rear tire changed. That left Nicole with eleven hundred dollars, which she thought would last her for two months easy.

Second, the brother of the Theta lived in a one-bedroom apartment facing an alley next to a dry cleaning plant that ran all night. It pumped out fumes that made Nicole feel as if she were going to vomit on a more or less nonstop basis. Nicole was allowed to sleep on a couch for one night. The couch had a strong smell of cat urine. In the middle of the night, Brad, the brother, a fat, pimply guy with peanut butter and beer on his breath, awakened Nicole by running his hand up under her sweatshirt and placing it on her left breast. She had to fight with him for a half-hour to get rid of him. In the morning, he told her that if she had "an attitude problem," she might just as well take herself somewhere else.

Third, Nicole had brought eight copies of her portfolio of sketches for advertising airlines, and also a few for cars. She believed those were by far her strongest work. On the first full day she was in Los Angeles, she dressed up in her gray wool suit because L.A. was far colder in June than she would have imagined and set off to show her stuff.

She left one set of sketches at Ogilvy and Mather, another at Doyle Dane Bernbach, and another at Young & Rubicam. At Scali McCabe Sloves, the thinnest woman that Nicole had ever seen came out from the executive offices. She introduced herself as Olivia Montgomery, said that she had a few minutes before she left for her sports training class, which she took in lieu of lunch, glanced accusingly at Nicole's full figure, said she would look at the Miller portfolio and that she had been "completely charmed" by Nicole's Tennessee accent, which had come through even in print in the letter Nicole had sent from Knoxville.

Olivia Montgomery looked at the sketches for three minutes, then closed the book and smiled at Nicole over a glass-topped coffee table. The smile was a kind of rictus over her purposefully emaciated face. "I am sure that for the University of Tennessee, these are perfectly good. But they are just a little pedestrian for us. For student work, they're fine. But the clients do not pay us for student work. Check back when you have a real portfolio." A beat. "You don't by any chance have a leotard in your car, do you? If you want to come to my class, I'm sure the teacher won't mind . . ."

Fourth, at J. Walter Thompson, a man named Larry Seidel, in charge of personnel, appeared when Nicole called. "I would very much like to look at your sketches," he said. He was offensively overweight, breathing heavily just from standing still, reeling back and forth in a cloud of stale cigarette smoke. "The problem is we just lost Lightwave Airlines, which was our biggest L.A. transportation client, and we won't be hiring at all for a long time. In fact, we'll be laying off. In fact, I'll probably be laid off," he added with a giggle. "But you're a good-looking trick. You won't have any problems getting along in this town."

Fifth, at six P.M. on the day that Nicole had her round of "interviews," she decided that she had better stop off someplace

77

and have a Diet Coke to keep her energy up. She was staying at a Holiday Inn in Burbank. She might not know much, but she knew she did not want to spend another day at a Holiday Inn in Burbank. J. Walter Thompson was in a high-rise down the street from a restaurant called Nicky Blair's. It looked cheerful and even elegant. There was certainly not any place like it in Jonesboro.

At its chrome, leather, and glass bar, Nicole sat on a stool and asked a beaming bartender for her Diet Coke. "Too late, babe," the bartender said. "These men have already bought you a Long Islander." He pointed with his thumb at three Iranian men in shiny silk suits who were lifting up martinis in her honor from the other side of the bar.

The Drum Major said, "I'll have a Diet Coke." She put three dollars on the counter. She drank her Diet Coke, left fifty cents for the bartender, and started for the door. "Don't be so fancy," said one of the men, with thick, curly, greasy hair combed low over his forehead. "We're all friends here. Where are you from, Miss Blondie?" Nicole shuddered and walked out.

The sixth bad thing was that the only apartment Nicole could find that was even remotely within her price range was in West Hollywood, in a low 1950s moderne building called Pacific View Terraces that housed sixteen tenants. Fifteen of them were men who worked as waiters, assistant art directors, buyers for high-end furniture shops, and hairdressers. That wasn't the bad part. That was the good part about the building on Holloway. The bad part was that for a one-room apartment with kitchen niche and bathroom, Nicole would have to pay five hundred dollars per month. Even that wasn't the worst part. The worst part was that Nicole had to pay first, last, and one month's security deposit, and she didn't have it. Before she had been in Los Angeles for even one week, she had to call home to ask for another thousand dollars.

"Honey, are you happy there?" Nicole's mother asked. "Do you think you're going to be happy there?"

"I think so," Nicole said. "I think so."

Nicole's parents sent her the check without a word of protest, without even a murmur. "We're just happy to hear from you, doll, that's all," Julie Miller said.

"You're just a little girl in a big city," Ray Miller said. "Of course we're glad to help you out. That's what we're here for. As long as I'm working, we're always here for you."

Here are some of the good things that happened to Nicole in her first month in Los Angeles. In the apartment building laundry room, which offered three industrial-size washers and three industrial-size dryers for all of the guests in the Pacific View Terraces, Nicole met a man who was a new stylist at Danni's Pour Le Chic in the Sunset Plaza area of Los Angeles. He told Nicole that he would get her lightened up and styled for free if she came in, just because she had "such perfect shiksa hair" and he was so sick of working on all that "yucky Persian stuff, no matter how much they pay me . . ."

When she went in the next morning, Nicole sat next to a woman with the reddest nails she had ever seen. The woman was bitching because her husband, a poor creature named Bernie, had just gotten a huge new account for his advertising agency, Sterling Grace Associates. His name was Bernie Labofish. The huge new account needed instant servicing and some visual people "a goddamn sight better than the shtickdreck he has working for him now."

The new account was an airline that serviced the West Coast and competed with PSA. It was called Lightwave Airlines.

Nicole Miller told Shirley Labofish, who had a good twenty years on Nicole, most of them spent scowling and demanding that people do things her way or not at all, that Shirley had the most beautiful nails Nicole had ever seen. Shirley looked at them as if she had not even realized that they were on the ends of her fingers.

"You think so, honey?" she asked as she drank a Perrier. "I'd give anything for blond hair like yours. You have to have a goyischekop to have hair like that, but I think it's worthwhile in your case."

By the time Nicole left Danni's Pour Le Chic, she had an interview with Bernie Labofish on the tenth floor of the ABC Entertainment Center, the next morning. That wasn't the good part. The good part was that at the meeting with Bernie, who looked as if he might just tear his own head off his neck and throw a grenade inside if it would put him out of his misery, genuinely loved Nicole's work.

Bernie Labofish had a Proton stereo in his office playing *The Magic Flute* while he talked to Nicole. He worked in a pair of large jeans and a sweatshirt that said "Kill Them All, Let God Decide," and featured a grinning Madame Defarge looking like Rosalynn Carter, next to a dripping tumbril. On his walls, he had one-sheets from some of his major campaigns. They included little items like Rainier Ale, Eastern Airlines, Metrorail, and Oreo Cookies. Nicole had actually studied the Oreo Cookie ads in school at U.T. With their cinema verité photos of famous heirs and heiresses in black tie and evening gowns, staring straight into the camera, holding an Oreo at eye level and saying, "We eat them for good taste," they had become almost as famous as "At sixty miles per hour, the loudest sound is the electric clock." And Nicole was there talking to the man who created them when he was still in his twenties.

"You wanna diet cream soda?" Bernie asked as he scanned a sketch of an airplane landing on a silver platter. "You want maybe some smoked salmon?" he asked as he appreciatively eyed a watercolor of a railroad train taking off from a runway, next to a stalled, overcrowded, stopped 747.

Even that wasn't the best part. The best part was that after Bernie put her on hold for a full fifteen minutes of discussion with his broker about something called "reverse straddles," which sounded sort of exciting to Nicole, he looked wordlessly at Nicole's final sketch, which was of a little girl holding a man's hand and watching a Lightwave Aviation 737 take off above a marshy bay scene and say to her father, "Daddy, what's it like to fly?"

"Did you do the copy, too, Nicole?" he asked as he ran his finger over the airplane in Nicole's sketch.

"Yes, sir, I did," Nicole answered.

Bernie Labofish let out a long sigh and Nicole's heart descended in time. At least, she thought, I can tell my friends that I had an interview with Bernie Labofish, who invented the Oreo campaign, and at the top of a huge building in Century City, where they eat smoked salmon during the day and listen to music on Proton monitors just as if they were at a party. At least I got that far.

Bernie sighed again and said, "The problem is that beginning creative people think they can really get the earth and the moon and the sun right off the bat. They don't know that I got to submit a bill to the client, and he thinks I'm padding if I tell him I got a brand-new chick right out of the University of Tennessee and I'm paying her a bill a week."

Before Nicole could say anything, Bernie said, "Of course, if Shirley likes you, that means you can get along with anyone, and that helps. Could we try four hundred a week to start, and if we keep Lightwave, we'll bump you up to five in six months."

That was the best part.

That night, Nicole went home to her apartment. She walked restlessly around the apartment for a half hour, calling everyone she knew in Knoxville. Then she decided that it was time to celebrate.

But where does a single woman of barely twenty-one, with dazzling blond hair and a full figure, go to celebrate in Los Angeles? She went down to the apartment of her friend Terry from Danni's Pour Le Chic and told him about her new job. Terry, who was about to make pasta for a new friend he had met at Rage on Santa Monica Boulevard, suggested that Nicole try a new club in Silver Lake called The Towering Inferno.

Nicole was in a daring mood, and so she went out with a map to find The Towering Inferno.

Silver Lake was a rundown neighborhood just south of Hollywood, just north of downtown, a mixture of Hispanic gangs, Hasidim, and yuppies in Volvos. The club was in a converted warehouse for electrical parts. It had a "pretty girl" admission policy. That meant twenty bucks a head for men, free for pretty girls, and fuck you to the damned who didn't make the cut.

Inside, the walls were black. The floors were black. Only the ceilings were white, and they were a delightful white indeed, with tiny Christmas tree lights twinkling in them. Somehow, against the white, in the virtually black room, they looked even better than they would have against black. It was as if it were dawn, but the stars were still out.

At the bar, Nicole met a man with a heavy leather jacket who manufactured medical vans with all of the equipment already built in. "It takes in a mill a year," he said, "and it's legal, which is a first for me."

She met a man with a thin leather jacket who wore an earring in his left ear. He was dressed in highly stylized rags, white tights, and elf boots. Although he was clearly American, he also clearly tried to imitate Mick Jagger whenever he could. Nicole, who played "Let It Bleed" on every possible occasion, could tell that he was using whole phrases from songs. "I saw her today at the demonstration," he said to Nicole with a straight face, pointing at a beautiful black girl dancing with a nationally known child star actress.

She met a man with a woman. They were both dressed in leather trousers and leather shirts. They both had small ponytails. They both wore rimless round glasses. They were both painters. "I can't tell you what kind of style I paint in," the woman said. "I don't want to be tied down to labels."

"I paint only light fixtures," the man said, inhaling so deeply on a Viceroy that in one puff he turned a third of the cigarette to ash. "Light fixtures that I see in public restrooms. I sell a lot of the fuckers, too, to people who don't even get it. Light fixtures in public bathrooms. Get it?"

Nicole danced with a black man who said he ran a record company. She told him she did not want to share some buds in his car outside. She danced with a man she had seen on MTV playing rhythm guitar with an English rock group of which he was now the only living member. She told him she did not want to go into the men's room and boot up.

At eleven o'clock, even though the two painters told her the place hadn't even started, she drove home. That night, she wrote a letter to Jeff Boone back in Tennessee.

She told him what had happened that day as well as she could remember it. Then she put out the light and listened as she heard the sirens and the car alarms (she had heard only one before in her life, on a trip to Nashville) and the two-hundred-watt-per-channel car stereos pumping out bass on Holloway.

Then she turned the light back on and added, in her letter to Jeff Boone, "I feel like I'm floating, like I'm not attached to anything, and it's good, and it's also scary, and I never thought I'd miss Jonesboro, but I do."

6

THE RAT AND
THE ELEPHANT

Notes from Nicole Miller's first months in Los Angeles:

*A*t Sterling Grace Associates, a.k.a Bernie Labofish, Inc., Nicole Miller did not get cheated. She was not put into the word-processing pool. She was given her own small office overlooking the Century Plaza and the West Side of Los Angeles. She was made an assistant account "creative supervisor," although she had no one to supervise. Her job was to attend all of the creative meetings on any subject even remotely touching on transportation.

This included meetings about Lightwave Airlines, about a Japanese van which was about to be introduced to the U.S. market called, of all things, the Divine Wind, and about a new brand of running shoes called Def Floaters, which were particularly favored in the inner-city areas of America.

At the meetings, Nicole was to make comments, show her own visuals for the ads, and appear intelligent. Unfortunately, at the meetings there were always at least two women and one man who were considerably senior to Nicole. One of the women had been with Bernie Labofish for twenty years. She had a tragically pock-marked face and walked with a comical bowlegged gait, which was a bad addition to an already grossly obese pair of hips. Her name was Marsha Grossman. After the first meeting, at which Nicole presented a drawing of a slightly African-American–looking Winged Mercury as a leitmotif for Def Floaters, Marsha Grossman spoke to Nicole in the ladies' room.

"I believe in you, honey," she said in a thick, tough Queens accent. "If Bernie thinks you got the stuff, then you got the stuff."

"I appreciate that," Nicole said, gingerly feeling the back of her neck.

"I just want you to know that there are a lot of dogs out there chasing Cadillacs, but not too many dogs driving Cadillacs, if you take my meaning."

"As a matter of fact, I don't take your meaning," Nicole said, smiling.

"It has to do with waiting your turn," Marsha said. "I think you knew that."

Nicole Miller was also expected to meet new and prospective clients. "I want you to do this, and you should know why," Bernie Labofish told her as he ate a pastrami sandwich and rode his bicycle machine one morning. "I want you to do this because, to be frank, and to be totally honest with you, you're the best-looking girl in the place, and you have that cute Kentucky accent, and it makes the customer think it's something other than a bunch of hustling Jewboys running the show. It makes them think, like, we got our feelers out there into middle America.

"It's Tennessee," Nicole said quietly.

"Somewhere," Bernie answered. "Somewhere other than Bialystok."

In her capacity as meeter and greeter, Nicole met a trio of Japanese manufacturers of a new camera that would take four pictures per 35-millimeter square. She took them to St. Germain. One of them asked if she would like to come back to his room with him and have some Napoleon brandy. He told her he had the best suite at the Bel-Air. She politely said she had work to do. Another group of visitors were from a Korean company that manufactured replicas of IBM personal computers, only they were microwave ovens. Yet another group was from Iowa. They had invented a kind of popcorn that contained therapeutic doses of calcium. The head of the company, a division of General Foods, a farm boy in a double-breasted suit with sharply notched lapels and white-on-white shirt, asked Nicole if she would like to take a drive out to Malibu by night with him. She told him she had to finish sketches, but she would take a rain check. "It never rains in California," he said.

Nicole shrugged. "Yes," she said, "but it pours."

The presence of the three agency men and women who were senior to Nicole, and the clearly flattering proposals by clients and prospective clients do not mean that Nicole had been duped, or was leading a painful life, or was the slave of the sex/class system she had read about in her class in Feminist Literature at U.T. Nicole was leading the life of the working girl in the big city. She was an almost uniquely attractive working girl, and she was in a fairly glamorous occupation, but she was a working girl in the big city. As Bernie Labofish used to tell her, "There's a thing like the Marine Corps about being in the ad game at any stage, but particularly where you are. It looks a lot better from the outside than from the inside. And at least in the Marines, they pay your chow bills and they have a nice ceremony when you die. In the ad game, your friends celebrate when you die, 'cause maybe they'll get your accounts."

To be a working girl in Los Angeles, and particularly one without well-connected parents and money forever at hand, meant many different things. It meant you had to tread carefully when you were in the spotlights of a Marsha Grossman. Marsha believed that the ideal way to do any campaign was simply to study what Chiat-Day did and do something almost illegally similar. To get along, you have to go along, and that meant Nicole could not stick her finger down her throat and gag when Marsha made her proposals in her Queens accent.

But there was a lot more and less to Nicole's life than that. For one crucial thing, Nicole had a new sensation she had never known in Tennessee: She was always broke. Four hundred a week had seemed like a fortune. That was before she saw that it came out to about three hundred and twenty dollars after tax and insurance deductions. Out of that three hundred and twenty dollars came her rent, which worked out, with utilities and phone, to about one-ninety per week. She was also supposed to pay for new clothes, because looking good was a key part of the ad game, too. She shopped only at sales at The Broadway and Ann Taylor, but she was still broke all the time. Out of that three hundred and twenty a week also had to come repairs to her feeble Subaru, a tip at Danni's Pour Le Chic, which was still doing her hair for free, but at least she had to give Terry a twenty every other week.

Also out of her wages had to come the occasional lunch at The Grille, a place she particularly loathed because it was filled with scary-looking unemployed producers and agents but was greatly favored by others in the office. Sometimes Nicole liked to buy herself something special—a color TV with remote or a clock radio or a few LP's for her battered Emerson stereo. These went on her Tennessee Bancard Visa, and she had to come up with about fifty-five dollars each month to clear her minimum and keep up her credit.

Then there were occasional books, especially the Ruth Rendell mysteries she loved so much from college days. There were also dry cleaning bills, monthly *Elle, Vogue,* and *Town & Country,* and the occasional grocery.

In a word, like almost every other working young woman in Los Angeles, Nicole lived from paycheck to paycheck, and very barely so at that. Her mail frequently had copies of charges for overdrafts, and that was ten dollars per item on top of everything else.

The glamorous life was going on somewhere in Los Angeles, Nicole knew, because she heard Bernie talking about it over the phone. She also heard out-of-town clients talking about it, and she actually took part on those rare occasions when she got invited out to a truly important dinner at Jimmy's or 72 Market Street.

But for the most part, she simply had her nose pressed up against the window, watching the people inside live it up at Morton's and Spago and places she drove by, but never went into.

For another thing, and something that Nicole had never really considered when she was making her plans to move to Sunny Cal, her life was lonely. It was lonely both at work and after work. She wrote about it in a letter to Jeff Boone just before Thanksgiving, telling him most if not all of the thoughts going through her mind, and most if not all of what she was doing about it.

Like you, I grew up in the same town for all of my life. For you it was Murfreesboro. For me it was Jonesboro. That meant dullsville. It also meant that people knew me. They didn't know the real me, whoever that is, but they knew me. They knew me even before I was Drum Major. They knew me as someone who knew them, whose father worked with them, whose mother taught their kids and their sisters and brothers. They knew we weren't rich and weren't poor, and most of all they knew we were like them. They knew if my mother was sick, and they knew when I started to smoke, and they knew the first time I was drunk and blew lunch behind the gym.

They knew too goddamned much, if you know what I mean. But at least they knew me, and at a certain level, they understood me. I was the pretty blond girl with the attitude and the teacher mother. I was the one with the ambition and then I was the Drum Major. So, at least some way, they knew me.

Now, at the time, that seemed like a great big drag. But now, looking back, it seems pretty wonderful. If people don't know you, you sort of don't exist except as something to be used. You're just a unit of merchandise, like a typewriter or a printer or scissors. The only value you have is what you can do for someone else, and other than that, you don't exist.

It's like, I hated that the people at Ertter's Market

*would tell my mother if I was smoking on the way home
from band practice. But at least they weren't trying to
make money off me or fuck me just because I have blond
hair and a Southern accent. I go into a bar here with my
friends, and everybody wants to do me, and no one wants
to know me, and I hate it. I talk to people who just want
to lay out that they make more money than I do, owning
quick print shops or dry cleaners or telephone banks that
sell Xerox toner, only it's not even real Xerox toner, and
the only reason they tell me how much money they make,
and how they have a house in "the Colony," wherever
that is, is so they can make me feel small, and then do
me. Then that makes them feel big, and in the process,
nobody even really knows who I am.*

*I hear about that kind of life is what I should say.
When I meet guys at the bars who act like that, I just
shine it on. I'd rather be at home reading a book, or
maybe seeing a movie, and I really mean that. People here
sort of sense that nobody knows them, and they pay
people to get to know them. Bernie, my boss, goes to a
shrink every day. It's not that he doesn't know enough
about his childhood already. He needs someone to talk to,
someone to be friends with, and in this town, that means
he needs to pay someone to be his friend and really
listen. It's kind of sad.*

*Anyway, maybe that's just the way life is when you
grow up, but I sure hope not. You have to write longer
letters, and tell me all about how you're doing. I got the
picture of you and your new Camaro . . .*

A fuller picture of Nicole's loneliness might have included more
about her visits to Le Dome and Rebecca's, a Mexican food
hangout in Venice Beach.

About one month after she moved into Pacific View Terraces,
a two-bedroom in the building came up for rent. About two
months later, a young woman named Mimi Keller, who worked

as a traffic researcher at Sterling Grace Associates, told Nicole that she needed a new place to live. Mimi, like Nicole, had just turned twenty-one. She was a perky little blonde from Beverly Hills by way of Westport, Connecticut. She had been forced to drop out of Stanford because she had taken part in an anti-Pentagon demonstration at a nearby Hewlett-Packard research lab. She had been arrested for assaulting a Palo Alto patrolman with a ball-peen hammer, and that was the end of Mom and Dad's support, and at least a temporary end to Mimi's days at Stanford.

She suggested to Nicole that the two of them save a hundred dollars per month by taking the two-bedroom together. They moved into it one week later. The first night that they were roommates, they went out to Rebecca's. Each of them had two Margaritas and then a good start on a bottle of Iron Horse Chardonnay.

When they asked for the tab, they learned it had been picked up by two youngish men in thin leather jackets who were standing down the bar from them.

The two men were in the music business. One was named John Franco. He was a heavy hitter in music law. The other was David Sonnenbaum. He was a heavy hitter in music publishing agentry at the Mark Cooperman Agency. Nicole and Mimi knew Sonnenbaum and Franco were heavy hitters because Sonnenbaum and Franco told them so.

Nicole and Mimi went back to David Sonnenbaum's house in Holmby Hills. From one in the morning until three, all four of them snorted cocaine. They snorted it while sitting on beige leather couches in a paneled living room looking out on a pool lit from underwater by blue lights.

For the first time since she had been in L.A., Nicole felt not only good, but great. Each new sniff made her feel as if she were more solidly hooked into the one element she had been lacking since she got out of Kefauver High School: power. Sitting on the couch, drinking Courvoisier while she inhaled cocaine, she felt as if she were almost back on the field after conducting Rachmaninoff with the kids whistling "Ballad of a Teenage Queen."

Nicole felt so good, and so grateful to David Sonnenbaum for making her feel that way, that she went back into his bedroom, also overlooking the blue-lit pool. She spent from three until about four trying to have sex with him. It wasn't easy, but not because she resisted. It wasn't easy because the drug has a way of making sexual desire incapable of realization in the human penis. But still, Nicole did her best, and when David finally came, she felt as if she had repaid her debt and as if, as she might say, she belonged.

After a few more hits out of the cocaine jar, Mimi and Nicole went home. "Did you do him?" Mimi asked, with a particularly weighty emphasis on the word "do." "I did Franco," Mimi added matter-of-factly. "He was all right. Only all right."

"You think David would make a good boyfriend?" Nicole asked.

"Are you kidding?" Mimi asked. "We'll be lucky if either of them ever calls us again. Are you kidding?"

Nicole gave her roommate a pitying smile. Maybe that was the way her life ran. That was not the way of the Drum Major. She had slept with only three men in her life: her second cousin from Knoxville, who had practically raped her while they were both high on marijuana, the quarterback of the Vols, and Jeff Boone. All three of them had asked her, no, *begged* her, to go out with only him, to be his *main squeeze,* to be there for him every night. The evidence of Nicole's physical attractiveness to men was pretty conclusive.

David Sonnenbaum did not call for three weeks, and when he did, he began the conversation by calling Nicole "babe." Nicole hung up on him. He sent flowers and called again. She went out with him that night, and again spent the night taking cocaine and watching the lights of the pool and trying to make love. "I won't be such a bad boy again," he said when she left in her battered Toyota. "You're too good for me to screw this up."

He did not call for one month, and when he did call, he began the conversation by saying, "What it is, babe," a then current black expression.

Nicole hung up on him.

It would be easy to say that David Sonnenbaum, his cocaine, his Porsche convertible, black on black, were somehow unusual. It would be easy to say that after David and his house in Holmby Hills and his cocaine and his thin leather jacket and his leather couches, Nicole learned her lesson and only went out with nice men. It would be easy, but it would be wrong.

The sadder fact was that instead Nicole learned something far more basic about the life of a single career girl in Los Angeles: *There are no nice men in Los Angeles.* Or, rather, there are no nice men in Los Angeles that she felt like going out with. As far as she could tell, there were basically three types of men in Los Angeles:

Type A, which stood for Asshole. It referred to a type of man who had a superficial appeal, the right kind of car, the right kind of job, the house at the right address, knew the right kind of Chardonnay to order (Grgich Hills or Cakebread or Far Niente or Iron Horse), and had a fairly cool line of patter. The type A man also was certified, guaranteed, to be one hundred percent self-obsessed, without even a discernible iota of feeling for any other human being. This lack of concern especially extended to women who had sex with him. It was this type's particular joy not to call women with whom he'd had sex or who expressed any tenderness or openness to him at all.

It was almost as if this type were engaged in a guerrilla war with women. Still, type A had a certain infuriating attractiveness, which haunted Nicole. David Sonnenbaum was not by any means the last type A she went out with. Life is lonely in L.A., and for a time, you take what's there.

Nicole never did cocaine again, though. The second night she used it with David Sonnenbaum was the fourth time in her life that she had used it. That night, after the initial euphoria, she had felt wave upon wave of panic, which subsided into anxiety, then into depression.

In her panic, Nicole imagined that she had been exposed on the playing field at Kefauver High, and that everyone knew she had taken home a strange man, or at least gone to his home and done him. The crowd also knew that she had taken cocaine, and when she threw back her head with the grenadier's cap and the feather, the crowd had not sung "Ballad of a Teenage Queen." Instead, the crowd had booed and hissed.

Then there was Type B, which stood for Boring. These were guys like the head of telecommunications at Sterling Grace, who drove a solid, reliable Volvo, had a two-bedroom condo in Sherman Oaks, and were almost nauseatingly nice. They took her to pretty good restaurants, ordered a pretty good bottle of wine (The Velvet Turtle, Firestone Vineyards—you get the picture). They talked about their work and about how lucky they felt to be working with Bernie Labofish.

Type B brought flowers, but flowers from Ralph's Grocery Store, on the first date. Type B listened to every word that Nicole had to say. Type B did that, Nicole came to believe, because Type B literally had nothing to say. Sitting at a dinner table with him, listening to him go through the motions of what human social intercourse should be like, was like reading instructions for operating a VCR. It's not even important to know the name of the Type B from Telecom. There were a few others, but Nicole did not remember their names either.

Then there was the third type. Type M, for Married Man. At the beginning of Nicole's exposure to Type M, he did the impossible. He combined a measure of sophistication, some substantial dash of cosmopolitan erudition, a real sense of humor, a confident sense of himself, and just enough caring to let Nicole know she was not alone. In a word, Type M, as far as Nicole could tell at first, was a personality type that did not exist in Los Angeles, California, in the unmarried form.

The first one who came into Nicole's life was from a national advertising firm far larger than Sterling Grace. The firm's name was Watson, Kerr Partners. The head of the West Coast office was Tony Morris. He was only a half inch taller than Nicole, a good twenty years older than she was, and slightly overweight, but he had a helluva way of telling a story.

He strolled into Nicole's office in Century City and put his smooth black leather Mark Cross look-alike briefcase on the floor. Nicole looked up at him and asked, in her most helpful shy Southern girl fashion, "May I help you?"

Immediately, she noticed a combination of boyish and grown-up that she liked. He cocked his head and answered, "I think you can. I'd just like to tell you that I've been working in the ad game for ten years here in Los Angeles, and you're about the best-looking woman I've ever met. I hear you're working on the Light-wave account."

Nicole did another take. The man had a rosy red face. He wore a gray Paul Stuart suit, a white shirt, and a staring green tie. He looked as if he had some authority. "I'm working on it in a small way," Nicole said. "I'm like the lowest man on the totem pole."

"It's all right," Morris said. "Because I'm the head of the L.A. office of Watson, Kerr, and we're teamed up with you for the presentation, and I want you to know that we're going to make it fly, and we're gonna make it bigger than Pan Am, and when they ask us how we did it, I'm just gonna say that Nicole Miller did it all, and the only question they're going to ask you is what color Mercedes convertible you'd like to have."

"Gray," Nicole said, "with black leather upholstery."

"Consider it done," he said. "I hear you burned up the University of Tennessee before you started to take over here."

Nicole Miller was impressed. The man had done his home-work. "I'm just starting here. I'm doing grunt work."

"Yeah," Morris said. "That's what David Ogilvy said when he started out. I've seen your drawings, Nicole, and I can tell you that the best people in New York would swipe them and put their initials on them if they could."

Nicole looked at Tony Morris's black leather briefcase and asked, "Is there a bomb in that thing?"

"Just to kill myself with if I couldn't get you to have dinner with me."

Nicole smiled and laid down her Pilot Fineliner and sighed. "You're awfully good at this," she said.

"I have to be," he said. "I'm an old fat guy and you're a beautiful young girl, and I'm starting out about five miles behind the pack."

"I couldn't possibly take off a whole evening to have dinner when I'm in the middle of preparing for a big presentation like Lightwave," Nicole said with an even bigger smile. "Where were you going to suggest we eat?"

Dinner at the Bistro Gardens, Cañon Drive, Beverly Hills, California, November 1982. At a nice little deuce on the terrace, right near the main inside room, with Tony Morris in a blue pinstripe suit and a white shirt and a red tie with little figures of dark blue facing Nicole Miller, in a white silk suit that had blue stripes running vertically, a long string of pearls, both borrowed from Mimi Keller, her hair up on top of her head, picking at a kind of fish she had never heard of before called John Dory, and which, incredibly, had been flown in all the way from New Zealand (probably first class) just so she could pick at it and eat it every now and then.

The wine: a Puligny-Montrachet for Tony, who was eating veal chops, and a Monterey County, California, Chardonnay for Nicole. Two bottles of wine for two people. Why not?

For the first fifteen minutes after she sat down, the man at the next table had been talking about such interesting recollections of his life in public office that Nicole had some difficulty paying attention to Tony Morris. But after Jerry Brown left, it was much easier to hear Tony. (As far as she recalled, and she would definitely have to write to Ginette about this, Linda Ronstadt had not said a word.)

In fact, even before she had finished with her endive salad, Nicole was wrapped up in a web of what Tony had to say.

"I was in about the first class of the Peace Corps," he said. "Right out of Villanova. It was a pretty hard adjustment, because I came from Elkins Park, this nice little suburb of Philadelphia, where I was the only Catholic boy in a whole high school filled with nice Jewish boys and girls, and then at Villanova, half of the boys wanted to be priests and all of the girls just wanted to get married and have a station wagon.

"So there I was, in a village in Madras called something I still can't pronounce, sleeping in a hut with a corrugated tin roof and such big spiders sleeping nearby that I used to give them names and share my breakfast with them.

"My job is to work with these three other losers, just as out of it as I am, only three of the four are engineers, and one—guess which one—is an art major, and we're supposed to be building a pipeline that's going to give them drinking water that won't kill them, and then we're supposed to teach them about boiling water before they drink it and not rubbing cow shit on their cuts and scrapes.

"The amazing thing was that it wasn't that hard to build the pipeline. The stuff just showed up there one morning, maybe from the CIA, maybe from the government, who the hell knows. And we just hooked it up to a well, and read some instructions from the Borg-Warner Company about how to hook up a pump to the pipe, and then we just ordered a gasoline generator from Central Stores, and next thing we knew, there was water coming out of a pipe and the people in the village weren't getting malaria or dysentery or whatever they had been getting before, and it was all stuff that an American plumber does just about every day."

For Nicole Miller, it was almost perfect. The two kinds of wine, the fresh fish flown ten thousand miles for her enjoyment, the movie star ex-governor, and then, the perfect spice—talking about saving poor dumb brown-skinned childlike people from themselves with a healthy dose of altruism and good old American know-how. The combination of luxury and doing good was overwhelmingly powerful.

Then it got better. "But remember," he said, "I was an art major. And all the time I was at Villanova, I had a sculpture teacher who used to talk about this little village called Rajaputra, just south of Madras. In this village, for more than fifteen hundred years, master sculptors have been doing just one thing, and doing it perfectly. It sounds incredible to Americans that anyone would do this, and it probably sounds stupid even, but all they want to do, from father to son, for fifteen hundred years, is to make statues, sculptures, of the Ganesh figure. Did you ever study Indian mythology in college?"

"No, I didn't. But I'd love to hear about it now."

"The Ganesha is a man with an elephant's face and tusk, but always a broken tusk, and the man is mounted on top of a rat."

"A rat?"

"The idea is that the man is melded into the elephant, which represents strength and dominance and closeness with eternity, but that because of the inherent failings in man's personality, he cannot ever quite merge totally with a godly creature like an elephant, and hence the broken tusk. And the man is riding a rat, because the man is also connected with the fertility, struggle, tenacity, and ultimate smallness of the life of the rat. Man is sort of a bridge between the sublime elephant and the sad but relentless rat.

"After I did two years in the Peace Corps, I was pretty much ready for going back to the States. And I wanted to go into advertising instead of teaching art history, which had been my plan, and I'll tell you why. When I was in that little village studying the Ganesh figures, I would just stand in front of them for hours admiring the perfection of line and depth. But the men who built them wanted to know if I really came from a country where every family had a car and a refrigerator and a TV set. To me, their art was a sort of perfection. But to them, and to everybody I met in India, having cars and refrigerators and TVs was an even better religion. And I knew myself, Nicole. I knew I couldn't stay in a classroom while the action of the world went on around me. I knew that as much as I loved the Ganesh, I was connected with the rats, too, and my religion was getting ahead, showing what I had in me, helping people to choose between a Buick and a Chrysler, and maybe exposing them to a little bit of the beauty of line and depth that I saw in the Ganesh every time they picked up a *Cosmo* or a *Life* or turned on 'Gunsmoke.' I could serve who I was, make my living, and maybe bring some elegance into people's lives in a way they never expected."

Nicole went to the ladies' room and called Mimi Keller. "This guy is fantastic," she whispered, because Linda was putting on lipstick nearby. "He's so great."

"I bet he's married," Mimi said.

"Not for long," the Drum Major said.

When she got back to the table, Nicole sat down, crossed her legs, and let her lower leg brush against Tony's calf. He smiled and blushed like a schoolboy.

"This was supposed to be a business dinner," he said. "To hear your thinking about logos for Lightwave."

"We can talk about that anytime at the office," Nicole said with uncharacteristic boldness. If you've got it, flaunt it. And ask for what you want out of life.

"Nicole, you should know something. You've totally bowled me over," Tony Morris said. "It's almost like a dream that you could be this smart and this beautiful and this young. But I'm married. It's on its last legs, and I'm already sort of separated, but in the eyes of the law, I'm definitely married."

"But you're separated."

"Well, I have a place of my own in Century City that Watson, Kerr lays on for me when I'm working late and don't want to drive all the way back to Pasadena or when visiting firemen are in town . . ."

But in the haze of the two kinds of wine, of hearing about the village in India and the Ganesh, and giving away two years of his

98

life so that villagers would not die of dysentery, and about the honesty of the man to his own needs, all that Nicole Miller heard were the word "separated" and the word "apartment." It's a lonely life starting out single and alone in the ad game in Los Angeles or anywhere else. And Tony Morris was a master of sales.

In addition, he knew that man had one finger touching the gray timeless eternity of the elephant and one grasping hand on the scurrying ambitious need of the rat.

The next morning, which was a Saturday, Nicole awoke in the airy one-bedroom apartment in Century City overlooking the playing field of Beverly Hills High School. It was an astonishingly smog-free day. Nicole could see the Santa Monica Mountains so clearly that she could make out individual palm trees. To the southeast, she could clearly see the Arco Towers of downtown. In the midrange, she could see her area, the boundary of West Hollywood. She would surely have been able to see her apartment on Holloway, near Tower Records, were it not obscured by the skeleton of an office building going up on Sunset.

To the west, she could see out to Catalina, the blindingly blue ocean, and an armada of sailboats skittering across the waves. They were adorable little white puffs on a perfect azure blanket. Even the air felt unusually fresh and clean and dry. She could quite literally smell orange blossoms from the backyards of Beverly Hills even though it was six months past spring.

She turned to Tony, who was still lying in bed reading the business section of *The Los Angeles Times.* "Wouldn't it be great to ride bicycles in Venice?" Nicole asked.

"I can't," Tony Morris answered.

"Why not?"

"It's Saturday, Nicole," Tony said with a surprising edge of weariness in his voice. "I have to go back to Pasadena and play softball with my boys."

"The office basketball team?"

"No, it's softball, not basketball. And I'm playing with my two sons, Kevin and Scott."

"You have two sons?"

"I have two sons and a daughter, Brigid. She's twelve. Kevin is fourteen and Scott is ten."

"How nice," Nicole said. "Evenly spaced like that. It must make things easy for your wife."

"Anyway, two guys from the Toronto office are coming in this afternoon and have to use this place, so we've got to go anyway."

When Nicole got into her little yellow Toyota, Tony Morris held her and said, "I feel shitty doing this. There are a lot of barnacles on an old hulk like me. I wish it were different, but it isn't."

"But you're separated."

"I'm getting separated. I've been married since I got back from India. That's more than twenty-two years. That's a long time."

"That's longer than I've been alive."

"I know. Can I see you Friday? I have some major hitters from Lightwave coming in. I'd like to just have you meet them informally. Don't do it if it'll get you in trouble with Bernie Labofish, but it would mean you'd be jumping over about ten levels of the bureaucracy to interface with them."

"Let me see what my schedule is," Nicole said.

She drove home alone, with tears in her eyes, feeling as if she had a bad flu that was making her dizzy, and that was her first brush with Type M, for Married Man.

That night, after she had gone bicycle riding in Venice with Mimi Keller, Nicole wrote the first entry in her diary. She had never kept a diary, and she really thought of herself as a visual woman rather than a literary type, but she went to Francis-Orr on Camden just before it closed and bought a blue leather diary with a little lock. She stayed up late watching "The Magnificent Seven" on Channel 13, and then watched "Saturday Night Live," which featured Chevy Chase playing in a skit about that finance whiz she had been reading about in the *Journal*, Barron Thomas, and then she started to write in her diary while the action a few feet away on Sunset was reaching its peak.

"This is what I'm going to try to do," she wrote.

100

I don't really have anybody here to talk to. Mom is so out of it that I can't really consult with her. Mimi is sweet, but she's been in L.A. too long. Its nonstandards are her standards. While I still have some values, what I'm going to do is imagine that I've been invited back to give the graduation speech at Kefauver High, and I'm going to try to tell kids about how to be true to yourself and get ahead and not be lonely, but still not hate yourself in a big city. So my idea is that after I give the speech, I go home, and all my pals from high school, Elizabeth Eastland and Traci Conner and all, are sitting in my little room, and they ask me what it's really like being a blond girl from Tennessee in the big city. So I'm going to try to only do things that I wouldn't be embarrassed to tell them. That's going to be my guide.

I wouldn't be embarrassed to tell them that I went out with Tony, because I didn't even know he was married. And I wouldn't even be embarrassed to say that I spent the night with him after I learned he was married, because, after all, he was awfully cute, and he was about the most educated, most aware guy I ever met, plus he does run a big ad agency, and that's something, too. But I definitely think that if I kept going out with him, I'd be stupid. And I know that if I let him take me to dinner with these big shots from Lightwave, all the people back at Bernie's shop would be really pissed, and it would be a perfect way for Marsha Grossman to get me fired. So I'll just play it by ear, and I'll just sort of cool around it if I can, and not get sucked into it. And I'll try to remember how I felt this morning when Tony said he had to play softball with his sons.

Nicole had not grown up the prettiest, most sought-after girl in Jonesboro, Tennessee, for nothing. Love is a junior high school student's game, and she knew how to play it once she had a man who was interested. She did not call Tony on Monday. When he called her on Tuesday, she did not return the call. When he called again on Thursday, she took the call and said she was really busy, but she hoped he would come by her desk next time he was at the office.

In fact, that afternoon, shortly before six, he strolled into her office again, looking slightly sporty in a blue, red, yellow, and white jacket from Polo with a white shirt and a solid dark red tie.

"Can I buy you a drink?" he asked.

"No," Nicole said. "But I have to tell you I can't go to dinner with you tomorrow. I'm really sorry."

Tony Morris looked genuinely unhappy. Without asking permission, he pulled the door to Nicole's office closed. "Don't do this to me," he said. "I can't stop thinking about you."

"Do what?"

"Turn cold on me."

"Tony," Nicole said. "I have to. I can't get my life wrecked around a married man. That's just got to be the way it is for me. I wish it could work out some other way, but it can't. You're fully married. Fully."

"I told you I was getting separated."

"You said you were already separated. Call me when you're divorced. In the meantime, I'd really like to hear about your ideas for the Lightwave logo."

Tony looked at her in amazement. "You're cool. You're very, very cool."

"Let me ask you a question," Nicole said, her voice quivering with anger. "How can a man totally trick a woman, rope her in, and play games around her that make her feel terrible about herself, and then, when she tries to stand up for her rights, how come she's cool, and a bitch, and awful? You studied art, Tony. You think that's pretty? You think it's got elegant lines?"

Morris looked at her and his face turned red. Then he smiled and laughed. "I think you should be in law school. That's what I think. You really know how to argue."

"Not really," Nicole said. "Underneath, I'm terrified."

"Okay," he said. He stuck out his hand. "Friends?"

Nicole laughed and stood up and walked to the front of her desk. "Friends," she said and stuck out her hand.

Tony grabbed her hand and pulled her to him. He wrapped his arms around her and started to kiss her. She pushed him away, but for reasons of tact and genuine affection, put her head on his chest. He started to stroke her hair.

Also, because man is related to both the elephant and the rat, he put his right hand on her breast. She began to push it away. Just as she did, her door opened and Marsha Grossman walked in without a moment's explanation. She flashed her angry brown eyes first at Tony and then at Nicole. "I'm so sorry," she said. "I had no idea you were in conference, dear. How are you, Tony? Everything okay with the family?"

And then she walked out.

Morris said, "She's a nut case, always has been, always, always, always."

But Nicole said, "Just leave. Please. Just leave me alone. I've got to think this out. Just leave . . ."

Nicole stayed in her office until eight o'clock, hoping against hope that by that time everyone in the office would be gone. In fact, when she came out, Marsha Grossman, and her best pal, Rhona Beck, a dyed blond rhinoceros in a dress, were waiting there for her, right down the corridor, a mere two doors away, ostensibly looking at proofs for printwork for Playtex tampons. In fact, of course, just waiting for a chance to stare.

When Nicole walked by, Marsha Grossman crooked her finger at her and pulled her into an empty conference room strewn with layouts for a candy bar.

"Nicole," Marsha hissed, "did you know that we're in competition with Watson, Kerr on about twenty accounts?"

"Good night, Marsha," Nicole said.

"I want to know what you two have been talking about. This agency means a lot to some of us. A really, really lot. Whatever it means to you, it's our life's work. It's not just for finding rich married men."

"I don't think you need to worry."

"But I am worried. I'm very worried. I want you to tell me what's been going on with you and Tony. I want you to come over to my apartment. I might be able to help you. It's right near you in West Hollywood. I want you to let your hair down and tell me, woman to woman, just what's been going on with you and Tony. Because I may be able to help you more than you think."

Nicole wondered if Marsha Grossman were also going to suggest that they go to an all-women's aerobics class together, if she perhaps had her leotard in the office. "Thanks anyway," Nicole said. "It's none of your business, and I have a lot of work to do tonight."

Marsha Grossman looked at Nicole and smiled tightly. "We'll see," she said. "This is a small little shop. We'll see."

At home that night, Nicole watched a show on PBS about a unique kind of gazelle called the Dorcas gazelle. It exists only in remote parts of the Arabian desert between Saudi Arabia and Kuwait. It resembles a full-sized gazelle, but in fact is only about twenty inches tall. Because of the frantic expansion of oil exploration and refining activities in the area, the gazelle had been having difficulty finding its natural food, a small desert plant that has leaves which taste surprisingly like squash.

Nicole watched the show and tears streamed down her face and she said to Mimi, "But I didn't do anything wrong. It was all his fault. He told me he was separated. He told me he thought I was a genius. He told me he would introduce me to people, and I still blew him off and did the right thing, and I'm still going to get screwed over for it."

"I think that's why they call it business. I think that's why they call them married men."

"But he was so nice. And I still stood up on my hind legs and did the right thing."

"Yeah," Mimi said. "It's a damned shame. You want some blow? This guy downstairs, Ed, deals and he's got incredible stuff."

"I don't care what happens at Sterling Grace," Nicole wrote in her diary that night after Mimi had left to rent videos. "I know

104

I did the right thing, and I know by doing the right thing, it's all going to come out okay in the end."

The next day, Nicole was visited at ten in the morning by Bernie Labofish. "Let's go down to the Sports Deli and have some coffee," he said.

In the darkened deli, cavernous and empty, with only a Hispanic waitress hovering next to a tank of brightly colored tropical fish for company, Bernie Labofish ate scrambled eggs, two orders of bacon, and coffee. Nicole had fresh orange juice.

"This is a political business," Bernie said. "You have to get along. I know it shouldn't be that way. Should be about talent. But it's not. It's about who likes you. Everybody in the biz knows what kind of guy Tony is. You are far from the first girl he's been interested in. We all know you're young. The problem is that you have real talent. That's already got Marsha and Rhona mad at you. They're already fighting me to keep you off the Candygram account. But see, they start out mad at you, and then Tony, and it just means that there's a big chink in the armor, and they're gonna try to get to you. And then there's Tony. His wife is from some rich meat-packing family in Kansas or someplace like that. She's got his nuts in a wringer. Shouldn't be that way, but it is. If there's any screaming about this at all, it's gonna be your ass. He's gonna say you led him on and seduced him and all this stuff, and then the word's gonna be out that you've got enemies and you're trouble. It shouldn't be that way, but that's the way it is."

"I understand," Nicole said softly. "Can you just give me a couple of weeks to find a new job?"

"Honey," Bernie said, biting off a huge hunk of bacon, so greasy that a transparent, barely viscous fluid ran down his thumb and dripped onto the table, "I'm not firing you. I like your work. I just want you to know the score."

Again, for the third time that day, for the tenth time in five days, tears came to Nicole's eyes.

"You don't need to thank me," Bernie said. "Another thing about my business is that Bernie Labofish doesn't like the idea that some putz can come in and play games with my smartest, hottest number, and start all kinds of problems at my agency, and then I'm going to take it out on you, like it's not his fault. I don't work that way."

That night, which was a Friday, Nicole slept well for the first time since she'd met Tony. She had a friend. She had a protector. Her talent and her genuine innocence of wrongdoing had protected her, given her justice.

For the first time since she left Jonesboro, she felt as if her life might really be like a movie. Bernie might shepherd her up to where she was meant to be. He might be her good angel, protecting her from herself while he ate pastrami on rye.

On Monday, after a weekend of seeing Van Gogh at the Norton Simon, she went into Sterling Grace with an entirely new lightness in her step.

As she rode up in the elevator, she felt euphoric until the second floor. After that, she felt a wave of panic so acute that she thought she might actually break into pieces. She felt as if her skin was about to fly apart, molecule by molecule, as if every atom in her was screaming to get back to outer space.

She was dizzy by the time she got into the Sterling Grace lobby. At that point, premonition and reality effected a merger.

Instead of the usual buzz of laughter and typing and printing and swish of papers, there was only silence at the desks along her corridor. There were not even any secretaries or assistants sitting at the desks. There were only empty work stations, empty offices, and a terrifyingly empty silence.

As Nicole turned a corner, she saw that even Marsha Grossman's office was empty. Her stacks of gourmet vitamins lay on her desk unattended. But just beyond that room, in the conference area where Marsha had spoken to Nicole two evenings ago, a meeting was going on. Nicole could barely see who was speaking because the room was so packed with her colleagues. Oddly, instead of the usual raised voices and competing squeals for attention and gusts of laughter, there was only one slightly familiar voice. Also, no one was sitting. In fact, men and women were standing behind empty chairs, facing a woman whose voice was coming from the window overlooking Century Park East. The voice: Shirley Labofish.

Shirley looked indescribably tired, fatigued, wrung out. There was no makeup to cover the hollows under her eyes. Her lips were a bare, colorless flesh tint. Even her teeth looked tired. She was wearing baggy jeans and a sweater and she looked as if she had been in them all night long.

". . . Bernie had been having angina for five years. Maybe longer. He had an angioplasty with one of those little balloons, but he just wouldn't stop eating the way he liked to eat. I guess that's my fault. Anyway, he loved all of you. He really liked being at work more than he liked being home, and that's the truth.

"I don't know what's going to happen to the agency now. I just have to think about the funeral arrangements, and I can't really think about business now. If it makes you feel any better, I don't think Bernie even felt a thing. He just went to sleep, listening through those damned earphones as usual, and then he didn't wake up. Massive heart attack. The first symptom was death. And that's it."

Despite herself, Nicole began to hyperventilate. Marsha Grossman looked over at her. She had a cruel, controlled, tight grimace on her face. Behind her stood a sobbing Mimi Keller.

On her way out, Nicole walked into Bernie's office. On his desk were his brand-new Proton stereo earphones, the ones he used only at work. Nicole picked them up and put them in her purse, and then walked out. A souvenir of a man she loved. As she rounded a turn near the ladies' room, she ran into Marsha Grossman walking and talking intently with Shirley Labofish. Shirley took both of Nicole's hands. "Bernie loved you, honey," Shirley said. "He thought you had what it takes. 'The people who have the goods get the goods' is what he used to say, and he thought you had the goods."

"He was a great guy," Nicole said in barely more than a whisper. "We're not going to see anyone like him for a long time."

For four days, Nicole drank a full bottle of Cypress Chardonnay each night before she went to sleep. On the weekend, she drove up to Montecito with Mimi to look at the pines and the mansions. On Monday morning, when she came into work, there was a note saying that because virtually all of the big clients of Sterling Grace chose to exercise their "key man" options and change their accounts, the agency was going to close in two weeks.

There was another note, this one Xeroxed on "From the desk of Marsha Grossman" stationery with a woman with frizzy hair holding a giant globe on her shoulders while she also bent over an easel and worked on a storyboard marked "God Consolidated Account."

The memo said that Marsha Grossman and Rhona Beck, in order to "take some of the burden off our dear friend Shirley Labofish," would henceforth be in charge of operations as the firm wound down. The memo further said that Misses Grossman and Beck would explore the possibility of starting a new firm, using the smaller clients who had stayed with the firm and making an effort to win back former clients and new clients.

Nicole took out her *Adweeks* for the past three months and began to look through them. In one day, she sent out eight letters and résumés. The next day she sent out fourteen. The day after that, her assistant, Roni, a Colombian woman with almost perfect command of English and a pure Inca face, was fired, and Nicole was told in an expressionless intercom voice that she was not to use the office Xerox facilities to look for another job. She was also told that in view of her close personal ties with the head of a competing agency, perhaps this might be the time to turn over all of her office files, "just to prevent any misunderstanding." Marsha Grossman added, "Of course, honey, you'll be paid until the end of the week, but the accounts are in such a mess that you might not actually get the check until another week after that, maybe longer. Looks like Bernie carried around where a lot of the money was in his head."

That was it. That was the chute down which the advertising

career of Nicole Miller slid with startling speed. At the time that Bernie Labofish's coronary arteries became so constricted that his heart muscle could no longer receive enough oxygenated blood to continue pumping, Nicole Miller had three hundred dollars in her checking account. She did not have a savings account. Out of that, she had to pay her rent and garage payment, a total of four hundred and ten dollars per month. She also had to pay her car insurance, which had recently been raised after its transfer to Los Angeles from Knoxville by a factor of around ten. She had to pay the minimum on her BankAmericard and on her Master-Card, plus the minimum on Ann Taylor and The Broadway. That amount totaled roughly three times her available money.

"You can't imagine how this worrying about money tears into me," Nicole wrote in her journal.

It must be similar to being hungry all of the time, except that you're not physically aching in your belly, but you're tearing yourself up inside all day long. What if they take away my credit cards? What if we get evicted? What if I literally can't afford to buy food? It's a state of mind that is like being kept awake by North Korean guards all night long, except that the North Korean guards are your own head telling you that tomorrow, definitely tomorrow, you'd better find some place to work, some place where they pay a lot and where they pay fast. I honestly can easily see why people rob 7-Elevens.

Of course, Nicole had only been in Los Angeles for a few months. She did not want to give up on her hopes about advertising. She sent out another five letters and résumés, using Mimi Keller's little Panasonic portable and the Quik-Print shop on Santa Monica Boulevard.

From that effort she got invitations to exactly two interviews. Both interviews were for jobs as assistants, which basically means secretary to junior copywriters and account executives in training. In other words, she was auditioning for a job that would have

109

been the equivalent of the job her Colombian assistant had at Sterling Grace.

At the first interview, her contact kept her waiting for one and a half hours. Then she gave Nicole a typing test. Nicole made five mistakes and typed forty words per minute. "Come back when your typing skills have improved," the woman said. "You definitely are well dressed enough."

At the second interview, a black man in Personnel kept putting his hand on her shoulder as he walked around behind her and talked to her. He, like the woman who kept her waiting for over an hour, did not even want to see her drawings. "The way it lays out," he said cheerfully, "is that there are only a few national agencies in Los Angeles. If they were doing well, there would be more, and there would be sort of a market in personnel. The way it is, in fact, is that hardly any of the agencies here is paying its way. At the most, they're just introduction services for the headquarters in New York. I hear you're buddies with Tony Morris. He must have told you all about this stuff."

Nicole could not bring herself to tell her mother and father about the collapse of Sterling Grace and her disappearance from that melting ice floe. Not at first. Within one week, when a little notice had been tacked to Mimi and Nicole's door telling them that they had one week to pay or vacate the premises, Nicole called Mom and Dad.

Within one day, by Federal Express, Nicole had a check for one thousand dollars. With it was a note in her mother's startlingly precise handwriting.

Dear Nicole,

Of course, Ray and I want to do anything we can to help, and Ray would kill me if he knew I was writing this to you. But the TVA is cutting back something fierce. Has to do with some big fuss in Washington. Ray says he's going to have to take early retirement. Of course, we'll do anything we can anytime we can, and you shouldn't ever feel you can't ask, but things are changing around here.

That was the trapdoor through which Nicole fell. If her mother and father had written that everything was great, her life would have been different indeed. For example, and this is a big example, Mimi Keller had been laid off, too. But Mimi had a major plan. Mimi's great idea, the one that was going to save their lives, was that they would both move to New York. "There are a thousand billion agency jobs there," she said. "We'd have it made."

"Apartments in New York are sky-high," Nicole said. "The agency business pays zilch to start. If we got there and didn't get jobs, we'd be freezing out on the street. It's scary enough going to New York at any time. If you go without money, and you desperately need a job, you're totally lost. You're just begging for trouble."

"You won't have any trouble. I've seen your drawings. Bernie used to rave about them."

"Mimi, I've seen what can happen. I've seen how you can get turned around when you least expect it. I'm not taking the chance."

"You can't let all this stuff about Tony Morris and Bernie wreck your confidence," Mimi said enthusiastically.

"Too late," Nicole answered. "I'm flat. I've got to get a little wind back before I can even start to think about trying again."

"Call Tony," Mimi suggested. "He owes you."

There was a moment's silence, and Nicole said, "I did call him. He told me I had a total attitude problem and had already wrecked my own life, and he didn't want me screwing around with his life. Then, if you can cop to this, he called back an hour later and said he was sorry, and that he'd like to make dinner for me, just him and me at that goddamned apartment in Century City. Can you really believe it?"

"What did you tell him?"

"Mimi."

"I mean it. You use what you have in this town."

"I'm an ad woman. I'm an artist. I work with my brains. I'm not a call girl. I'll go back to Jonesboro a lot faster."

"Yeah. But if a guy likes you and can do something for you . . . I mean, there are so many dorks here who are gonna use you and can't do anything for you in return. Besides, Tony's cute."

"You go out with him, then. He once told me he thought you were really cute."

"I might," Mimi said. "No, I'm kidding," she laughed. "Girls just want to have fun."

*F*rom an entry in Nicole's diary in the spring of 1984, roughly eighteen months after the day that Bernie Labofish entered immortality:

When I was in eighth grade, they took a few of us from Loudun Junior High and spent about six weeks teaching us calculus. I really don't remember much of it except that I remember that the teacher, a guy from the Weapons Research Lab at Oak Ridge, explained to us how a ballistic missile works. It's not like a 747, where someone is turning knobs and making fins come in and out to move it around the sky.

Instead, it is given a certain angle and a certain speed within the first two minutes of its flight. Sort of like a rock that you throw. After that, you can't change anything about the whole rest of its flight path, even if it's going all the way from North Dakota to Moscow. It's just the same as when a rock is thrown. How it starts out is exactly how it's gonna finish.

I feel a lot like that about what happened to me back at Sterling Grace. It was like knowing Tony Morris, and getting Marsha Grossman mad at me, and losing the job at Sterling Grace because Bernie died, and not having any

112

money in the bank . . . all those things set me on a particular angle of flight, and after that, things were just totally set permanently. That was it, and that explains an awful lot of everything else that's happened.

I'm trying desperately to exert some free will and some little sense of my own motion and control, but no matter how hard I try, I just get myself further along a trajectory that some facts that happened a long time ago determined. It really makes me understand about why people feel so lost. I feel like a homeless person about to happen, maybe already happening.

*S*ome of what happened to Nicole after she left Sterling Grace:

Eventually, she began to work as a temp for a variety of agencies that promised glamorous work in glamorous fields. To her credit, Nicole realized almost immediately that the concept of "glamorous temp work" was something of a contradiction in terms. Her first few jobs basically involved sitting in offices where she knew no one and no one knew her, answering phones for men who did not even look at her as they came in and out, filing away masses of papers in file rooms with no windows, bending over bottom drawers of file cabinets until her back felt as if it would break in two.

For this work, she was generally paid seven dollars per hour. The temp agency was paid another seven dollars per hour on top of that, or a commission of one hundred percent.

The only interesting job that Nicole found in the temp world was a three-week assignment for a well-known legal consultant in securities fraud. He had been hired by a law firm in San Diego to analyze a case involving a casino. He had worked for a month and submitted a bill. His clients simply refused to pay or answer his calls. In order to sue, he had to find his contract with the law firm. His office had hundreds of cardboard boxes filled with papers, and Nicole's job was to find the contract in those boxes.

It would have been boring, and especially dirty because the

expert witness had five Dalmatians who all tried to climb in the boxes once Nicole opened them, but the expert, a reclusive maniac of forty-four, insisted on keeping Nicole company and talking to her as she filed.

His name was Mark Cooper. He had a theory about the reasons that some people succeeded and some people failed. It had to do with acquiring human capital through education. In aid of his theory, he preached endlessly to Nicole about the vital importance of law school, film school, business school—any school, he said, that would "add value beyond its marginal cost."

Mark Cooper made a number of calls and got Nicole accepted to a month-long program in the legal aspects of advertising at UCLA Law School. As a gift, because she found his missing contract in a box filled with articles about ancient Roman Dalmatians, he paid for the course. It met every Monday and Wednesday from seven to nine P.M. From it, Nicole learned a number of case holdings about right to privacy, secondary meaning, fair use, copyright and trademark, and the limit of free speech when product disparagement is involved.

However, when Nicole applied to advertising agencies, citing her new knowledge of the field of advertising law, they all told her that they employed law firms to study that kind of problem. At the three major law firms to which she applied for work as a paralegal, the personnel officers said they would indeed be interested if she could take a one-year course in paralegal research, which met from ten to four every day at UCLA Law School.

Mark Cooper did not have any ideas about how she might support herself during that time. He, in any event, was called away to Bartlesville, Oklahoma, for a trial involving fraud by an oil drilling company and simply vanished from her life with his theories and his Dalmatians, except to send her an occasional cryptic note warning her not to buy junk bonds, along with a portable C.D. player one Christmas.

Nicole temped for twenty different employers. She never made more than four hundred dollars a week, except for the one time she was typing for yet another lawyer and discovered what looked to her to be a major contradiction between two of his arguments in a breach of contract and unjust enrichment action. For that discovery, Nicole was given a bonus of five hundred dollars and an offer (declined) to spend the weekend in Cabo San Lucas with the lawyer.

In the two years that followed Bernie Labofish's passing, Nicole went out on exactly twenty-five dates.

She went out with several men she met at temp jobs, a few men she met at the Hughes Market on Doheny Drive and Burton Way, and three fix-ups by Mimi Keller, who seemed to have men coming in and out of her life constantly.

"I think that the young, with-it L.A. man may very well set an entirely new standard for self-obsession, lack of feeling, and lack of the most basic skills of human interaction," Nicole wrote in a letter to Jeff Boone.

I sometimes think they are making these men in a factory somewhere on Mars, and because they haven't had much experience with human feelings, they just left out the parts of the brain that are supposed to deal with empathy, caring, or even communication. (The only men I ever meet who have even basic skills of asking about me and assuming I'm human and can talk and think are married, and that's taboo after some recent history.)

The usual man that I meet wants to brag about how much money he's making, not hear one word about me if at all possible, show me off to anyone he knows at the restaurant or party or whatever, and then expects me to do anything he wants just because he happens to be there. I keep expecting that one day I'm going to meet one who has some idea that I'm a person, too, with feelings, and that I have something to say, but I never do. Has there been some kind of neutron bomb detonated in Los Angeles that doesn't hurt Porsches or BMWs but does destroy men with feelings? I know you follow scientific literature and maybe you know something about a virus

that takes away only the parts of the male brain that deal
with being funny or nice or intelligent or giving a
goddamn about anything except having your head up
somewhere dark. I often think Mimi and I are the only
human beings left in Los Angeles, and when I talk to
other women here, they tell me that they think the exact
same thing about themselves.

In other words, in her time in Los Angeles, Nicole had been fed a steady diet of discouragement, chaos, and rejection. In return for her hopes of success, her work, her creative accomplishment, she had been sent to the lowest subbasement of the urban, female, educated proletariat, the army of those who have been promised by magazines that they can have it all (whatever that means), and who get nothing but frustration.

For example, on three separate occasions, Nicole performed her duties as a temp so successfully that she was asked to stay on: once at the California headquarters of Mrs. See's Candy on La Cienega Boulevard (a province of Warren Buffett's far-flung empire), another time at the intake center of the Burbank Lifesavers program for teenage drug abuse, and finally at the office of Bob Gabriel Associates, an insurance agency in Santa Monica.

But in every case, there was something that kept her from taking the job. She was not offered enough money at Mrs. See's. She was told she would have to work with potentially violent addicts without protection at the hospital. At the insurance agency, the agents were cheerful and lively. The whole office laughed all day. But the future was to become an insurance agent, a much maligned if generally excellent occupation. Head of Creative at an advertising agency was much more what the Drum Major had in mind.

That is, Nicole was imprisoned not only by what was out there and the reality of the job market for female college graduates from Tennessee in a big city, without family connections, without family money, without unique skills or a medical or legal degree. She was also cruelly hobbled by her own ambition. She was able to see all too clearly the immense gap between what she wanted and felt was her due on one hand and what was available on the other. The women's revolution of rising expectations threw her madly forward. The facts of life for a woman who has made a few small mistakes and had some bad breaks and has no powerful relatives to help her were an unbreakable Plexiglas wall into which she crashed every hour of the day. But on the other side of that wall, seen through the agency of her own ambition, was the carrot that kept her thrashing and grasping to get through.

"You are a prisoner of cultural illusion and market reality," Mark Cooper had said, and the only word that lingered in Nicole's mind was "prisoner."

The walls were of missing four-thousand-dollar-per-week paychecks, absent Gold American Express cards, a strangely lacking house with a pool in Brentwood Park, a ghost saleswoman who knew her and her size at the designer floor of Bullock's-Wilshire, but they were keeping her in all the same.

Thank you, Valu-King Liquor Empire, for your specials on California Chardonnay, to help me get through the nights, Nicole often said. Thank you for a way out that's available every day for almost no money. Other times she thought that she would be in trouble if she ever had to stop having her white wine, and instead face up to what her life had become.

Surely though, fairly soon, her luck would change, and she would have the life she needed, a life that would not require that bottle to get to sleep at night. How long? Not long.

7

HELLO, STRANGER

On a day in January 1985, when Nicole came home from temping as a receptionist at the Los Angeles office of Goldman, Sachs, she stopped in the lobby of her building to pick up her mail. There was a letter from Jeff Boone, a letter from The Broadway suspending her charge account, a letter from MasterCard canceling forever her credit privileges with them, a note from the superintendent of the building saying that she was about to be evicted for late payment of her rent, and a letter from her mother telling her that she ought to write to her father more often. "His spirits are very low, what with being laid up with that colitis, and I really think that a few lines from you would charge him up."

Nicole went up to her apartment and walked past Mimi's door. Mimi was painting her toenails, listening to a compact disc of one of the horrible rap music groups she adored. She was eating a huge chocolate bar and simultaneously watching a rerun of "I Love Lucy" and laughing out loud at it—even with the sound turned off.

Surprise, surprise, it was about Lucy forgetting to turn on the oven just when Ricky was bringing Cesar Romero home from the club. Wahhhhh!

Nicole flopped down on Mimi's bed and sighed. A light drizzle was falling outside. Nicole felt as if she had brought most of it inside with her.

"I don't get it. Today I worked at a place where young dweeby guys just out of school are making eighty thousand dollars a year. They aren't any smarter than I am. I just don't get it. Is it because they can add and subtract? Is that it? I could learn to do that."

"Listen," Mimi said without taking her eyes off the screen. "Today, while I was getting my nails done at the Sayonara Nail Club, I sat next to this really good-looking girl. I mean, really good-looking. And classy-looking. And she was wearing a gorge red fox coat. Gorge. So I asked her what she did, and she asked me to come to lunch with her at the Border Cafe, and guess what."

"She hooks."

"Right. She works for this woman in Beverly Hills and she goes out with these Japanese guys and Korean guys and rich American guys who are in town, and she sometimes just has to have dinner with them and hear about their jobs. And sometimes she might just give them a little head . . ."

"Mimi, what's 'a little head'?"

"Well, you know. And once in a while they get to do her, and she always makes sure they wear a condom, and she gets like five hundred bucks a time."

"I'm not going to be a hooker, Mimi."

"It's not like you're out on a street corner, and anyway, you only have to do it if you need money. It's like temp work. Only you go out with guys."

"Mimi, have you been doing it?"

"No, but I'd sure consider it if I didn't have to do anything but have dinner with the guys."

Nicole held up the stack of bills in her hand. She thought of the stack already on her dresser in her walk-in closet, next to her photos of Jeff Boone and of her family.

"I'd like to meet her," Mimi said. "The woman in Beverly Hills. Maybe we could make a deal where we just went to dinner and then we got less money, but we didn't have to do anybody."

"It's a little far-fetched, but I'll go with you, just to keep you company."

Two hours later, after a mere one telephone call, Mimi and Nicole were on their way over to the Polo Lounge in Nicole's battered yellow Toyota. They decided to park on the side. It was too humiliating to park "the yellow peril" in front among the Beemers and the Ferraris. They walked through the pathways amidst the bungalows, passed two agents talking about money from Taiwan for a movie to be set in Bangladesh, and then walked into the Polo Lounge.

"We're here to see Ms. Middle," Mimi said authoritatively. She wore a blue leather dress and high-heeled shoes. Nicole wore a white silk dress with delicate red stripes running vertically along its length, and white leather pumps.

Bernardo showed them to a table where a woman of about fifty sat smoking a More cigarette. The woman wore a gray business suit and a veritable silver mine of jewelry around her neck and wrists. She smiled up at Mimi with watery blue eyes and then at Nicole with a look of hunger.

"I'm going to lay this out for you really clearly," Elaine Middle said. "I run this thing as a business. It's the hospitality business. It's like owning a hotel or a casino in Vegas. I supply hospitality to men who are lonely and can afford to pay for it. You're both young. You're both good-looking and got good figures and blue eyes and look like real American cheerleader types. That's money in the bank."

"What I'd like to know," Nicole asked, "is if there's some way I can work for you so that I go out to dinner and look really nice, and make conversation, and then don't have to, like, do anything with them afterwards."

"Well," Elaine Middle said, "what you do with them afterwards is totally up to you. You don't have to do anything at all with them. Or, you can do whatever you feel like doing. I just get half. And if I get a complaint that you copped an attitude or were difficult or uncooperative, naturally that affects my decision about whether or not to keep on sending you out on calls. Because

120

you're both cute, and men love that little girl look of Mimi's and they love big tits like Nicole's, but there's a lot of other girls who'd like to have the gig."

"I don't know," Nicole said.

"What I think you're going to find," said Elaine Middle, "is that if you try it, you'll find that it's not that incredibly different from just the usual dating stuff that goes on in L.A. right now, only you get paid for it."

"I'd like to think about it," Mimi said.

"Look," said Elaine Middle, "instead of that, tonight, I have these two guys from Argentina. They make shoes or something and they're totally loaded. And they're here and I was going to fix them up with two of my best girls, models from Robinson's or somewhere. But they got better offers. So maybe you two would like to go out to dinner with them and just see how you like it. It's a minimum of two bills each, which I'll give you right outside no matter how it shakes down. Just think of it as business. The companionship business. These guys won't hate you. They'll like you. I never yet have had a girl beat up."

At nine-thirty, Mimi and Nicole, fortified with half a bottle of Grgich Hills and a large joint, appeared at the desk of the Beverly-Wilshire Hotel and asked for Mr. Vargas and Mr. Gusmann.

The effeminate man at the desk looked down an aquiline nose at them and said, "Oh, yes. They're in Suite 1102. They're expecting you."

Nicole and Mimi took the elevator in the old part of the complex up to the eleventh floor. They held each other's hands for confidence. They walked down a seemingly endless hall with a garish red carpet. They heard couples laughing and ice cubes tinkling. They saw a bellhop carrying in Mark Cross luggage marked with a return address of Knoxville, Tennessee. Then they came to Suite 1102.

Mimi knocked on the door. "I just want you to know," she said, "that if you don't want to stay, I don't want to stay either."

"Okay. I swear I won't let them touch me."

The door opened. Two fat middle-aged men stood at the door

in white terrycloth bathrobes. They wore a cologne so sweet that Nicole gagged. Both men had their hair slicked back. Just from the door, Nicole could see two black girls in startlingly high heels holding up champagne glasses. One of them was pouring wine into the glass held by the other. They were both laughing a peculiar, high-pitched giggle and tripping as they laughed and poured champagne. The two black girls wore transparent pink bathrobes, through which Nicole could see their nipples, and infinitesimal gauzy panties.

"Here she comes," sang one of the men in highly Spanish-accented English, although he also looked distinctly Iranian. "Miss America, with major-league knockers, just like we ordered . . ."

"Come in, blond darlings," the other man said. "Black and white and black and white. This is going to be wonderful. What are you drinking?"

Nicole said, "I think we're in the wrong room. We're looking for the Beverly Hills Police Department immigration meeting. Sorry."

A look of terror crossed the men's faces. "You are kidding, no?" one of them asked.

But before Nicole could answer, the other man slammed shut the door amid a torrent of screaming Spanish.

Mimi and Nicole did not take the elevators. They ran through the first fire door exit they could find. They did not stop running until they were at the yellow Toyota on the corner of Rodeo and Charleville. They did not stop laughing until they got back to the little liquor store at the corner of Crescent Heights and Wilshire, where they bought two bottles of a California Chardonnay and a fifth of house gin.

They stayed up drinking the wine and telling stories about the men who had fucked them over and the men who had been losers and how nothing at all ever seemed to go the way Betty Friedan had promised it would After The Revolution.

At about one A.M., there was a shrieking angry telephone call from Elaine Middle. Nicole hung up on her. In an excess of caution, however, she tore up both two-hundred-dollar checks that Elaine had given them. No sense in leaving a trail of obligation or anything else. At one-thirty A.M., Mimi passed out while listening to The Fat Boys and watching a rerun of "Lassie," which made her cry, so that she fell asleep while crying, so to speak.

At two A.M., Nicole drank the rest of the remaining bottle of wine and wondered if she would ever get the security and family and warmth and, towering above those things, the sense that she had accomplished something with her one and only life, that she had made anything out of what God had given her.

She also wondered if there was a liquor store nearby still open where she might possibly get another bottle of Chardonnay. Then she realized that she was actually scared, no, terrified, that there might not be another bottle available for her that night.

When she had that thought, something of the Drum Major from Kefauver High School kicked in. Instead of buying wine, she called 411 and asked if they had a number for Alcoholics Anonymous in Los Angeles. When she got the number, she asked the man who answered the telephone if there were a meeting in West Hollywood the next day.

"There are about twenty meetings," the man said. "Are you sober now?"

"No," Nicole said.

"Would you like to say the Lord's Prayer with me right now, over the phone?" the man asked.

"Yes, I would," Nicole said.

"Our Father," the man began, "who art in Heaven, hallowed be Thy name . . ." and Nicole joined in, warm tears streaming down her cheeks. "Thy kingdom come. Thy will be done . . ."

8

FURRY CREATURES

You might think that if you were a man not yet forty, who had created a financial entity so potent that a relatively small amount of debt and equity mixed up together in a stew, seasoned with a small airline, yielded him three hundred million dollars' worth of stock, you would be a happy guy.

After all, you could go into a Porsche dealer, any Ferrari shop, any branch of Tiffany, and buy anything that struck you. You could open up the country living section of *The New York Times* Sunday magazine and pick out all of the Connecticut estates listed there and buy all of them.

If you had three hundred million dollars, essentially money would be what economists call a "free good." You could use as much of it as your little heart desired without having to forego anything else. It would be like water or air. It would be as easy— and as free of cost—for you to buy a farm overlooking the Mediterranean above Cap d'Antibes as to buy a pack of Clorets gum. In either case, there would be no requirement that you sacrifice any other thing to have the farm or the gum, and so you would be basically getting either or both for free.

The most basic of man's problems on earth, scarcity, would simply not exist for you. You would not have to figure out at any time what you could or could not afford. You would not have to create your own economic system for dealing with scarcity. You would basically be outside the whole science of economics as it relates to individual human beings. Instead, you would have a strong purchase on something like economic weightlessness. The gravity of scarcity and the necessity of making choices would be somebody else's problems.

That's what you might think.

By the same token, if you were Barron Thomas of Barron Thomas Aviation, you would also have escaped the problem of anonymity in mass society. The scary emptiness of knowing that you were just a cipher in a nation of two hundred and fifty million hustling people who did not care whether you lived or died would just be gone.

You would not be a traveling salesman in a cheap motel in Indianapolis with a neon sign flashing VACANCY outside your room for the rest of your life.

You would not be a frantic newsboy running alongside a car with rolled-up windows as it approached the toll booths on the Triborough Bridge, desperately trying to get some slight notice from your fellow ciphers as they sped toward the airports on their way to eternity.

No, if you were Barron Thomas, you would have had your picture in *Forbes* not once but many times. You would have been in a section on businessmen with "Guts and Glory" in *Fortune.* You would have been interviewed on CNN's "Pinnacle." You would have had your photo in *SkyNews,* the in-flight magazine of BTA. You would have been interviewed on CBS News when Eastern had a labor disturbance. You would have been seen going into and out of fundraisers for the various wings of the Metropolitan Museum of Art that were being built by various financiers in New York.

While you would not be David Bowie, you would be recognized more than enough for you to feel far from anonymous. As you walked down Fifth Avenue to meet your two lawyers, Si Lazarus and Abe Cohen, at the Harmonie Club, you would have

total strangers approach you—well-dressed strangers to be sure—
and ask you what you thought about Carl Icahn buying TWA or
about the prospects for solvency of Pan Am. You would have
people in restaurants look at you as you passed by, then give you
the celebrity double-take, then whisper to their dining companions, and then the dining companions would give you the celebrity double-take, too.

No one is saying that Barron Thomas sought out such attention. In fact, he didn't. He did not even have the 1980s equivalent of the alchemist, the modern publicist who can turn the most
hopeless bore of a businessman into a glamorous figure. He did
talk about what he thought was important, but he did not try to
make himself into a yachtsman or a country squire or a baronial
figure in Charlottesville, or any of the other things that creative
accountants do when they get rich.

Still, if you were Barron Thomas, you would not be anonymous. You would feel that anywhere in America, you were
known, you had some respect, you were among family.

Now, you might think that if you had licked the twin demons
of scarcity and insignificance, you would have life sussed out. You
would have no constraints of cost, no limits of being unknown.
At any moment, the only real threats would be the health and
happiness of those close to you.

That's what you might think. But then you might only think
that the way that people who have never been to Rome imagine
that when they get near the Trevi Fountain there will be young
lovers holding hands while Cary Grant and Audrey Hepburn kiss
in the foreground. Those people who haven't been near the Trevi
Fountain imagine that it will be the way it is in the movies—
pristine and perfect and available. They don't think about the
swarms of tourists, the pickpocket Gypsies, the thick haze of
smog, the fact that by the time you get to the fountain, it's often
not even working—in fact, it's often quite dry.

In other words, you might think all these things if, you did not
actually know Barron Thomas and have a pretty good idea of just
what his life was like, say, in the spring of 1984.

Life is not static but dynamic, as long as people are alive and in a body. Accordingly, after Barron Thomas made his major strike on the airline, he felt compelled to come up with other ideas.

The one he liked the best had to do with real estate. He observed, as others had before him, that real estate had been on a mostly straight ride up from about 1941 to about 1984. It was expensive to buy it from a real-estate broker, though. Luckily, there was a way to buy it wholesale, so to speak.

Real-estate investment trusts (REITs) were big in the go-go 1960s. They were brought public, raised money, and bought real estate. Almost axiomatically, they were then wildly misrun by the promoters, who had just wanted some up-front cash anyway. The scandalous mistakes of a few tarred the others, whose errors were just routine. The result was that the prices of shares tended to drift down, down, down through the 1970s and early 1980s.

In addition, and this was really the killer part, REITs tended to pay extremely modest dividends. In a world wracked with inflation, where investors could get fifteen percent on risk-free Treasury debt, not many wanted to own shares in an REIT, which paid maybe one percent, and whose management was far more likely to show up in the *Police Gazette* than in *The New York Times* business section, to the extent the two were once different.

Again, the shares were hammered down, down, down.

The lavish irony which so appealed to the dramatist in Barron Thomas was that the real estate commanded by these shares tended to go up, up, up.

Thus, to make something simple even simpler, it was possible to buy real estate at wholesale by taking over an REIT at a bargain price through the shares and then liquidating the selfsame REIT.

In March and April of 1984, Barron Thomas floated a private placement of the Real Estate Equalization Fund. With equity players at five million a pop, and insurance companies flocking to get their paws near Barron Thomas, the issue soon had two hundred million of privately held stock.

With this equity, and with the real estate owned by the REITs as collateral for debt, Barron could buy several REITs at a time, liquidate them as fast as possible, and pocket the difference between the liquidation price and the stock price—along with his fellow equity players.

"The problem with this gig," as Si Lazarus told Barron after they had entered the fifth such transaction by June 1984, "is that it's too easy."

Barron, Si Lazarus, and Abe Cohen were all sitting by the backyard pool in the twenty-acre expanse of Barron and Saundra Thomas's new home in Bedford. It was a cloudy but warm day, and Saundra was in the glassed-in terrace reading a book about the fashions of colonial wives in the British Raj. Within Barron's view, she was regularly lifting a glass of clear liquid to her lips, like a stripper oil derrick pumping old oil. In the pool, a mechanized cleaner floated in circles picking up pine needles.

"I don't doubt it," Barron said. "There'll be other players in the field soon. Maybe by tomorrow. That's okay. We'll get out when the deals aren't there anymore."

"When you've got an internal rate of return on your equity of sixty percent, there's bound to be lots of competition," Abe Cohen said. "Word's gonna get out. Word's already out."

"I don't care if word gets out," Barron Thomas said again. "By that time, we'll be on to something else." He paused and watched a robin walking on the edge of the pool, staring at the pool-sweeping machine. "Anyway, don't be so sure that other people will come into the market. There are a lot of reasons why markets don't work quite as smoothly as John Stuart Mill said they did. People are lazy. People get confused. The idea that every opportunity that exists will automatically be seized is just plain wrong. If it were right, the stock market would only need to be open once a month."

"Then what'll we do next?" said Si Lazarus, senior corporate finance partner at Crutch, Marley. "You must have some ideas."

"I still love real-estate gigs," Barron said. "It's hard to sell, but it's so easy to buy on the right side of it. It's got a lot of allure."

"What about something in high tech?" Abe Cohen, Lazarus's

128

partner asked. "There's a lot of venture capital money chasing deals in the Silicon Valley. Could be that there's some product we could latch on to, maybe develop it . . ."

"Are you kidding? Do you know anything about semiconductors, Abe? Do you, Si? I sure as hell don't. You know what I know? That every time some halfway decent hardware comes on the market, the Japanese can make it better, cheaper, faster."

"Then maybe some way to invest in Japanese high tech would be the ticket," Cohen suggested.

Barron got up, walked to a table with food on it, passed by the food, and went to a bottle of Bombay gin. He poured a jigger over ice, mixed it with tonic, and went back to his chair.

"Why? Why compete with the guys who've been studying this crap for years? You speak Japanese? You have any clue who's hot and who isn't in that market? Not only does none of us have a clue about high tech, none of us has even a hint about what's real and what's not in Japan."

"The man is making some sense," Si Lazarus said to his partner.

"You know what the first rule of making money is?" Barron asked.

"Never pay retail," Cohen suggested with a laugh.

"No. The first rule of making money is don't lose money," Barron said. "I learned that from Warren Buffett. Let's just do what we can with the real-estate thing. That's easy. That's not in San Jose. That's not in Osaka. That's pretty straightforward."

"Yeah, but what—" Abe Cohen started before Barron cut him off.

"Abe, you don't need to think about it right now. Let's try doing what's in front of us. This Bay Bridge Investors Trust is a lovely shot. Let's get the appraisers out there, start buying a few shares, make sure the management knows we're going to treat them right when we buy the company."

"Okay. Consider it done." Cohen nodded.

"I think a straight three percent on the profit on an allocated basis per piece of property for the managers makes a lot of sense," Barron said cheerily. "It turns out to be cheap. Whatever we pay to the managers is one tenth of what we don't have to pay to the lawyers."

"I love that it's so blatant," Lazarus said. "Just give it to the managers and you can be sure they'll do what you want. But we'll disclose everything and offer a stub to anyone who wants to stay in."

"It's the iron law of corporate decision making," Barron laughed. "All decisions will be made solely in the best interest of the decision makers."

"You should write a book," Cohen chuckled.

"Why? Why share something so obvious?" Barron asked.

The three men laughed for a little longer in the early-summer sunshine, and then Lazarus and Cohen got up and walked across the lawn with Barron for the ride home. When Barron stopped at the terrace to look in on Saundra, Lazarus said to his partner, "I wish I knew ten guys with his confidence."

"It's great. Like a twenty-game winner, only in business. I love it a lot. I wish we had just one other client who was so decisive, who figured things out so clearly."

"The guy really has got things so figured out it's amazing," Lazarus said. "A very happening guy."

"A guy who really is in charge."

"A success machine," Lazarus said. "A very fortunate son."

*A*fter Lazarus and Cohen drove off in Lazarus's "identify with the aggressor–mobile," as Barron called the 1983 Mercedes 450SEL sedan, Barron turned back from the circular driveway of crushed gravel. He walked through the house, down the hallway, through the sunroom, past his downstairs office, and out onto the terrace.

Saundra was sitting in her padded lawn recliner reading her book, *The Raj and the Origins of Modern Leisure.* She looked particularly lovely, Barron thought, in her white Bermuda shorts and a cotton sweater.

"Hi, Barron," she said as he walked up. "Did you make any money today?"

"I guess so," Barron said. "How are you feeling today?"

Barron stood about three feet from Saundra's face. A huge draft of vodka-laden air passed from her to him. "I'm fine," she said. "Just great."

"No headaches?"

"Well, I have my usual headache," Saundra said. "The one that I get because you're always trying to make me feel guilty about drinking."

"You don't really believe that, do you?"

"Of course I do," Saundra said emphatically. "I know that's what you do. You're talking with your two lawyers and you're thinking how you can come in here afterwards and make me feel shitty just because I'm not making tons of money the way you are, just because I'm trying to live my own life the way I want to live it."

"You can't be serious," Barron said. "You don't really think that."

"Oh, but I do," Saundra said. "I know that after making your little piles of money, the thing you like best is to control people by making them feel guilty."

Barron took a deep breath and walked around in a circle and then sat down on an adjoining chaise. As he did, he felt something hard under his left thigh. He picked out a bottle of pills from Dr. Auguste Greenthal, of Bedford Hills. "Valium, 10 mg. For anxiety as needed," said the label.

"This is another doctor you're seeing?" Barron asked.

"I need this doctor," Saundra said, "because what if you called up from one of your trips where you buy apartments or whatever you do, and you asked me what I did today, and I told you I just enjoyed myself."

"Well?"

"Then you'd make me feel shitty by telling me all the things you did that day and how I was a complete failure because I just read a book. And then if my usual doctor wasn't around, and I needed something to calm me down so I could be a decent human being to myself, then I could reach Dr. Greenberg and get some medication."

"Greenthal, I think," Barron said.

"Typical," Saundra snapped. "I suppose that makes me stupid that I can't remember his name. You really think he cares as long as he gets paid?"

"The point is that I care," Barron said. "I *never,* not *ever* try to make you feel bad about anything, except your taking all of these pills and drinking with them. I never care about what you do with your day as long as it's not hurting you."

"You think maybe I could be the judge of that? I am a college graduate even if I didn't go to Yale Law School, you know."

"I wonder," Barron said. "How many of these pills have you had today?"

"I don't remember. As many as I thought I needed," Saundra said. "As many as I thought I needed because I knew you were going to come in here and try to make me feel shitty about wasting my day."

Barron sighed. "All right. Let's get off this kick. What are we going to do about dinner? We were supposed to go into town to meet the Kiewits, the guy who runs the real-estate lending part of MetLife. I think maybe it makes sense for us to start getting ready. He's a nice guy, and his wife is supposed to be a big children's book writer somewhere. We have a table at Côte Basque."

"You go. It's your business. You'll just be talking about real-estate and interest rates, and the wife will probably be some kind of bleeding-heart drip whining about children or something. So you go, and I'll stay here and read."

Barron let out a long breath. "We made this plan about a month ago," he said. "I'd really like for you to come. It's just sort of the way the game is played."

"Not my game," Saundra said. "You come in here and start a fight with me, and then expect me to ride all the way into New

York and sit there and be bored so you can make even more money than you already have? Forget it. I don't work for you."

"Please," Barron asked. "It would be a nice change. We can go in on the Merritt, and it'll be really pretty, and we'll have a good meal."

"No. I have a show on PBS about a murder in Hampshire that I want to watch. Ask one of your lawyers to go with you."

With that, Saundra got up unsteadily from her reclining chair. As she did, her eyes went momentarily white, as if she were about to pass out. She righted herself though, paused for a moment, and then walked directly into a floor-to-ceiling plate glass window. She had taken a good, strong stride, so she could have possibly walked through the window and bought a bloody ticket to immortality; except that the same thing had happened twice before, and Barron had replaced all of the glass in the terrace with triple-pane tempered panels.

Saundra literally bounced off the glass, slid to the floor clutching her forehead with her right hand, and then fell to the floor, narrowly missing the shards of glass that leapt from the tumbler she had been holding.

Barron knelt down and held her. "Jesus, Sandy," he said. " What are you doing?"

"Barron," Saundra sobbed. "I'm scared. I'm so scared I can't stop. I'm so scared."

"I know, Sandy," Barron said. "But we're in it together. I'll cancel dinner. We'll just stay home. It'll be fine. Just fine. It'll be like it was when you were visiting me in the hospital in North Carolina. It'll be just fine. We'll take care of each other."

That night, Barron and Sandy lay in bed watching a videotape of *A Dandy in Aspic,* a particularly cryptic English spy mystery of the genre that Barron and Sandy particularly loved, a movie with almost no explanation, and everything left to the viewer to figure out. Sandy fell asleep leaning on Barron, and on Sunday, she awakened and said that she was not going to take any pills that day, and she would just drink wine.

For three days after that, Saundra did not drink again. But on

Thursday, Barron came home from a trip to Florida's Cedar Key to find that Saundra was asleep with a cup of coffee still in her hand in front of a television set showing a rerun of "M*A*S*H." She reeked of alcohol. In the coffee cup was a thin coating of coffee on top of six ounces of vodka. When Barron carried her into bed and put her bathrobe away, he found a bottle of a new drug called Xanax and a half-pint of Wolfschmidt vodka with about one ounce remaining in it.

Saundra did not drink after that for one full week. On the following Friday, Barron brought home his two lawyers, Abe Cohen and Si Lazarus, to talk about how much leverage he might add to his REIT acquisition fund. With a day's notice, Saundra had the cook make a meal of fresh salmon fillets, broiled, with a lime butter sauce and homemade Caesar salad with croutons that had been cooked by the house of Thomas, specifically the cook, Marla, a Trinidadian woman who never spoke.

Saundra was the picture of vivid lucidity at eight P.M. By ten, as she carried a tray of Courvoisier and berries to the party, she simply passed out in the kitchen with a huge clatter.

When Barron rushed into the kitchen, he found Saundra struggling to get up. She was squirming on the white tile floor in front of the Jenn-Air, with her eyes still closed. With the help of Abe Cohen, who was discretion in an eight-hundred-dollar suit, Barron put Saundra to bed. As he rolled down her bedcovers, he found eight little purple pills, shaped very much like footballs, in the Pratesi sheets. In infinitesimal letters, each one read "Xanax, 1.0 mg."

The next morning Barron canceled a trip he was going to make to Michigan to see about acquiring an REIT that specialized in shopping centers in and around Bloomfield Hills. Instead, he walked out to the poolhouse with Saundra and asked her what the hell was going on.

"I don't know," she said, and started to cry. "I just know that I start to feel really wonderful, like my life made sense, and then suddenly I'm on the floor or it's the next morning, and I've done something, and I don't even know what I've done."

134

"Does Dr. Greenthal know about this?"

Saundra sighed and wrapped her red silk robe tightly around her. "Dr. Greenthal thinks I should be taking even more Xanax than I am. He says it's like Valium, only without the side effects. I suppose you know more about it than he does, right? I suppose you know more about everything than everyone, especially if it allows you to order them around. Right? And make them feel shitty about themselves?"

"I think that things have gotten a lot worse since you started taking the Xanax," Barron said, struggling to be calm. "You never were passing out until you had the Xanax."

"You're right," Saundra agreed. "On the other hand, I never really quite felt as good about myself or about life in general before I started taking the Xanax. You just can't imagine what it's like to take them. You feel on edge and like you're going to start screaming or like you never had a friend in the whole world and you're husband thinks you're a loser, then you start taking the Xanax and in about fifteen minutes, it's suddenly as if a heavenly hand started to untie all the knots. Not just the knots in your head. The knots about everything in your life, about every problem you've ever had. I feel better about you than I ever did since we got rich."

"That's strong medicine."

"I know, but Dr. Greenthal says that it's totally not addictive and that you can stop taking it at any time. No withdrawal, no shakes. Just stop and, boom."

"But I guess you don't want to stop if it makes you feel that good," Barron said.

"No, I want to stop. I'd rather have these shitty feelings than pass out and embarrass you. But you have to stop making me feel bad about myself, too. You've just got to stop making me feel so small, and in return, I'll stop embarrassing you."

"You think the main problem is that it's embarrassing to me?" Barron asked in shock. Outside on the lawn around the swimming pool, one lone robin was pecking at the well-tended grass, looking for something warm and juicy and nourishing. Bloody, too.

"No, I know it's bad for me, too. But frankly, Barron, I'm really scared to live without Xanax. I take one in the morning, and then another at lunch, and by the time I'm finished with lunch, I feel a lot better than I've felt for the first thirty-five years of my life. I don't have that committee in my head holding hearings all day and all night asking me what I've done to justify my existence. I don't have a pair of cops giving me the third degree about what I've done that day that keeps me from being a total ingrate and not worthy of life."

Barron looked at the robin again, which was still in the search-and-destroy mode. Then he looked at Saundra. "Look," he said. "You don't have to feel that way. You were so good to me when I was at Yale and in the Corps that you don't ever have to do anything again for me. Not ever. If you just read all day long and played bridge, it would be totally jake. You aren't being cross-examined."

"That's what you say now," Saundra shot back. "But when you come home and tell me what you did, and I know I didn't do anything but spend your money, it makes me crazy. It makes me feel like dog dirt."

"All right. Then if you feel that way, and only if you want to, start teaching again. Start a school. I don't know what exactly you should do. But do something that makes you feel better."

"I thought you weren't going to tell me what to do," Saundra said with surprising resignation.

"All right. Let's just begin with the Xanax," Barron said. "Let's see if you can just stop taking them the way Dr. Greenthal said. They obviously screw you up in some way, so let's just see if we can get you off them. Okay?"

"You don't need to talk to me like I'm a child, Barron," Saundra retorted. "You're not my father, who used to slap me across the face when I couldn't learn to deal cards at age four. You're not my father, who used to hit me on my legs with a belt if my French lessons were wrong when I was ten."

Barron sat down. He felt as if he weighed a thousand pounds and might never be able to get up again. He remembered something a second lieutenant he had met in Saigon had told him just before they were carried off in trucks to the U Minh Forest.

"If you're really totally scared, and feel like you can't do a goddamn thing about it, and can't do anything, and are just stuck, pretend you're someone else, and pretend someone big. Pretend you're John Wayne. Pretend you're Jack Nicholson or Audie Murphy. Just pretend, and you'll be fine, and after a while, you may even see yourself like that."

That's what Second Lieutenant Larry Hyde had told him at the barracks near the Saigon River, the BOQ that was later blown up by VC sappers, right around the time that Larry Hyde had flown back happily to his family farm in Kentucky.

In his glassed terrace, Barron Thomas told himself that he was Robert Young, Family Doctor. In a tone of almost eerie patience, Baron said, "We can deal with all of that later. I'm sure we can work out anything. Just let's get you off the Xanax. How you do it is your business."

"You bet it is."

"But if you don't do it, you're going to kill someone in your car some day. I'm sure of that. You know it, too."

Saundra's mood changed abruptly. "That's exactly right," she admitted. "I'm just not going to take any Xanax for the next year. I'll just stop, and we'll see how it goes. But I won't stop the Mellaril. Just the Xanax, and that should do the trick." She sounded almost cocky.

"Good. And then we can work on the other things."

"Right. And then we can maybe talk about setting up a school for kids who can't read but have promise. That would be a great thing to do with your money."

"A great thing, and it's something you can do better than anyone else I have ever known. Your patience with those kids is phenomenal."

"I learned it dealing with a big, confident, aggressive guy like you. It takes a lot of patience." Saundra sounded almost coquettish. She took Barron's hand and squeezed it.

"Fine," Barron said. "Let's try it. I think I'll stay home and we'll drive up to Sharon, just to look around and see what's what, and then you won't be alone, and maybe that'll make it easier."

For two days, Saundra, true to her promise, did not take Xanax. She did have an old-fashioned at the Sharon Pestle Inn for lunch. She did take her canary yellow Compazine and her lustrous Mellaril. At dinner she had two vodka martinis, but she did not pass out, and indeed lay in bed reading a French mystery until after Barron fell asleep.

The next day, she decided it might be fair, all things considered, if she upped her dose of Mellaril slightly before breakfast. But she still did not take any Xanax and only had three drinks during the day.

On the third day, she started to feel shaky. A rash of perspiration broke out on her forehead and on her upper lip. She took twice her normal morning dose of Mellaril, and then just before lunch doubled her dose again. She tried to call Dr. Greenthal, but she got only a recording that told her Dr. Greenthal was not available, but that she might leave a message. She left a message and then went off to meet her college roommate, Lavinia Hearn, who was a private investigator of securities fraud for a large insurance company that frequently invested in leveraged buyouts and had been stung by dishonest accounting for the proceeds of deals on more than one occasion. The insurance company had gotten tired of the equity partners taking fictitious charges for expenses and losses before passing out the goodies. Now Lavinia Hearn, an MBA and a lawyer from Harvard, was their lead sleuth in trying to ferret out the truth about where the money went from the deals.

The two women met at L'Auberge Bretonne, which had been a favorite watering hole for them when they were at Vassar. They oohed and aahed over each other's sapphire earrings, both pairs of which had been gifts from Barron Thomas. Lavinia Hearn had been the first human to alert Barron to the real-life fact that the equity partners in buyout deals routinely screwed over the next layer of the deal, taking out chunks for million-dollar legal bills that had never happened. Armed with this information, Barron had built into his real-estate fund guarantees of monthly inspections of all underlying expenses. This had allowed him to pay one eighth of a point less on loan commitments from insurance companies. On $300 million of debt, he had been able to save $375,000 in organizational fees. He figured that Lavinia, however incidentally, had earned a $13,000 pair of sapphire earrings.

The two women, who were remarkably similar in appearance aside from their earrings, sat at a table in a corner overlooking a field that sloped down to the north and ordered Gibsons. They both loved drinks from the 1940s and '50s. As Saundra liked to remind Lavinia, "The liquor is from today."

About thirty minutes into their reminiscences about a former roommate named Suzette who was rumored to be working as a madam at a resort in Libertyville, New York, Saundra felt an acute rash break out on her upper lip. She had an uncontrollably strong desire to defecate. She hurled herself toward the ladies' room. After fifteen minutes there, she emerged and started to walk back into the dining room. Just as she passed the kitchen, she was hit by a powerful blast of cigarette smoke from a passing guest.

She felt a strong urge to vomit. Almost instantaneously afterward, she passed out. As she lay in a heap in front of the kitchen, she began to have powerful seizures that shook her whole body and made her choke in her stupor. Lavinia jumped up and pulled Saundra into the carpeted lobby of the restaurant. She yelled at the maître d', a silly college student with pimples, and ordered him to call the paramedics.

Now, if this were a TV movie, in the next scene we would see the ambulance deposit Saundra in the ER of Mount Vernon Hospital. Then we would see white-jacketed men and women conversing solemnly with Barron Thomas while Saundra lay in the background gasping or sleeping lightly.

However, this was life. The maître d' had no idea of how to call the paramedics. Once Lavinia had called them, they took almost thirty minutes to arrive, because they took a wrong turn, plus they were not exactly sure where the restaurant was, plus they had to stop for gasoline because the man who had been supposed to fill the ambulance with gasoline turned out to have forgotten because he was so high on cough medicine the night before.

In addition, the paramedics were not exactly sure where to take Saundra for an overdose of drugs, especially because they did not know what drugs she had been taking. Plus, the driver had been promised that he would get a bag of ganja if he brought the next drug patient to Westchester Lady of the Angels Hospital. But, as the paramedic in the back said, "We don't even know for sure that she's a drug patient. She looks like she is from the seizures, but we can't be sure. And if she isn't, and Lady of the Angels can't handle her, we get sued and we're fucked."

So, while Saundra passed in and out of seizures and tremors, and Lavinia Hearn followed closely behind in her Jaguar coupe, the ambulance made its way slowly and reluctantly to Mount Vernon Hospital.

At that point, normal salutary procedures began. Saundra was attached to an IV for irrigating her system. She was given a substantial dose of Vistaril to end the seizures. She was given an IV administration of Probanthine to control nausea and, yes, liquid Compazine to keep her sedated.

She remained unconscious for twenty hours. At the end of that time, an anesthesiologist named Sam Fairstein took Barron Thomas aside. Dr. Fairstein, a kind, weary-looking man in his sixties with surprisingly merry eyes of a deep, thoughtful brown, said, "When you tell me how many different kinds of drugs she's been taking, I can only tell you it's a miracle that this didn't happen when she was driving, and that it didn't happen months ago."

"She was taking them under a doctor's care," Barron Thomas said.

"They always are," Sam Fairstein said. "She's cross-addicted to so many things that it's hard to even know where to begin to get her off the drugs and the booze. I just know that it can't go on. It stops either with her quitting or with her dying pretty soon."

140

One week later, Saundra Logan and Barron Thomas flew to the Betty Ford Center on Eisenhower Drive in Palm Springs. They left the Falcon 50 at the Palm Springs Airport and took a limousine to the entrance to the center. In sunlight so dazzling that Barron had to squint even inside, he escorted Saundra to a place that would, he hoped and prayed, give her a start on living out the rest of her life without her customary torment. In a hallway with beige carpeting and a portrait of both Gerald and Betty Ford, Barron kissed Saundra goodbye and walked back out to the car. As he reached the door of the Cadillac, he turned back to see a nurse holding Saundra at the elbow and leading her into the bowels of the Betty Ford Center. She looked small and beaten. He ran back inside and overtook her. For five minutes, he held her in his arms and sobbed, while she held still and sniffled.

"Sandy," he said, "Sandy, Sandy, Sandy. Please come back soon."

Then he kissed her and watched her leave. She looked as if all of her spirit had gone to another planet, leaving only her body behind. With the missing Xanax, he thought, with the missing -zine sisters and -ril brothers went the mainspring that kept her moving. Maybe that wasn't right, Barron thought. Maybe something else kept her moving and it was gone. Anyway, something was gone, and all the jokes that he and Saundra had made in the Falcon about their friends from Yale were hollow, mechanical failures. Saundra just wasn't there.

On the way back to Teterboro, Barron lay on the horseshoe-shaped couch in the rear of the Falcon's cabin. He stared at the off-white ceiling of the craft. He sought to let his mind be lulled into some state of forgetting by the soft hum of the Garrett TFE-731's.

All history is the history of class struggle. All history is coincidence. All history is human longing. All history is loss.

Somewhere above western Pennsylvania, the telephone rang in the Falcon. "I just want you to know that I feel totally humiliated by your locking me in here," Saundra said in a whisper. "I don't belong here. I'm just here because you're such a paranoid maniac about alcohol. This is the ultimate control trip for you, right?"

"I thought you weren't allowed to make calls for a few days," Barron said.

"Well, hubby, who taught me that money buys things? Who taught me you can give a hundred-dollar bill to a maid and she'll get you to a phone even if you're not supposed to be there? I just want you to know that I am completely hip as to why you're doing this. You're not fooling anyone. I won't forget it."

"I hope you will forget it," Barron answered, but by then the connection was gone.

At home, he lay in bed and thought about what had happened. In the morning, he went to the Westchester County Pound in Scarsdale and picked out a terrified but beautiful brown-and-white German short-haired pointer. The dog had been abandoned a few weeks before by a plastic surgeon who had a weekend place near Croton. The dog, who cried when left alone, had been a hindrance to the doctor's "lifestyle," according to the pet-rescue group that took her in.

Barron took the dog home, washed her by the pool, fed her, then took her for a walk around his lake. At the end of the walk, Barron got into bed for a nap with his 10-K's. The dog, whom Barron had decided to call Miss Vicki, jumped onto the bed and put her head on Barron's chest and fell asleep. Something was missing from the house, Barron thought as he awakened later. The something was fear.

9

S T A I R W A Y   T O   H E A V E N

In July 1984, when Saundra was still at Betty Ford, occasionally sending angry postcards—"I don't belong here and you know it" or "I hope this makes you happy because I feel like nothing"— Barron Thomas had just made the news again for acquiring a 4.9 percent stake in the Los Angeles Chemical Corporation. LACC was a virtually defunct company which had once made household floor coatings and a lower-grade commercial product for hotels and office buildings. LACC also made dry-cleaning solvent. The company had long since been unable to compete with Monsanto or Dow Chemical. But its old plant, now sputtering along at five percent of capacity, occupied fully twenty-five acres just south of the intersection of the 10 Freeway and the 5, only about half a mile from where forty-story office towers were under construction.

Land nearby was already selling for fifty dollars per square foot. LACC had two million square feet of buildable land. There were six hundred thousand shares outstanding. When they traded, which was infrequently to be sure, they went for about twenty dollars per share, purely as a very mistaken asset play, since the company had not made a profit for almost eight years.

Barron could buy the land incalculably cheaper through ownership of the stock than by buying the land. Even if he doubled the current market price, he would have to pay only twenty-four million dollars for the stock. The land had to be worth three times that at a fire sale.

The problem was that fifteen percent of the stock of LACC was in the hands of a family named Walsh. The Walsh family also owned a good helping of the stock of two local racetrack companies, as well as land near the Jockey Club in Las Vegas. They had nominated the officers and directors of LACC forever.

The attorneys for the Walsh family, who occupied all management positions at LACC, told Si Lazarus that while they certainly welcomed Barron as a passive investor, they hoped he would not do anything to jeopardize the Walsh family's "long-term plans for the growth of the company and the long-term benefit of the shareholders." What these were or had ever been was not specified.

A few days later, a man named Jack McCahill, who identified himself as a lawyer for the Walsh family, called on Barron Thomas in his office in New York City. McCahill, a lean man with extraordinarily pale lips, a high-collar white shirt, and a deep blue tie, wore the only diamond cuff links that Barron had ever seen. They were shaped roughly like small dice.

"We know about your resources," Jack McCahill said, rolling his shoulders as he talked in a way remarkably evocative of Jimmy Cagney. "But we also know that the Walsh family intends to develop this property for the benefit of all the stockholders, and we would like for you to receive a special benefit as befits your particular expertise." McCahill shot his cuffs, eerily like James Caan in *The Godfather*, adjusted his cuff links minutely, and went on. "The way we'd like to structure it is that you'll be a nonexclusive consultant to us. A half-million per year for ten years. On top of that, we'll make you a consultant on each building as it gets developed, once we have the plans approved for large-scale development, and we'll give you a piece, maybe two percent, of the gross construction budget on each structure. Of course you can audit the figures. We might even be able to give you guarantees on the buildings before they're finished."

"I'll think about it," Barron said. "I'd be a lot more interested in buying out the Walsh family and making a deal for them to be consultants to me. What kind of price do you think we're talking about?"

Jack McCahill looked at Barron with eyes that were more amused than curious. "You think you're the first guy that's walked in the door with a few bucks thinking he can take this property away from us? Every swinging dick in L.A. knows what that property is worth. There's a reason nobody's ever made a serious move on it."

"What's the reason?"

McCahill looked at him incredulously, then said, in the tone of a teacher helping a slow child, "Look, the Walsh family is a well-respected family in Southern California. There are two buildings, a classroom building and a cafeteria, named after them at UCLA. That's how it goes. You can't just walk in and make moves on a family like that."

"The stock is publicly traded. I guess they could have made it into a private company by buying in all the stock if they'd wanted to."

McCahill looked at Barron as if he had just discovered a new, totally naive species of financier. He smiled pityingly. "They don't want to right now. The great-grandmother, Priscilla Walsh, is ninety-three. She's in a nursing home in Pasadena. Nice place. Her kids make sure she's got everything she wants. Sees the father every day. She's got eleven percent of the shares. Price. Estate tax. Figure it out."

"Okay. I'll take it all into account," Barron said.

"Mr. Thomas, you're forty years old. You've got a great family. Lovely mother back in Dallas that you're very attached to, and with good reason. Wife has some health problems, from what we hear, but she's very well taken care of. Lovely house in Bedford. Beautiful pool, lovely glassed-in pool house or something right next to the pool. Great cook from Trinidad. Never talks but she's a helluva cook. Marla."

Barron stood up from the gray armchair where he had been listening to Jack McCahill. "You had better leave now," he said. "I don't like threats very much." He felt the way he used to when he walked down a particularly slippery path in the Iron Triangle. The hairs on the back of his neck were standing up.

"Neither do the Walsh family," Jack McCahill said evenly, looking as calm as a man can look. "You have a perfectly nice life. Your wife will come around. That's a great hospital. I know a lot of people who got well there. Why screw around with a good thing?"

"Get out." Barron could feel his fingers tensing for his M-14.

"I'm going, and I'm sure you heard every word I said. Smart guy like you."

A few days later, Barron interviewed a young woman to be a statistical researcher. The woman, whom he had found by advertising at the economics department and also the business school at Columbia, was a well-dressed twenty-four-year-old named Shannon Savage. She had thick black hair, rich blue eyes, white even teeth, and a full, almost voluptuous figure. She wore a businesslike flannel suit, but even so, she was a highly attractive woman.

"I've had mathematical statistics and also economic statistics," Shannon Savage said. "I'm planning to go into marketing, so I like to know my math."

"Have you got any experience in doing real-estate comparables?" Barron asked.

"Definitely," the woman answered.

"The thing is that I'm thinking of buying this piece of property in Los Angeles. I want to have a pretty clear idea of what land all around it went for. I also want to know how long it took for the builders to get approvals, how long it took to get the buildings up, whether there were any kind of union problems."

"I'll do it. I was a history major as an undergraduate at Smith.

I know very well how to find out things at libraries. I'm glad to do it."

"I have two real-estate appraising companies in L.A. working on it," Barron said. "I just want some backstop from here. Someone who has no interest in jacking the figures up or down."

"I'm hip."

That was on a Monday. On Friday, Shannon Savage reappeared in Barron's office at six in the evening. This time she wore a more casual outfit. Jeans, a silk blouse with a long strand of pearls, surprisingly high-heeled shoes.

She hovered over his teak desk and went through her columns of figures. She smelled of a wonderfully alluring perfume he had never been around.

"What's that perfume?" he asked.

"It's called K.L.," Shannon said. "Do you like it? I want to wear something you'll like. Maybe we could go over some of these figures at my apartment. I'm a helluva cook, and I hate being alone."

Barron did not hesitate this time. He did not even argue with himself as he left for her apartment.

For a graduate student, Shannon Savage had an extraordinarily lovely apartment on East End Avenue, overlooking the river. It had one wall of glass, and adjoining it, two large bookcases packed with well-worn paperbacks by Myrdal, Marx, Wassilieff, Stigler, and other mainstays of the world of economics.

Shannon herself appeared at the door in tight jeans and a Yale T-shirt, under which she clearly wore no brassiere. She gave Barron a Chivas straight up, and asked him to help her as she made veal scallopini. As she repeatedly moved by him in the tiny kitchen, she brushed him, perhaps at first accidentally, with her breasts. Even through his sports jacket, he could feel their youthful density and firmness.

At dinner, she talked about how she rarely dated in New York because she only liked older, more successful men, not the ones her age who were just trying to get laid and had nothing to say about how the world worked. She also liked particularly men who had actually accomplished something in their lives, she said.

"Give me a man who's built something, who knows how to operate in the real world, who doesn't just sit in a bar bragging all day," Shannon said. "That's what turns me on."

For a trained economic statistician, Shannon was an unusual specimen, Barron thought, even as he marveled at her beauty and seeming availability. For example, she seemed to genuinely believe that "supply side" economics was a valid branch of the dismal science. She seemed to have only the slightest grasp of the fact that "penny stocks" and "junk bonds" were not real securities but just media for fraud. On the other hand, there were economists at Harvard and Stanford who believed the same thing, and some in the Executive Office Building as well.

After dinner, she asked him if he liked Frank Sinatra. She put on a disk of Sinatra singing, "Some day, when I'm old and gray . . . and the world is cold . . . I will feel a thrill just thinking of you . . . and the way you look tonight . . ." Then on her white couch she put her head on his shoulder. A few minutes later, she took his hand and led him into her bedroom.

In the dim light of her bedroom, which had a solid-looking blond wood king-size bed as its main furniture, she took off her T-shirt and her jeans. As far as Barron could recall, he had never seen a figure quite like hers. Like a Playboy Bunny, he thought. Or a Penthouse Pet. Perfect, large, upswept breasts. A thin waist. Long, tapering legs. A rear end like an apple.

For sure, Barron thought to himself, this woman has about the best physique of any economic statistician in America. By a long, long way. No one else that I know of would even be close.

"Just hold me," Shannon Savage said. "Just hold me."

"I really can't do this," Barron said. "I would like to do it. I feel like doing it. I don't think I've ever been with a better-looking woman in my life. Certainly not with her clothes off. But I'm a married guy."

"Who cares?" Shannon asked. "Who cares right now?"

"I know," Barron said. "I didn't when we were in the kitchen.

I didn't at the dinner table. You made me feel like I was a college kid again. But I don't know. It's just not right. Maybe the next time. Maybe . . ."

"Don't argue with me," Shannon Savage said. "Just lie down and I'll do everything."

"It's just not . . ."

But by then, Barron was on the bed, and really unable, unwilling to stop her hands and her mouth and the rest of her. God, he thought, what are they teaching these kids in econ grad school these days?

Later, when Shannon had fallen asleep next to him, breathing rhythmically, he stroked her black hair, and she actually purred. He took her hand, and she held it against her cheek in her sleep.

Out the bedroom window, he could see airplanes banking and gliding in for landings at La Guardia. How long, he asked himself, since he'd had this feeling of rest next to a woman? Since New Haven? Maybe since before New Haven? At three in the morning, he left her apartment, left her a check for her week's research, paid out of his BTA account, and went home to his own apartment in town at the Carlyle, and fell asleep with his pointer, Miss Vicki. I actually feel good, he said to himself. Better than money good. Actually great. Actually like I belong. Like I did the first few times with Katy Lane and with Saundra. I belong here on earth.

So Barron thought to himself.

The next morning, at his office on Fifth Avenue, Barron got a telephone call from Saundra, at the Royal Hunt Hotel. Nairobi. Kenya.

"The thing is," Saundra said, "that I felt so much better after just a few weeks at Betty Ford that I decided I really needed to get some distance on myself, and take a break, and some of the women I know in Bedford were already here, so I left, and flew here. It's really great."

Even across the world, Barron could hear the vodka in her voice. "I've always wanted to go on safari. We're going to have this thing called 'private tenting,' where there are five servants to every American, and they bring you tea any time of the day or night. I'm telling you, I already feel a lot better than I did in that hospital."

"You left before the end of the treatment? Is that right?"

"See, there you go. Making me feel shitty about myself. I haven't done anything bad. I'm just trying to have a good time. Is that so bad? Everybody else brought her husband or else the husband at least brought her to the airport. I had to get here by myself."

"So, wait a minute. Let me get this straight. You're mad at me because I didn't help you leave a treatment program you desperately need so you could go on a trip to Africa that I didn't even know about. Is that right, so far?"

"See. Now you've made me feel guilty. Is that how you get your kicks, Barron? By being the master of guilt?"

"No, but you need to be in treatment. How did they ever let you leave? That's not supposed to happen."

But by then there was a trans-world click, and Barron was holding a dead phone. What did people ever do to express frustration in communications before there were telephones to hang up? How else was there such an easy, inexpensive way to make people feel cut off?

But, in fact, Barron was feeling so good about his previous night that he did not even get angry. When Saundra came back, there would be time enough to try to fix things up. Time enough. Nothing pressing. No races to run. A good feeling to have. He tried to call Shannon three times but got no answer.

Did he feel guilty about last night? A little. But after all, Saundra hardly had been acting like a wife. Hardly at all. On the other hand, Barron recalled, as a leaden weight came falling into his chest, what did Shannon Savage do when he was in base hospital in Camp Lejeune? What did Shannon Savage know about a guy having a breakdown in law school? Suddenly, Barron stopped feeling good about Shannon Savage.

The next day at his office, while he was going over a spreadsheet of financing options for LACC, not even a particularly large

150

deal, talking seriously with Si Lazarus about bank rates for commitments, Barron got a call from Jack McCahill.

"I know you're busy," McCahill said. "I know I must have come on a little strong last time I was over there. I feel bad about the way I acted."

"What is it?"

"I just want you to know that I'm glad you had time to relax with Shannon Savage. She's a nice girl. We use her a lot at some of the places the Walsh family hangs out in Vegas and in Tahoe. The stats are real, too. We had enough respect for you to get some professor at USC to get them for you. Getting the books was the hard part. You want them now? We won't need them anymore. By the way, I like that perfume Shannon uses myself."

Barron tensed up and turned toward the window overlooking the Fifty-ninth Street Bridge. He felt as if he were transparent and dirty, a soiled windshield.

"There's just going to be a little teaser about a major corporate hotshot boy-wonder type who's hanging with call girls while he buys up America. Just a little one. In the *Herald-Examiner*. We have a guy there who owes us some favor. Some money, too, when you come right down to it."

"This is illegal extortion," Barron said. Si Lazarus's ears pricked up like those of a dog who has heard a Galton whistle.

"No. We're not asking you for a thing. We didn't make you fuck Shannon while your wife was in the hospital. That was up to you, pal. I think you should know that we mean business about working for the good of all the stockholders," McCahill said.

There was another click. Barron wearily explained the call to Si Lazarus. Lazarus seemed even more weary, but went into lawyer mode, technical, careful, analytical. "He has you dead to rights," Lazarus said. "If he's not asking you for anything, or making you do anything, it's not extortion."

The next morning, Barron got a call from the Los Angeles office of Si Lazarus's firm. A young associate read him the item from Moishe Ratner's "About Town" column in the *Herald Examiner*.

"What boy genius luftmensch—that's airman, stupid—financier has found solace in the arms of a Reno party girl while his wife tries to stay on the water wagon in Palm Springs? The Rat will never tell, but watch this space."

"If they're fighting this hard," Barron said to Si Lazarus after he thought about the call, "there's a lot of money in this deal. Maybe more than we think. Let's put together the papers for a tender at thirty-five dollars. Let them fight me. We can make out if it goes to forty. After that, they can buy me out. Maybe they've just given me the clue I needed. Anyway, I don't like blackmail. And I don't like to run away."

"Sometimes it's best to run away," Si said flatly.

"Maybe so," Barron said. "It's just that they're practically advertising what a fantastic deal this is. I'll bite."

By working Lazarus and Cohen around the clock, by dragooning the new boutique investment bank of Leitch & Co. for eight days without sleep, with the usual incredibly fast turnaround from Pandick Press, Barron had made his tender within nine days of McCahill's call.

The Walsh family sent lawyers—not Jack McCahill—to talk to Barron Thomas. There were press conferences. There were lawsuits for failure to disclose and attempted evasion of state securities laws. There was a flurry of motions for temporary restraining orders in the Delaware Court of Chancery.

But within one month of spending the night with Shannon Savage, two days after Saundra Logan Thomas stepped off a British Airways 747 at JFK, staggering and almost incoherent from vodka, the Walsh family capitulated and agreed to tender all of their shares, including the ones held in trust for Priscilla Walsh, age ninety-three, for thirty-six dollars per share. Their only condition was that the closing be done quickly, preferably within another four weeks.

In the richly carpeted offices of Leitch & Co., sitting in front of a custom-made chromium and glass desk lit from above by four suspended halogen lamps, Barron Thomas asked Don Leitch and Si Lazarus if they had the horses to do the due diligence within

152

four weeks. "It's not a problem," Leitch, a thirty-one-year-old genius M&A man from Salomon Brothers, said. "I'll put five associates on it tonight," Si Lazarus said. "It can't be that big a deal. They were making laundry detergent or something. They weren't involved in making poisonous gas in India or making payoffs to generals in Brazil. They don't even have any operations outside California."

With those assurances, on August 15, 1985, the Real Property Equalization Fund, L.P., closed on the acquisition of LACC by LACC Acquisition Holdings, a wholly owned subsidiary of RPEF L.P. In a small rented room of the Biltmore Hotel on Pershing Square, Barron and his colleagues toasted one another. The Walsh family did not show up. A somber Saundra, just up from visiting the ruins of Chichicastenango, Guatemala, did appear, only slightly buzzed.

In the two months since she had left Betty Ford, she had traveled constantly, and had only spent the night under the same roof with Barron three times. On each occasion, she ostentatiously slept in a guest bedroom and locked the door, like Scarlett O'Hara. She also explained to him that her drinking was not anyone's problem but her own, and he should just worry about his precious lawyers and his deals, and she would live her own life, thank you very much.

Barron was too tired and despairing about her to fight about it. And he now remembered another Saundra, and to that woman he owed a great deal. How exactly the debt should be paid was for another day.

In the Falcon 50, on the way back to Teterboro, Saundra ostentatiously had a Bloody Mary in front of Barron. As she drank it, she also took a white 1-milligram Xanax and another much larger pill that Barron had never seen before.

"I know you think that my problems aren't important," Saundra said.

"No, just insoluble," Barron said.

"I know you think that my problems are unimportant, but when I was in Kenya, I spent a lot of time talking to a woman named Dracena Shlepkis. Her husband isn't a big wheeler-dealer like you. He just owns a few hospitals in various parts of America like Beverly Hills and Pacific Palisades. But she was the one who first tipped me off that I might have a chemical predisposition to anxiety, and that it might require more chemicals to get things right in my bloodstream."

"So she was the one who told you that you needed to take vodka every few hours to get your chemicals straightened out, right?"

"No, but she was the one who had me see a doctor back in New York who found out that I was that type of person."

"What type is that?" Barron asked.

"Inherited chemical deficiency. That's what these are for," she said and she held up a huge jar of the new pills. Under the name of the Bedford Value-Rite Pharmacy and the name of Dr. Wishniak was the name of the drug: Tofranil. "Much more sophisticated antidepressants than I was taking before. Tricyclics. They can restore the right balance in my system."

"What does Dr. Wishniak say about taking them with vodka?"

Saundra Logan flushed. "The vodka is not because of what I inherited. It's because of who I married. It's because I'm married to someone who doesn't really give that much of a shit that I'm alive, someone who doesn't think twice about screwing some hooker from Vegas while I'm still in the hospital, and at the same instant practically is trying to make *me* feel guilty."

Barron stared stonily out the window of the Falcon. He could see below him the lights of a small community in Tennessee, as he guessed by how long they had been in the air. Probably, he imagined, there was a Tastee-Freez and a Safeway and probably something like a Presbyterian church hall where there were Sunday meat loaf dinners. As tiny as the lights looked, they still radiated a warmth that Barron could feel in the cabin of the Falcon.

"Oh, yes. Someone sent the article to us when we were in the Masai Mara. That was when I started drinking again."

"I thought the program taught you not to blame your drinking on someone else," Baron said. "That it was between you and God."

"I agree." Saundra nodded. "But that's the ideal. I'm working toward that. I'm not in the program, but I am working toward that ideal. I'm not there yet. I'm hurt inside in a lot of places. I have to patch myself up in a lot of different ways before I can even start to love and forgive others. First I have to love and forgive myself."

Barron did not talk anymore for almost an hour. Then Saundra put down her magazine (what was the mystic bond between women and slick-sheet paper?) and moved close to Barron on the seat. "I love you, Baron. I never loved anyone the way I love you. I don't blame you for that call girl. I wasn't that much of a wife. I really want to be better for you. I really do. I know it makes life shit for you to have a wife like me."

Barron held her and squeezed her hard. "It's all right," he said.

"It's not. I'm going to be a lot better. I'm going to start paying attention to your deals, for one thing. Give me the merger agreement. I'm going to read it. By the way, this is the way the Xanax makes me feel, so be thankful I have it."

Ten minutes later, Saundra was asleep in a horizontal position on the couch in the Falcon's cabin. She had the unopened merger agreement on her stomach. She did not even stir when the Wolfsburg Four rang.

Barron picked it up and said hello.

On the other end, through the night air at twenty-six thousand feet, came the voice of Abe Cohen. He sounded as tired as anyone Barron had ever heard.

"Barron, I have some bad news for you. It's about LACC."

Barron laughed. "Abe, you're a little too late. The deal's already closed."

"That's just it. Turns out that LACC and those guys from the Walsh family own some other property out near Riverside. They used the property for fifty years as a dump for chemicals from the L.A. plant that they couldn't even come close to disposing of in L.A. County."

"Oh, Christ."

"Yeah. Part of the land was next to an Indian reservation for the Morongo Indians. One tank underground apparently ruptured about five years ago. The stuff—dioxins, PCVs, everything—spilled into the aquifer that feeds the well for the reservation's elementary school."

"Oh, Christ, no . . ."

"I'm afraid so. We've got over a hundred lawsuits. They're being consolidated into a class action. Make that two class actions. One for permanent, irreversible injuries and one for wrongful deaths."

"Oh, no."

"Yeah. We have about forty wrongful deaths. Bad stuff. Cancer, mostly, but also strokes, kidney failure, just plain poisoning. Then there are retarded kids, lots of them, deformations at birth. It's really a bad story. One time the stuff bubbled up to the surface and started foaming, like root beer, and the Indian kids played in it and splashed in it. It melted the rubber off their tennis shoes. Every one of those kids is either dead or has some big problem. We've got kids with three sets of teeth, kids with one eye. There was a hearing and one kid who was slightly retarded stood up in front of the TV cameras and said, 'Now I'll never know what I could have been.' It's a fucking nightmare."

"How could you conceivably, possibly have missed this? Possibly?"

"Leitch and Company didn't catch one thing. I've been on the phone with Don Leitch for two hours. Apparently they didn't think there was anything there. They turned it over to two college interns from NYU. They didn't even know where to start."

"My God, those kids. Think of those Indian kids," Barron said. "It was as if the Walsh family just used them as laboratory animals."

"Worse."

"Yeah, worse," Barron said. "Just basically killed them to save a few bucks."

"It's not a pretty picture," Abe Cohen said.

156

"And you guys didn't catch it either? How come?"

"We screwed up," Cohen said. "We screwed up something fierce. We just got it wrong. We figured that if Leitch and Company were onto it, they would find out everything. Plus, LACC had it all under another corporate name, some Cayman Islands company. You'll have to sue us, too."

"The suit is against the Walsh family and the guys on LACC's side. They've got to indemnify us."

"I agree. The problem is that the Walshes are just going to declare bankruptcy the minute you file papers. They probably have already filed. They know the casino business. I guarantee you that they already have wired the money for their stock to the Cayman Islands. You're going to have a job getting anything out of them."

"They have insurance carriers."

"Yeah, they do. But the insurance carriers on the deal are going to say they were defrauded, too. And the insurance carriers for the company are going to say you assumed their liability. They're going to say you can't get all of the good parts of the company and none of the bad parts. And believe me, don't count on the California courts, even the federal courts, to straighten this mess out. They couldn't find their asses with both hands. All they know is that they've got a lot of poor people out there on the reservation who get on TV a lot, and they've also got a rich guy from New York, and he's healthy and somebody's got to pay."

"I can't believe this has happened. I can't believe the Walshes could have killed those children. Most of all, I really can't believe that with all the people I have working for me, they could have put this over on me. How could it have happened?" Barron was screaming.

"Barron, it was an incredible series of fuck-ups on our end, and some very bad hombres on the other end. There are bad people out there. Sometimes they have buildings at USC named after them."

"So, the business with McCahill and the threats, with the girl and the item in the newspaper. That was all just to suck me in and make me think it was an incredible deal? They just totally suckered me?"

"Looks that way."

"All right," Barron said after a long pause. "This is my preliminary thinking. First, if it's not in the news, we just fight like hell in the courts. Second, if it is in the news—"

"It's already on the Dow wire. Long story moving for tomorrow's *Journal.*"

"Shit on a stick. All right. Then we call the people from Hill and Knowlton. We have a press conference. We get some really pretty, sweet-looking woman, maybe an Indian herself, to say that this was outright fraud. We also say that we are not going to walk away from what is finally adjudged to be our legal duty. Also, that we're going beyond that. We're having the ground tested everywhere near that reservation. We're setting up a lab to test everyone there. We're calling in ten experts from Harvard and UCLA to study the situation. Whoever's legally responsible, we're going to take moral responsibility."

"You're going to get sued by the other partners in the fund. They're going to find out about Shannon Savage, about your wife being in that place, about everything."

"I have to believe that the limited partnership has insurance for this kind of thing," Barron said.

"We have insurance. Whether it covers liability for toxic wastes based on gross negligence on our part, I really don't know. And I strongly suggest that you get someone else to handle it. We're conflicted out from here on in."

"So, I'm on my own right as the shit is crashing into the fan and flying all over the room, right?"

"I guess so. I'm sorry. I'm not even going to say anything more than that, because our insurance carrier will kill me if I do. I'm just sorry."

Barron hung up the telephone and held his hands over his face. He moved his hands away and looked out the window. He did not know where he was. He could not see any lights on the ground. It was just black out there, and, in fact, pretty dim inside the cabin as well.

Barron got up and walked back and forth in the cabin. This is the way the world ends. Not with a bang but with a multidistrict class-action litigation. Not with a whimper but with everyone suing everyone else, not with a kiss or a gunshot but with depositions.

All history is the history of someone fucking up. All history is the history of lawyers. Baron had never felt as alone in his life as he did at that moment.

Saundra stirred. She lifted up her head and said, "Money, money, money all day and all night. Can I just have one little drink of wine?"

10

GIMME SHELTER

From a conversation between Barron Thomas and his psychoanalyst, Paul Loehmann, at Dr. Loehmann's office at Sixty-third and Park, in January 1986:

Barron was sitting in a stark wooden and fabric chair with distinct worn spots on its arms, resting his feet on an ottoman which also bore signs of wear. Dr. Loehmann, a thin man over six feet four inches tall, sat eight feet away from him on a far more worn easy chair with a high back and wings. It was covered in a faintly nauseating orange cotton fabric. On the wall was a drawing of a guitar hovering over a city like a huge blimp from outer space.

Dr. Loehmann had a pad of paper on his lap and was writing furiously in a tiny hand that Barron could never make out even when Dr. Loehmann left the pad open as he reached to refill his Mont Blanc fountain pen.

Next to Barron, on a round end table, was Barron's wallet, a bottle of .25 milligram Xanax, a bottle of Tylenol with Codeine No. 3, a package of Clorets, and a stack of quarters.

"I know that you can't stop the people who are picketing in front of my office," Barron told Dr. Loehmann. "I know you can't stop the women from Brooklyn who are dressed up like what they think squaws look like, with silver and topaz jewelry, from throwing red paint on my gate in Bedford. I know you can't stop the kids without feet from getting wheeled up and down outside restaurants when I eat there.

"I know you're not a lawyer and you're not a publicist, and you're just a doctor. I know you can't do anything about Saundra. You're not a marriage counselor. And I know you can't fix anything except in years and years."

"If then," Dr. Loehmann said in his deep placid voice. "But tell me what you think I can do."

"I'm lonely," Barron said. "That's the main thing. It's like I'm under attack, and I don't have anyone to talk to. It's like I'm scared all the fucking time, and nobody's on my side except the people I pay, like my lawyers, and God help you if your main friends are your lawyers."

"Or doctors," Dr. Loehmann said.

"So true," Barron said. "But you're someone I can talk to who's not looking to cover his ass or maybe write about me. You're my hired best friend."

"That I can do," Dr. Loehmann said.

"All right. Then here's the way it is. For the last five or six years, I have been so lucky in my work that it's beyond any rational expectation. Then, for the last few months, the roof has fallen in. I spend half my time at depositions. I spend so much time in L.A. giving depositions that I've bought a place there on the beach. I hear the surf crashing, and the whole place shakes, but at the end of the day, that sounds good compared with what I've been going through in depositions. It's not scary at all that the building shakes. It's scary that there are lawyers out to crucify me.

"And even though I didn't do anything about those poor kids, even though I'm not the one who poisoned them, I still feel terrible about it all of the time. I'm under siege from everyone, even from myself, just because I bought LACC, and none of it was my fault at all. I bought it to make money, and somehow this is my punishment, which is crazy. But it all gets connected in my head. It's like retribution for all of the good luck I had before, with NatSted and BTA and everything else.

"I just feel like it's payback for being lucky, for surviving in Vietnam, and that it's never gonna end at all."

"The mind attacking itself, just like the body attacking itself in rheumatism and multiple sclerosis," Dr. Loehmann said.

"Right. Set off by something beyond my control, it's now like I have this acid pouring out of my brain burning it up. It hurts. It's actually painful, so that I have to take these pills, and I take too many of them. A trick I learned from my wife.

"As far as Saundra is concerned, it's like the whole thing with the dioxins is happening to someone else. I tell her about it, and she listens, and then she tells me about how tired she is and how Dr. Greenthal thinks that maybe he should have a meeting with Dr. Schechter and maybe she should have some more blood work done at Mayo to see exactly what other chemicals she might have poured into her system, to save her from her terrible fate.

"Her total response to this crisis has been to become utterly and absolutely obsessed with her health. It's amazing. I've never seen anything so self-obsessive. I mean, she has manicures and pedicures and massages and then she has all these pills, and that's all she can talk about."

"She feels threatened, too. It could be that she's feeling it as a threat to her health."

"That may be. I've thought of that. But what makes me crazy is that she feels it as a personal threat, but she's unable to do anything but guard herself. She has no energy or will power left over to do anything for anyone else."

"She probably is doing all she's capable of doing."

"I don't doubt it, Paul. But what I keep thinking is that if this is all she's capable of, I get left out in the cold. I'm expected to do every fucking thing in terms of making sure that the money spigot is kept running, but I don't have anything to do at all in terms of getting help from my wife. I mean, I can tell her every detail of everything that's happened in court that day, and it doesn't do one damned bit of good."

"It's probably too scary for her to focus on. I'm sure she thinks of it as terribly dangerous."

"Paul, I am sure you're right. And I'm scared, too. I'm not one of those looters who don't have feelings. It's scary stuff. And I'm sure that Saundra doesn't wake up in the morning and say, 'Gee, how can I be totally unavailable and unhelpful to Barron this morning?' I know she's in pain. When I'm back in Bedford with her and I see the way she looks in the morning, with those perfect features, but completely drained, as if she's been wrestling with an angel of the lord of fear all night, I know she's suffering. It's just that I'm still helping her, and she's not really reaching out to do a damned thing to help me. That's what bothers me. I get a lot more support from Miss Vicki, the German short-haired pointer, than I do from Saundra, the mate."

"Have you thought about any action consequences?"

"No. Because I love Saundra. As scared as she is, she has the best sense of humor in the world. We have all that history in Washington and North Carolina and New Haven, and I think I really don't have any hope of ever finding anyone who'll know me any better. And she was so good to me back then. No one else could ever be that good."

"Why? You still have money. You still have the wherewithal to meet anyone in the world you want to meet. You're a major catch. Lawsuits and all."

"Yeah. In theory. But go out there into the world. I fly on American back and forth to L.A. at least once a week. I walk up and down the streets in Beverly Hills, I see women. I don't even know where they come from. They're so hardened-looking. Sometimes I talk to them on the plane. They're tough. They don't know me. They know what I'm wearing. They know whether I'm in first class or business class. That's what they know.

"I'm so goddamned alone. That's the problem. If Saundra were having these problems and couldn't help me when I was going nuts and we were still in law school, it would have been all right, because I would have people to hang around with at the graduate student union building and at Hungry Charlie's and the

Howe Street pizza place. But now, now I'm so alone I can't stand it anymore. I sit at the conference table, and there are all of these people just hoping I'll say something stupid and then they can take away every single thing I ever owned and make me look like a criminal, and even my own lawyers look like aliens with armor on their faces and little slitty eyes, and I can't fucking stand how alone I am.

"Sometimes in Malibu, on the weekends, I just make myself a TV dinner and I eat it and I watch 'The Dating Game' and I wish I were one of those people. They have so much hope. I feel as if someone has a needle in my hope gland and is sucking all the hope out of my life.

"Saundra keeps saying, 'Well, we'll be rich anyway, won't we?' and I keep saying, 'Hell, no. We could be bankrupt.' My insurance carriers are contesting liability. My partners in the fund are saying they want declaratory judgments against me just in case, so they won't be on the hook, and in the meantime, if there's a huge judgment in these cases, and the insurance carriers walk away, I have to defend it all myself. I feel so scared I can't swallow. And then there's the airline business. Some smart guy from Shearson wrote a report saying that if Delta and AMR moved into my hub cities, my company would fold up. And I'd be left with a lot of airplanes in a market that thinks airplanes are worthless. The price of a five-year-old 747 has fallen by half in the last few years. If the routes aren't worth anything and the planes aren't worth anything . . . The stock has lost thirty percent of its value in the last six months. It isn't even close to enough to satisfy all the claims I could have against me.

"You wonder why I have all this medicine? Why I'm so glad to have these pills? Because I would have jumped out the door of my Falcon by now if I didn't have them to take. That's why. I know they're bad. I saw what they did to Saundra. I know that killing myself would be worse. A lot more final. Although I also know it would make a lot of lawyers very sad. I just feel so alone. Like everybody's after me and nobody's on my side."

Paul Loehmann got up from his chair in a peculiar crouch, so that he was walking almost bent over, almost at right angles to himself. He moved thus to his rosewood desk, covered with books and articles about Egyptology ("Victoria and Albert Team Question Validity of Insect Glyph Codes at Alexandria Conference").

Dr. Loehmann picked up a piece of paper and studied it as if it, too, were a hieroglyph, susceptible of more than one meaning, even though it was in his own handwriting. "Barron," he said as he returned to his seat, "I get in a lot of trouble with my colleagues because they say that things like this are not analytical. But I think they have some value. One of my patients who had just lost a son was not an alcoholic. But a friend told him about meetings of Alcoholics Anonymous. He had business in L.A. and was out there a lot.

"He started going to them. That was six months ago. The guy was the most beaten-down dog I ever saw. Not even remotely in command of the resources you have personally and in every other way. But the meetings changed his life. And he said he found a lot of nice people at them. He got some kind of strength from them that he never had from anything else in his life. He's a new guy. Will it last? Will he go back to being an Encino garmento with a Rolls that he can't pay for? Who knows. But it works for him.

"There are a lot of meetings every week. But I think that he said the meetings at Cedars-Sinai on Saturday nights was a good meeting. He particularly liked it because it was a time he used to feel really lonely. It's in West Hollywood, in L.A., but you're there a lot, aren't you?"

Barron smiled as he looked at Dr. Loehmann's notepaper. "You think I'm a drug addict? These pills are from a prescription."

"They always are," Paul Loehmann answered. "I just think that maybe, just maybe there's some kind of company there, maybe not quite the same as what you had at Yale, but maybe enough alike so it means something. How much can it hurt to try it? If you don't like it, you can have your loneliness back."

165

11

ADMISSIONS

The young man wore a black leather jacket that was wrinkled and battered. On its back, which Barron could see as the young man walked up to the podium, was writing. In awkward white lettering, the jacket read FROM ANARCHY TO SURRENDER. Then, under it, there were symbols. On the left was a large, staring A, and then an arrow leading to a triangle within a circle.

The man had acne scars on his face, but was otherwise startlingly handsome, with perfect, almost delicate features and deep blue eyes under black eyebrows. He reminded Baron of the young Alain Delon.

"I really can't tell you what a miracle it is for me to be here," the young man said. "I really can't even tell you what a miracle it is for me to be alive." He smiled and the crowd nodded and laughed and then burst into applause. The room was shaped like an extremely oblique octagon, with both front and back walls folded twice at the center like a fan. In the front of the room was a podium with a blackboard. On it, someone had written SATURDAY NIGHT LIVE. At the back of the room were tables with coffee and cookies.

The great majority of the other people in the room were much younger than Barron. About half, Barron guessed, were gay, mostly gay women. They sat, often holding hands, sometimes with their heads on each other's shoulders, sometimes stroking each other's hair. Other attendees were musicians, Barron thought. They had long hair, wore T-shirts with leather jackets over them, or else just leather jackets with nothing under them but skin. Certainly they did not work at Morgan Stanley or Skadden, Arps.

"I'm here to talk about what life was like when I was drinking and using, how it changed, and what my life is like now," the young man said. "By the way, my name is Dave, and I'm a cross-addicted alcoholic and drug addict."

"Hi, Dave," the whole room answered back.

"Hi," Dave said and grinned boyishly. "Well, I guess we start with my father. I'm not from here. I'm from Seattle, and my father was foreman at a brewery. Mount Rainier Ale, or at least something like it," he said, to the chuckles of the room. "He thought it was part of his job to get really and truly loaded every night. It would have been disloyal to the brewery otherwise.

"So starting for as long as I can remember, the whole house was afraid. It was like there was this fog of fear hanging over our house. On the outside, it looked as if we were a perfectly normal house, with three bedrooms and a dog and two kids and a wife in the PTA. But on the inside, it was like House of Wax.

"My father would come home from work, and he'd have dinner, which was always fine, and then he'd go out just to have a few with his best buds from the brewery. My mother would beg and plead with him to stay home. But she'd never say, 'Stay home because if you go out you'll get drunk and terrorize our family.' No, she'd ask him to help re-shelfpaper the closet or make storm windows or stay because there was something great on TV. And he'd always say whatever it was could wait, and then out he'd go, just like a shot.

"And we'd wait at home for him. We'd make jokes about it, like 'I wonder how many beers he's had by now' or 'I wonder if Dad's sitting up or lying down by now.' But we were scared shitless anyway.

167

"So, about eleven at night, always very punctual even if he was in a blackout, Dad would get home. As soon as we heard his car in the driveway, my brother and I would head for the rec room and for the pool table. Because if we were in the basement, in the rec room, we figured we were safe. First of all, Dad didn't always like to walk down those stairs if he was really plastered. He knew damn well he might fall, and break his goddamned neck.

"And even if he did get down the stairs, he knew he'd probably fall over on his face if he bent over and tried to reach us under the pool table. And we knew to stay under there. Because it didn't matter what we had done that day. If Dad was drunk, and that was just about every night, if he was drunk, he'd beat the shit out of us. That was just our home and our dad. That was alcoholism in our family. Bruises all over my face if I got caught. A blanket and a pillow I kept under the pool table, and my mother even would wash the pillowcase and change it for me. She couldn't hide herself, and she just locked the door to the bedroom, and we'd hear him screaming that he'd kill her if she didn't open the door. But she didn't open it.

"So that was our life, and I used to vow that no matter what, I didn't care what, no matter what, I wasn't going to end up like my dad."

At that, a few isolated laughs went through the room. Barron, a complete newcomer, could understand them easily: Everyone in the room had probably vowed that they would never get to be like that, like Mom, like Dad, like an alcoholic.

"My mom used to sit with me and pray that I would never drink. And I always promised her that I wouldn't. But that's the way of an alcoholic even when he's fifteen years old. At fifteen, I had the worst acne you could imagine. I mean, I could hardly bear to even look at my own self in the mirror. That's how bad I looked. Just like the worst nightmare of acne. And girls wouldn't talk to me. I couldn't beg, borrow, or steal a date. Not for anything. And I was a loser.

"So, like I say, at fifteen, some guys in my class started the Club Six Hundred. The way it worked was that if you could drink a six-pack of beer at lunchtime and maintain for the rest of the day, you were in the club.

"The first day I tried it, out in the woods behind the boys' gym, I got sick as a dog. Really and truly retching awful sick. But the next day I ate a whole half a loaf of bread, because a guy told me that if you did that, you'd be able to coat your stomach and you wouldn't get sick. The technology of how to become an alcoholic. Passed around at age fifteen, like the names of girls who would fuck you on the first date."

At that, there were scattered hisses in the room. Dave went on as if he hadn't heard them.

"So, the next day, with all the bread in my stomach and everything, I drank the six beers, all Rainiers, and I managed to stay awake through sixth period, and I was in the club. Great stuff. From then on it was a six-pack every day until they changed it to a fifth of bourbon, and I still stayed in, and by the time I was eighteen, I was drinking more than my dad. And my mother cried and told me that her life was over and actually got down on her knees and begged me not to drink again, and of course, I got down on my knees with her and promised, because denial is part of the disease, and I prayed with her, and of course, the next day I drank *and* I took Percocet."

Barron looked around the room. There had been a distinct change. In front of him and three seats to the right, where an elderly man with a cane had been sitting, a blond woman in her mid-twenties now sat. As far as Barron could recall, she had the finest features he had ever seen. Well, maybe about as fine as Saundra's when he first met her. Long, perfectly shaped nose, absolutely flawless chin and lips, wispy but magnificently arched eyebrows, and blue eyes. Her skin was pale and firm. The first time he looked over at her, Barron noticed that as she concentrated on what Dave said, a tiny blue vein in her left temple fluttered minutely.

". . . the thing is," Dave continued, "even if it was a club of dumb-ass guys getting bombed when they should have been learning trig, at least it was a club of some kind. And belonging

169

like that, feeling that there was somewhere I felt as if I were at home, that was worth as much as lying to my mother. It never occurred to me at all that probably my father felt the exact same thing every night when he got loaded.

"Anyway, right after that, I left home. I was already big enough to knock down my father, but it got pretty horrible having to lie to my mother and confront her all the time. So, instead of being a good son and just stopping all that drinking and pill taking, I moved out where I could be comfortable with my disease.

"I was then about eighteen, and about that time, two things happened. First, the heavy metal scene came to Seattle in a big, big way. Judas Priest. Twisted Sister. There was this club called The Cross, and I got a job there as a bartender, and it was heavy metal all night long.

"And about the same time, my doctor told me there was this new thing called Accutane. It was supposed to clear up acne. Now, I had used every possible kind of drug you can imagine— and some for the acne, too," David said, getting the obligatory laugh. "But this one worked. It was a miracle. In less than a month, my skin was as clear as it had been since I was eleven years old. So, I was the bartender at this club, and my skin was clear, and for the first time, I looked pretty great to girls, I guess, and I had girls who liked me for the first time in my life.

"They wanted drugs, too. And they also had drugs to give me. So, the way it worked out was that every day before I opened the bar, I had two Absolut martinis and then about ten lines and then a few number-three Tylenol and codeine. Then, all through the night, I'd hit up whenever I felt like it with a few more lines, and then about one, I'd switch to Margaritas, and then when the place closed down, I'd snort heroin to really mellow me out. And I can tell you, based on a year's experience, that there is nothing quite like ending the workday with a few lines of smack and a blow job."

At that, there were still more hisses. Barron noticed that the girl with the blue vein was smiling a small smile to herself. She did not look around the room but only down at her lap. She wore a dark blue skirt and a white linen blouse. To Barron, who had been sensitized to such things, the outfit was not complete without an opera-length string of pearls.

"By the time I had been at the bar for a year, I was also doing acid about the middle of the shift, too. So with the acid and the alcohol and everything else, I was totally fried by the end of a year. Maybe a few of you can relate to what I'm about to say, too, because in a very, very short time, I was taking money out of the cash register to buy my lines. And sometimes I would trade guys free drinks for lines, and I guarantee you that the babes never, ever paid for anything."

Barron looked again at the woman with the blue vein. Her hair was about halfway to her shoulders. She wore a black and white barrette at the back of it. Barron noticed that she was playing with a pack of matches from someplace called The Reel Inn. Her eyes only occasionally left her lap.

"So, as you might guess, I was fired. I don't blame the guys who owned the place. Shit, I would have fired me, too. I was a thieving, lying, totally dishonest junkie kind of guy. The day after I was fired, I ran into a friend from the bar. He told me that I was really good-looking and that I should head down to L.A., that guys who looked like me were getting huge, huge deals to make records, and they didn't actually have to know how to play any instruments. So the next thing, I was off in my Dodge Dart headed down Highway 101, drinking Mount Rainier beer and stopping every fifty miles or so to have a few lines and then some white crosses, and I drove the whole way, about fifteen hundred miles, without stopping.

"I was here for about a month before I realized I had been totally stupid. Guys who can play Mozart with their eyes closed, with cinderblocks on their shoulders, who look like Robert Redford on a good day, couldn't get gigs. Guys who looked like me, and as junked up as I was, were a dime a dozen. I mean, I was far from home, broke, without any way to make money, and addicted to every drug in the PDR and alcohol and smack and coke, too. And one day, I was washing dishes at a restaurant on

171

Melrose, and there was this black guy who was washing dishes with me, and he always seemed like really, really cheerful, and one day I said to him, 'Hey, man, you're just a fucking dishwasher at a shit restaurant and you're always singing. How come?' And he said, 'Because acceptance is my answer to every single thing that ever happens in my life. Everything.' "

Once again, Barron looked over at the girl. She seemed to be saying something under her breath. Suddenly she looked over at him. Barron smiled at her and to his surprise, she smiled back. She had even, incredibly white teeth. She only smiled for an instant, and then her eyes went back to her lap.

"So I went to one meeting, and I sat in the back, in this very room, and it was three years ago to this day, and I looked at all of you, and I hated you. I mean, I totally and completely hated you. I thought you were Hare Krishnas, only more nuts, and crazy in twenty different ways, and copping an attitude, and I just really hated you. I mean, well, anyway, so I started to leave at the break, and this really pretty girl came up to me." Barron heard hisses again. "And she said, 'If you leave at the break, you miss the best part.' So I stayed until the end, and then I saw the girl again and I asked her, 'Well, what's the best part?' and she said, 'The best part is that you stayed to the end.'

"I haven't had a drink or a pill since that day," Dave said, wiping sweat off his forehead. "And I can truly say that for the first six months, it was the hardest thing I have ever done. The absolutely hardest. By fucking far the hardest. I mean, I made the admission that my life was out of control. I made the conscious decision to turn over my problems to God. I asked for the guidance of my higher power. I said the serenity prayer over and over again.

"But I still had the shakes. I still felt as if I were going to kill myself. I still wanted to kill myself. I still hung around with the same people, places, and things. I would hang around at the Egyptian Gardens and then I'd walk home to the absolutely worst apartment in Hollywood, and I'd feel so much like I wanted to die, so much like I was out of my head, that I'd walk next to

172

stucco buildings and drag my face along them until it bled and blood poured down my face and my whole body and everything and there would be blood on my shoes by the time I got home.

"Other times, I would hold my arm over this fish tank, and I'd roll up my sleeve, and I'd tie off like I was going to shoot up and I'd bring a razor along my vein, not so much that blood shot all over the room, but just enough so that blood dripped into the fish tank and turned the water all pink and the fish went nuts. Then I'd think, 'Well the fish at least are having a good time.' At least they're doing something fun, and I'm doing something for them, making it all possible, so to speak, and maybe I'm not worthless after all.

"That was me at the beginning of my sobriety. But every day I would say to myself, 'Whatever happens is supposed to happen. It's all part of God's plan.' And that would mean that I was where I was supposed to be. And pretty soon I was feeling a lot better . . ."

At that point, Barron left the room. He had an uncontrollable urge to talk to someone, to let someone know where he was, to not sink into wherever Dave had been, where Dave had come from. He also felt as if he were a tourist in an amazing new country, one where gravity had been repealed. He wanted to phone home.

Barron got up from his chair and walked up the aisle past the cookie and coffee tables and through double steel doors to a linoleum-floored lobby where he found a pay phone. He put in a quarter and dialed his number in Bedford. No answer. He dialed the number of his tiny pied-à-terre at Seventy-second and Third in New York. His machine told him that he had received three calls. Two of them were about scheduling depositions. One was also about document production at yet another deposition as well. He called the answering machine at his apartment in Malibu. Four calls. Two from newspapers in Riverside County, to whom he had become the living demon, wanting interviews and wanting to know if he would be willing to debate someone named Lazaro Gomez, who was a "people's rights advocate for *La Raza Unida.*"

One of the others was from lawyers in Los Angeles about whether or not he had received a fax of certain requests for admissions from lawyers for a group of parents of deceased children. The other was from Saundra. She wanted Barron to know that she might go up to Boston for the weekend to spend some time with her friend Lavinia, who was now divorced and dating the owner of a rib and chop restaurant near Harvard Square. Her speech was distinctly slurred.

"I know you think this is just a way for me to escape," Saundra's voice on the message machine said. "But it really isn't. It's just a way of my taking care of myself and being good to myself, since it looks as if I can't really count on anyone else to do it."

Barron hung up the phone and turned back toward the room. In front of him was the blond woman with the blue vein. Now that she was standing, Barron could see she was surprisingly bosomy. The thought flashed through Barron's mind that he did not recall ever having had a bosomy girlfriend.

"I'm Nicole," the woman said with a distinct Southern accent, with an arch, slightly teasing inflection, the voice of the prettiest girl in the high school. "I'm in charge of the cleanup for this meeting. You look like you could probably be trusted to help put away the coffee cups. Wanna help?"

"I'll be glad to help," Barron answered.

"The catch is that you have to wait until the meeting is over, and it's still got another half-hour."

"It would be an honor," Barron said. "Where are you from? Virginia? North Carolina?"

"Close. Tennessee. How about you? Texas?"

"Very, very close."

"You don't look like an alcoholic. Let me guess. Pills and coke? Plus just looking?"

"You're half right."

"Listen. If you help with the cleanup, there's a few of us who go out after each meeting to this place in Beverly Hills for coffee. It's called The Old World. If you do a really good job, I'll buy your coffee. Anyway, you don't want to leave before the Miracle."

174

12

M I R A C L E S

Dream on, dream on, teenage queen.
From the diary of Nicole Miller, at a time when she learned
that, for reasons which have not yet been reduced to a formula
or to digital resolution, falling in love is wonderful:

> I still cannot believe this has happened. At the meetings,
> we always say it's a program of miracles, and I certainly
> believe it, because I never use drugs anymore, and I never
> do things that hurt me just because other people try to
> hurt me.
>
> But I never expected this kind of real-life miracle, I
> mean, a miracle outside of not drinking and using. This is
> like what I used to think about when I was out on the field
> with my hat on in high school.
>
> This guy helps me clean up, and I mean he's cleaning
> out the coffeepot and really, really scrubbing, but he's got
> on this Hermès tie, a gorgeous one, yellow with little blue
> crosshatches. I ask him what he does. He says he's in the
> airplane business. I ask him what his name is, and he says,
> "Barron." So I make a joke about how people must get
> confused because there's this guy named Barron Thomas

who owns an airline, and that must make it easy for him to sell planes, and he laughs and laughs.

So then it dawns on me why he's laughing. I ask him if he's the guy who owns the airline. "I work for the stockholders," he says, "but I own some of it." Then this girl Sheryl who's the treasurer of the meeting drags me away to meet this guy, this musician, who she thinks is really cute, and he's a loser in a leather jacket like most of the people she thinks are cute. And I go back to Barron, and he says maybe I'd like to go with him to get a late supper at La Scala instead of going to The Old World.

La Scala is like a movie version of a Beverly Hills restaurant. Thick red leather seats. Banquettes with bottles of wine all around them. We're sitting at this one in the front room, and right across from us, and I'm not kidding, is Laurence Olivier, drinking from an enormous glass of wine, and he's sort of just staring at the tablecloth, totally ignoring Johnny Carson, who's sitting right next to him.

The waiters are all sort of doing a ballet around Barron, and we don't even have to look around for anyone to help us. The greatest part is that Barron wanted to know what kind of wine I wanted. I told him that I was in the program and didn't drink at all.

He didn't have a clue. He thought you just weren't supposed to drink so much that you got drunk. He didn't have any idea that you weren't supposed to drink anything or take any pills at all.

He told me that he's not really an alcoholic, but that he went to the meeting for some spiritual help. I told him that if that's true, he should just not drink for a month, and if it's totally easy for him, then do whatever he likes.

So we talk about the program for a long time, and all these people are coming by and looking at him and whispering, and he's kind of shy about it, and then just as I'm telling him about how you don't think it'll work and then it starts to work, he says that he'll try it just because

176

he'll see me at meetings. And he says he wants to hear about me.

I tell him about life in L.A. for the Drum Major, and about Bernie Labofish and Marsha Grossman, and about what a struggle it's been, and about Mimi, and he wants to know about every little detail in my life. Like about how much my father watches sports games, and about what I used to wear to school, and then about what I wanted to do in advertising, and really smart questions, too. Did I have a creative goal, or a career goal, or just what kind of goal was it?

It's been so long since anyone asked me anything beyond how fast I could type and if I knew word processing, or if I wanted some blow, that I really could hardly even remember what I used to want in advertising.

I started to cry just because the idea that I would ever amount to anything is so incredibly far away from what's happened to me in the last few years. So I didn't say anything, but I took a napkin, a cloth one, and I drew a sketch on it. It was the thing that I showed Bernie Labofish. It came to me that it was a vision that I had when I was a little girl and I was driving across the Tennessee River with my mother, and there were cars next to us, and they were stopped, and a boat below us, and it was going really slow, and above us, there was a plane, and it was moving, glittering in the sky, and I said to my father, "Daddy, what's it like to fly?"

So, I drew that sketch, and Barron looked at it for a long time, and then he said, "How about if we break it down as a storyboard and have the little girl say it, and then we see a head-on shot of the airplane going through the clouds which really shows us how fast an airplane goes . . . and then we have the little girl get off the plane and throw her arms around her grandparents, and in the background, a guy is shaking hands with somebody in a business suit, and the voice-over is someone like Orson Welles, and he says,

"Putting people together with people. The wonder of flight."

Then he asks me if that sounds good to me. I would have told him it sounded good no matter what, but the truth was that it really did sound awfully good. In fact, I was sort of amazed that this businessman guy in a suit had any idea of how to write copy, or design an ad, or anything.

We're eating this chicken cannelloni, and he tells me that what the two of us just did would have cost BTA about fifty thousand dollars. Plus, he says, he would have had to fight and argue with people all day long just to get it done the way he wanted it.

"Yes," I said, "but this is a sketch on a napkin. That's different." And he says, "But if I'm the chairman and you're my liaison with Foote Cone and Belding, at least maybe we have a shot at getting it done right."

So, when he takes me back to my car, he doesn't put the moves on me or anything, or even kiss me. He just says, the way Bernie did, "Now, I can't pay you what you're worth. I know that. But maybe I can pay you enough to live on." And the guy is serious. He wasn't jerking me around like most of the people in this town. In this world.

I started two days later at the BTA offices in Century City, which are close enough to where Sterling Grace used to be that I can practically smell Bernie's corned beef sandwiches. It's actually a dream come true. I have an office overlooking Santa Monica and the ocean, and I have a secretary from Van Nuys who talks like a Valley girl, and when we have meetings with the people from FCB, they look at me with that same *extremely* respectful look that all clients get from their agencies.

The thing we drew on the napkin has been totally storyboarded out now, and it's getting done, and Richard Basehart is going to do the voice. I get a paycheck *net* of seven hundred a week. After taxes and everything. I get health insurance, and an expense account, and I may even be able to get Mimi something over here.

I spend part of my day just hanging around with Barron. He has this big lawsuit thing about some chemical spill that happened a long time before he even bought the company that spilled the chemicals. It's really sad because some Indian kids were terribly poisoned, but it wasn't Barron's fault at all, and he's really tormented about it, inside and out.

I go to depositions with him, and while the lawyers yell and scream, Barron's just sitting there smiling at me. He says he'd rather have me at the deposition than Edward Bennett Williams, who's some really huge lawyer back East.

The amazing part is that he's not gay, in fact he's married, and he never comes on to me. He hardly ever spends time with his wife, and he doesn't seem to have a girlfriend. He just works and then lies around with his dog, this big thing named Miss Vicki. It's making me a tiny bit crazy that he absolutely never ever comes on to me. Why? I'm getting old, I guess. I can see cellulite on my thighs in the mirror. Pretty scary. What'll I look like when I'm thirty? Probably like my mother.

But I know he likes me, because last week I was out one day getting my teeth cleaned, and he called three times to find out if I was all right. That's something.

He's even got this thing where if I have an account at the BTA credit union, they lend me enough to pay off all my bills, and I pay it back a little bit at a time. Can you even believe it? I'm not broke, and I'm moving. I feel like the girl in the ad Barron and I wrote. Well, really I wrote most of it.

I'm moving. I'm really moving. All the friction that used to hold me down is just gone. Effortless. Like in a dream.

Thank you, God. For the first time since I've been here, I can connect what I'm doing right now with who I wanted to be when I was out on that field in Jonesboro. All because of Barron and the program. And I don't feel like I'm robbing him. He is a so much happier guy than he was when I met him. In a couple of months, he's a new guy. It's mostly the program, but he just likes being around me, I think. I just wonder why he never comes on to me. I'm going to have to diet all month. I'm not fishing, but at least I'd like for him to think I'm all right looking.

Please show me Your will for me and give me the strength to carry it out.

13

A VERY WHITE LIGHT

Barron Thomas sat in the tiny waiting room outside Paul Loeh-
mann's office. He studied a copy of *Antiquities* and then a copy
of *New York* magazine. As always, he carefully examined the
Personals at the back of the magazine. As usual, the ads were for
perfect Jewish women looking for perfect Jewish men. Some day,
Barron thought, he would have to ask Milton Friedman or
George Stigler or some other economist how it was possible that
in a functioning market for human companionship, there should
be so many lonely people.

Barron heard the door open from Paul's office to the escape
hatch through which patients left without being observed by the
incoming patients. In the instant before Paul opened the door,
Barron thought how strange it was that the alienists still used the
hidden door exit method. Patients with AIDS, patients with
syphilis, patients with great running sores passed blithely in and
out of public waiting rooms. But people who were frightened or
anxious or depressed had to keep that hidden. It was all right
for the world at large to know if your penis dripped blood. But it
was not all right for another sad person to know that you were
also sad.

The human mind is so terrifying, Barron thought, that any hint that it might be out of control is too horrible to be known. For some balance wheel to be awry in the unconscious was potentially more dangerous than typhoid or polio. Don't admit it. Keep it hidden. Whatever happens, don't let anyone know that you might be sad. It might be catching, and soon everyone would be sad, and where could that end?

"Come in," Paul Loehmann said. "Is that a new suit?" He smiled his tall, gangly Abe Lincoln smile.

Barron Thomas settled in his usual chair—in fact, the only chair in the room besides Paul's chair. He swung his left leg over his right leg, and then rummaged in his pockets. "No drugs today, Paul," he said. "I can offer you some Clorets."

"Tell me everything," Paul said. He was smiling. "This is the new Barron Thomas. You actually have a spring in your step."

"Paul," Barron said, "not only do I have a very noticeable spring in my step. I also have a new suit on my back, and new shoes on my feet, and a new shirt, and a new tie. And I feel as if I have some hope in my life for the first time in a very long time."

"It's a great suit," Paul said. "I love those tiny little gray-dot suits. I think they're about as good-looking as any suits can be. Where's it from? Paul Stuart?"

"No, it's from the new Polo store on Rodeo Drive. It's a lot like the Polo store on Madison, only not quite as crowded with investment bankers and lawyers. A lot more agents. Hollywood agents. With two-tone shoes and everything. Would you like to know why I have all these new clothes? Why I have a spring in my step?"

"I certainly would," Paul Loehmann said. "I'd like to share your secret with my other patients."

"All right," Barron said. "I'm going to tell you, and then I'm going to give you a large kiss on the cheek, because I really and truly believe that you, Paul Loehmann, started me out of the fucking tunnel of craziness that I was in. You, and your little note about AA."

"Did you go to a meeting?"

"Is Fred Astaire Jewish? You bet I went to a meeting. But first, I want to back up. Take me, Barron Thomas, as I was, say, four weeks ago. To the world at large, I'm this big corporate guy, wheeling and dealing, like Frederick the Great, fighting off six armies simultaneously, meeting lawyers, meeting bankers, going to depositions, moving from place to place in limos and in first-class seats. And to the rest of the world, I'm like a face in *Forbes* that they know, and a guy to be envied. But inside the fuselage of the Falcon, inside the Paul Stuart suit, inside the skin that gets massages twice a week, the guy that's at home, receiving guests, is a guy so wrecked they wouldn't even let him into a homeless shelter on the Lower East Side.

"Just a screaming, out-of-control guy. His wife is utterly unable to help, scaring him to death that some day he's going to find out that she's crashed into a van filled with children from a convent school. The lawyers are baying at his heels. The newspapers are baying at his throat. *La Raza Unida* wants to crucify him for something he didn't do. He's got thirteen thousand employees at the airline, and a few hundred investors who would like to see him dead, because then they would get their paws on his key-man life insurance. In a word, he's out there, and he's alone, and he's hunted. Barron, the Hunted."

"You do have me."

"I know I have you. And that's great. Because that's why I'm not dead. Because I kept hoping that you'd get me a ticket out of there. Okay, so I went to the meeting at Cedars-Sinai in L.A. I was totally unprepared for it. It wasn't like a group of alkies hanging around spitting. It was like a religion, only a really old-time, evangelical religion, with people getting up and confessing and crying and the group saying Amen. Only they don't say Amen. They raise their hands to say they're alcoholics. And it all makes you feel as if you're not the only person in the world who's suffering, and I like it a lot. Really, very, very much.

"They have these rules, like 'Turn your problems over to God,' and 'Just take it one day at a time,' and 'Whatever happens is supposed to happen.' And even though the speakers are sometimes very nutty and very, very scary, I still like it a very, very lot."

"Very good."

"Yes. Very. Anyway, so at the first meeting I went to, I met the girl of my dreams. That's all. Nothing much. Just the girl of my dreams."

"The spring in the step. The new clothes."

"She just came up to me and started talking to me. The first thing I said to myself was that she looked just exactly like the girls I used to be insanely in love with when I was at St. Mark's."

"You went to St. Mark's?"

"Paul. The one in North Dallas. Not the one in Southborough, Massachusetts."

"I was just kidding, Baron. Psychoanalysts can make jokes, too, I hope."

"Anyway, so she has just that look. Chiseled features, blue eyes, perfect, incredibly perfect white teeth—just her teeth are so unbelievably perfect—and she's got this white skin, and nice legs, and really big tits, which is definitely rare for me."

"Correct me if I'm wrong," Paul Loehmann said. "But I don't recall you ever discussing whether a woman had large breasts or not. I don't think that's ever been discussed here, has it?"

"You're the one who writes down all the notes in that little book you never show me," Barron said. "You tell me. Access it. Don't you have it on Word Perfect?"

"Go, Barron, go. I love it when you're so up. Go on with your story."

"So, bear in mind that I've just been sitting in a room hearing a guy who likes to cut open his veins and hold his arm over a fish tank so he can feed his fish. And bear in mind that I'm thinking that my life is getting to be just like that guy's, only worse, because when I do it, my picture is going to be in the *Times,* and the fish I'm feeding are called lawyers, and they'll just jump out of the tank and take my whole arm. And I'm like one of these Hogarth prints or somebody else maybe of a guy with all these monsters inside him eating him up, and instead of these guys, there's me and my guilt about Saundra, and about those kids who

184

died from the formaldehyde in their drinking water—and never mind that it's not my fault, that I didn't even know about it. Guilt is not rational. Guilt is not logical. Guilt is a psycho out-of-control cannibal from hell.

"And he's running with a gang that also includes fear and self-loathing and a feeling that I'm a goddamned long way from home. And I'm thinking that this kid and his fish tank and I could be very good friends. We could write our names in shit on the wall together and maybe play Scrabble with it.

"Suddenly, out of nowhere, comes the girl of my dreams."

"I love this. I wish that Hans Kohut could be here to listen to this."

"I wish he could, too. Did I ever tell you that I used to see her in a dream? Yes. When I was twelve or thirteen years old and I was a pimply kid at St. Mark's—the one in North Dallas, Paul. I would see her in my dreams. She would be coming down the stairs. Don't ask me what stairs. The stairs at Twelve Oaks. The stairs of the Lincoln Memorial. Some stairs somewhere."

"I think I heard something about stairs."

"Yeah. And she had this light behind her. This heavenly light coming out from behind her blond head. It was so bright that even from behind it lit up her blue eyes. And she would just come down the stairs and look at me and say, 'I always loved you. I was just too shy to tell you.' Or 'You always turned me on. I just never wanted to tell you.'

"And I'm trying to make a call, and she comes up to me and talks to me. Asks me to help her clean up. She's not even wearing any jewelry. That's how perfect she is. Not even any jewelry."

"That is perfect."

"No, but I mean, she's a country girl. Just a simple country girl. That's what I mean."

"Go on, Barron."

"And we go out for dinner, and before she knows who I am, she offers to split the bill. She offers to split the bill, Paul, and she's a temp, filing all day until her back is breaking, or so she says. And I talk to her about advertising at La Scala, and Christ, the kid has so much talent it's almost scary. She's related some-how to Andrew Johnson or Andrew Jackson or Madison or some-one, and she's really talented. I mean, I don't think that Bob Greenhill at Morgan Stanley has to worry that she's going to take his job, but she's smart. Really, really smart.

"She's in the program, and she doesn't drink, and I think that's a gigantic start. She has the softest skin you've ever seen in your whole life. Or touched. Dense. Soft. It's like a baby's skin. And she's so smart. I tell her things about Vietnam, and she remem-bers every detail. I tell her the name of the guy whose eardrums were blown out the first day we were in country, Larry Hyde, and the next time we hear a loud song on the radio, she says she doesn't want to end up like Larry Hyde. And she remembers what I like to eat. Like, she knows that I like to get chicken with the skin on, and then take it off before I eat it. That's pretty smart. Very smart, I'd say."

"She works at it."

"Exactly. It's like, even before she found out that I run an airline and could hire her, she was working at making me like her. Not at deposing me. Not at getting money out of me. She's twenty-five. Or maybe twenty-four. Don't hold me to it. But she looks sophisticated and country at the same time. She has a real serious look on her face. God, she tells me stories about the guys who have treated her like shit in L.A. It's terrifying. I feel scared just listening to it."

"There's going to be a seminar in a month at UCLA, analysts only," Loehmann said, "about the war between men and women. It's a big subject out there. Kill or be killed. There is an actual plague of impotence, and the women wonder why, and women are becoming lesbians and turning suicidal, and the men wonder why. Too many rats in too small a space."

"Only this one isn't a rat. I hired her to work for BTA. Not much money. She gets in a day what a lawyer gets for one phone call. Maybe she gets in a week what a lawyer gets for one phone call. I'll have to try to figure that out some day. It has to do with price fixing, I guess . . ."

186

"Go on, Barron. About the girl."

"I can't exactly tell what's right about her. I guess it has something to do with enthusiasm. One day, when we were coming out of a meeting with FCB about a campaign that she had very largely dreamed up while she was still at the University of Tennessee, she was so happy that she did a cartwheel on the cement plaza at Century City. Can you beat that? In modern America?

"When I think about it, it's like I'm seeing her in slow motion. She was wearing a white pants-type suit, and her legs and her hair and her little white arms just went flying through the sunlight. Magnificent. Perfect. Like the girl coming down the stairs, only somehow better. More alive. More girlish."

"Just what the doctor ordered."

"Exactly, Doctor."

"And Saundra? Is she bothering you less?"

"She's bothering me a little less right now because she and her gal pals went to Srinagar or somewhere to live on a houseboat and try to figure out what's going on in their lives. They say they want to feel good about themselves. I told Saundra that when she used to teach ghetto kids how to read she felt good about herself, and maybe she should give that a whirl. She just looked at me as if I had thrown up on the table, as if I were so lost in space that she couldn't ever bring me back."

"Well, so she's gone for now."

"Exactly. And if I'm living in a fool's paradise, if all of this is about to come crashing down on my head, well, that's life. That's it. It's a fool's paradise, but that may be the only kind of paradise there ever is. I just know I feel free. 'A free man in Paris,' as the song says. 'Unfettered and alive. Nobody calling me up for favors, and no one's future to decide.' "

"And the lawsuit?"

"It's a nightmare. Human leeches in the form of lawyers clustering all around. But it doesn't torment me the way it used to. It's part of my day, and my day goes on whatever happens in the conference room."

"I'm happy for you, Barron," Dr. Loehmann said. "I wish all of my patients could take the same cure."

"The point is that I can, and for right now, that's enough. I live one day at a time. I dream one dream at a time. That's enough."

"And will you make her your girlfriend?" Dr. Loehmann asked.

"I haven't even touched her so far," Barron said. "I don't know what's next. It's plenty that I feel as good as I do right now. Plenty. You're looking at a very happy guy."

14

S O U T H E R N   S O N G S

On Valentine's Day, 1986, Baron Thomas arrived at LAX, at the Barron Thomas Aviation Terminal, and saw Nicole Miller waiting to meet him. She wore a long yellow-and-black hippie skirt and a dark blue sweater. When Barron first stepped through the gate, she was reading a copy of *People* magazine. As soon as she saw him, in one fluid motion, she curled it up, tossed it into a nearby trash can, took one step forward, and went from a serious reading look to a face of completely unself-conscious joy. Her mouth widened to a smile. Her perfect white teeth shone out across twenty feet of crowded space. Her eyes lit up, and she glided across the floor and hugged Barron from her head to her toes.

As she did, he recalled that when he was in high school, you could tell who the girls really liked. If they liked you a lot, they hugged you from their knees to their shoulders. If they only liked you "as a friend," they hugged you from the waist up. No potential touching of the genital areas. In high school, no girls hugged Barron below the waist. Katy Lane had been the first woman to ever hug Barron like she meant it.

Even after almost twenty years together, off and on, Saundra Logan Thomas still hugged Barron only from the waist up.

In the arrival area of Gate 49 of Barron Thomas Aviation, on Valentine's Day, Nicole Miller, assistant and gofer of Barron Thomas, hugged him with her whole body. Only for a few seconds, but from the knees up. Barron noticed, and felt flooded with happiness and desire. For the first time in two years, he actually felt a stirring in his groin just being near a woman. The sensation was so unexpected and so comparatively new to Barron that he felt lightheaded.

"I have some wonderful new space to show you," Nicole Miller said as they drove up the San Diego Freeway in her little Toyota toward Century City. "It's just one floor up from where our offices are now. For the private office you wanted, to rest and think. It was a computer facility for someone. I think that when I was with Sterling Grace, I once saw it. The good thing about it is that because it used to have all these printers, it's soundproofed. An architect took it over, and it still has her stuff. Really gorgeous Knoll furniture and rugs. I think she went bankrupt and the furniture is still there. Great stuff. White-and-red Oriental rugs."

Just north of the Slauson interchange, a huge, rusting semitrailer from Safeway roared past. Nicole's yellow Toyota literally shook, like a wet, frightened dog. The air wash from the passing truck made the Tercel swerve partly into another lane. The driver behind them in that lane, in a black Mustang with tinted windows, beeped furiously and gave them the finger as he drove past.

"Let me ask you a question," Barron said when his heart stopped pounding. "Let's put aside that additional space for just a moment. Do you think that just possibly you might let me buy you a new car? Maybe something a little more solid? If you're going to be driving me around, I think it's only fair that we might go in and get you something newer, maybe that could hold its own on the freeway."

"I don't want you to do that," Nicole said cheerfully. "I know you have a lot of other things on your mind. In a year, I'm going to look for a car. Maybe a used VW Rabbit convertible. Triple white. That would be a perfect kind of car for me, don't you think?"

"A little flimsy," Barron said. "I thought maybe a three twenty-five."

"A three twenty-five BMW?" Nicole's voice was thrilled, disbelieving. "For me to drive around in?"

Barron felt a sense of power almost as wonderful as the feeling he had when he had gotten his full body hug from Nicole at the airport. He threw down the *Wall Street Journal* he had been reading while they were driving (in little snatches so that he did not get a headache). "I think if we get it, I'll just have it be your car, and that way, it won't look like I'm having the company give you a car out of stockholder money. I'll just get it for you on a three-year lease and I'll pay off the lease when you get it. No, wait a minute. That doesn't make sense. If you like it, I'll just give it to you and it'll be part of your wages."

"A BMW? For me?"

As they turned off the freeway and onto Santa Monica Boulevard, Nicole composed herself. "I don't really think I should take the car. Can we talk about it?"

"Of course," Barron said. He laughed inwardly at the thought that he was going to spend ten minutes talking about a twenty-five-thousand-dollar investment. Usually, his concentration segments were about investments of million-dollar, more often ten-million-dollar, increments. If Nicole could know how little a car meant in his world, she would probably cry. Abruptly, Barron was sobered. It was sick and unrealistic for him to even make the comparison. His colleagues were talking about inanimate lumps of computer spreadsheet money buying lumps of assets they never saw. To Nicole, the money and the car were real, powerful, frightening parts of daily life. Parts that made her as a person feel larger or smaller. Shots into the main line.

"I don't want to take the car because then you would think that you just had me hanging around because of the car. And, in a way, I don't want the Beemer exactly because I do want it so badly.

I want you to know that I really like being around you, and I find you really interesting, and you've been really good to me, and you don't need to do any more for me."

"I don't want to get killed on the freeway either," Barron said.

"Well. Okay. That's one thing. But also, you're rich—"

"Or else bankrupt."

"Yeah. Anyway, you never had the experience of having to watch every cent and wonder if you're going to be evicted. You've never had to take the bus because your car was broken—"

"Are you kidding? I had to do that all the time when I was your age," Barron said. It might have been when he was in high school, he realized, but who was counting?

"Yeah, but you never were sitting at a bus stop feeling like you were just a big nothing, and then you saw some other blond girl cruise by in a Beemer and you just thought you'd kill her for that car. It was never the difference between being someone and being no one. And I just feel as if it's so important and it means so much that if you got it for me, I'd have turned over too much of my self-esteem to you. I know that's not what you're trying to do . . ."

"Well, suit yourself," Barron said. "But it's really a safety measure. If I get killed because you were being proud about a piece of tin, I don't think you're going to win any medals for altruism."

"I don't know. We'll talk about it another time," Nicole said. "I want you to see this space. It's so private. It's like being in a turret of a castle tower, only you're in the middle of Century City. It would be perfect for a place for you to just get away from everybody . . . just be by yourself and rest . . ."

The office was very much like what Nicole had described. It was bright, but tucked behind an outcropping of the wall, so that it gave the impression of being sheltered from the rest of the complex of towers. It was just one room with a secretary's outer office, and a bathroom of its own. The main room had no lights except for one small desk lamp over a rosewood surface. Facing it was a tan linen couch with a painting above it of a yacht

192

anchorage in Nassau. In front of it was an ivory-and-red Bokhara rug of silk with wool fringes. It seemed to glow in the rays of the winter sun that came through the window.

Barron opened his Mark Cross briefcase (perfect black calfskin, twelve hundred dollars, a gift from stockholders, of course) and took out a little blue box with a white silk bow. "I'd like for you to have this," he said to Nicole. "You've become a big part of my otherwise collapsing life, and I think you've earned it."

"You already pay me really well . . ."

"It's just for telling me that we're always in God's hands and that everything that happens is supposed to happen."

Nicole opened the box. Inside was a heart of gold with tiny blue sapphires around its rim. "It's just a little nothing," Barron said. The heart had a long gold chain.

"It's from Tiffany," Nicole said. "I've never had anything from Tiffany before. Put it around my neck."

Nicole turned her back to Barron and pulled down the back of her sweater. Barron felt intoxicated at the sight of her pale skin with a barely perceptible ridge of infinitely fine blond hairs running from her scalp down to her first vertebra, almost like girl peach fuzz. A smell of perfume rose up from her skin. It was K.L., one of Barron's favorite scents. Nicole's skin was warm to the touch. He felt giddy from her smile, the fatigue of the trip, the perfume, the relief of having a friend, the temperature of her skin, the fine blond hairs. He locked the catch of the gold chain. She turned around and faced him. Her long fingers stroked the heart. "Does it look pretty?" she asked. "Do I look pretty?"

Barron felt as if a magnetic field were pulling him toward Nicole. The power of the field was Tennessee blond girl with halo behind her hair, the end of loneliness, cartwheels, K.L., and a place to rest. He said, "You look beautiful." Then he leaned forward and kissed her. She leaned into him and kissed him back with a young girl's kiss, enthusiastic, welcoming, energetic, smelling fresh and hopeful.

"You look beautiful," Barron said again.

"Only to you."

"Would you like to look at yourself in the mirror? I think there's probably a mirror in the bathroom," Barron said.

"If I look pretty to you, that's enough," Nicole answered. "I never in my life thought I would have jewelry from Tiffany."

"I feel so tired," Barron said. "If you want, you can take me back to my car, and I'll go back to the beach. I don't think I'm going to get much work done today."

"Lie down here," Nicole said. "I'll go get you some low-fat chocolate yogurt. Maybe with some brownie crumbles on top."

"I don't know . . ."

"Go ahead. I won't hurt you."

"You know what I'd really like," Barron said, and he did not know why. "I'd like to lie down and have you sing me a Southern song. 'Dixie' or 'The Bonny Blue Flag.' Just sing to me until I fall asleep, and you'll have earned that heart."

"Okay." Nicole sat down at the end of the couch. She patted her lap. "Lie down with your head in my lap and I'll sing you 'The Tennessee Waltz.' Or I'll hum it for you. Go ahead."

Barron could feel the fabric of the yellow-and-black hippie skirt. He could feel the soft fuzz of the blue sweater. "I imagine that she's still in Tennessee, by God, I wish I was there, too," sang Nicole in a girlishly out-of-tune voice. She stroked his hair and he could feel her fingertips driving the darkness out of his brain under his scalp. It was as if each stroke were soothing light.

Barron turned so that he was facing Nicole's stomach. Her breasts brushed the top of his cheek. He held out his right arm and hugged Nicole behind her waist. She leaned over and kissed him lightly on the side of his mouth. He turned upward. She kissed him on his lips. He pulled her down to him and kissed her for a long time on her lips. Then he lifted up her sweater and buried his face in her taut skin.

Nicole reached around behind her back and undid her brassiere. Barron lifted himself up and started to nuzzle her nipples.

"God," he said, "you are perfect."

"Most of my friends tell me I'm too fat," Nicole said. "They say it's like a cow to have big breasts."

194

"They're jealous," Barron said. "You're the one with the perfect body. They're jealous because you look like what they'd like to look like."

Barron sat up and hugged her to him. When he kissed her, he noticed that a little blue vein in her temple flickered. It was that same blue vein he had seen at the meeting. It was the magnetic blue true north of what he had always wanted and needed.

"Let's just stay here," Nicole said. "Let's just stay here where no one can find us."

Nicole lifted up her arms and Barron drew off her sweater. He started to take off his shirt.

"Let me," Nicole said. "Let me."

Later that night, in Nicole's apartment, where she took Barron because she wanted to show him her college annuals and what she looked like when she was Drum Major in high school, Barron looked at her again, holding her in front of him in a full-length mirror while next door, her roommate, Mimi, played Billy Joel on the stereo (". . . and we're living here in Allentown, and they've taken all the coal from the ground . . ."), Barron held her and squeezed her.

"Don't let them ever tell you you're not beautiful. They're just jealous," he repeated. "Because you look like a woman is supposed to look. Because you have that perfect blue vein that quivers when you're concentrating. Because you can sing Southern songs . . ."

"If you think I'm pretty, that's enough," Nicole said. "More than enough."

Barron took Nicole in his arms and held her against him and started to stroke her back. As he did, his foot brushed against the *Panther Logue* for the year 1978 and just touched a photo of a Drum Major wearing a short red felt skirt with black piping, high white leather boots, a red wool blazer with a white cotton blouse underneath, and a hat. The hat was a tall grenadier's cap with a huge, enormous, incredibly unlikely cavalier's feather arching at least eighteen inches above it, waving and twisting in the East Tennessee breeze coming off the Smoky Mountains.

15

WHEN THE GETTING WAS GOOD

From a diary entry in the journal of Nicole Miller on a day in the fall of 1986. The diary had been bought two weeks before at Mark Cross. It was bound in red leather that felt like warm but firm butter to the touch. Its pages were Crane vellum, with thin brown horizontal lines. In the inside front cover, in Barron's handwriting, was a message: *From Barron, for Nicole, who saved my life. I will always love you. Barron.* The diary entry went like this:

Wednesday. I'd like to try to get a little bit analytical about this. I'd like to at least try to explain to myself just why being around Barron makes me so incredibly happy. I don't think I can, which is the nature of being in love, as our English Lit teacher told us when we were going over Shakespeare's sonnets. But I'll try, with examples, because maybe the examples are the analysis.

For the last few months, I've been talking about the lawsuit with Barron. The beauty of the job with BTA is that by virtue of being Barron's girlfriend as well as his employee, I get a lot of time off from the advertising venue and get to spend it learning about the business.

So, I've been calling up law professors and economists all

over the country about the lawsuit. The best guy I talked to was this poli sci professor at my alma mater, Jack Rothschild. Professor Rothschild told me that the whole thing was a political problem, not a legal problem, and then he sat me down, over the phone, and explained to me about Milken's Law and about externalities. When he was done, I felt as if I had seen the aurora borealis.

I went in to see Barron and I told him what I had learned. The first thing is that it's an externality if something happens which is so big that it can't be paid for by any one person and also if it's not clearly the fault of any one person.

That would be like air pollution in Los Angeles. It's caused by so many people and affects so many people that we can't expect any one person to pay for it.

Same thing with the chemical spill at the Morongo reservation, as Professor Rothschild told me. It wasn't Barron's fault. The people whose fault it was are unavailable to pay for it. A lot of innocent people are suffering because of it. The solution is to have the taxpayers pay for it, just the way they do with air pollution or defense or airports.

"The problem is," Barron said, "that even when a bankrupt organization is responsible, if there's any possible way to pin it on someone connected with the bankrupt, they'll do it. That's the way California works its participation in the Superfund. If California law allowed it to come under the Superfund, we'd be all set. But I'm the successor to the guilty party, so they go after me."

"Exactly," I told Barron. "But that analysis is based upon a basic mistake. You are assuming that the law cannot be changed. That's where Milken's Law comes in."

"What's Milken's Law?" Barron asked me. "Something to do with the junk bond guy?"

"No. That's his cousin. This is Somerville Milken of Virginia. He teaches a course in the intersections of finance, government, and psychology. His law is simply that the constant factor ME is always greater than the variable factor U."

"Wait a minute! I thought that up. I said it to my lawyers a long time ago. At least I think I thought it up. Maybe I read it somewhere," Barron said. "Some economist guy who used to work for Nixon . . ."

"Doesn't matter who thought it up. The issue isn't who's getting into Bartlett's. The issue is simply this application of the law of infinite selfishness: The legislators and executive branch of the state of California are not interested in the rights and wrongs of what happened in the chemical spill. They're interested in what's in it for them. Put enough into it for them, and the deal is done. Make it so important for them to get the spill into the Superfund that they can't ignore it, and it's off your back."

Now, the part that I, Nicole Miller, particularly love, is that Barron thought about it for an hour. After an hour, he called some lobbyist woman in Sacramento and talked to her for two hours. The next day, he talked to his new lawyer, Marty Singer, for another hour.

Two days after that, there was a press conference, a small one, and Barron announced the founding of the Environmental Protection Institute in San Francisco. Funding, ten million dollars, or what RPEF spends on litigation in a month. (That's Barron's holding company, which owns the chemical company.)

The foundation without any publicity at all announces a conference for one week later. In Sacramento. Speakers get ten thou per speech, or just to be on a panel to talk about the environment. Governor's reelection committee campaign advisers get fifty thousand to set up the conference.

Two weeks later, a bill sails through, and I mean *sails* through—no discussion, no debate, no hearings. The legislature says that spills in Indian boundaries are

198

automatically brought under the Superfund unless there's a compelling reason why not.

Bam. It's done. Barron just gets a call from Marty Singer saying that the Superfund has assumed the defendant's position in the lawsuit.

That's it. Now, Professor Rothschild thought up the approach. Barron made it happen. But I, who used to get yelled at if I didn't file things in chronological order, suddenly am Barron's guru about things political, legal, and spiritual. He trusts me. He listened to me. He got great results.

I am the conveyor belt, but it's conveying some very big things. I used to be like a Drum Major playing in a little stadium in Tennessee. Then I was a Drum Major playing to an empty room. Now I have a whole world listening via Barron.

I'm the best me I've ever been since I met Barron. Sometimes Mimi asks me if I don't feel bad that he's married. Of course I feel a little bit bad about it. A little bit, and I'd rather he wasn't married. But the point is that no one who was single ever made me feel so good about me.

Like, for example, after we get pulled into the Superfund, in the great tradition of the rich getting the poor to bail them out, Barron felt bad about it. So he put in ten million of his own bucks, out of his own pocket, to set up a foundation to do real research about the genetic effects of the environment. What is smog doing to people's genes? What is mercury in fish doing to our grandchildren? That kind of thing. Not my idea.

So, we also set that up in Sacramento, and the Governor came to the ceremony, and even some Indians, and it was low key, but it was nice, and it was real. And Barron made me a director, so I read the proposals and pass on them, and like that. So, now I'm plugged in, and I have a lot of stuff going on in my life that makes me feel as if I am somebody connected with the currents of life. I'm not just a lump any longer.

Not just in terms of my work, but in terms of having a man like Barron love me and believe in me.

And I obviously make Barron so happy. That's another thing. It's great to be around a man you obviously have such a big effect on, and such a good effect. It's great to be hooked up to something big and happening. That makes me feel big and happening.

For another example, after we had the foundation thing in Sacramento, we flew back to L.A., and it was time for lunch. So both Barron and I had taken a nap on the Falcon, and we're ready to rock and roll. He drives us up from LAX to Malibu. We go to this incredibly cute community center in Point Dume. It's in the middle of all these fancy houses, and you can tell that the whole area just screams money, and there's this abandoned school that's been made into a community center, and it looks just like the place where I went to junior high, Beauregard Junior High, only way far in the distance you can see the Malibu Mountains.

Anyway, in one of the classrooms, there's a meeting. It's just twelve people around a table. It's an Eleventh Step meeting, and everyone is talking about getting in touch with God and asking Him only for knowledge of His will for us and the strength to carry that out.

The people are amazing. I'm not even going to tell you, dear diary, who they all were. One guy was a movie star who has a TV series now. He's talking about surrendering to God and His will. He says there are a lot of agents and studio executives who think they are his Higher Power, but they're not. He only has one Higher Power now, and it's not William Morris and it's not ICM. It's God. And he says that he looks at the people who are fighting and trying to control the whole world, and he looks at them, and he sees them swallowing gobs of Xanax all day long, and he says to them, "Man, you'd better surrender or you're gonna be fucking *forced* to surrender." And then he just stared.

Then there was this other guy, this big, hippie-looking middle-aged guy, and he says, "I want to tell you about the miracle of asking God for His will for me. A long time ago, I used to keep goats. Not to sell. To eat. And every few months, I would slaughter a few of them. And the first one I slaughtered, his blood would go everywhere. And the other goats would smell it and they would just go out of their minds. They'd do everything they could to get away, and sometimes they got away.

"Anyway," the guy said, "that's how I feel about intimacy. That's how I used to feel. I just ran like I was going to get my throat cut. But now that's changed. And I feel totally different. Next month, I'm getting married, to a woman in the program, and I love her, and I really would like to say thanks. To you in this room, and to my Higher Power and to the program."

And then this other woman starts to talk, and her hands are shaking, and she says, "I wake up every morning, or almost every morning, and I think I'm going to have to kill myself, and that I'm going to drink and lose my mind, and that I want God to take me right then and there.

"And then I tell myself that feelings come and feelings go. That I'm powerless, even over my own feelings. That I can pray over my feelings, and then I'll be in God's hands a little tighter, or I can just lie down, or I can go about my day. But no matter what I do, my feelings are going to change. Feelings come and feelings go. That's what keeps me sober, one day at a time."

By that time, I'm feeling like I've found the place where I want to be for the rest of my life.

When it came to my turn, I just said my name was Nicole, and I was a grateful alcoholic, trying to stay sober one day at a time.

When we all stood up to say the Lord's Prayer, I felt like

I was going to go sailing off right over the baseball field outside the room and just go off into outer space somewhere and float.

On the way back to Century City, I asked Barron if he really thought he was an alcoholic. He says, "Not exactly addicted to alcohol, but really, I'm more of a pillhead than you think. I was getting so I just lived for every four hours when I could take my next Xanax. I really didn't want to be present and accounted for for my own life."

So then we're back in Century City, and Barron has all these faxes from Tokyo. He's doing this incredible deal whereby he's selling off fifteen percent of BTA to All-Nippon Airlines. Only instead of taking cash, he's getting stock in ANA, equal to the dollar value of his shares, and he's going to distribute them to his stockholders. Each stockholder gets one share of ANA for every eleven shares of BTA or something like that. And Barron thinks it's this great thing to get the American stockholder to have a piece of Japan, just like the Japanese are buying up pieces of America.

Anyway, he's talking back and forth with somebody in Tokyo for an hour, and then he works out all these numbers on his Lotus 1-2-3, and he keeps smiling and saying how it'll work, and then the people from Doyle Dane Bernbach come in and we're all sitting around looking at sketches for the new campaign about encouraging fliers to stop carrying their own luggage on board, and Barron lets me run the meeting.

It's so great. All these agency people, and one of them tells me that Marsha Grossman is looking for a new job, and what do I think about her. So I start to trash her, and then I remember the program, and I just say, "I really can't talk about her." That way, it gets the point across, only I don't have to do her dirt.

The theme we decided to go with is the one I suggested.

It's got a plane cabin looking like a living room, all cluttered with bags, and then they disappear, and the announcer says, "This . . . or this. It's your choice on BTA." It's not going to win any awards, but it tells people the truth, and that's a new one for airline ads.

Then we went off to Morton's for dinner. It's so great, because Barron is really great buds with Gil, the captain, because Gil is dying to be a pilot some day, and Barron keeps offering to let him sit in on pilot school for a week to see how he likes it. Anyway, so Gil always gives us the best table, this little deuce near the window, and we're sitting there, and first, and this is really great, in comes David Sonnenbaum, this loser from Rebecca's, looking like he thinks he's so cool, all dressed in black, and he comes in, and Gil starts to take him to the total back of the room, where the people from Simi Valley sit, and David sees me, and he's with this bim, and I can see his lips move, and he's really asking Gil who I'm with, and Gil is saying "Barron Thomas," and David starts to walk over and kiss some rich-person ass, and Gil holds up a hand in front of him and says, "Peter doesn't like for our diners to be disturbed," like David is some tourist from Pacoima and he was going to ask Kim Basinger for her autograph.

And the bim is like holding her hands on her hips because she's so totally embarrassed, and it's great. I mean, great. And David just walks out, and the bim stops and talks to some sleaze at the bar, and I never did see her leave with David, and I heard him yelling out in the parking lot because one of the valets forgot his car or something. Since this is all not really my doing, I'm enjoying it a lot.

Why not? He treated me like a doormat. Why shouldn't I be glad he gets his? I'm not Mother Teresa. I like to see bad people get it back. The program says that everything is in the hands of everyone's Higher Power. I'm not exactly sure what that means, but I guess that David Sonnenbaum's Higher Power really wanted him to be humiliated at Morton's, and who am I to get in his way?

Anyway, I'm sitting there, eating my crab cakes, and all I can think of is, I can't believe the whole thing. Until that meeting where I found Barron, my life was just insecurity with a capital I. I was just a leaf, floating for a few instants on the ground before it hit bottom and got swept away and burned in some big pile.

All my dreams and hopes and everything I carried out here in my little car were just a joke. They were a sick joke. They were mocking me all of the time. In my head, there was this committee telling me I had wasted my youth, and wasted my strength, and I basically had thrown away my one and only life, on the likes of David Sonnenbaum and Ms. Middle and Tony Morris. I mean, I could just hear myself every day saying that I had already seen my best days, and they were long past, and everything else would be a long slide down into confusion and smallness.

Now, I think about what happens in a day. Every single day, I have some scope in my life. I can use my brains. I can pay my bills in every way. Not just to Southern California Edison and Adrienne Vittadini. But to my hopes and plans and expectations. Every single day, I feel like I'm the woman that the girl out on the Panther field wanted to be.

Basically, a big guy came into my life. Now, he could have made me feel like a little piece of shit, the way David Sonnenbaum and all those Hollywood losers did. Or, he could have ignored me.

Or, he could share some of his bigness with me. That's what he did. So, if happiness is the exercise of one's creative powers in large ways, then I'm a very happy girl. Very, very happy.

Anyway, so we're all through with dinner, and suddenly all of the waiters, Skippy and Randy and Doug and Mike and Rick, all gather around and start singing "Happy

Birthday" to me. And I hadn't even *remembered* that it was my birthday. I'm twenty-five. I've been so busy that I didn't even remember. That's a first for someone who's usually sulking on her birthday that nothing is going right.

They all sing "Happy Birthday," and then they bring over one of those great flourless chocolate cakes that give you pimples but taste unbelievably sweet, and then everybody goes away.

Barron says, "Nicole, you did something pretty great for me. A lot of things. Thank you. You saved my life." He's always saying I saved his life, which is pretty strange, since he really saved *my* life. But, I guess that's what it means to find the right guy.

Anyway, we went back to his place in Century City and lay in bed. It was really sweet. It was really wonderful just having him hold me.

I always hate to walk through his den and see his answering machine with its little red light blinking, because I know that means his wife has called. She's the only one who would call him at his condo, except for me.

He never takes the calls, and I guess he answers them after I leave. Maybe the next morning. Maybe that's why he doesn't like for me to stay over. I don't know. I can't think about that. Tomorrow, or some other day, I'll think about that. But for right now, I'm thinking about where I was six months ago, and where I am now.

Anyway, I went back to bed after I went past Barron's study, and I saw that he was sitting up in bed looking all proud and happy, like he had just picked ten stocks in a row that were takeover candidates. And he takes out from under the covers this long light-blue box from Tiffany. It's really long and thin. He hands it to me, and he says, "This is for you, because you were good to me when I was all alone. Because you saved my life. Because I love you."

I opened it up. Get ready to faint. It's pearls. I mean, major, heavy-duty pearls. A double strand. Opera length.

Great big giant ones. Eight millimeter. Maybe more. With a catch and little diamonds on the catch. I mean, totally righteous. Do you know what it means to have pearls like that at twenty-five? Do you? How many twenty-five-year-olds in the whole world have opera-length eight-millimeter pearls?

As far as I'm concerned, they're better than diamonds. Mimi does this hilarious imitation of a JAP in Beverly Hills saying classy like "cleeassy." That's what I feel like. They're so *cleeassy*. I actually feel like a different woman when they're next to my chest.

Anyway, I guess I started to cry, and Barron held me, and then he did me again, while I was crying. I don't know why, but Barron just loves to do me when I'm crying or when I'm really sad. I mean, he gets really excited when I'm crying or when I'm sad. Sometimes it scares me.

Anyway, after he did me, we both slept for a while, and I could hear the answering machine clicking on and off, and of course, Barron never answered it. Never. Then, about one in the morning, Barron goes to his desk, all solemn like, like he was going to take out his Last Will and Testament.

And he says, "I'm not immortal. I may not always be here." That scared me. "I mean, I'll never leave you, but things happen."

"Like what?"

"Some lawyer could kill me for cutting off his livelihood. That could happen. Some guy from O'Melveny who was planning on a house in Carpinteria and now has to suck some air and do some other work. Anyway, I just don't want you to ever feel like you're just a floating atom out there on the ocean. So, I want you to have this. And it's just between us.

"It's not from the stockholders of BTA and I didn't even ask my lawyers if I should report it to the Commission. I'll ask them some other day." Then he hands me this really

official-looking gray envelope. Inside is a stock certificate
from BTA. Ten thousand shares. It's trading at twelve and
a half. That's 125 K. The stock certificate is made out to
Nicole Elizabeth Miller.

Now, everyone has heard the expression "I can't believe
it." It can mean anything from mild surprise to mild
condemnation. But when I say I couldn't believe it, I mean
I really couldn't believe it. I COULD NOT BELIEVE IT
WAS HAPPENING. That's what I mean.

It made me feel all different ways, I guess, and probably
he shouldn't have done it.

The first thought I had was that I must be dreaming.
But then right out of nowhere, like a freight train, I started
to feel really angry. It was the first time I had ever felt
angry at Barron. The first time. But I didn't want to say
anything.

I'm lying on Barron's bed in Barron's apartment on the
twenty-first floor of this building looking out at the
airplanes landing at LAX, and I'm wearing the pearls
Barron gave me against my chest, and Barron's just handed
me something worth over a hundred thousand dollars, and I
know I shouldn't feel mad at him, but I did.

I didn't say anything except I sort of stammered and I
walked over to this built-in desk Barron has in his bedroom
with a stock market ticker hooked up to a CRT, and the
quotes from some shit in Tokyo that I don't even know
about are going across it, and I just held my head in my
hands and started to cry.

Barron said, "What's wrong?" and I said, "Nothing. I'm
just so happy." But you never can fool that dude. I mean,
like never. It's like he has a third ear or something. And he
says, "I guess I shouldn't have done that."

I said, "I guess not" or something like that.

"Why?" he asked. "Do you mind telling me?"

So I thought and then I said, "Well, for one thing, I
don't like you talking about being dead."

Barron shakes his head. "I don't really think that's it," he says.

"I don't know," I said to him. "I think it's because every other thing you've done for me makes me feel big, and this makes me feel small. This makes me feel like a little match girl. This makes me feel as if I were just a little peon getting thrown a peso by a rich person. This makes me feel like you're trying to just bribe me to love you, and you don't have to do that. It makes me feel like you think you have to bribe me to love you because of that answering machine that's always clicking and the little red light and you never answer it or even pick it up while I'm here."

Barron didn't say anything for a long time. Then he says, "I make a lot of mistakes. I'm really sorry. Can I explain it to you?"

So, naturally, I start to cry like there's no tomorrow. I mean, really sobbing. And I hug him and he hugs me. And then, while I'm lying next to him, he says, "I guess I knew there was a risk in doing this. But here's the thing: The money isn't to make you feel small. It's to make you feel as if you have some independence. It's so that if I ever start to behave like a total loser, which I am perfectly capable of doing, you'll be able to just say 'Fuck off' and walk out the door and know that you can live perfectly all right for as long as it takes for you to get another job just as good as what you have.

"I know it makes you feel small right now," Barron tells me. "But tomorrow morning, or the next day, you'll get up, and you'll feel really pissed about something I did, and you'll think you're trapped being with me because of the job and the car and the pearls. Then you'll remember the stock and you'll say, 'Hey, I'm not trapped after all. I'm not trapped at all. I'm a free woman. I have all that stock, and maybe Barron gave it to me, but it means he loves me, and it means I'm free.' "

So I just thought about that for a minute, and then I

said to him, "I'm the biggest loser and jerk in the whole world. I am totally sorry. But I can't take it. It's too much money."

"No, it's just the right amount. Because it's one year's pay, so you can live for a year on it if you have to."

"I think you'd better work on your math, Barron," I said to him. "I get eight hundred dollars a week. That's three years' pay."

"Haven't you read tomorrow's newspaper, or even the BTA press release?" Barron asks. He hands me the press release, with the airplane and the bridge and the river, the logo I designed, and it says, "Nicole Miller to head advertising and government relations of Barron Thomas Aviation." It has a little bio and Barron saying how glad he is to have me on board, and how much help I was to the Real Property Equalization Fund on the dump thing, of which BTA is general partner, and I still don't even know what that means, and tears are just pouring down my cheek, and I'm thinking, God, what did I do to deserve this guy . . . and Barron says, "It pays one and a quarter a year. I think you're worth it."

Anyway, he didn't take me home until about three in the morning, and I was pretty much in a trance the whole way. And when I got home, I couldn't sleep, and I had to write all this down. I don't care about that answering machine. I don't care about Saundra. As far as I'm concerned, she gave him to me.

It's all just perfect, and I'm not going to let a small thing like that get in the way of the best thing in my life. And I'm only twenty-five. And I know he won't be married to her for long. We can't be this happy and have him stay married. It just can't happen. I'm not going to get upset about it anyway. What happens happens, and that's it, and I'm not going to start crying about it like a big baby. I love him, and that's plenty for now. Plenty. More will be revealed, and I know it'll go our way.

16

W R A P A R O U N D

Just as Nicole's 325 rounded the corner into LAX from Sepulveda Boulevard, across from an immense billboard advertising Bora Bora with a smiling maiden and a volcano spouting a white substance, Nicole remembered to set the "on board computer" for the observed fact that it was not September 30, but October 1, 1986. That was the only thing wrong with the car, and Nicole loved it a lot. Still, there was this one little nagging thing about the clock and the calendar. If you were going to have it, it might as well work right.

"I still don't understand," Nicole said. "Why do you have to go to New York right now? You said you were going to speak at my seminar at UCLA on marketing, and now you're going off to New York."

"It's like I already told you," Barron said. "Saundra called me and told me she's getting out of Chestnut Lodge, and she's done incredibly well in the program and this time she's sure it'll work."

"Barron, she said that when she got out of Hazelden and when she got out of Mount Sinai, too."

"I know," Barron said. "But I have to show her that I'm there for her."

210

"Why?" Nicole asked. "When was the last time she was there for you?"

By this time, the Beemer was stuck behind an immense airline shuttle bus pouring out exhaust into the cars behind it. The sky had turned the color of a used cigarette filter all around the airport access road.

"Nicole, that's too difficult. Ask me something easier. She was there for me a long time ago."

"I hate this," Nicole said. "You're going to see your wife. For all I know, one of these times, you're going to see her, and she's going to have stopped drinking, and you're going to stay with her. I'm scared, Barron. I'm really scared."

"How many times have I told you that I will never stop loving you?"

"Barron, that's what people say when they're about to break up. We both know that."

"We have this thing," Barron said. He looked down at the flashing red lights on the clock that Nicole had just reset in the dashboard. "We don't lie to each other. Now, you know I'm going to see Saundra. She's flying up from Washington, and we're going to meet in New York, and then go out to Bedford. I won't sleep in the same bed with her. I won't even be in the same room."

"I know," Nicole said. She flushed, and paused. "I really have no right to go at you like this. Just forget I even said anything."

The light changed ahead of the bus. Still, as busses will do, the airline shuttle express did not move. It simply sat and spewed out more exhaust. Nicole raised the windows on the BMW and turned on the air conditioning. Immediately, with the air filtered and cleaned, she felt better. As if she could breathe. Whatever had been choking her was now shut out.

"Saundra is a person," Barron said. "We have a long history."

"I hear you," Nicole said. "Listen, shall I fax you the new one sheets on the routes to New Orleans, or what do you want me to do with them? Also, we have an option on another four thou-

211

sand square feet in Century City. I think we might consider starting our own data-processing unit. We're getting royally hosed by NCR . . ."

Barron held her forearm. He rolled up her sleeve and pulled her right arm gently away from the steering wheel. He turned her arm palm up. Then he began to stroke the inside of her forearm. In spite of herself, Nicole began to smile. She almost purred, even as she awkwardly shifted gears with one hand and lurched forward behind the bus.

"We can't be all business all the time," Barron said. "That's what makes us dull."

The traffic thinned out and then bunched up again in front of the Barron Thomas Aviation Terminal. "When is the Falcon going to be ready? Wasn't it supposed to be ready today?" Nicole asked.

"It's ready. I'm just having Steve check it. If it doesn't work, it's no joke. Not like having a flat tire in your driveway. In the meantime, it looks good to fly commercial every so often. Shows concern for the stockholders."

Nicole found a space next to the curb and rocketed the little car into it. Barron still held her arm and stroked its inside. "I'm so glad Mimi told me you like this," Barron said. "It's a whole new way to talk."

"It's better than talk," Nicole said. She leaned over and kissed Barron. As always, she smelled perfectly of K.L. "It's just that I love you," Nicole said. "I don't really feel like me if I'm not with you. I feel like somebody else if I'm not with you. I don't feel good about myself . . ."

"I'll be back in two days."

"Yeah, but some day . . ."

"Some day," Barron said, "some sweet day, we'll be together, yes we will, yes we will," he continued, sending up the Supremes. "I'll be back in two days, and it'll be swell and you'll see it's all right. Saundra is the past. You're the present and the future. Who controls the present controls the future," he added.

"I think the line is, 'Who controls the present controls the

212

past. Who controls the past controls the future.' It's from Orwell."

"You've gotten to be awfully smart since I met you, haven't you?" Barron demanded with a smile.

"No," she said. "Awfully stupid."

Barron suddenly looked sad. "I hope you're kidding."

"Of course I am," Nicole said eagerly. "Just call me a lot. A real, real lot."

"I will," Barron said.

A smiling skycap stepped up to the car. In a surprisingly thick Southern accent, the man said, "Flying with us today, Mr. Thomas?"

"You bet, Willie," Barron said.

Nicole pressed a button on the door that made the trunk flip open. The skycap took the suitcase and Barron's ticket. "New York," he said. "Yes, sir."

"That's the way to behave, right?" Nicole asked.

Barron stared at her in frank disbelief. "Where does this come from?" he demanded. "Where? What have I done to you?"

He opened the car. In one fluid motion, he stepped out, handed the skycap a twenty, took his claim check, and walked into the terminal.

Nicole leapt out of her side of the car. "It comes from the fact that I love you," she said. "That's where it comes from," she called after him. But she did not know whether or not he heard her, because by then he was inside the terminal. When she began to run into it herself, a policeman with an impossibly neat mustache followed her and tapped her on the shoulder.

"You want your car towed?" he demanded. "You want it impounded?"

"No," she said softly. "No. I'll move it."

That night, Nicole called her answering machine every fifteen minutes. She asked her secretary and Barron's secretary, also named K.L., if either of them might have heard from Mr. Thomas. "There's a big decision that has to be made with D'Arcy Masius, and I just know he wants to tell me about it," she told each of them. She did not leave work until nine o'clock, in case Barron sent her a fax or wanted to call her at the office.

At nine-thirty, at home, Mimi walked into the living room carrying her pocketbook and Nicole's. "Time to go out and party," she said. "No time to spend just hanging around at home brooding about your married boyfriend."

"I don't know why I snapped at him," Nicole said. "He really didn't do anything wrong. I was just being a bitch."

"How are your hormones?" Mimi asked. "I know that when I get near my period, I start to act like a crazy woman. Especially if I haven't been drinking."

"If you *haven't* been drinking?" Nicole asked. She sat on her green silk couch, a gift from Barron, and flipped the remote control on her television. Lately, as far as she could tell, everyone on TV had a bug-eyed insane look. There was an intensity about everyone, from the dancers on Club MTV to Peter Jennings to Ted Koppel to Brent Musburger to Jane Curtin that was almost unbearable. She had begun to dread turning on the TV because it sounded like a chorus of magpies, all screaming "Me! Me! Me! Me!" over and over again, with slightly changed background graphics. Yet, as much as she felt repelled and even nauseated by what she saw, she also felt compelled to watch, as if she were watching a whole culture swirl around and around the bottom of a drain before vanishing into eternity.

"Yeah. Drinking mellows me out," Mimi said. "I haven't ever had a problem with it. It makes me feel good."

"Our public relations policy is based on attraction rather than promotion," Nicole said. "But I don't really feel like going out to eat. I have some Weight Watchers in the refrigerator."

"Fuck Weight Watchers," Mimi said. "You don't have to wait at home for him to call. He's not a lost puppy you have to stay up waiting for. He's a big powerful wheel. You yelled at him. Nicole, he's a grown man. He's had people yell at him before."

"Yeah, but it came out of nothing," Nicole said. "I mean, the guy is a prince to me. He's nicer than anyone else has ever been in my whole life. That's a fact. He loves me more unconditionally than my mother or my father."

"Nicole," Mimi said, "he's nice to you because he controls you by being nice to you. That's the way guys are. If he could control you by treating you like shit, he'd do that." She sat on a leather and canvas chair and swung her legs. "You really don't know guys at all." She opened an issue of *Elle* and began to read it, circling the items she would pray for later that night.

"Okay. Let's just agree that you don't know Barron. He's not like that. He's nice to me because he loves me. Because he wants to protect me. Because he sees something in me that he wants to see get bigger."

"Yeah. That's why he's always sending you all that stuff from Victoria's Secret. I know what things in you he wants to see get bigger."

"Bad girl," Nicole said. "You are such a dirty bad girl. Bad girl, bad, bad, girl."

They both began to laugh. In a half-hour, Nicole had her diamond earrings on, her hair pulled back with a barrette from Neiman-Marcus with little inlaid silver airplanes on it, and a white silk dress with thin blue lines running vertically along its length. It showed her breasts and her legs in a way that her mother would have described as ladylike but unmistakable.

Veronica's was full, so the two girls sat at its bar. It was a Thursday night, and the room was packed with people, many of them younger than Nicole and Mimi. Boys with looks of angry concentration with slicked-back hair and steel-rimmed glasses that looked as if they were meant to be scalpels.

The men were talking among themselves, shooting their cuffs, checking their appearance in a mirror behind the bar, occasionally looking at girls along the bar.

The girls wore tight dresses with slits up to their thighs, tight blue jeans, even tight shorts. Nicole was astonished at how many of the women were overweight. When you leave the land of

Morton's and Spago, she thought, when you leave the first-class cabin, people have normal weights once again.

The men and the women talked too animatedly, too loud, with too much studied concentration to show that they were not even aware of anyone else being in the room. They certainly did not need any help finding a mate, thank you very much.

Mimi was on her third Stoli martini before the surfer-captain, himself obviously only standing in for the real captain, since he could not speak without giggling, as if he were testing the lethal tolerance for Quaaludes, showed them to their table.

Half an hour passed before a waiter took their order. He sneezed on them. He did not know what the specials were. He told them they were a couple of hot babes, and maybe he and his friend, who was working as captain tonight, could buy them a few brewskis and then take them dancing afterward.

The food was a dispiriting mass of lukewarm cheese and chewy chicken strips. Nicole was sure that a year ago, she would not even have known what good food was supposed to taste like. Whatever that was, the food they had at Veronica's wasn't it. Maybe it was just an off night, or maybe Nicole couldn't taste anything.

After pecking at her food for a few minutes, she got up and walked to the ladies' room. She dialed her answering machine. No messages. She dialed her voice mail at BTA. Only one call, from a decorator about the new offices and what kind of bleached wood they wanted.

She ate another few bites of food while she waited for Mimi to tell her about how much she hated men. Then, at two-thirty A.M. New York time, she called Barron's apartment on Fifth Avenue in Manhattan. The telephone rang twice and a groggy Barron picked it up.

"You can't imagine how glad I am to talk to you," Barron said. "It's been a nightmare. Saundra was drunk when I got to the Côte Basque. She reeked of wine. She denied it when the smell was so strong I thought I would pass out. She could barely make it out to her car. Yeah, she has decided she has to have a car and driver. I'm not kidding. Then she told me about how wonderful the program was, and how grateful she is to be in it. God, I miss you. Let's not ever fight anymore."

"Why didn't you call me?"

The noise from the restaurant was deafening, but Nicole could hear Barron say, "Because I copped such a ridiculous attitude at the airport, and because you did, too, and I just had been through enough today."

"Let's never fight anymore," Nicole said. "Let's never ever fight. I'll pick you up at the airport, and let's never fight anymore."

"I love that idea," Barron said.

Nicole walked back into the dining room. She felt a wave of relief washing over her, as if she had been gracefully immersed in the warm ocean off Kuilima Point on a warm summer night. She felt cleansed, relieved, protected. The loose ends that had been sputtering with undirected electricity were covered up. The edge was just a memory.

She was literally a different woman from the confused wreck who had walked over to the telephone in the ladies' room five minutes earlier. "I am powerless over my fears," she heard her say to herself, "and also over my happiness."

Back at the table, David Sonnenbaum and a friend who looked even more devoid of human intelligence and compassion were sitting with Mimi. Both men wore "Miami Vice" double-breasted blazers with T-shirts and had their long hair slicked back. The man with David Sonnenbaum had a slight rat's tail on the back of his head. He stared at Nicole's breasts as if he were choosing a dessert from a pastry tray at Marie Callender's.

"This is Lanny Shlepkis," Sonnenbaum said. "He's in our music division. Just out of Wharton."

"Hey, pretty lady," Shlepkis said. His breath smelled of garlic. "Want to dance?"

"No, I'm on my way home," Nicole said.

"Hey, I'm having a great time," Mimi said in a gurgling, barely conscious voice. "I'm not going anywhere."

"No, you have work tomorrow, Mimi," Nicole said. "We have to go."

"Oh, all right," Mimi said good-naturedly. "Woman's got to earn a living. Got to pay my bill at Ann Taylor somehow."

"Hey, you're just crabby because you need what I've got," Shlepkis said, suggestively throwing forward his pelvis, as if he were in a Run DMC rap video.

"You look like you're maybe in a bad mood because you're a little tired of dealing with older men, and you need what young men have to give," said Sonnenbaum, making a similar but even lamer gesture.

"What is this?" Nicole asked. "Are you guys high or coming from some acid trip or what? You're acting like maniacs. I mean, you're acting crazy. We've got to go home."

"Hey, my mother, back in New York, is pals with Saundra Thomas. She says she's really a nice lady. Kind of lonely, though," Lanny Shlepkis said. "Husband's always running around with cute blond girls."

"Hey, leave us alone," Nicole said. "We're just trying to get out of here and go home. We were just out to have a good time," Nicole said.

"We'll show you a good time," Shlepkis said. "Better than some old businessman can show you."

Mimi suddenly slammed her fist down on their table. It made a surprisingly loud noise, sending two martini glasses hurtling to the floor. "Hey, dickless!" she shouted at Shlepkis. "If we want any shit from you, we'll squeeze your head. Now butt the fuck out."

Nicole had never really understood how much she loved Mimi until she saw Sonnenbaum's jaw drop and Shlepkis's eyes bug out. They were still mumbling when Mimi and Nicole walked out the door.

At home that night, Nicole and Mimi lay in bed watching TV for half an hour until Mimi fell asleep. Then Nicole got up and tucked Mimi into bed and went back into her room.

She walked into her closet and took off her clothes. She looked at herself in the full-length mirror to see if she would still look good to Barron. She thought she would. Then she took a shower. Under the steaming water, she sang to herself, "Day

218

by day. Day by day. Oh, dear Lord, three things I pray . . ." It was from a production of *Godspell* in which she had starred as an eleventh-grader in Jonesboro. It soothed her, and she felt as if it also taught her.

When she got out of the bathroom, she walked nude into her closet. In the back of it, where even Mimi could not find it when she was looking for something to borrow, was a man's shirt. It was a plain blue Oxford cloth button-down shirt from Brooks Brothers, size 15-35. She had taken it from the dirty clothes pile at Barron's apartment in Malibu, the one he kept for nights when he wanted to hear the ocean.

The shirt smelled of Barron. It smelled of his sweat and of his Lime Eau Sauvage After Shave, and just smelled of Barron as he was when she held him against her.

She put on the shirt and wrapped herself in it tightly. She smelled its arms, its collar, its everything. it smelled like Barron. She got into bed, wrapped the covers over her, took a long smell of Barron, and went to sleep.

17

SWINGING ON A STAR

On an evening in June 1987, Barron Thomas and Nicole Miller drove from Barron's apartment on Malibu Road to the Community Center on Point Dume, at the corner of Greyfox and Fernhill Roads. Barron had bought his new Toyota Cressida only that afternoon and was still puttering with its controls. He was having a particularly hard time with its self-locking seatbelt. The device was attached to the top of his door. It swung shut on his neck and chest when he closed the door. Once, minutes after he left the showroom, he opened the door to ask a gas station attendant for help in opening the self-locking gas cap. As he stuck his head through the open window, the strap began to tangle around his neck. Only by quick thinking, instantly closing the door, did Barron escape strangulation at the remote-control hand of an engineering team in Tokyo. Revenge for the fire bombing of Tokyo.

The Wednesday night AA group—"Reality as Bill Sees it"—filled the erstwhile classroom in the erstwhile school. Across the back of the room, teenagers from various substance abuse houses lounged on folding chairs, trying to look cool, clearly tormented in a hundred different ways. In the front of the room, a dozen regulars whom Barron and Nicole recognized from the noon meeting talked animatedly among themselves. In the middle of the room, others, most of whom Barron recognized from other encounters in the program, sat awkwardly in chairs that were slightly askew.

The meeting began with the Lord's Prayer, a brief reading from the Big Book about how surrender is the beginning of triumph, and then was open for discussion. A movie star told about how he used to feel lonely all of the time until he found his Higher Power. The best thing about the Higher Power is that the calls to him are free. Another man described how he had recently been to a Thrifty Drug in Koreatown and had been threatened by killer Koreans from a gang. They had menaced him with a gun. When he called the police, they had laughed at him as they were led off to jail. The policeman had told him that he should consider himself incredibly lucky to be alive.

"Those zipperheads just don't care about wasting a guy like you, an Anglo, a huero. Doesn't mean a thing to them whether they're in jail or out." That's what the policeman who arrested the Koreans had told him. The problem was that he had so much anger toward them that he really felt as if he were going to lose his mind, and no amount of praying or meditating helped. He said he told himself the Serenity Prayer over and over again, and all he could think of was what kind of guns to buy.

Nicole whispered to Barron that she had to go to the bathroom. She edged her way out of the room. A man with a flaming red beard was saying that he had grown up in South Chicago, in a tenement near an elevated railroad line. All day and all night, he could hear the trains going by, rattling the dishes and the glasses. His mother and father used to have fistfights every day. His mother used to hit his father with a baseball bat when his father came home drunk, which was every night. That did not even slow his father down. He was in the Army, then a drifter, then in mental hospitals most of his adult life. He used to think that however low his father had fallen, he had fallen further. Then he could not get out of bed for a year and hurt all over from a mysterious ailment.

221

Barron squeezed past an astonishingly fat man with suspenders, who beamed at Barron and whispered, "Best airline I ever flew on. Best stewardesses. That's what makes an airline." Barron patted him on the back. "Thanks," he said.

Barron walked to the water fountains near the bathrooms. They were outdoors. The whole school had no indoor corridors. Everything was set around concrete breezeways and patios. The water fountain was only about two feet off the ground. This school must have been an elementary school, Barron realized. As he bent over to drink, he remembered a story his mother had told him. When she had been in high school in Nortex, Texas, she had been bending over to drink from a fountain when a classmate had knocked her from behind. He had only meant to get her face wet, but instead, he had chipped her tooth, and it had stayed chipped for all of her life.

That was her way of teaching caution.

Barron drank his water. It still tasted of youth, even though it was far from where he had gone to elementary school, at Silverado Elementary School in University Park, Dallas. The low fountain and the institutionalized taste of the water flooded him with memories of his confusion in Texas, when he tried desperately to figure out what made the world go around, before he knew about Marx or lawyers or Bill Wilson or luck. The water made him feel lonely.

Barron walked back toward the meeting room. He figured that Nicole must have taken another route back. As he rounded a bend near the playground, he heard a squeaking sound. He turned to his right. There, in the moonlight, a blond girl was swinging from a swing. She swung her legs and made herself fly higher with each arc. She was flying so high that her blond hair was silhouetted by the moon. He could see its fine filaments floating through the air with impossibly white light behind them.

In the moonlight, Nicole looked like a child herself, a child who was not attached to the swing or to the ground at all. Nicole was a child with moonlight filtering through her hair, sailing into the graying blue night sky above Point Dume.

Barron could see her pale skin and hear her giggling with a completely unself-conscious glee. He could see her swing so high that she was on a line with Sirius and the Big Dipper.

He walked over to the swings and stood in front of her. "You get on, too," she said.

Barron slid onto the swing next to her. He pushed against the familiar sand at the bottom of the swing and forced himself up until he was swinging with her, cycle for cycle, high, high into the night sky.

As they reached the highest point of the swing, so high that Barron thought they were going to flip over the steel bar that held the steel chains of the swings, Nicole reached out her hand to hold Barron's hand. Barron hesitated, fearful that he might lose his grip and fall off onto the ground. Nicole smiled at him anyway, and blew him a kiss.

Then the meeting broke up and someone called to Barron. He stopped swinging, slowed down, and then jumped off the seat.

Five beats behind him, Nicole still swung through the sky, her hair still floating somewhere up near Canis Major, where she belonged.

18

W O M E N ' S   D A Y

"Miss Miller," said the receptionist's voice. *"Miss Miller, there's* a woman here to see you, and she looks really unhappy, and she's already on her way down the hall . . ."

Nicole Miller swung her gaze away from the window where she was watching a blimp float across the sky above Santa Monica trailing a sign reading JAY LENO TONIGHT AT . . . and then the name of a club she had not heard of. She put down her sketch of a logo for a child's mileage accumulation card that kids would carry in their pockets along with their Mickey Mouse Club cards. Or maybe with their condoms and their baggies of crack these days, she reflected sadly.

The door flew open. Saundra Logan, whom Nicole recognized immediately just from glimpses of photos and from the rage in her eyes, strode into the room. She slammed the door after her theatrically. A calendar of Cap d'Antibes in summer fell to the floor.

"What the hell have you got, Nineteen eighty-six, that makes you so damned smug and so damned great and gives me such a headache?" she snarled.

Nicole studied her rival. Tall, thin, elegant even in a rage. Model thin. Model elegant. The bones of a wealthy woman.

Long, lean. Intelligent face. Large nose, but intelligent. Thin hair, too. The face and body of an aristocrat. But an angry, confused aristocrat.

After that, the main impression on Nicole was the jewelry. On each wrist, Saundra wore a diamond bracelet, a bangle with two rows of diamonds. On her wedding ring finger, she wore an emerald as large as a postage stamp. On the other hand on the same finger was a topaz of even larger size. It occurred to Nicole that she had never seen so much jewelry on any one woman except in advertisements.

Nicole Miller looked at her evenly. "Who are you?" she asked, stalling for time.

"You know goddamned well who I am. I'm Saundra Logan Thomas. I'm Barron's *wife. Wife,* get it? What you'll never be, in other words. *Wife.* Not hooker, not mistress, not plaything. Wife."

"I see," Nicole said. "Is there anything I can help you with?" She turned her back, sucked in her breath, prayed for calm.

"Yes. You can get the hell out of my husband's life. You can stop stealing him away from me. You can take your blond hair and your big tits and take your broom and fly away to some other planet and ruin people's lives there."

Saundra Logan was panting, out of breath, angry, drunk. Nicole could smell the alcohol on her breath across the room. Probably vodka.

"You think I wrecked your life?" Nicole asked.

"I don't think so. I know so," Saundra Logan Thomas said.

"Have a seat," Nicole said.

"Fuck you."

"All right, then. Get the hell out of my office. I have work to do and I don't need someone coming in here reeking of alcohol screaming at me, wrecking my day. I have work to do. Get out of my office."

"Your office?" Saundra asked with an effort at mockery and condescension. "Your office? I don't think so, sweetheart. This is my husband's company. It's his whole building, as far as I'm concerned. I'm his wife. You get out. You just get the hell out of my building." Her face was red. Her voice flew up and down, with instants of high indignation mixed with instants of complete confusion and fear.

"Wait a minute," Nicole said. "I work for the stockholders of BTA. Maybe you're one and maybe you're not. I report to the board of directors. I don't think you're one of them. You don't have any more right to order me around than a shopping-bag lady in Venice."

This stumped Saundra for a moment. "Don't give me your fancy talk," Saundra said an instant later, after she had recovered. "I'm not a lawyer. But I know this. You stole my husband right out from under my nose. You can't argue with me about that. I want him back."

"I didn't steal him from you. You gave him to me. That's a big difference. A very, very big difference." Nicole was sitting now, but hiding her hands under the table, digging her nails into her palms to keep control.

"I didn't give him to you," Saundra Logan said with an attempt at a laugh. "You think I would give away a husband like Barron Thomas? Are you out of your mind?"

"You gave him to me, Mrs. Thomas, when you completely abandoned him when he was in pain. You gave him to me when you went off into vodka land when he needed somebody," Nicole said. She paused then as she noticed a look of pure confusion on Saundra's face. "You want some coffee?" Nicole asked. "You look tired."

Saundra laughed. It was an entirely unexpected, girlish, high-pitched laugh, like the sound of bells on a sled. "Thank you, I am tired. I came here straight from the airport to roust you out of my husband's life," she said with another laugh, as if for a moment she realized how bizarre and chaotic her situation was.

Nicole handed Saundra a cup of coffee from her black Braun coffeemaker. "You want milk?" she asked.

"No, I need the caffeine," Saundra said. After she had a gulp, during which it occurred to Nicole to wonder just what the

226

connection was between milk and caffeine in coffee, Saundra went on, in a far calmer voice. "Look, I know it must look like I abandoned Barron after that thing at the Indian reservation. I know you see it from your perspective. But you don't know the past. I was there for him in a very, very big way when he needed me then."

"He knows it and I know it," Nicole said. "We're both grateful."

"Don't be sarcastic. When he was cracking up at Yale, I was there. When he was flying off to Vietnam, when he was terrified, I was there. When he was in the hospital at Camp Lejeune, when he was wrapped up in bandages like a mummy, when he was barely alive, I was there. Before you even knew him. Before he was a huge star in *Fortune* and *Forbes*. Before he could give away millions to charity. I was there. What can you possibly ever do to make that up to him? What can you possibly ever do in your wildest dreams that would be the same?" Saundra's voice was calm at first, then becoming steadily closer to hysterical.

"I don't know how to answer you exactly," Nicole said. "The only thing that occurs to me is that it's like a mother saying to her kid that she fed him a year ago, and he shouldn't be mad at her if she didn't feed him this month."

"Barron's not a kid. He shouldn't need feeding all the time. Look, when he was a poverty lawyer in D.C., when he was broke, when he couldn't take me to a decent restaurant for years on end, I was there. I never complained. Never. Not ever. Not once. Not one time. When I had to take a bus to work because the car was broken, I didn't say a word. When all the girls I had gone to school with had Mercedes and I was on the bus, I never complained. What can you possibly say? You knew him when he was rich and famous. You knew him when he was a celebrity. What can you possibly say to me?"

Nicole sighed. "I can say that if you had continued to be there, we would never have met. Barron's a person, Mrs. Thomas. He's not like some kind of nuclear reactor that you put fuel into once and you don't have to do it again for fifty years. He's a person.

You need feeding. He needs feeding, too. You stopped being there, and he was in trouble, and he found me."

"All right," Saundra said. "I had a little lapse. I agree. He was there for me and I wasn't for him. But that's over now. I'm ready to start doing what I should have done. I'm going to stop drinking. I really am."

"So?"

"So, I want him back. You can keep your job. I'll get you a better job. But just get out of Barron's life. Give him back to me. I'm his wife. I need him. I need him badly." Saundra looked washed out, wrung out, pale.

"You know, I don't really have any way of saying this that doesn't sound mean," Nicole answered after a moment's thought. "But I wouldn't give him back if you pulled out my fingernails one by one. I love him. We have a good life together. You had the past. Something happened. I don't know what. But Barron's with me now. He's the best thing I've ever had in my life. I'm not giving him back. Not a chance."

"But when he was in the hospital, so wounded he could hardly talk . . ."

"That was then and this is now," Nicole said. "I don't think you understand. You have the past. You'll always have it. This is now, and I'm the now. I'm the future."

"What about me? What am I supposed to do?" Saundra's voice was plaintive, vulnerable.

"You'll think of something. Stop drinking, for one thing. That'll be a start."

"You mean Barron will come back if I stop drinking?"

"No, I mean stop drinking and you can start putting your life together. I'm not your doctor. I can't tell you what to do. I just know what is, and that's me and Barron. That's the way it is right now."

Saundra did not say anything for thirty seconds and then she drew out her ace of trumps and laid it on the table. "I just guess that you must wonder why he's still married to me then. In California, all you need is irreconcilable differences. He doesn't

228

even need my permission. How come he's never even *mentioned* divorce to me?" For the first time in the interview, Saundra looked as if she might have some control of the room.

Nicole inhaled sharply. "I don't know," she said. "I don't own Barron. Maybe I'll ask him. Maybe he feels sorry for you." A pause. "No, I don't mean that, even though it's probably true. I don't know why men don't leave their wives even when things aren't working out. Ask Joyce Brothers. Anyway, this has gone on long enough. I have a meeting to get ready for."

"Doesn't it bother you that you're with another woman's man? Doesn't it bother Barron that he's still married?" Saundra asked the questions in a meandering, almost amused tone, as if for a moment she was asking a question about someone else's life. The moods of alcohol, Nicole thought.

"You know what?" Nicole snapped. "This isn't 'Sixty Minutes' and I don't have to answer any more of your questions. Maybe it bothers us and maybe it doesn't. I don't work for you. I don't have to answer your questions. That's it. Now, if you don't mind, I have work to do."

Saundra Logan stood up and neatly placed her half-empty cup of coffee on the edge of Nicole's coffee table. Half-empty, Nicole thought. On the edge.

"Thank you," said Saundra. "I can see what Barron sees in you. Very high value-added. Looks. Brains. Spirit. In the end, it all comes down to staying power. Nothing else. I just wish I could be as cool as you are."

"And I wish I could be the woman who nursed Barron and took care of him. I wish I could be the woman who taught ghetto kids without fathers how to read *A Tale of Two Cities*. Barron told me about that. You're quite a woman after all. I can see why Barron doesn't want to divorce you. Quite a woman."

Saundra nodded and actually laughed. "Oh, yes," she said. "Quite a woman." Then she went out the door. "Well, I just came to town to see the woman my husband is in love with, and now I'll be heading back to my own world. Goodbye, Nicole."

Nicole walked to the door and snapped the DO NOT DISTURB

button that she used for important meetings. She hit the same button on her GTE PhoneMaster, which shifted all of her calls to Voice Mail. She went to her window and lowered the blond wood Levolor shades. Then she took off her shoes, lay on her tan cotton sofa, and sobbed until she could not sob anymore, long after every other employee of BTA had left, and she was in the office all by herself, in the building all by herself, in the whole world all by herself as far as she could tell.

19

DREAM GIRL

Late on the night of the day that Saundra Logan Thomas had come to call, Nicole Miller lay in bed at Barron's small apartment on Malibu Road. At every breaking wave, the house shook. It was a frame duplex, built to be disposable, and Nicole could feel its impermanence every fifteen seconds. Some waves were so powerful, crashed with such resonance, that the cottage shook as if it were in the realm of earthquake, the demon god of California.

At midnight, Barron came into the house from his limousine, back from a day of arranging a line of credit to buy new Airbus aircraft from the Europeans. As usual, Nicole could hear the Cadillac door open outside, hear Barron thanking the driver, hear him walk down the used-brick path to the front of the cottage, and then into the living room, which faced the ocean.

Miss Vicki barked, and Nicole got up from her bed, put down her book by David Ogilvy about the advertising business, about how to sell without seeming to sell, and walked down the hall into the living room. She passed several sketches of giveaway BTA calendars she had been working on. Surely, she thought, Pan Am had been incredibly right to give away calendars with photos of South America decades ago.

A traveler needs to consult a calendar before he makes reservations. Why not, why the hell not, Nicole thought, why the fuck not have BTA right in front of him when he was marking his days of flight? Printed right, they would cost virtually zilch, and Barron could get even richer. Wouldn't that be grand?

When Nicole entered the whitewashed living room, with a particularly terrifying wave breaking behind Barron's head as he walked toward her, she saw that he was carrying a bunch of Stargazer lilies. He offered them to her as he folded her into his arms.

"I heard," Barron said. He took off his gray suit jacket and tossed it onto the white couch. "I heard about Saundra. I'm sorry. I don't even know what to say. It's horrible. I had no idea she would even have thought of doing something like that."

Nicole kissed Barron, more of a brush along his lips than a kiss, really, and hugged him so that she could feel his heart beating against her breast. It was a strong heartbeat. Faster than usual, but strong.

Then she stood back from him and looked at him. "The problem is that I love you so much," she said. "If I didn't love you so much, it wouldn't hurt."

Barron took Nicole and sat her on the couch. He handed her a small blue box from his pocket. It said TIFFANY in tiny black letters. "Something I got for you as a guilt present," Barron said truthfully.

Nicole opened the box. Inside was a round gold pin with diamonds running along its circumference.

"It's incredibly beautiful," Nicole said. "You didn't need to do it. You don't need to feel guilty. You didn't make Saundra come to see me."

"I know," Barron agreed.

"And you know what?" Nicole added. "I don't even blame her that much. I mean, after all, you're her husband. Why shouldn't she come see me? What's really wrong with it, all things considered? Why shouldn't she try to get some control over what's going on? She doesn't have to be in Siberia somewhere. She's not in exile. She's a person, too, same as you or me."

232

"I know that," Barron said.

"You have to think of her sitting in that huge house in Bedford, getting drunk, stoking up her grievances. She's there thinking about how she took such good care of you when you came back from Vietnam. She's got a point of view. She's thinking that when you were a nobody, she still loved you. Now that you're somebody, you're not around."

"Nicole, why are you doing this?" Barron got up and got a bottle of Evian water from the refrigerator. He poured himself a glass, then one for Nicole. "These are the times when I wish I had never heard of AA," Barron said. "I wish I were pouring Cutty."

"Go right ahead," Nicole said. "It wouldn't change anything. Saundra's got her points. She doesn't take account of how badly she neglected you, but then, she didn't have a boyfriend, did she? She never had a relationship outside the marriage, did she?"

"Nicole, maybe you should go home," Barron said. "You already knew all of this, and now you're going to make me crazy about it."

"That's great, Barron. First think about escaping by having a drink. Then think about just sending me home. I don't think so, Barron. I don't think that's quite going to work this time. I can go home, but we've got to talk sometime. The truth is that there's something wrong."

"What?"

"You have a wife," Nicole said crisply, more crisply than she meant to sound. "You have a wife, and that makes me a mistress, and I don't know that I like the mistress role."

"You knew I had a wife when you met me. I never made it a secret. Never tried to hide what was going on in my life. You know that's true."

"Of course. But that was when I thought maybe I'd know you for a few weeks or maybe just a few days. When we started being lovers, I was so in love that I didn't even think very much about the next day. And I'm still in love. That's the problem. But it's so fucking hard, Barron. I'm the fifth wheel. I'm the back-street gal. That's not what I had in mind. I didn't plan to go from Drum Major to back-street kept woman.

"I didn't plan to have people whispering about me all the time. It's not like what I'm doing is disgraceful or criminal or even bad compared with what other people do in this world. I'm not dropping poison gas on people. But it's all so damned complicated. It's like clockwork, and the pieces don't ever quite fit, because there are too many damned pieces in this puzzle."

Barron got up again and walked out onto the deck overlooking the crashing waves. He flipped on the halogen spotlights that threw the white spray into a crazy, circus-clown-white relief.

After a minute, he walked back into the living room. Nicole was not there. She was in the bedroom, taking her belongings out of her drawers in the built-in cabinets, stuffing them into the dark blue duffel bag Barron had bought her at Mark Cross a few weeks earlier.

"I know it's hard," Barron said. "Please don't go home. Please stay here. I'm sorry I suggested that you go home. I do love you, and I'm really sad that you're suffering."

"I am suffering right now," Nicole said. "That's real. I don't like it. Nobody would like it."

"I know. But you're my dream girl."

"Barron, I'm your dream girl, but this is my real life. This is my one and only life, and it's hard spending it in love with a married man." Nicole said it with a kind of conclusive flatness, an overpowering sincere pain that Barron could not mistake.

Barron took Nicole by her hand and led her to the bed. He pulled her down onto it. He did not even start to take off her clothes. Instead, he hugged her and stroked her hair. "I don't know what to say," he told her. "What can I say?"

"You can say why you're still married to her. That would be a smart beginning. I know I'm maybe not even entitled to know, because after all, I got into this with my eyes open, and I'm a big girl and everything, but still, it would be nice to know. Why don't you just divorce Saundra? Barron, to put it all in your terms, where's the value-added?"

234

"I don't even know how to answer that question," Barron said. "Maybe it's because I feel guilty. But then I'd probably feel even guiltier if I stayed like this for very long than if I just made a clean break."

"I think so," Nicole said. "Why not just cut it off? Go on to the next thing. Let her go on to the next thing. Let life go on."

"I agree." Barron nodded, his chin brushing Nicole's golden hair. "I agree entirely. Every so often, even in my personal life, maybe I should do the smart thing. The sensible thing."

"It's a little late for that." Nicole laughed.

"Exactly," Barron agreed, also with a laugh. "God, I wish I knew just why I don't leave her. I should. If someone came to me and described his life, and it was my life, I would say that it'll hurt like hell, and there'll be all kinds of pain around it, but you've got to do it. This isn't Italy, where you can't get divorced. This isn't *1984.* People get divorced when marriages don't work. People get divorced when they don't like someone's perfume or after-shave."

"So?"

"I don't know. I think of her sitting by my bed at Camp Lejeune. I think of her going off to teach those little ghetto kids. I think of her cheering me up at Yale . . ."

Nicole stood up and grabbed her duffel bag. "Barron, I'm leaving for tonight, but before I do, I'll just tell you one thing. That's another girl. That's another Saundra Logan Thomas. That girl's not here now. She's as gone as the Barron Thomas that was worried about paying his rent. She's as gone as the Barron Thomas that thought being a public defender was the best way to live. She's a gone kid. If you're hoping she's coming back, you've got another thing coming."

Nicole zipped her duffel and went on. "You do whatever you feel like doing. I don't own you. If you want to chase the past, go ahead. Keep doing it. A lot of people throw away their lives doing that. But know what you're doing. Going after something that just gets farther and farther away the harder you chase it. It gets farther away if you just lay low and have another girl, too. You're looking for something that's not there.

"You think one day you're going to wake up and it's going to be perfect with her and you'll both be young and enthusiastic and everything will be like when you first saw her at the State Department party again? Barron, how can someone so smart be so incredibly stupid? You're just ignoring the good things you have now to chase the past that's never coming back and probably wasn't so great even then."

"All of the really smart people are really stupid. Didn't you know that?"

"No jokes right now, Barron. This is real."

"All right. I'm not ignoring the present, Nicole. You really think I'm ignoring you? You can't really think that, can you? Not really?"

Some of the momentum went out of Nicole's voice. "Of course you don't neglect me. Of course you don't ignore me. The point is that you're neglecting making it solid. Making it secure. You keep it so temporary, like you were renting furniture."

"How would you have me make it more permanent? Divorce Saundra and marry you?"

"I'm not saying you have to marry me," Nicole said, conscious even as she said it that a hundred million other other women had probably said the same words before and *not* meant them every bit as much. "Just divorce Saundra and then we'll see where we are."

"But you know that's where the locomotive of history is leading. That's where you want it to go, anyway. Down the aisle. Not a bad thing. Right?" Barron's tone was open, kind, thinking as he spoke.

"Not so bad. Lends a hint of permanence, anyway," Nicole said with a light laugh covering her churning feelings.

"Yes. The same permanence I have with Saundra. The same permanence that made me crazy. The same permanence that went so totally wrong. I know you're going to say, 'Hey, pal, it's the woman, not the institution. Get hip.' And you'd be right. But the institution is part of it.

"A friend once said that when you're lovers, you're soulmates. When you get married, you're cellmates. It's a joke, and it's silly, and the only problem is that it's true for a helluva lot of people who didn't think it would be true for them."

"So," Nicole shot back, "are you going to rent forever?"

"No, but I'd like to make sure it is the woman and not the institution. It hasn't been that long, has it? Not really so long. Less than a year. Is that so long?"

"But it doesn't say anything about why you won't divorce Saundra. I see your hesitation about getting married again. Perfectly understandable. But you can divorce Saundra. Make me at least a little bit honest."

"You're getting too smart," Barron said. "But I think you're so smart you already know the answer."

"Yeah, I do. If you divorce her, there's no protection from me and the other girls looking for a rich guy, right? The old wife's real-world function: Ward off the next wife."

"Maybe. Maybe. But look, Nicole. How bad off are you? How would it be if you had never met me? How would it be if we broke up tomorrow? Would it be perfect that way? It would be better than it was, because you would have some money. But do you think the men out there have gotten dramatically better? You think loneliness and cruelty have been abolished? I don't think so."

"But I wouldn't be a mistress, Barron. That would be something."

"It would," Barron said sadly. "And you have every possible right to feel frustrated about it. But if something can't go on forever, it will stop. A famous economist said that."

"But let's see what else happens. If you can't stand it anymore, it'll stop. And some day soon, it's just got to be that I'll wake up and I'll be smart enough to make you an honest woman. In the meantime, you'll still be the woman I love. *The woman I love.*

"Now we know that there's a fuse on this thing. That's worth something. Let's not let it blow up the best thing in our lives. Let's just be patient. Just stay on it. Not get crazy."

Nicole paced back and forth, and then lay down next to Barron and kissed his neck. "I told you this was the problem," she said. "I love you too much."

20

FACSIMILES

For one week after Barron's talk with Nicole at the earthquake house, Barron tried to call his wife. For two days, she did not return his calls. Marla, the Trinidadian cook, said that Saundra was sleeping, possibly recuperating from a flu. For five days after that, Marla said that Saundra was out and would call back. On the eighth day, while Barron was in a meeting with officials of the Sumitomo Bank about a line of credit to allow him to put down deposits on new Boeing 767's, Saundra called. She left the message that she was sailing off Nantucket with her friend Arleen Pincus, wife of Mark Pincus, the well-known hospital magnate and, recently, aluminum siding distributor. She said she would call when she got back if she felt well enough.

Barron sent her a letter by fax to their home in Bedford.

"I'd like to talk to you about our situation," the letter said. "It's really getting to be a terrible strain on everyone, including me and you. There is so much good that you did in the past, and so much feeling I still have for you that I would hate like hell to just let it slip away to lawyers without in any way trying to see, just between the two of us, exactly what happened. Please call me back."

By fax, the next morning, Barron got a reply, from the fax number of a "Whale-of-a-Copy" on Nantucket, in handwriting.

I was so moved by your letter that I can hardly tell you. I really don't know what's happened between us. I'm sure some of it is your fault and some of it is my fault. I still remember sitting by your bedside at Camp Lejeune for hours on end reading to you from A Tale of Two Cities. *I still remember how after we were both exhausted from working in Washington, and we didn't have enough money to go out for dinner, we'd get a pizza to take out and eat it while we watched "Mannix" on TV.*

I would really like to discuss all of it with you, but unfortunately, I have been so upset by my meeting with your friend Nicole that I'm not sure I can calmly focus on anything useful for several months. In any event, I am now planning to rent a sailboat with my friend Faith Koen and sail around the Indonesian archipelago, which is something I have been wanting to do all my life.

I am sure that you probably think that this is incredibly selfish and spendthrift of me, and maybe it is. But it's something I've been really not just wanting, but needing to do. I think you'll agree that after all I've been through, a rest is very much in order. Anyway, when I get back, I'll be rested enough to really go over our lives sensibly and see what's lost and what can be reclaimed. I will always love you, Barron, and I'll always, always, always remember only the good times.

After Barron got that letter, he felt dizzy for the rest of the afternoon. He felt a swelling in his throat and a decided pain in the back of his neck. Endless, he thought to himself. Endless.

21

THE HOME FIRES

Life goes on, in conflict and in resolution. In the fall of 1987, Barron Thomas had an idea. Of course, he had ideas every day and every night, like any other human being. Usually Barron's best ideas came just before he went to sleep, when rest had washed away the clutter of the day. He would have an idea such as forming a mutual fund that would concentrate on certain regions of the nation. There would be a Midwest Fund, a California Fund, a Florida Fund, for example. In that way, the attention of its stock pickers could be concentrated on a smaller universe of stocks. In that way also, by raising the ratio of time devoted to each stock, the return on each investment could be raised.

Barron firmly believed that the returns to equity in stock picking were a function primarily of the amount of time spent researching each and every equity situation. If he or some other person he trusted spent a lot of time on study, his returns were usually excellent. If he was tempted by a rumor or a guess, he usually did considerably less well. Hot tips invariably produced a negative return.

Return, in a word, was a function of interest rates, real inflation rates, the quality of a company's management, but above all, of the time and intelligence spent studying the stock.

At any rate, on one autumn day, Barron had an idea closely related to his notions about time and study. It had to do with the importation of talent. As far as Barron could tell, the great mass of MBAs in America were being taught mainly sophisticated means of theft. Asset stripping, management buyouts, front-end-loaded deals of every description, totally unproductive shuffling and reshuffling of capital already in hand. "This is just the same as teaching scientifically advanced pickpocketing," Barron told Nicole one night as they lay in bed watching Cable News Network. Two incredibly smug-looking men, rugs, collagen, and all, were belching into the camera, picking their noses, and telling about what insiders in Washington thought about herring quotas.

"Business is like that," Nicole said. "I think that John Kennedy's father said something about that at one time, if I remember my history."

"Yes, but that's not what lasts. Anyway, it's not what lasts for me. Now, when I find a securities analyst, he's usually just a guy who knows how to use Lotus, but would rather read and rewrite a company press release."

"The one given in man's affairs. Inertia," Nicole added. "And entropy."

Barron got out of bed in his light blue pajamas and took out a book about the social history of England. "But, you see, I was reading this little thing, and it tells me that England has a perpetual problem with having too many well-educated people. There is not enough employment for all of them. Their brains turn to drink and sex instead of finding good stock buys. What a waste."

"Exactly," Nicole said.

"So, here's my idea. We go to England and hire a few super-brainos from Cambridge or Oxford or somewhere else, pay them well, and see if they are far enough out of the rut to find us some good stocks and not just follow the herd. It's sort of like the way builders here in L.A. hire Mexicans instead of our homegrown lazy redneck labor. Get it? Only instead of Mexicans carrying hods, we have Oxford graduates carrying spreadsheets. At roughly similar wages. Also, not already sucked into some PR agent's maw."

"It sounds right to me," Nicole said.

One week later, Nicole and Barron got on a TWA flight to London. Ten and a half hours nonstop from LAX to Heathrow. On a new pro-stockholders bender, Barron and Nicole flew business class. Barron had to admit that it was tolerable, although only barely.

"The fastest way to get spoiled in the entire world is to fly on private planes," he said to Nicole. "The second fastest way is to fly first class. After that, everything else in the world is McDonald's."

In Cambridge, Barron spoke to Sir Winston Fundador, the Chairman of Comparative Statistics. Sir Winston, a tall man with a florid face, innumerable broken capillaries in his nose, and spectacles that looked as if they had been manufactured in the eighteenth century, towered above his desk. When he looked for anything on it, clouds of dust rose into the closed room. He seemed to have been at that desk, at his office, for all of his six decades on the planet. Nicole and Barron sat across from him. Nicole wore a navy blue pin-striped suit and pearls. Both of them had been gifts from Barron. On her right hand, fourth finger, she wore a square-cut emerald, also a new guilt gift from Barron. She smiled frequently at Sir Winston. He explained about his ancestors, who had been Portuguese nobles fleeing the wrath of King Philip for having helped Queen Elizabeth defeat the Armada. Nicole was too polite to ask what King Philip was doing in Portugal, since he was King of Spain. Maybe they were one country then, but Nicole didn't think so.

The don drank from a heavy, heavily dusty glass, which he repeatedly refilled with sherry from an equally dusty decanter. Outside, on the lawn of Magdalene College, pronounced "maudlin," young men and woman lounged in the fall air. Incredibly, two young men seemed to be listening to a tape recorder playing rap music. L.L. Cool J. "The Great Satan," Nicole mused. "Mass culture. The American imperium. It doesn't matter if our cars don't work. Our music works."

"What you propose is to make our young men into moneymakers for your company. Is that right, Mr. Thompson?" the don asked.

"Not at all," Barron said, ignoring the slight. "I propose to allow them the chance to use their full mental faculties, along lines of creativity and excellence, to enrich themselves and our stockholders, many of whom are widows and orphans."

"In other words, the logic of the enterprise is that by increasing individual wealth, the wealth of the society is increased," said Sir Winston.

"Precisely."

"And, of course, they won't be indentured servants," Nicole added. "If they don't like it, they can go right home."

"How are you gonna keep them down on the farm after they've seen Paree?" said the don out of nowhere.

"This place is hardly a farm," Barron said.

"No. Not a farm," the professor said sadly. "But there's not money to be made here. Just a quiet life, and repression and not getting what one wants and pretending that it doesn't matter, that you're happy leading part of a life."

The professor took a huge gulp of sherry. "And this is how the equation gets evened out," he said as he swallowed. His face changed from red to gray and back again.

Two nights later, at the Commons of Magdalene College, a room lined with oak paneling and hung with portraits of scholars who had changed the world by inventing concepts like standard deviations and linear regressions, and who now were in a place where there was only one number, and that number was zero, Barron hosted a meeting.

Around a heavy maple table, Barron and Nicole sat with five scholars, three British and two Pakistani, and four wives. The men asked questions about the nature of their work, about the kinds of software they would be using for their analyses, about the work load. A Pakistani asked if pay would be proportional to financial results achieved. "Absolutely," Barron said. "That's the point of the exercise. Very closely proportioned."

"I think that is a sound principle," the Pakistani said.

"I find it highly questionable," said a young British man with an extremely upper-class South of England accent. "My whole training has been that effort and scholarship should be maintained, not money-grubbing." His voice dripped contempt.

"Perhaps this is the wrong field for you then," Nicole said evenly. "Your point of view is legitimate, but it's not really what we're looking for at BTA."

"We have accumulated cash in excess of depreciation requirements," Barron said. "We invest it. If we do it well, it helps the shareholders, many of whom are just ordinary workers and stewardesses and mechanics at BTA and, as I like to say, widows and orphans. We're not just making money to spend it on call girls and drugs."

"I entirely agree," said the wife of the man with the upper-upper accent. "Perhaps we ought to think of money-grubbing for people who need money as something better than mere greed. Let's talk about homes and schools. One hears Los Angeles is frightfully expensive."

"It's nowhere near as expensive as central London," Nicole said. "But it's probably a lot more expensive than Cambridgeshire."

Barron was impressed by Nicole. He had not known that fact. Nor had he realized that the area around Cambridge was called Cambridgeshire. Nicole's knowing those facts made him slightly uneasy. She was getting *really* smart, he thought.

"The schools in Los Angeles . . ." another Pakistani began. He had a plump blond English wife with a distinctly working-class kind of pinkish shiny makeup. "One hears that there are problems . . . uh, one doesn't like to say foolish things about non-whites, especially if one is nonwhite, but . . ."

"You heard right," Barron said. "The public school system of Los Angeles is gone. Finished. History. It was murdered by just the threat of busing in the late seventies. It was a good idea in concept, but the white families who could afford it all pulled out. That left the minorities, poorer whites, and a thoroughly demoralized teaching staff. It's a textbook case of public school demoralization through well-meant but catastrophic policy."

"So, it's public schools, then. Is that what I'm hearing?" asked a pretty young wife of another don-in-training. She had freckles on her nose and owlish horn-rimmed glasses. She had a warm, self-effacing smile and a deep, intellectual voice. In a way Barron could not explain to himself, she reminded him of Katy Lane twenty years earlier. He stared at her, and Nicole looked at him sharply.

"Private schools. That's what we call them in America," Nicole said. "Same as your public schools. But unless a miracle happens, it's private schools. But at the college level, we have excellent state-supported universities, and there's some savings there." Nicole smiled.

"I can tell you that you will be able to live in good suburban neighborhoods," Barron said. "Not great, not perfect, not the places where movie stars live. But definitely fine homes. I think you will find that if you do well for BTA, you will soon be able to live next door to William Hurt or Madonna."

"I have two teenage girls," said the woman who looked like Katy Lane, who looked far too young to have children of that age. "I worry about the precociousness of every kind of experience there in Los Angeles. From what I read, there is no childhood in L.A. Only a rapid movement from a pampered and emotionally impoverished infancy into a garish mimicry of adulthood, with sex and drugs and alcohol and disillusionment. I don't want to see my Page and my Blair exchange their St. Agatha's jumpers for rubber dresses and tattoos."

"I don't deny that it's there," Nicole said.

"But surely it's a matter for individual parental concern," Barron said. "I have never yet heard of a family where a mother and father paid full attention to a child, taught him and disciplined him, and then saw him turn into a monster."

"Or her," Nicole added.

246

"Have you children, Mrs. Thomas?" a Pakistani wife asked cheerfully.

"I'm not Mrs. Thomas," Nicole said, about ten times too cheerfully. The rest of the table looked embarrassed. Had they heard? Nicole wondered. Did they know, even here in Cambridge?

"We're not married to each other," Barron said, again, too hastily, too cheerfully, too heartily. "But neither of us has children, and, as far as we know, it's still true that parents make the difference."

"May I ask another question?" said the Pakistani husband of the woman who had asked the question about Nicole's children. "In your analysis, do you follow technical analysis or fundamentals?"

"That's like asking if I believe in the Ptolemaic system of planetary movement or the Newtonian/Galilean theory," Barron answered. He was deeply relieved to have gotten away from whether or not Nicole was his wife or had any children. "Technical analysis is just a selling proposition. It never touches the ground of reality at all. It is not tied to anything but its own tail. Reading tea leaves would be more productive. There is only one kind of analysis: fundamentals of value and management.

"I have one rule above every other," he said, warming to his subject. "I don't buy markets. I buy companies, and if they're good, I hold them forever. If they go down, that's just an opportunity to buy more. I learned that from Warren Buffett."

"Hear, hear," said the woman who looked like Katy Lane. "My father worked in the City for forty years, and he used to say exactly the same thing. Did well for his clients, too, although they never thanked him for it in any lingering way. I shall speak with Nigel about it, but I am definitely in your corner, and if you can't sell him, perhaps I shall work for you myself via PC over the international telephone wire."

"And I would be glad to have you," Barron said.

By the time the meeting was finished, it was dark. Barron hailed a taxi to take Nicole and him to the railway station. As they arrived, they saw a commotion of some sort. An immense black Daimler was pulling away from the station. Two motorcycle police rode in front of it and two behind. In front and behind also were police cars with rotating blue lights. The crowd was waving gaily at the car.

Queen Elizabeth II waved back and smiled.

Perhaps it was because she was preoccupied with what had happened at the meeting. Perhaps it was jet lag. Perhaps it was the accumulation of a stream dammed up by the strongest and weakest of adhesives, human denial, or perhaps because she was excited at seeing the Queen, but as she stepped out from the curb to get to the ticket windows at the Cambridge station, Nicole Miller did not see a young woman student on a bicycle passing by. The woman tried to stop, but she was on top of Nicole instantly. There was a cry and a thud and a screech, and Nicole was lying in the street, with a bicycle on top of her, a gash in her shin, and blood seeping out from her leg onto the street.

"Jesus," she said, "this hurts."

Barron picked up Nicole in his arms and carried her to a taxi rank. The first driver Barron saw said he would not take a passenger who was bleeding. Barron told him he had better take her or he would be the one who was bleeding, and would lose his cab as well.

In a few minutes, they were at the Royal Hospital, Cambridgeshire. Barron helped the hobbling Nicole into the emergency room. A bored woman reading *The Sun* did not even look up when they entered.

"I have a hurt woman here," Barron said. "Bicycle accident."

"Fill out these forms," the woman said without lifting her face out of the newspaper.

"Get a doctor right now," Barron said, "or you're going to be in court for the rest of your life. Right now."

The doctor was a young West Indian. His name, incredibly enough, was Stafford Cripps Mombasa. He wore dark glasses and cornrows, but had an astonishingly poised manner of exclamation and explanation. Contusions of the calf and the Achilles tendon.

248

Minor lesions of small veins. A possibly bruised femoral artery. Definite bruising of the femur. "Keep her in bed for a week at least, mon," he said. "No more disco dancing. No more reggae. No more party-hearty for this woman."

Barron took two adjoining suites at the Cambridge Varsity Apartments. They were usually employed to house visiting firemen and well-to-do parents of undergraduates. Now Barron had them rigged into a sort of hospital room, with three shifts of nurses, a sitting room, a dining room, and two bathrooms. There was also a tiny kitchen in each suite, and Barron hired the chef from Jean-Pierre, the topnotch restaurant next to Magdalene College, to make lunch and dinner.

For one week, Nicole was taken care of in a way she could not have dreamed of before she met Barron. He stayed by her side and read while she read. He talked on the phone to his associates in New York, Tokyo, and L.A. while she dozed fitfully.

When she awakened, or wanted to be told a story, he explained to her about the decline and fall of the Roman Empire. Like all successful men and many unsuccessful ones, he had his own theory about the parallels between the fall of the Roman Empire and what was happening in America.

He told her about how the Romans had brought in Goths to do their fighting and manual labor. Eventually, the Romans became habituated to leisure. The Goths became habituated to work and struggle. That was how the Roman Empire fell. It was because the Goths inside the Empire became powerful and numerous, but felt no loyalty to the Empire. When it was challenged from outside, largely by other Goths, it had no able-bodied Romans to defend it.

"It's just the same in the West," he said. "We bring in all of these black people and Mexicans and Orientals. We expect them to do our dirty work. We expect them to empty our bedpans and be our actuaries and harvest our crops. And we think they'll be happy always to be at the servant's table. But it won't work like that. They know they're growing. They know they're tough. They'll take over in some fields, just the way they have in boxing and basketball. They deserve to. They'll have enormous political power. They deserve to be there as well. That's why it's called democracy. But don't expect them to fight for us endlessly unless they're made full partners.

"You either integrate for real or expect the society to collapse. If it turns out it's just plain against people's nature to really integrate, then there'll just be chaos for a long time. But societies don't die from wars with other countries. Never. You can't find a single example in three centuries. Societies died from the inside out, and that's happening to us.

"Look at L.A. It's a colonial city like Delhi in 1935. Dark-skinned people do all the hard work. They're the ditchdiggers and the nannies. They're just lying around on street corners waiting to work. But they're also waiting to vote and take power. When they do, we've got to make damned sure they're committed to the system and feel like it's their system."

Nicole would lie next to Barron in the dark, with the omnibuses and the taxis and the drunken university boys roaring past their windows. She would hold Barron's arm until she fell asleep. When she woke up in the morning, Barron would be on the speaker phone to Tokyo, checking on the prices of Yen-denominated notes, marvelously reset so that the interest rate kept falling as the dollar fell, and making her coffee with one hand as he wrote down numbers with the other.

In the afternoon, he rented videos. They lay in bed and watched *Gone With the Wind* and *Funeral in Berlin.* Then Barron and Nicole would take a nap until Klaus, the Alsatian cook from Jean-Pierre, came over.

Oh, happy day. Nicole sang it over and over in her head when Barron was singing to her about how unimportant trade ratios were and how the only things that made a country great were willpower and education. He might have been a crank. He might have been a genius. Nicole didn't care. He was there.

After one week and one day, Dr. Mombasa came over and palpated Nicole's leg below the knee. "This leg is healed, woman," he said. "Get up and walk and sin no more."

"You mean we can go home?" Nicole asked.

"I mean you can go anywhere you damn well please," Dr. Mombasa said. "I mean you had better start getting some exercise on that leg or it'll stop healing. That's what I mean," said Dr. Mombasa.

Nicole felt a sudden, intolerable wave of rage and panic like the gushing of an oil well. All of the happiness she had felt turned to nitroglycerin.

When Barron went out to talk to Professor Fundador about the care and feeding of Cambridge statisticians, Nicole packed her few belongings. She took out her Nikon and took photos of the apartment. Then she sat on a couch, alone in the dim light of late afternoon, and cried.

When Barron came back, she would not let him touch her. "I want to go home on another flight from you. When we get back, I think it might be better if we didn't see each other for a while."

"What are you talking about? We've just had the best week in human history. Are you kidding? Is this a joke? Is Mrs. Thatcher going to jump out of the closet?"

Nicole stared at the floor. She ran her hands through her blond hair. She cried and shivered like a wet mouse. "It's not a joke," she said. "It's gone far enough. It's been wonderful. More than wonderful. But it's gone far enough. I'll never stop loving you. I'll think of you every minute. But it's over. You'll always be in my heart, Barron, but I can't live like this anymore."

"Like what?" Barron asked. "Tell me, and I'll fix it."

"You can't fix it," Nicole said. "If you could have fixed it, it would be fixed. I saw those couples, talking about their kids, about their futures together. I saw them, and I felt so jealous I felt sick. I saw you looking at that little mousy wife. How long until one like her comes along and I'm history? I want to have a life with some future, Barron."

"We have a future," Barron answered, taking her hand. "We also have every day, and that's better."

Nicole slowly, very, very slowly, drew back her hand.

"No." Nicole shook her head. "We have a past now, and it's

a wonderful past. The best past anyone could ever have. But go to that mousy little woman with the glasses or back to Saundra or back to somewhere. I'll never stop thinking about you, Barron.

"But when we were together for this week and you took care of me, it was just the way it should be. I just can't go out into the world again, back into the real world where you're married to another woman. I just can't take the change ever again. This time just about killed me. The shift between having it right in a dark apartment and having it wrong in the sun is just too much, Barron. Too much."

"We have to talk about this," Barron pleaded. "This is like two high school kids—"

"No. Hug me, Barron."

She got up and leaned into Barron as he stood. He hugged her and started to stroke her hair. But this time it didn't work. She did not melt into him the way she usually did. She pressed against him for just a few seconds, and then she slung her bag over her shoulder, kissed him fleetingly on the lips, opened the door, walked through it, and was gone.

Barron looked at the closed door. It had marks from old coat-hooks. He could still smell her K.L. perfume. He walked rapidly into the bedroom. The maid had not yet made the bed. It smelled still of Nicole, of her perfume, of her hair, of her sweat. He lay on it where she had lain for that week. He held his hands over his eyes and smelled her smell.

22

A SEARCHING AND FEARLESS MORAL INVENTORY

For one day after Nicole flew back to Los Angeles, Barron stayed in the Cambridge apartment. Amazingly, the apartment came with a heavily built-in and fortified compact disc player and a Philips stereo system. Barron made a quick trip to a nearby student-run record shop and bought four CDs of Mozart piano concertos. For twelve hours, he listened to them each three times. His favorite, he decided, was a disc of numbers 23 and 19, played by Maurizio Pollini with the Vienna Philharmonic. He normally considered Pollini slightly maudlin and even schmaltzy. But in his mood, Pollini was perfect.

He lay on a couch in his living room, got under some covers, and let the music bathe him. He got up twice to have lunch and dinner, but other than those interruptions, he simply let Wolfgang Amadeus Mozart's genius, feeling, and acute sensitivity to life carry him along. He was, so to say, floating in salty, buoyant water, borne up by the greatest talent who ever lived.

Barron had often found himself thinking about Mozart at odd moments. For example, he would be waiting for a meeting with Bob Greenhill at Morgan Stanley, when suddenly he would see a young executive in the full Paul Stuart gray suit, yellow suspenders, white shirt, and red necktie pass by. The young man would carry a sheaf of papers and look as if the world would end if he did not get to his destination within the next five seconds. A clause in a breakup-fee agreement might not be changed. An equity player in Cincinnati might have to be paid ten thousand dollars more in commitment fees. Joe Flom might not get a fax of a missing page of an indenture. The world might end. Utter triviality, yet the lad was rich.

Mozart, on the other hand, had made the most beautiful, perfect art in the history of mankind. He had lived in pain and poverty and abandonment. What that said about the human condition was important. Perhaps it was all that was important.

At about ten o'clock one night, out of nowhere, there was a knock on Barron's apartment door in Cambridge. It was a porter with a sheaf of phone messages and three Federal Express envelopes. Barron handed him a five-pound note and went back to his sofa.

A few minutes later, there was another knock on Barron's door. "Just slide them through the slot," Barron said.

"I don't see how I can do that," said a refined woman's voice.

Barron got up and walked to the door. There, in a raincoat (Barron had not realized that rain was falling), her hair in a bun, carrying a dripping umbrella, was the don's wife who looked like Katy Lane.

"May I come in?" she asked.

"Well . . ." Barron said.

Barron tried to put a smile on his face. Pinning the wagging tail on the whipped dog.

"Remember me? My name is Astrid Anspacher. May I come in?" the woman said.

The woman looked at Barron. "I just wanted to talk to you," she said. "I had the impression that you were looking at me as if you knew me." Her eyes were glistening.

Barron wordlessly got out of her way. She walked into the room. She took off her raincoat and put it neatly on a chair. She was wearing under it a black silk dress with a surprisingly low neckline. She was also wearing magnificent pearls and no bra.

When she bent over to run her fingers through her hair and dry it, Barron could see her competent English breasts.

"What do you have to drink?" she asked eagerly as she sat down and crossed her legs. "Nigel is away in Glasgow for two days, and I heard from the manager that your colleague has left. I thought we might reminisce about the times we apparently had in some other life. You're about the most exciting thing to come through the statistics department since a buzz bomb blew it up in 1944. Decades before I was born, of course. What do you have to drink?"

Barron looked at Astrid Anspacher. She recrossed her legs and smiled again at Barron. Her teeth were slightly brownish. Still, she had that edge of want, that mixture of thin, intense whippet intelligence, and those firm breasts and much longer legs than Barron would have guessed. A superb package for the visiting American businessman. Perhaps she needed some footnotes for a study on the precocity of experience. Certainly, she was not there to compare theories of the efficient market.

"You know," he said, "you remind me of a woman I used to be hopelessly in love with. A woman whom I met in a jail where I had been arrested for demonstrating for civil rights. That was a long time ago now."

"Do tell," she said, "and by the way, who do I have to screw to get that drink?"

Barron sighed wearily. "Not me," he said. "You are really beautiful. Flat out. And just the kind of woman I like."

Astrid laughed and said warily, "But?"

"But my life is complicated. And I don't feel so happy today. So maybe we had better continue this at another time."

Astrid Anspacher looked intensely at Barron. Her eyes misted up again. "You know," she said, "I think I will move to Los Angeles. It's not all Sodom and Gomorrah, is it?"

"Just parts of the San Fernando Valley," Barron said. "I will always remember that you thought of me," he added. "It's the only good part of the trip."

"Yes, well, you'll get her back," Astrid said. She got up and slipped on her raincoat. She picked up her umbrella. "It's impossible that this kind of feeling should go unrewarded."

"Let's ask Mozart."

"Yes, well, not right away," Astrid said, and then she was gone.

When Astrid Anspacher left, Barron went into the bedroom. He took a deep whiff of K.L., and lay down. In about ten minutes, he fell asleep. When he awakened, it was late at night. He looked for a book he carried with him. He read a passage about everything that happened in life being supposed to happen. Then he threw the book against the wall.

He picked up that day's *Financial Times* and looked at it. Its print might as well have been in Sanskrit. He threw it into the corner as well.

He went into the bathroom and washed his face. As he did, he suddenly started to sing, without premonition, "We shall overcome, we shall overcome, we shall overcome, some day . . ." His voice swelled with feeling as he sang five different verses. He sang as tears streamed down his cheeks. He sang as he laughed. He even sang as he called his London office to make airplane reservations to go home, wherever that would be. For the next few days, it would be New York City.

23

THE CHARMER

Nicole Miller could not get over how much the man looked like Robert De Niro. She first saw him standing in line at Heathrow to get on her TWA flight back to LAX. She noticed through her fog of confusion, resolution, and doubt. He had that same boyish look mixed with an almost frightening aspect of self-absorption. He wore a professorial brown suit with leather elbow patches and a blue shirt, with a red-and-blue tie that she immediately recognized as Hermès.

He was sitting one row behind her in business class. In the second hour, when she got up to ask for hot water for tea (astounding, the difference in service between first class and business), he was also at the stewardess station, asking for fresh, not canned, orange juice.

The stewardess told him there was no fresh in business class. He looked at Nicole, smiled that boyish De Niro smile, and shrugged as if to say, "You can't stop a guy from trying."

An hour later, he came by looking for a magazine and asked if he could sit next to her. "There are two men who smell like ashtrays next to me," he said. "Asleep. Snoring."

He was a professor of archeology, he said. At Brown, in Providence, Rhode Island. He had just been on a dig near Tartus,

Syria. A major find of Phoenician artifacts. Apparently something akin to the Port Authority, only in the Levant, more than three thousand years ago. Many extraordinarily well-preserved chests of coins and jewelry. He was supported by the Los Angeles County Museum of Art, he said, and he was on his way back to give his report to Mrs. Chandler, among others. He might well have to stay in Los Angeles for as much as a year to "fully digest the magnitude of the find and process the artifacts" as they returned from Syria.

His name was Arturo Karras. His mother had been Persian, from a family in Qum, Iran. Distantly related to Shah Reza Pahlavi. His father had been a professor of antiquities at the University of Athens. For himself, he had grown up mostly in London and New York, where his father had enjoyed visiting sinecures at the Victoria and Albert Museum and at Columbia University.

He was thirty-two years old, but Nicole must not hold that against him. "I was the youngest full professor in the Archeology Department at Brown," he said, "and I had to fight against youth bias there, too."

At LAX, when the arriving passengers were wrung out as if they were dirty, hot, wet towels, Nicole had a car and driver waiting. After all, she was still an officer of BTA. She still had standards. Arturo said that he was on a scholar's stipend, and he would take a bus to the room at the Hollywood Holiday Inn that the Trustees of the LACMA had reserved for him. Nicole insisted on giving him a ride. "I do so little for culture," she said. "This is one little thing I can do. Anyway, I'm not paying."

Since Madame was being so kind, perhaps Arturo might return the favor by taking her to dinner on any evening at her convenience. Perhaps also, since Madame was being so kind, she would drop him off not at the Holiday Inn, but at the home of a friend on Westknoll Drive in West Hollywood. By taking her car, he had a few extra minutes, and he would visit a friend who had been an undergraduate with him at Columbia, now a composer at MGM-UA.

258

It would be easy to think that Nicole's politesse toward Arturo—frankly, her interest in him—showed that she was callous or had already forgotten about Barron. It would be easy, but it would be wrong, and that's for sure. In fact, it would do an injustice to love.

Nicole listened to Arturo with one ear. She watched him with one eye. The other parts of her were still watching a documentary entitled *The Nicole and Barron Story*. She was seeing him at the meetings. She was hearing him explain about his business. She was seeing them together in bed, with her head on his chest. She was hearing him do a deal, hearing him praise her work, seeing him visit her in her office. She was seeing him bring her pastries in their apartment in Cambridge. She was seeing his stunned face when she walked out.

If she showed an interest in Arturo, that did not mean that Barron was out of her thoughts, any more than if she had cut her wrists and put a tourniquet on them meant that she was only thinking about the tourniquet and not about the blood.

On the third night she was back in town, when she had been in to work only once and had spent the rest of her time bicycling on the cement boardwalk in Venice, Arturo took her to dinner at a little Greek place on Cahuenga and Mesa in Hollywood. It had a belly dancer. A number of people dashed in from cars with the motors running, talked frantically with the captain, and then ran out with something clutched in their palm. The food, mostly chicken livers of various kinds, was incredibly greasy. She ate salad. Arturo ate everything with relish. He insisted on ordering ouzo. Nicole, of course, did not drink.

He politely kissed her on the cheek when they stood on the sidewalk and waited for the valet to bring his rental car. "I see your sorrow," he said. "I respect it. I know you need it. But I also see your promise," he said. "God does not make a woman as beautiful, as overflowing with love as you, to be left alone to grieve. I hope I may speak so impertinently."

On their next date, by which time Barron had not called her and she had not called him even though she knew he was back in New York, he took her to a café in a tiny cabin above a rise in Topanga Canyon. From it, they could see the lights of Santa Monica stretched out and glittering below, ten miles away.

She ate delicious fresh salmon grilled over a mesquite fire. There were only two other diners in the minute restaurant. In the middle of the room there was a potbellied stove crackling and hissing.

"I love this spot because it is timeless," Arturo said. "Like you. Like the beauty of antiquity that is my life's work, it is not something of the moment."

"I'm just a marketing woman having a bit of a problem right now," Nicole said. "I'm not a timeless beauty. I'm just another loser."

"No," Arturo said with surprising vehemence. "It does not matter if you have no money or no power in this world. In your face, in your body, is all of the promise of eternity. I have seen faces like yours on vases from the time of the pharaohs. I have seen figures like yours on reliefs from the temples of the Acropolis. There is something in you like this spot. Timeless. Money is paper. Power is an autumn leaf. Beauty is forever." He did not mention rats or elephants or broken tusks.

Remember, Nicole was from Jonesboro, Tennessee. She had met college boys and sports fans and a gym teacher and agents and businessmen. She had not met any poets or international travelers or archeologists, and only one ex–Peace Corps volunteer, and she had been charmed by him. She had lately been around power and money. She had not been around words about time-lessness and sculpture.

"May I pour you just a hint of Chardonnay?" Arturo asked. "You are safe here, in the mountains, in the granite, in the timelessness that matches your own."

On Nicole's shoulder, an imp appeared. The imp said that Nicole had been so incredibly good about alcohol for so long that she had in fact defeated the imp. He told her that in point of fact, she was no longer powerless over alcohol. In point of fact, alcohol was powerless over her. At this stage of her life, she could drink,

260

take drugs, enjoy herself like a normal person. She was no longer in any danger from anything as insubstantial as alcohol. In this beautiful spot, starting a new chapter in her life, with as much shrieking pain as she was trying to keep mute, one drink could not possibly hurt her. She was not an addict after all. She had beaten the problem. That was what the imp said.

From now on, the imp said, you need not avoid the scenic regions of France and the Napa Valley, the lochs of Scotland, the hollows of Kentucky, the majestic icy steppes of Russia, the high plateaus of the Andes, that you were once afraid to visit. You are no longer an addict, said the imp. You are free, and you should celebrate your independence.

"One glass," said Nicole. She looked around to make sure that no one she knew from the program was nearby, and then she lifted the glass to her lips and drank.

The problem was that as soon as the first taste of Far Niente hit her throat, she had a wave of remembrance of how her life had been before she met Barron. David Sonnenbaum. Tony. Marsha Grossman. Terror about money. Ms. Middle. The Iranians. The black girls in the see-through panties. The months and years of losing everything, of being an atom in a whirlwind of confusion and attack.

The further problem was that when she thought about that, she then thought about how Barron had lifted her above all of that, how he had taken her from nowhere to somewhere high and dry and magnificent.

The third problem was that when she remembered that, she also recalled a rush of pearls, and waking up with a man next to her whom she was not ashamed of, and having a man read to her while she dozed in a warm room in Cambridge.

And then she felt that she desperately needed another glass of wine.

When she had that, when she had that peculiar rush of agitation and excitement that one feels before the buzz hits, she remembered walking out on the man who had saved her life.

When she remembered all of that, and thought that she would

now be plunged immediately back into the world she had known before Barron, only with a few dollars in the bank, she decided that she had better order another bottle of Far Niente.

"Do you have any coke?" she asked. "To level this off?" By total chance, he did.

At four in the morning, naked in bed, with a distinctly bad-smelling, touching, pushing, invading Arturo next to her, she heard her telephone ringing. She had an idea who could be calling at that hour. She did not want to know for sure. No matter who was calling, she did not want to be in touch. There was just too much terror at that moment. Of loss, of guilt, of the future, of retribution, of a world that no longer had any order.

Nicole finally fell asleep at noon, with the crucial help of four Tuinal that she had been given by Mimi just in case.

When she woke up at eight that night, she felt the worst she had ever felt. The physical effects of the hangover of alcohol and cocaine and barbiturates worked beautifully with the guilt and idiocy she felt about herself to pound her feelings into a vicious, swampy, self-loathing, catastrophic mush.

She walked into Mimi's room. Mimi was lying naked on her bed with her hands over her breasts watching a rerun of "I Love Lucy," giggling.

"That guy was sure a greaseball," Mimi said. "He tried to put some moves on me when I got back from work. You were passed out cold. Off the program?"

"I hurt, Mimi," Nicole said. "I hurt so bad."

Then she collapsed onto Mimi's bed. With Lucille Ball in the background saying "Wahhhhhh" as usual, Nicole Miller cried real tears. They were the saltiest tears she had ever cried. She could hear the traffic going by on Holloway. She could hear the shouting of people coming out of Tower Records. She could feel the power bass of fools riding by in Jeeps with 300-watt amplifiers playing Tone Loc. But what she mostly felt was tears so salty that they burned her cheeks as they fell. And total despair.

"God," she cried. "What the hell happened?"

262

"You're confused," Mimi said, stroking Nicole's blond hair. "You're confused. You sleep with me tonight."

"I wish I were dead," Nicole said. "Just dead, dead, dead."

At nine that night, when Nicole was still crying, she got a telephone call. It came in on her Phone-Mate. It was from her mother. "Darling, it's been raining and miserable for several days now, but when we think of you enjoying your wonderful life in California with that nice Mr. Thomas, we feel as if you are truly living for the whole family."

Nicole listened to the message and went back into her room. She walked into her walk-in closet and looked at herself naked in her full-length mirror. She looked horrible. Not just bad. Horrible. Incredibly different from the way she had looked that day she left England. Just ghastly. Like an old woman. Like she had gone in forty-eight hours from young to old and defeated, skipping middle age altogether.

She wanted to see if perhaps she would look better if she put on some makeup. Just an idea. When she was looking for the Chanel kit that Barron had given her, she noticed that her jewelry box was open.

The pearls were gone, of course. So was the diamond promise ring from Fred. So were the emerald earrings from Beverly Hills Stones. So were the diamond twist earrings from California Jewelsmiths. So was the set of diamond-and-pearl earrings. So was the circular brooch rimmed with diamonds. So was a little plastic sack with one thousand dollars in cash and another one with five hundred pounds that Barron had insisted she carry around with her in case of dire emergency in Margaret Thatcher's England.

He had even taken her forty-five dollar amethyst earrings that Jeff Boone had given her for the Sigma Chi U.T. Christmas Dance in 1981.

Her Merrill Lynch statement was gone. So was her checkbook. So were her wallet and her credit cards.

Of course, the next day no one at the Los Angeles County Museum of Art had ever heard of an Arturo Karras. There was no such person on the faculty at Brown. He was not a graduate of Columbia.

It took Nicole Miller a day to make sure that the First Credit and Assurance Bank, a private bank whose largest customer was Barron Thomas, would not honor any of the fifty thousand dollars in checks that had been written on her account in one day. On the same day, she was able to stop her MasterCard, her Visa, her Diner's Club, and her American Express. Four hundred dollars was gone from the ATM, and that was gone forever. Kevin Hanley, her man at Merrill Lynch, had hung up on the man and called the FBI when he tried to sell her stock and get cash for it on the same day.

*T*hrough that whole day of telephone calls, Nicole could think of only one phrase, which she said to herself over and over again, on her knees, in her bedroom: We admitted that we were powerless over alcohol and that our lives had become unmanageable.

Unmanageable. Before she went to sleep, Nicole threw away the sheets and pillowcases that Arturo Karras or whoever he was had lain upon. She took the longest, hottest shower she had ever taken. It was not enough. She felt as she fell asleep as if she were a refugee from West Beirut who had moved to Beverly Hills and in one day found herself back on the Green Line again. When she slept, she dreamed of drowning in a whirlpool of confusion. When she awoke, she wished she were still asleep.

24

CUNNING, BAFFLING AND POWERFUL

A few words about Barron's visit to New York: Saundra Logan Thomas actually picked up Barron at the airport. She was waiting for him at his gate. He did not even know that she knew he was arriving. She looked spectacular in a black silk dress and magnificent pearls. She had red hair, which looked as if it had been colored by Botticelli. She was smiling and enthusiastic. She hugged Barron and slipped her arm through his and asked him about his trip.

As they walked out of the terminal, Saundra's Cadillac sedan, a discreet black Fleetwood, far smaller than what Barron had expected, glided forward and scooped Barron and his wife up. The driver was a trim, athletic black man named Todd. He took Barron's luggage and put it in the trunk.

On the curb, other passengers stared at Barron and his red-haired, beautiful wife, and their driver, and their car. God, they must think I'm lucky, Barron thought. They must think this is what any sensible human being has always wanted out of life.

In fact, Barron felt pretty good about the tableau himself. He looked like a winner. Saundra looked like a winner. For an instant, Barron thought that it all looked right. There was nothing wrong with the picture. It looked great. Listen to him. Even after Cambridge.

Barron was with his wife. He was not with his mistress. His wife was sober and cheerful. He was rich, hurtling down the Van Wyck in a Cadillac. His wife was holding his arm and acting as if she did not hate him.

"Thank you, God," Barron said to himself.

That night, Barron took a tour of his and Saundra's home in Bedford. She had redecorated it, and done a beautiful job. Everything was up to the moment. The floors were no longer tile. Instead, they were bleached hardwood. The windows were all white French sashes, with brass fixtures. The walls were white, with the photorealist art that Barron had always loved: Goings and his diners, Estes and his trucks, Lichtenstein and his crying comic-book characters. Lithographs, in lucite frames. It was as if she had redone the house just to suit him.

Before he fell asleep in bed next to Saundra, he talked to her about the days in New Haven. Helping the cafeteria workers to strike. Lying down in front of police cars on Elm Street. Always, the haunting message at the cemetery gate across from the Sterling Law Building: THE DEAD SHALL BE RAISED.

"And remember when we showed *Zabriskie Point,* and someone in the movie was talking about how beautiful it was just to see the sunset and feel the wind, and right behind us in the audience, Dick Player whispered real loud, 'Oh, wow,' and everyone in Linsley-Chittenden cracked up?"

"And remember when you told Gordon Sputak that law school was just boot camp for the lackeys of the rich?" Saundra asked. "And everyone cracked up?"

"I only said that because the really smart guy, Duncan Mac-Lean, said it to me," Barron said. "I only said it because my stomach had been super upset that morning, and the infirmary had given me paregoric, and I was as high as a kite."

"Still, it was brave," Saundra said. "And speaking of paregoric, I've really been so good in the program. I mean, I'm doing it for you, and it's really working. And it really means a lot to me for you to know it."

"I can see it," Barron said. "You can't imagine how much it means to me. It's a miracle, Saundra. A true miracle."

Barron fell asleep holding her hand, listening to the sound of the waves of Westchester breezes blowing through the maples in the back around the pond. Maybe, he thought, maybe it's all over. Maybe the fever is broken. Maybe I can really be back with the woman who owns the past. Who controls the present controls the past. Who controls the past controls the future. Something like that. Maybe everything was just a bad dream and now it's all right.

At about three in the morning by the Nakamichi clock radio next to the bed, Barron was awakened by a crashing sound. He opened his eyes. Saundra was not in bed. He threw himself out of the bed, ran out the bedroom door and down the stairs. He could still hear crashing noise coming from the kitchen. He pushed through the swinging louvered door and walked into the brightly lit room.

On a stool at the white Formica table sat Saundra. She was in her robe and her silk pajamas. About her feet were dozens of broken glasses and a few broken wine bottles. She ignored them. Her eyes were red, bulging, bloodshot. Her face was broken out in red splotches, with a sheen of sweat over her pale skin. She held a tumbler with ice and clear liquid.

"What the hell are you looking at?" she asked.

"I'm looking at you. What are you drinking?"

"Just tonic," Saundra said. "Just tonic. Go back to bed."

The room reeked—not just smelled, but reeked of vodka. Barron was afraid of the pilot light from the Jenn-Air meeting the fumes.

"How did this happen?" Barron asked, pointing at the broken glass. He noticed that Saundra's left foot was bare and bleeding. She had a pink ballet slipper on the other foot.

"I don't know," Saundra said. "What do you care? Go back

to sleep. Go back to sleep and dream about your little prostitute from Mississippi. Go lie in bed and jerk off about that whore. I don't need you. I don't need your precious dick. There are plenty of men around and they do it just the same as you, and they're not in such a goddamned hurry to stop and get back to the *Wall Street Journal.*"

"Your foot is bleeding," Barron said. He picked up a towel and ran it under scalding water in the sink. Then he leaned down and started to pick pieces of glass out of Saundra's skin. At that range, the smell of alcohol was even more overpowering. Barron took out one long sliver and several smaller fragments. He could feel how warm Saundra's blood was. To him, even her blood smelled of Stoli.

"Don't try to kiss up to me," Saundra said. She kicked at him with her ballet slipper foot. Barron was not expecting the blow. He lifted up his hand to fend off her foot, and briefly lost his balance. When he stuck out his hand to balance himself, he pressed his right palm down on what was once the neck of a bottle of Absolut vodka.

Instantly, a ray of pain like an electric paper cut raced through his hand. He saw that it was bleeding, with the blood dripping fast onto the white tile floor. Barron got up to find another towel.

"Don't expect me to feel sorry for you," Saundra said. "Find that little slut and get her to bandage your hand."

Barron wrapped a Martex dishtowel around his palm. If he ever wanted a change of career, he might like to go into research on the origin of brand names, he thought. Better to think about anything than what was going on right in front of him.

"I want to take you over to Scarsdale Memorial right now," Barron said. "I want you to pray with me right now and then go over to the alcohol unit."

"Go fuck yourself," Saundra said. "I'm not drinking anymore. This is just tonic." She held up her glass. Barron could smell the vodka from two feet away. "Don't pull that hypocritical crap on me with your praying shit. You're the one who has the little whore. I didn't start with men until after you started with that little wisecracking tramp. Why are you even back here? What the hell gives you the nerve to even be in this house? What if I had a man here? What if I weren't alone? How would I explain this whole thing?"

"You need to go to the hospital. You're sick. I've never seen you this bad. This is the bottle talking and it's really bad."

"I'm not bad. You're a paranoid maniac. You think I'm drinking when I'm totally sober. I'm just tired. That's all. I'm just tired of your shit and your persecuting me and your crazy delusions that I'm still drinking. You're the one who belongs in a straitjacket for thinking that I'm still drinking and thinking you can get away with having that little hooker in your life and that I'll let you get away with it.

"I want half of everything we have," she added. "Right away. Half. Call Si Lazarus or whatever smart Jew we have as our lawyer these days. Half. And don't try to fool me. I'm not stupid, you know. I'll go over everything with a fine-tooth comb. I'm not stupid. I want half. Right away. I want my share for all the work I've done."

Barron saw that blood was still dripping from Saundra's left foot. He bent down again and started to dab at it with another dishtowel. Saundra took a huge pull from her tumbler of vodka. "You are the biggest liar in the world," she said. "You don't fool me for one second. Fucking around, screwing every little slut that walks by, dripping little slits, and you expect me to just take you back? Forget it."

"Hold still," Barron said. He poured vodka from the bottom of a still intact bottle onto the towel and wiped it over Saundra's wounds.

"That hurts," Saundra said. "Don't touch me."

"You need to go to the hospital," Barron said. "Right now."

"Don't threaten me, you shit, you psychopathic shit," Saundra said. "I know you. You should be at the hospital, checking to see if you have any diseases I should know about. For all I know, you got something horrible from that bitch. Crabs or something."

Barron stood up. God grant me the serenity to accept the

person I cannot change, he said to himself. He took the glass gently out of Saundra's hand. "I'm not saying you're wrong," he said. "I'm not denying about Nicole. But I think that we're never going to get to the bottom of this unless you go into the hospital. Maybe we could make a start by just walking into the living room and getting on our knees and asking God to show us His will for us. Can you do that right now? Just for old times' sake?"

"No!" Saundra shrieked. "I can't do it now for any fucking sake. And I'm perfectly all right. You're trying to gaslight me, trying to make me think I'm crazy, so you won't have to pay me any alimony, so you can cheat me."

"I just want you to pray with me," Barron said softly, trying not to upset her further.

"Don't give me your phony, fake, sickening lowered voice!" Saundra screamed. "Like a TV preacher. You have a helluva nerve even talking about praying after the way you betrayed our marriage."

"Come on," Barron said. "I want you to go to the hospital, to the recovery unit. Right now. Right fucking now." He started to lift her off her stool.

Saundra suddenly picked up her glass of vodka and threw it in Barron's face. It stung his eyes. At the next instant, she started to scream and press a button under the counter. "Help!" she screamed. "He's trying to kill me!"

While Barron was still wiping his eyes, trying to see clearly, Todd, the athletic black man, walked into the kitchen through a swinging door that led to the servants' quarters.

"He's trying to kill me, Todd!" she screamed in a frenzy. "He's trying to make me insane!"

Todd looked at Barron and then at Saundra. "You'd best go to bed now," he said, as if he had said it many times before. "You'd best get some rest, madam. You're tired."

"That's it," Saundra said. "I'm tired."

"She's just tired, Mr. Thomas," Todd said. "Just very, very tired."

He walked over to Saundra and put his arm under her shoulder.

270

He lifted her smoothly off her stool. "Time to sleep now," he said.

"Yes," Saundra said. "And you stay with me in case that monster tries to get back into my bed and do anything to me."

Barron watched, numb, as Saundra and Todd glided out of the room. He could hear them going up the stairs. About ten minutes later, a slightly disheveled Todd reappeared in the kitchen, smoothing the collar of his pajamas.

"Mrs. Thomas drinks too much," Todd said. "She says wild things when she's drunk. She gets crazy. When she's sober, she's a wonderful woman to work for."

"Are you her lover?"

"No, I am not," Todd said, easing the white upper-class husband's greatest fear, that of being supplanted between the sheets by a burly handful of Afro-American proletarian potency. "But she is not a well woman. I have tried to pray with her, and she will not hear of it. Just will not hear of it."

"What do you try to get her to pray?" Barron asked.

"The Twenty-third psalm," Todd said. "The Lord is my Shepherd, I shall not want."

"Well," Barron said. "We'll pray for her." And then he and Todd did just that, on their knees, in the living room.

Barron went up to the bedroom and started to pack. He had his airline executives meeting in the morning. A fatigue so deep that it was a river of dense gravity, seeming to pull him under permanently unless he could float on a raft of willpower, tugged at him as he packed. Once, when he snapped open a suitcase from Mark Cross that Nicole had given him six months earlier, Saundra woke up and stared at him as if he were a complete stranger, then passed out again. God, he wished he were back in Malibu, with his dog, Miss Vicki. He wished he could even hear Miss Vicki breathe into the phone.

Another time, as he snapped shut his briefcase, Saundra awakened again. "Are you still here?" she asked, then passed out again.

As he left, he kissed her on her forehead. It was dank with sweat. Her breath was a hurricane of vodka. When he kissed her, she looked at him but said nothing.

271

In the kitchen, Barron asked Todd if he could drive him into Manhattan.

"I really shouldn't," Todd said. "If she gets up and gets confused, Serena really isn't strong enough to keep her quiet."

"Will you call a cab, then?" Barron asked.

While Barron waited for the cab, he sat in the living room. It was cavernous, white, ghostly, frighteningly empty, an ice cube of a room not beautiful at all in this light. He picked up a Trimline phone and dialed his number in Malibu. A message from Warren Barber at Morgan Stanley. A message from K.L., his secretary at BTA. A message from a reporter for *Barron's* doing a piece about the effects of monopolistic competition in airline hubs. That was all.

The taxi appeared in the circular driveway. It beeped its horn. Barron got up and walked to the door. As he did, he saw Saundra on the staircase that descended into the hallway. "Get out and don't come back," she said. She held a glass in her hand.

"You have to go to a hospital," Barron said. "You just have to."

In a sadly uncoordinated way, Saundra threw her glass at Barron. It hit the wall six feet from where he stood. "Get out of my house," she slurred.

Todd suddenly appeared and walked stoically toward her. He took her around the shoulders and led her back up to the bedroom again. Just as she reached the top of the stairs, Barron heard her scream, "No one's afraid of you anymore! No one. Just get out."

Then Todd took her into her room and closed the door.

In the lobby of the Helmsley Palace (Barron's pied-à-terre was being painted), Barron saw two Japanese who had invested successfully in his real-estate program for liquidating REITs. He saw a banker from San Francisco who had lent him money for a new purchase of 757's. He saw a young pale-blond woman sitting alone at the bar of Harry's. She smiled at him and asked if he would buy her a drink. She had watery blue eyes that reminded him of Katy Lane's eyes.

"Here," Barron said, flipping her a one-hundred-dollar bill. "Take it and go home and rest. That's what we all need. Rest."

"Let me rest next to you," the woman said. "You're halfway there already."

"No, thanks," Barron said. "I can only rest by myself these days."

"Then I'll owe you," the woman said.

Barron's room looked out over the spires of St. Patrick's. A dazzling ultrawhite frosty light bathed the tower and its cross. Behind it, the towers of Rockefeller Center swam in the same halogen light, like the castle turrets of Oz, remote, invincible, unmoved by human pain. Barron lay in his bed and watched the tower. At six A.M., the city began to stir and hammer and accelerate and honk, and Barron could rest no longer.

25

MERGERS AND ACQUISITIONS

In the time that Barron stayed in New York City after hell night in Bedford, he took "bold new initiatives," as *Fortune* later described them, to "dramatically raise the stakes in the private crap game that Wall Street knows as mergers and acquisitions."

First, he followed up on the airline owner's perpetual agenda of raising and fixing prices by ordering a rapid study of fares to all BTA destinations. He had one of his statisticians generate random numbers between six and thirty. He then had the same programmer randomize all of the destinations and routes. This might seem to be a simple exercise. But in fact the computer power necessary to truly randomize a grid that is already almost random is huge. It then took as much computing power to match the random fare increases between six and thirty percent with the random cities and different fares per route as it took to schedule an entire day's travel for almost one hundred thousand customers.

Market analysts responded to the resulting fare increases with wild enthusiasm. One analyst tried to figure out the logic of the different magnitudes of fare increases. He had his employer, Smith Barney, issue a press release explaining that they were related to the lift efficiency of the various kinds of aircraft used on each route, further refined by the load factor at that time of year.

To Barron, the securities analysts with their explanations were what the Three Stooges were to teenagers. In their fumbling, heartbreakingly obtuse efforts to mimic understanding, the analysts spoke volumes about human pretensions and limitations. They reminded Barron of the Three Stooges trying to convince someone that they were college professors, preverbal infants trying to sound like Oxford dons, simians trying to mimic genuine understanding.

The securities analyst, Barron often thought, was the perfect crystallization of man's helplessness before events and his endless aspiration to seem to be the master of phenomena over which he was totally powerless and uncomprehending.

Second, with the zooming BTA stock behind him, even as the market was clearly retreating from its July and August froth, Barron met for an early breakfast meeting with the five top M&A men and women at Morgan Stanley. In Warren Barber's spectacular aerie over the Avenue of the Americas, glittering with little lucite cubes marked with the first page of proxies announcing deals, Barron and Si Lazarus, recently rehired by Barron, went over the possible objects that might be traded for stock in BTA.

Five companies were considered. Viacom, an astounding powerhouse of cable TV and film library assets. No. Hollywood was for insiders, pure and simple. Delta Airlines, with probably the best routes and gates in America, but a board of directors who would literally pour gasoline on themselves on Broad Street rather than allow the company to be merged. Statue of Liberty Savings & Loan, an S&L in San Francisco that had grown from a tiny mom-and-pop operation into the largest S&L in the Bay Area. It had grown by taking in brokered deposits and using the money to buy immense quantities of junk bonds. Its CEO, Manuel Lopez, was the survivor of a Cuban concentration camp. He was rumored to have eaten cockroaches to survive. Now he was best friends with the powerful Ellis Lifschitz, head of high-yield debt at Lumpen Frères, a major hitter in junk debt.

"As far as I can tell," Barron said, "that S and L is bankrupt. It won't break out its holding of junk. Its top people are getting warrants for the bust-up deals Lumpen has done in the past five years that have made them all rich."

"Statue of Liberty has a lot of those warrants, too," said Barber, a tall man with coppery-colored hair and a perfectly fitting blue suit. "That's where the value is. In those warrants."

"Horse shit" Barron said. "I know Ellis Lifschitz. He wouldn't be giving out those warrants unless he was getting Statue of Liberty and Lopez to take down the junkiest junk he has in his inventory. You don't need to bribe people to buy good junk. You bribe them to buy the stuff you know is going to default."

"So?" asked Sheila Kryer, a whippet-thin woman banker with a prominent chin and distinct ketchup stains on her white silk blouse. "How much junk can there be compared with the warrants?"

"Quite a lot," Barron said. "If he's got sixty percent of assets in junk, and only five percent has gone bad, he's insolvent right now. It's much more likely that it's seventy-five percent gone. And I'll tell you something else. Those warrants are in there for Manny Lopez. Even the ones owned by the S and L. He'll buy them away from the S and L for two bits and make a billion dollars on them. But if anyone else buys Statue of Liberty that isn't in the Ellis Lifschitz Daisy Chain, those warrants are suddenly going to become worthless. So let's leave Statue of Liberty to the feds, who are going to wind up eating it anyway."

The fourth company on the screen was Eastman Kodak. "Quality through and through," Barron said. "Except for Johnson and Johnson, as blue chip as you can get. Top-notch management. I love that company. Two problems. No, three problems. One, Fuji is making a better thirty-five film right now. Pretty soon, they'll make every size better. I don't want to have to compete with Fuji. You get your ass handed to you when you compete with Fuji. Second, even if there were no Fuji, the company is fully priced. Third, they're going to have huge environmental claims down the road. I've had it with that."

276

"Okay," said Warren Barber. "A huge bite. Westinghouse Electric. The financing operation is manufacturing money. The appliance division is lean and mean. The heavy industry part is operating in a monopoly environment. No competition in a lot of lines. They're totally out of the hole on the nuclear stuff. The cable operations are a license to steal, not now, but down the road. The broadcast properties are the best or second best in every market."

"Sounds like Viacom only not as hard to deal with," Barron said.

"There's one big other way that Westinghouse is better," Warren Barber said. "It doesn't have Sumner Redstone owning a great big hunk of it. Ownership is widely dispersed. Just take this breakdown we made. Nothing confidential. Just some stuff we thought up, and tell us what you think."

"I'll tell you when I've read it," Barron said. "I'll tell you something else I'm worried about. The market has fallen by three hundred points in the last three weeks. It's going to open in about half an hour. I think it's got a lot more to go down. If I buy now, I'm gambling on stock value now and on break-up values. I'm trying to make paper ballerinas while the hurricane is blowing down buildings."

"I won't fight you on that," Warren Barber said. "You don't have to move today."

"I'll think about it," Barron said. "I'll think about all of it."

On his way out of the office, Barron watched a screen in the trading room that registered order imbalances. He saw something he had never seen before: According to the futures/cash ratio projections, the market was going to be down a hundred points within five minutes after it opened.

Barron was suddenly frozen with a realization. If the market were about to collapse, he was about to lose hundreds of millions of dollars in one day. His stake in BTA was now worth about $1.2 billion. It would be nothing for it to lose one-third of its value after its huge run-up after the fare increases. He could short it right then and there. If he did, he would save himself hundreds of millions of dollars. By just one order to the traders at Morgan Stanley, he could avoid a truly staggering debacle for himself, even if one were going to happen to the rest of the market.

On the other hand, if he did sell short any large block of his own holdings, he would hammer his stock into dust. Dumping even a part of his holdings would take away any of the blocks keeping the stock from free fall. He would be devastating the value of his stockholders' assets exactly as he protected his own. Furthermore, BTA was built to last, and the founder does not short a company built to last. Leave that to Lumpen Frères.

But he could do something. "Look," he suddenly said to Warren Barber and Si Lazarus, "I think the best move I could possibly make with my personal money is to buy more of BTA. I may very well take it private. I want you to tell the Big Board. I'll make an announcement at the end of the day. We'd better suspend trading."

Warren Barber and Si Lazarus looked at each other, then they looked at Barron, and then they laughed out loud. "You are a fucking pirate," Warren Barber said. "But a pirate for your own stockholders, and that's rare. I'll give you that."

As it happened, BTA did not trade at all on that day, October 19, 1987, or for the rest of the week. "By this one maneuver, which had other CEOs chewing the rug with envy," *Forbes* later wrote, "Barron Thomas saved his stockholders as much as a billion dollars and made himself the envy of the Dow Transportation Index. When the stock did open the next week, it was up six points, by far the largest gainer in the transports list, all on rumors of a management buyout that eventually did get proposed, only to get shelved when management instead went on the prowl for Westinghouse."

That was hindsight. On The Day itself, Barron was a basket case of anxiety and premonition. He had managed to stave off disaster on the BTA stock itself. But he had no idea of just how long that good fortune would last. The market was down five hundred in one day. For all that Barron knew, BTA would open the next morning and the market would be down another five hundred. For all that Barron knew, the world was coming to an end.

God, he wished Nicole were nearby. God, he wished the Saundra of 1969 was still alive. In fact, he had not heard from Nicole since Cambridge. K.L. had told him she was on a prolonged leave from BTA, but more he did not know. Saundra was with Faith Koen on a barge trip in Belgium.

He sat in his office on Fifth Avenue and watched the trades as they came across his monitor. They were a torrent, down, down, down, then a brief break, and then down again and again and again.

Barron called Warren Barber. "Is this based on some secret news that everyone else knows and I don't know?" Barron asked.

"The word is that it's selling out of Japan because the dollar is falling against the yen and we're going to need higher interest rates to get back the Japanese money, and the higher interest rates are going to hit the market really hard."

"You believe that?"

"Of course not," Warren Barber agreed.

"That kind of adjustment goes on over a year, not over a few hours," Barron said. "Anyway, the Japanese still get a better return on their stocks in Japan than they do here, and those stocks are getting murdered. My pals at Nomura tell me the imbalance there on the sell side is bigger than it is here. So what's happening? It's not the Japanese, or else the Tokyo market wouldn't be going down, too."

"You tell me. Some action on the Hill? Nahhh. Only the supply-siders would buy that."

"It has to be the portfolio insurance dumping index futures, sucking down the stock. No matter how much stock gets sold, there are so many index futures getting unwound on the portfolio insurance programs that the futures are always at a discount to the cash, so it makes sense to sell the cash part all day. It's that simple."

"If it's that simple, how come it doesn't stop? How come people don't say it's just a momentary thing and then buy back in?"

"Because the futures keep trading at a discount to the cash, and there's always money to be made selling the stock," Barron said. "Or it could be that I'm wrong, and that we really are in for a Depression. Or it could be something else. It could just be that all the traders in the Persian rug bazaar are getting a panic attack. Or it could be that *plus* the portfolio insurance. I'm going to think about it."

Barron went through his small library of economic statistics. He had his temporary secretary, a stoic Jamaican woman who could not possibly have cared less about the stock market, go out to Roy Rogers and bring him back fried chicken and a chocolate milk shake. The foods of his youth made him feel as if his life would go on.

He pored over what he had: Money supply was increasing rapidly; interest rates were stable; inventories were falling, not growing; the trade deficit was falling very slightly; industrial profits were climbing. There was a rumor about a House committee reducing the deductibility of interest used for takeovers. Journalist-lobbyists for Lumpen were already on the TV saying that this proposal was causing the crash.

Barron figured it out on his PC. The total cost to all businesses from the proposed deduction change would be about eight billion dollars per year. The loss on the Big Board so far that day was estimated to be above eight hundred billion dollars. No, the deductibility was not big enough to cause a crash.

By about two o'clock, Barron was convinced. The whole crash was an epiphenomenon. It just did not mean a thing except that there was a panic on the casino floor, probably caused by the sell programs of the portfolio insurers. There was nothing basic that was about to cave in.

Just as Barron realized that this meant that October 19 was the biggest buying bargain day in history if he had the steel balls necessary to do the deals, Ms. Reynolds, Ms. Sweetness Priscilla Reynolds of Jamaica, buzzed.

"Your wife on the line," she said.

Barron was concentrating so hard that he did not even think about whether to take the call. He just took it.

"Are we poor, Barron?" Saundra Logan asked by long distance. She sounded incredibly cheerful. "It's all over the news here in Flanders."

"No, we aren't poor."

"It's not going to make you jump out the window?" Again, she sounded amazingly cheerful.

"No."

"I just want you to know how horrible I feel about the way I acted the other night," Saundra Logan said. "I know I was really bad. I sort of black out but then I remember what I did. I am ashamed of myself, if that means anything to you. I really feel terrible about the whole thing. I must have acted like a monster."

"You bet."

"I'm going to the rehab unit of Mount Sinai when I get back," Saundra said. "I really think this time it's going to work. If you can just not do anything to set me off, I just know I can stay away from drinking, one day at a time."

Barron sighed. He looked out at the invisible torrents of despair pouring over the ghastly, Addamsesque Plaza Hotel, at the pigeons roosting in its crenellations. "I've heard it said at meetings that if you blame your drinking on anyone but yourself, you'll never stop," Barron said.

"Yes, of course. It's all up to my acceptance," Saundra agreed too quickly. "But I just want to be sure you're on my team, and not on that little slut's team."

"I want you to stop drinking, if that's what you mean," Barron said. "But I can't control you, and you can't control me, and if you use me as an excuse to stop drinking or to start drinking, you're not going to stop."

"That's exactly what I mean," Saundra said giddily. "You won't lift a finger to help me. I'm out there all alone."

"I've lifted quite a few fingers," Barron said. "I still have a gash on my hand from where I lifted a finger. I lifted a lot of fingers before I even met Nicole. If you think that's going to fly as an excuse, forget it. No excuses. You stop drinking no matter what I do or what anyone else does, or you don't stop. That's the program. You can have it if you want it, or you can make excuses."

"Fuck you," Saundra snapped. "Now when I see what kind of a shit you are, I see why I need the Xanax."

"You need it because you're a drug addict," Barron said. "If you stopped using it, you wouldn't need it."

"Let me know when you're about to jump out the window," Saundra said, and then she laughed, and then she hung up.

Barron rubbed his temples with both hands, then went back to the stock quotes. He got three calls from Warren Barber about the huge buying opportunities in the market, in GE, in Johnson & Johnson, in Ford. "I'll buy into the first two, but the auto industry in this country is a dead duck. The Japanese can kill it any time they want. But bring me other ideas."

The next call was from K.L. in Los Angeles. She wanted to be able to tell the people there something. "Are we in trouble, Barron?" she asked, with real concern in her voice. "Are we going to have a Depression?"

"I want you to tell everyone in the company that the airline business is in good shape, that BTA is the strongest carrier in the country, and that I do not contemplate any trouble at all because of a few days' market craziness. Also that I wouldn't be planning to buy it if I thought it had anything but a great future."

Such is the magic of myth that K.L. sounded genuinely relieved after she spoke to Barron. Employees of companies actually believe their bosses know something, Barron mused. It's incredible.

About ten minutes after K.L.'s call, Barron got a rushed telephone call from Si Lazarus. "You aren't going to believe this," he said. "But I just got a call from a lawyer at the SEC. They're real interested in just exactly how you happened to know to stop trading in BTA when the market was collapsing. They think there's something going on there. They also think maybe it's illegal market manipulation."

"To keep the stock from moving at all?"

"When the rest of the market is in the toilet? Absolutely."

"They think I rigged the whole crash, then rigged BTA to stay the same? Are they insane?"

"Barron, it's the SEC. It's federal bureaucrats."

"You've got a point."

"So, they want to come up to New York and ask you a few questions. About your relationship with portfolio insurers, about your short sales, about how serious you are about the buyout."

"About what steps I took to cause a crash, then protect my stockholders, in other words."

"Exactly."

"They want to ask a few questions?"

"Right. They want you to have counsel present."

"So the short sellers and the portfolio insurers and the program traders and Ellis Lifschitz and Lumpen Frères are taking eight hundred billion dollars out of the economy and the SEC wants to know why I bothered to protect my stockholders?"

"Right."

"You know what? Fuck 'em. Fuck them and the horse they rode in on. Make them subpoena me. Then appeal the subpoena. Then appeal that. Then sue for malicious prosecution. Then sue the guys at the SEC personally for interference with business advantage."

"Are you serious?"

"Goddamn right. I am sick of being pushed around. After L.A. Chemical and the Walsh family, I'm not going to just sit around and be the patsy anymore. If they want me, they're going to have to go after me. Come and get me. Like Little Caesar."

"Are you sure?" Si Lazarus asked. "Sometimes that just makes them mad."

"Fuck 'em," Barron said. He was suddenly energized with rage. He felt better than he had felt all day. The anger organized all of the confusion that had been disorganizing him all day.

The next call was from Saundra. Barron would not have taken it except that his secretary was not at her desk, and he was so stoked from his fighting words with Si that he wanted to fight with someone else.

"I just want you to know something," Saundra said. "Last night, I dreamed we were back in Washington, and I was in the backyard of our house near Georgetown, and suddenly I saw all the fireflies I used to see when I was a little girl, and I said, 'Barron, Barron, the fireflies are back.' I just wish everything were the same."

"I do, too," Barron said.

"It would be if you would just stop torturing me about having a little drink every so often. There's really nothing wrong with it. It's just that you're so strict about everything . . ."

But then the connection was broken and Barron did not even know where to call to get it back. All he knew was that the story about the fireflies, along with the talk about the drinking, made him feel as if his spine had been removed from his body.

By seven o'clock, as he was going over his own losses on his portfolio—his best stock, the *Washington Post,* had so many sell orders that it had never opened at all, but was reported to be off sixty points—he got a call from Steve Gage, his pilot and pal.

"Barron, it's been a hard day," he said. "I have a new Falcon Nine Hundred. Let's take it up and play with it. Let's take it to LAX and get away from all of this mess."

"You got it," Barron said.

From his limousine, he called Warren Barber. The young investment banker sounded as if he had just been through the spin-dry cycle on an industrial washing machine. "It's all hell out there on the street today. I think I'll see if my poolman needs help on his route in Peapack. Maybe the gardener will need people."

"Maybe I'd like for you to pick up a million Westinghouse," Barron said. "At market. From that guy in L.A. But no funny business. The real market."

" 'Funny business'? This is Morgan Stanley."

There was a pause on the line and then both men burst out laughing.

The bad energy of the day was faltering. Barron could feel it as he got out to the airport in Teterboro. The sky was dark and overcast. On the runway, the Falcon gleamed, white with gray pinstripes, its jet engines whistling softly in the nighttime silence of New Jersey. Barron waved at Steve in the cockpit, then climbed the few steps into the cabin.

It, too, was dark. Barron could make out leather seats and a chrome-ribbed coffee table. He was not familiar with the control module for the new Falcon, so he did not know how to operate the lights. In any event, he was far too tired to need or want lights. He sank into a seat on the airplane and waited for the welcome sound of the engines revving up. He could see the orange flames not quite totally hooded by the cowls of the engines. He could feel the strength of the jets pulling the airplane forward. He began to fall asleep. Perhaps, he thought, as he felt the threads of rationality unravel, as he started to imagine shopping centers in swimming pools, perhaps everything would come together eventually. Some day. Some sweet day, when the resistance of life was as slight as the resistance of sleep, everything would come together again.

He awoke over Memphis because of medium turbulence. The Falcon was bouncing about in the atmosphere, its wings reflecting far-off lightning, the lightning in turn making eerie blue-gray bubbles of light far to the south. It was as if the clouds and the night were manufacturing light and some of it was escaping from the factory, oozing into the night illegally.

Just to be a child, Barron thought. Just to be a little boy looking from his Memphis backyard at the blue light oozing into the night and to be bathed clean in that light. Just to be bathed clean. Just to be.

In his half-sleep, Barron sought to recall when he had last felt clean and alive and uncomplicated. It had something to do with a girl in a swing, in a park, in Point Dume, Malibu, with Canis Major floating high above.

Still largely asleep, Barron picked up the Wolfsburg and dialed Nicole's number in West Hollywood. She answered the phone on the second ring.

"Nicole," Barron said, "this has been the most horrible day. I miss you. I need you. I love you."

"Barron," Nicole said, "I am so happy you called. I'm such a jerk for not calling you when I was wrong. When is your plane getting in? I'll meet you at the airport. God, I've missed you. Barron, I'm sorry about what I did in Cambridge. I'm not going to promise to never get crazy again, but I'm sure going to try. From now on, all I want to know isn't who you're married to or what my name is. I just want you to love me tomorrow, forever, one day at a time."

26

DR. LOVE

December 22, 1987

Barron Thomas was worried. It was nine weeks after the crash. He sat in that most vulnerable of modern peacetime positions, chest bare, wearing only his underpants, on Dr. Clay Lewin's examining table. Through the double-pane windows, he could hear the traffic going by on Park Avenue. A Haitian nurse giggled loudly outside the door to the examining room. Dr. Lewin, a startlingly healthy specimen in his sixties, with a bushy black mustache, was fumbling with his charts and saying, "There's a problem here with your chest X-ray. That's really the only thing I'm seriously concerned about."

Goddammit, Barron thought. It wasn't enough that he was having this ongoing three-day fight with Nicole, and she was in fucking Tennessee, unable to stand next to him right now. It wasn't enough that Westinghouse was showing the resilience of a Bengal Tiger ball in fighting him off. It wasn't enough that the SEC seemed to have made a collective vow to give him heart disease.

What was that horror that Steve McQueen, star of his favorite movie, *The Great Escape,* had died from? Small-cell lung cancer?

287

Large-cell? Whatever it was, it had killed him in a few weeks. With no prior symptoms, as Barron recalled. Surely Steve McQueen had access to the best in medical care. If that's what the "problem" on Barron's X-ray was, how long did Barron have? How long to delay making decisions? How long to keep screwing up with the sure and certain belief that all Americans have that no matter how badly they hurt themselves today, all can be saved in the final reel. Maybe this was the final reel. Maybe this was one of those horrible European movies where things did not work out well in the end. Where issues did not get resolved, and life was endless frustration and sorrow. That was what a "problem" on the X-ray might mean. Easily.

"What, specifically, is the problem?" Barron heard himself asking in a voice that came from far away. A calm voice. The voice of a calm, confident man. Someone else's voice.

"Just a minute," Dr. Lewin said, fumbling through still more piles of folders.

No. He had not even been feeling any physical symptoms, and he had just come to Dr. Lewin for an annual physical, without the slightest hint that he had anything wrong with him except the dull edge of concern that he got when he was fighting with Nicole. And now, there was something wrong with his chest X-ray.

As far as Barron knew, there was absolutely no good at all that could come from having something wrong with his chest X-ray. Lung cancer. Heart disease. Maybe something else altogether. Nothing good.

Nothing but a far, far faster journey into eternity than he had been counting on. Nothing but a change from private planes and boardrooms and bedrooms to hospital corridors. Nothing but a constant diet of fear until the very end. That was what a problem with a chest X-ray meant, as far as Barron could think at that moment.

Life would not go on forever.

Barron Thomas, of St. Mark's School, North Dallas, and Yale, now of Barron Thomas Aviation, also of Bedford, Malibu, Los

Angeles, and Manhattan, also of Docket Number 579-65-8247 of the Securities Exchange Commission, would not have forever to keep making his mistakes. He would not have forever to keep figuring out what to do.

Finally, after what seemed like an hour but was probably thirty seconds, Dr. Lewin fished out a file, and drew from it an X-ray.

He stared cursorily at the negative and then at his diploma from the University of Cincinnati Medical School. "This is something they never prepare you for at med school," he said. "But it's something that you, as a man who runs an airline, must have happen all of the time."

"Just please tell me what the problem is with my chest," Barron said. "I'm concerned."

"Concerned." That was vintage Barron in negotiations. "Concerned." How about "screaming crazy"? Maybe that would be closer to the mark.

"The problem is my nurses," Dr. Lewin said. "I have the best equipment, up-to-the-minute technology, but nurses who don't know how to file. Nurses who can't put a patient's chest X-ray file in with his other charts. It took me a half-hour this morning, time I could have spent with other patients, to find your X-ray. You're a businessman. Surely you appreciate that waste of my time. My time goes for about twenty times what my nurse's time goes for, and yet I had to spend—"

"That's it?" Barron Thomas asked in a rush. "That's the problem?"

"Well, your X-ray looks perfect. Excellent for a middle-aged man. But the waste of time in my looking . . . Surely you can see it? What if you had to clean up all of your airplanes yourself—"

"Clay, I don't know whether to kiss you or strangle you," Barron said. "I'm outta here. Thanks."

Barron walked down the street to his office. A reprieve. Time enough. More time. That most precious of assets. More time in the sun washing over Park Avenue. More time to see shoppers with their last-minute gifts. More time to fly over empty prairies and lit cities.

Still, he thought as a cab narrowly missed him while he crossed Park at Fifty-seventh, still, it's not a circle. It doesn't go on forever.

Back in his office, where he ordered a green salad for lunch instead of the cheeseburger celebration of life he was craving, Barron went through his neatly typed list of telephone calls. One of them struck his eye: Ginette Miller. Nicole's baby sister. What was she? An eighth-grader? At some school in Jonesboro? P.G.T. Beauregard Junior High? Something like that. Or maybe she was in high school at Estes Kefauver. That's right, she was probably about an eleventh-grader now.

Ginette had called only once before, for an autograph of Carlos Wilde, the fifteen-year-old star of "Twelve Ways to Grow," the hit sitcom about a robot who lived with a family in Santa Barbara, and who also made ads for BTA.

There were also calls from his lawyer in Washington about the SEC, from his lawyers in New York, his lawyers in Los Angeles, and, of course, from Warren Barber, his man at Morgan Stanley, still hanging in for the kill on Westinghouse, as remote as that now seemed.

Better to call Ginette. She might have a message from Nicole, which would be what he really wanted that day.

K.L. put the call through. In a hushed voice, Ginette said, "Is this really you, Barron, or is this someone else who works for you?"

"It's me."

"Okay, because this is really secret," Ginette said in an even more hushed voice.

"Is it about Nicole?"

"Yes, it is."

"Is she all right?" Barron asked sincerely.

"Well, in a manner of speaking," Ginette said, a phrase which sounded odd in her child's Tennessee voice. "But this is definitely serious."

"Please tell me," Barron said.

"Well, did Nicole ever tell you about this guy Jeff Boone, who

290

she dated at U.T.? I mean, he's really cute, like this guy in Whitesnake, and he's not a big businessman like you, but he's doing great in his father's tractor business, and he just broke up with his girlfriend, and he's coming to town to take Nicole to lunch at the country club . . ."

Barron listened and asked questions for another few minutes. Then he politely thanked Ginette and got off the phone. Then he laughed out loud. Of all the eleventh-grade girl tricks! No, no, worse, an eighth-grade trick. Of all the jokes that happen to the CEO of a public company every day! How perfect! What a blast from the past.

He tried to laugh more. But it was a hollow laugh all the same. He told K.L. to hold his calls. He looked out the window at the Christmas lights starting to come on in the stores. He went to his bookcase and took down an album with photos of his and Saundra's days at Yale. He looked at just one photo, of Saundra and him practicing snake dancing for a demonstration in Washington, only the snake dancing was in front of the Yale Law School. They were in a line with some other students and their wives. Barron could only remember one of their names. Only one. Twenty years. Long time passing. Where have all the names gone, long time ago? One of them died of lymphoma right after law school. A sweet, hardworking boy named Michael Eggers. The other names had vanished.

Tears started to fall down Barron's face. Detachment—from love. That's what they called it. Not just from a woman he still loved. But from the past. From the magnetic, gravitational pull of the whole miracle that had been youth, the way that Saundra had taken care of him at Yale and at Camp Lejeune. Like cutting off a huge part of himself, a big healthy part along with a sick part of himself.

Please, God, he said to himself, free me from the burden of the past and let me go into the present.

Then he called Saundra in Bedford. Amazingly, she was at home. Between trips to Finland a few days earlier and to Celebes (again) tomorrow.

"Saundra," he said, "I will always love you. Always. And I will always be grateful for what you have done for me and for us. And I will always provide for you. But we are over as a married couple. You might want to see a lawyer about this . . ."

"Can it wait?" Saundra asked. "I'm really busy packing for my trip. Can we put it on hold for a few more months? I mean, it's gone on for so long, surely it can wait a little longer, can't it?"

"No," Barron said. "It can't wait."

"That's you all over, trying to upset me, trying to ruin my trip, which is about saving the Celebes rain forest, for your information—"

But she did not get to finish, because Barron had hung up. He slammed the scrapbook closed and went out to K.L.'s office to tell her to get in touch with Steve Gage.

27

BALLAD OF A
TEENAGE QUEEN

December 23, 1987

Panther Stadium at Estes Kefauver High School. Night. It was between semesters, Nicole figured. Anyway, the place was totally empty. Usually, at least some rooms in the high school were lit up. But not tonight. There was not a soul in the offices of the student paper, which used to be called *The Volunteer,* and then *The Loser,* and then, for a few months when Pink Floyd was hot, *The Floyd.* Nicole could remember it as if it were yesterday. The whole student body voted to change the school anthem from "The Tennessee Waltz" to "We don't need no education. We don't need no thought control. No dark sarcasm in the classroom. Teacher leave those kids alone."

Now, according to Ginette, in Reagan Amerika it was probably *The Volunteer* again. With ads for the Mercedes dealership in Knoxville. Anyway, that office was dark. So was the office of the yearbook, *The Great Smoky Annual.* No one working late there pasting up, making layouts. Nicole remembered that one, too. The kids used to call it The Great Smoker, and the year she graduated, there had been a drawing of a student hefting a great big Bob Marley–sized joint with a stunned Robert E. Lee looking on. Right on the flyleaf of the yearbook. Right on.

Oh, happy days, before she even dreamed that there were people on earth like David Sonnenbaum or Marsha Grossman or Ms. Middle. "The dear dead days beyond recall." Wasn't that how it went?

History. But then, as she saw it, a lot was history. Her friends from high school were dispersed, gone, *gar nicht*, as Bernie Labofish used to say. Pretty soon she would have her high school reunion at the nearby Lenoir City Holiday Inn, and her pals would be very impressed by Nicole and would try to pretend that time had not passed. Wasn't that the whole point of reunions? To pretend that by renting a room and sending out a few invitations, you could reverse the flow of history? Low-impact aerobics of futility.

Meanwhile, it was freezing on the field. A wind swept down from the Smokies, down the cement bleachers, down the sidelines, onto the field. How many, many, many Friday nights and Saturday afternoons she had felt that wind. Blowing against her sixteen- and seventeen-year-old legs in that ridiculous costume of a felt skirt and a grenadier's cap with an impossibly tall feather on top. Talk about dear dead days beyond recall. "Nor call back time in its wingèd flight." Flight. Time. On the wings of Barron Thomas Air. A clock going backward on a wing? Not bad. But let it be. Just let it be for right now.

Where the hell was Ginette? The little demon was supposed to have met her there ten minutes ago. To show her how well she could cheer. She was bound and determined, no matter what, to make the squad. She told Nicole that she was sure that if she could practice in front of Nicole, lit only by the headlights of the Buick Regal, she could get some tip-top pointers from the old Drum Major.

Frankly, Nicole did not trust Ginette as far as she could throw her. Ginette had been talking a lot lately about Jeff Boone. How he was "back on the market." How he was doing really well in the tractor and farm implement business. How handsome he was.

How single he was. How he might be in town that night to meet somebody at the Elks. Yes, indeed. Ginette was up to something. Nicole knew her well.

Meanwhile, Nicole had read in the morning's *Wall Street Journal,* now sold in front of Ertter's Market, about the rumors linking Barron and the SEC. She felt certain that at this moment, Barron was probably the busiest person in America. As she walked out to the middle of the field, the spot where she would be at the top of the marching band ziggurat, she imagined Barron yelling at his lawyers, madly dialing the telephone, screaming bloody murder to make the government of the United States say "uncle."

Nicole turned around on the field and realized she was at a familiar spot: the place in the field where she used to stand when she would lift her arms and begin to conduct. The Drum Major conducting Mahler. The Drum Major who always got a huge cheer no matter how well or how badly the football team was doing.

Alone on the field, she could literally feel the power, the strength, the feeling that she was at the head of a limitless parade of music, marching down an endless opportunity of chance and opportunity and promise and success. When she was standing there, she was holding in her hand the promise that she would live forever. More than that, that she would be forever young and in charge and blond and beautiful. Forever young. How did that go again? "May your heart always be grateful, may your song always be sung, and may you stay forever young . . ."

Really, how many times after those fall afternoons had she had those feelings? Not when she got fired by Marsha Grossman. Not when she got tricked by Terry McCoy. Not when she was temping and staying up at night worrying about her bills. No, only when she was flying on Barron Thomas Air.

Suddenly Nicole started. She knew she was at her accustomed top-of-the-pyramid spot because she could center C building, above the bleachers, between the two speaker towers, which in turn were between the four night-light towers on that side of the field. Nicole started because she was sure that she had just heard an amplified squawk out of the loudspeakers. She knew that start-up of the old MacIntosh amp extremely well by now. It was the precursor to the announcement by Ric Wurst, "And now, the nationally famous Kefauver Marching Panthers under Jonesboro's Teenage Queen, Nicole Miller!"

Oh, yes, she knew that sound.

Squawwwk . . . There it was again. "Ginette! Ginette!" Nicole called out. The kid was a devil. She was easily capable, *easily* capable of playing some kind of game with the loudspeakers. Some kind of sixteen-year-old clever game. She had wormed every detail out of Nicole about Barron, and surely she could get the key to the audiovisual shack out of somewhere and play her Guns 'n' Roses tape over the loudspeaker. The kid was a born trickster.

Then, *squawk, squawwk,* music came on. It was Johnny Cash. Singing "Folsom Prison." "But I shot a man in Reno, just to watch him die . . ."

Then there was a squawk and someone changed the track on the tape, and a huge arc-closing electric *clack* as the ancient field lights went on.

Alone, in the center of the Panther Stadium field, Nicole was flooded with light. It was as bright as it had been when they were playing the Mechanicsburg Titans a long time ago.

"Ginette!" Nicole yelled. "You little maniac . . ."

Then there was the sound of the tape starting again. Out of the loudspeaker came Johnny Cash's voice again. This time, even before the first note, Nicole knew what it would be.

> *There's a story in our town,*
> *Of the prettiest girl around,*
> *Golden hair and eyes of blue,*
> *How those eyes could flash at you,*
> *Boys around her by the score,*
> *But she loved the boy next door,*
> *Who worked at the candy store.*

Dream on, dream on, teenage queen,
Prettiest girl we've ever seen . . .

Then two of the light towers went black so that Nicole was no longer blinded by their brilliance. Onto the field, from the center of the bleachers, walked not Ginette Miller, and not even Jeff Boone.

Barron said, "Step one. We admitted that we were hopelessly in love with Nicole Miller, that our lives would be impossible without her. Step two, we filed for divorce from our wife . . ."

Then the music came up again, about a teenage queen hugging her boyfriend or something or about Hollywood, but it didn't matter by then, because Nicole was running to Barron, holding him, pressing herself against him, kissing him in the floodlights in the Tennessee night.

Nicole gasped, stared, amazed at Barron holding out a little light-blue box to her. This could not be happening. It would be less strange if it really were 1978 again and Nicole were in high school than to see this. And divorcing his wife? But Barron did not lie. Not about Saundra or about her. This spot, this blessed top of the pyramid, Nicole thought. Where dreams are dreamt, and where they come true.

"Step three," Barron went on, now holding her left hand while he put the box in the right hand, "we begged and pleaded with Nicole to at least consider marrying us."

"Barron," Nicole said, "you're really doing it? You're really leaving her."

"It's done," Barron answered. "I was insane to drag it out so long. It's done. It won't be easy being married to me," Barron added. "The SEC is after my ass. It's bogus, but it'll be hell. I'm a compulsive maniac. I'm a crazy, psycho guy who can't hear that well. You'll probably wind up visiting me in jail for something I didn't do . . ."

"Just shut up," Nicole said. "Just shut up and hold me." He held her. Then a beat. "You really told Saundra?"

"I told her and I've already filed in New York."

"So, it's just you and me?"

"And Ginette. And Steve. And the SEC. And Morgan Stanley. Ginette was the one who got me to move with that story about you and Jeff Boone, that little high school trick, about you and him getting back together . . ."

"Love's a high school thing, Barron," Nicole said as they started to walk off the field. "Everything that lasts is from high school or junior high school."

"Maybe so," Barron said. "But you didn't wind up with the boy next door."

"Yes, I did," Nicole said. "You were always next door. Always in my dream, always what I wanted out of life, even before I knew you." Then she squeezed Barron around his waist. "Anyway, how do you know Jeff and I weren't about to get back together? Might be true. Could very well be true. Anyway, you'll never know," she said with a truly happy laugh.

"I guess I won't," Barron said. "Anyway, it's freezing here. I want to go back to your house and get a sweater and take your mother and father and Ginette out to dinner and talk about the wedding."

"They know, too? Ginette worked it all out in a couple of days? Didn't she think I might like to be consulted?" Nicole was too happy to be angry.

"Maybe she thought she knew you already," Barron said. "Maybe she thought she knew what was best for you."

"Maybe she did," Nicole answered, and they walked off toward Barron's waiting car.

Behind them, on the hill behind the bleachers, Ginette Miller slapped Steve Gage and gave him a high five. "I knew it would work," she said.

"I guess you know men," Steve Gage said.

"You know what else?" Ginette asked. "When I grow up, I want to be just like her. Out on the field with that big tall feather, blowing in the breeze off the mountains. And after that, I want to do everything she did. More than anything. Just like my big sister."

298